Mike + Vick —

Thanks for buying one of the 1st copies of my new book. I hope it lives up to expectations. You guys are two of my most favorite people that I've met through RED Spot. I hope we can stay in touch.

ENJOY —

B

7/23/08

For my wife, who encouraged me to dream big and then chase those dreams with passion matched only by the dreaming itself.

And for my son, who has taught me that imagination can change everything and is bound by nothing.

Printed in the United States of America

ISBN 978-0-9801186-0-5 (regular hardcover ed.)

Book design by Brandon A. Willis
Cover design by Brandon A. Willis

Capable of Anything

A work of fiction by

Brandon A. Willis

Is paranoia the source of our worry, or is worry the source of all things paranoid and at what point does paranoia become certifiable fact? Must it take the soft black veil of death to don the mantle of truth…

I.

Summer of '95

I. Emery Takes a Ride

Death comes unbidden and steals us away with life yet to be lived. The words rose from the depths of Emery's memory and cut into his consciousness, embedding themselves there like shrapnel. He couldn't remember where he'd first heard the phrase, but it had never felt more apropos than at this very moment. He could feel the cool sweat on his skin as he looked out the windshield of the big International semi-tractor. He was due home in two hours, but would never again see the white farmhouse with the wrap-around porch he'd spent so many weekends building. He could only go there in his mind. On a cool breezy afternoon, there he sat in the swing holding a glass of lemonade and staring out at the manicured lawn, or the big blue sky, or nothing much at all. He liked to sit in the swing and go to that place we all know. The space between life and dreams, where anything is possible and everything is perfect. He would never see his loving Julia, who had complained each Saturday and Sunday night that Emery was spending too much of his time working and not enough time loving her. Though she complained, she always kept his Igloo insulated jug full of water or lemonade, or sometimes even freshly made sun tea.

The porch had been Julia's idea, of course. He could remember the conversation perfectly. It was Sunday afternoon, and he had a whole week off before his next run. They sat in the living room, watching the *Home and Garden* station on their aging 27 inch Sylvania television. There was some show on about remodeling your house. Emery was only half-paying attention, more interested in how long it would be until the Bears pre-season football game came on. Julia was enthralled, as she always was with home improvement shows. Amazing how interesting those shitty shows can be when you aren't the one doing the work!

"Look honey, this is exactly what we need," she had said. "A wrap-around porch would really give this old farmhouse some spunk!"

Emery gave her the stunned and surprised look that he was so famous for. "Sure sweetie, let me go ahead and get one up real quick before the Bears come on," he replied with a smug sense of gratification and a little bit of guilt.

Julia sighed and said, "Come on, I'm being serious. I think it would really be nice. We could put up a swing too. In the fall, we could wrap up in a blanket on the swing in the early evenings and cuddle."

Emery thought about that proposition. With a mischievous smile firmly planted on his face he asked, "What happens after the cuddling?"

"Come to the bedroom and I'll show you," she replied.

And that little, not-so-discreet invite had sealed the deal. An hour later, he was on his way to the Home Depot to get plans and wood to begin constructing the porch. The Bears could wait 'till next Sunday; they were going to be pathetic this year anyway. Same old Bears team he followed every year. It seemed like another life when they were in the Super Bowl. That conversation was 12 years ago, but seemed so fresh in his mind now. Unfortunately, there would be no more cuddling in the swing with Julia or the lovemaking that had generally ensued. These thoughts careened through his head at a rate almost as fast as that of the big white International truck speeding towards what he knew would undoubtedly be his final destination.

He frantically looked at the speedometer. It continued to climb, 75, 80, 85 miles per hour. He saw the pocket-sized picture of himself and Julia taped to the instrument panel. It was taken on their wedding day, outside the First Street Methodist Church. He flashed back to that day. It had been absolutely fantastic.

His buddies had begged him to go to the strip club the night before, but he knew how much Julia despised that sort of less than G rated fun, so he had declined. Actually, he had declined over and over for about six hours. Instead, they had gone to the small karaoke bar down on the corner of First and Main. God knows how many drinks he had polished off, or how many songs he had ruined on stage. You could bet the set included "Hey Jude" and "Take Me Home, Country Roads". You couldn't get away from the Beatles, and John Denver was one of the all-time greats in his humble opinion. He had probably paid homage to Denver multiple times that evening at Hal's. He only remembered that he had a blast and finally got to bed about 4 a.m. At noon, he felt good enough to drag himself back out.

After he had taken three extra-strength Tylenol, two Advil, and a hot shower, it was 2:30 and time to head to the church. The rest of the day was a blur, but there were many things that stuck in his head from that day forward. The worst had been the anxiety.

He remembered being so nervous that he nearly passed out in the waiting room off of the sanctuary. He was afraid that he smelled of body odor from all the sweat. It seemed crazy, but it was possible. His tux shirt was soaked with sweat just 45 minutes after he'd changed into it. That hadn't been the only irrational thought to make a pass at his sanity on that bright, sunny Saturday in June either. At one point, he was convinced that Julia didn't love him at all and was just marrying him out of pity. Surely she could find someone better than him. She couldn't really *want* to marry him, could she? What if she decided not to go through with the wedding? What if she realized that she didn't love him and would be better off not marrying him? They would start to play "Here comes the bride," but there wouldn't be a bride. She'd be long gone before the first note is played. Of course, it hadn't been true.

Everything had "come off without a hitch" as his grandma Betty had been so fond of saying. It had only been his mind playing tricks on him. Most people called it cold feet, and apparently it happened to everyone. Otherwise, they wouldn't have a name for it, would they? He remembered the look on Julia's face when the doors opened in the back of the sanctuary. Her smile had been so warm that it could have melted all the ice in the Arctic Circle. And she had been so adorable, picking the rice from of her hair in the limo. That day had truly been the beginning of a wonderful new life for him and Julia.

In a snap, the image was gone.

"Holy Shit; I'm a dead man," he thought. "How could this happen to me?"

He was a good husband. And a damn good truck driver too. He had never missed a delivery. Why do bad things happen to good people? Maybe he could ask God when he got there, which would be much sooner than he had always anticipated. He thought again about Julia, standing in the doorway with that stunned look on her face as Sheriff Bergdolt told her about his final moments. How she would undoubtedly hold her cupped hand to her mouth as if to stifle the cry that would not leave her throat.

"I'm so sorry Julia," Clancy would say, "Emery was a good man; one of the best of us."

Then he would no doubt hold her as she wept; hold her as Emery would never do again. The horns broke him out of his trance. Benton Grove 17 miles, the sign read. The speed limit had come down to 50 miles an hour, but the International continued at it's breakneck pace.

"Goddamn it," he muttered under his breath.

What was he going to do? He had to reduce the speed of the big rig. The road was going to start winding soon and even the most experienced driver couldn't keep a rig this size on the road at nearly 95 miles an hour.

He had already gone through the sequence he'd learned at driving school some 25 years ago. When he had realized he had no brakes, he tried to repressurize them by quickly pumping the pedal. No luck. At first, the feeling had been one of disbelief. He tried to pry the gas pedal off the floorboard with his foot. No good; this truck was determined to do him in. Next, he tried the emergency brake. It was like pulling a lever connected to air. Oddly, this brought back memories of the clown shows he saw at the circus as a child. He had loved going to the circus to see the clowns. It was always a family event at Thanksgiving.

After polishing off the turkey with all of the fixings you could imagine, his whole family would pile into the cars and take off to the stadium for a night of amusement. The cotton candy, ice cream, Cracker Jacks, and popcorn were almost as big a hit as the turkey, dressing, and pies that Mom had tirelessly slaved over. His favorite was when the clown car would come out, the front end bouncing up in the air and the driver frantically trying to keep it under control. What a hoot! Now he was the clown trying to keep this seventy thousand-pound clown-mobile on the highway, bouncing front end or not.

At this point, he was really beginning to freak out. He frantically looked around the cabin wondering what to do next.

"Shit! Shit! OK what the hell do I try now?"

He saw the CB hanging from its connector on the dashboard. He grabbed it and ripped it off the dash, pulling the U-shaped connector completely out of the dash and leaving a hole in the plastic, marking the place where it had just been. He didn't bother with the formalities of CB talk or the common lingo that you hear on CB's across the country; he didn't have time for any of that shit.

"Hello, is anyone out there? I need some serious help! I've lost my brakes, my throttle is stuck, and I can't stop my rig. Somebody please help me!"

His answer came back - complete and utter silence. Unbelieveable! How could there be no one on the road? When you just wanted to quietly cruise down the highway, it was littered with truckers and the CB gushed with chatter about smokies, pigs, and hot chicks. Tonight, when he really needed some serious help, it seemed that he was the only truck on the road. How ironic. Disgusted, he threw the CB into the floorboard. *Wait a second!* He could downshift, allowing the transmission to slow the truck. Sure, it could work. It would work. He would make it home yet! He moved his foot to the clutch pedal and pushed.

"Holy Mother Fuck!"

The pedal went all the way to the floor, but the engine refused to disengage. No brakes, no clutch, and no help - he was certain that this was one nightmare from which he would not wake. All he could do was keep this puppy on the road as long as possible and try to think of another way out of this mess.

Shit! He was coming up on traffic. Ahead, there were cars in both lanes. He pulled the horn, signaling them to get out of the way. Neither of the cars responded. They both continued cruising down the road, oblivious to Emery and his eighteen-wheeled coffin eating up the highway behind them. He honked again and flickered his brights at the cars in front of him. The Toyota Camry directly ahead of him hit his brakes as if he was unsure of what was going on. This was getting too close for Emery's liking. The Camry was only 150 feet in front of him now. At this pace, he would be right on top of the car before he could do anything to avoid it. He repeated his warning. The big International roared, "HONK, HONK, HOOOONK," with the lights flickering in the Camry's rear view mirror like lightning. He flipped on his flood lights, filling the car with daylight.

The Camry braked hard and quickly reduced his speed. The driver must have thought that Emery was just trying to pass, and was being a dickhead semi driver while doing it! This was a common reaction of drivers and Emery had seen it many times, although he never experienced it quite like this. He had seen countless accidents on the road in his time as a professional truck driver, many caused by this very scenario. An aggressive driver rides someone's bumper, trying to get them to switch lanes so that they can pass. The lead driver refuses, so the follower flashes his brights, honks, or both. The other driver taps his brakes as if to say

"I'm going fast enough, back off!"

The aggressive driver will do no such thing, because he believes the road is his. The lead driver becomes impatient and decides to teach the guy behind him a lesson, so he hits the brakes hard. Generally, the second driver reacts quickly enough to avoid an accident. However, many times he is already too close and going too fast. He either rams the car in front of him, or he swerves into the median, wreaking all kinds of damage on his car.

Emery never saw it coming - he was too panicked over the situation. He was concentrating so hard that his eyes actually stung. His head drummed with pain. His hands and arms were soaked with sweat and the wheel was becoming slick with his perspiration. Unfortunately, it was too late to react. His last glimpse of the car was that of the bright red taillights and the rear bumper rising to meet the challenge of the front end of the International. It was no contest. The semi connected with the car, and it began to spin sideways. For a split second, the Camry was wedged under the front of Emery's truck. The International seemed to push harder, as if to clear the debris from the roadway.

The Camry slowly slid off the left side of the front bumper of the rig and began rolling as it left the shoulder and entered the grassy median. Emery watched in horror as the car finally came to a stop, wrapping itself around a tree in the median. The car was now totally unrecognizable. It appeared as a mass of junk steel and tailpipe tied in a horrific bow around the tree. The big International had plowed right through the late model Toyota, unconcerned about the welfare of the driver or his family. Emery was unsure if anything other than a government-issued tank could have survived that collision. The five person passenger vehicle certainly didn't, crash test safety rating or not. The truck was unfazed through the whole ordeal and had quickly recovered its lost speed. It was again hurtling along the interstate at better than 90 mph.

II. Have a Drink on Me

The Texan Inn Bar and Grill wasn't really much of a grill at all. The only solid food worth a shit was the stale trail mix that partially filled the bowls scattered along the length of the bar. Daniel Bramstow had been a daily patron here for 12 of the 16 months that he had lived in Graisville, Mississippi. He still remembered the very first words out of his mouth when he first entered what he now considered a second home.

"How about that, a redneck cowboy bar in the middle of a faggoty-ass French town?"

It may or may not have been ironic, but it was the place that Danny-boy, as they called him, had latched onto.

The bar was a tangle of confusion tonight. Della, the barmaid (and janitor) had separated the tables into two distinct sections, one on each side of the bar room. Della split time with Frank Brumley, who owned the place. Frank and Della alternated nights during the week, while they both worked the weekends. Danny wasn't sure, but he thought Frank might be putting it to Della in their off shift time; they seemed awfully cozy on those weekend nights.

Della's separation technique left a section of empty wooden floor where "The Firestones" were supposed to play. Unfortunately, or maybe not so unfortunately in Danny's mind, The Firestones had determined that a gig at The Texan Inn and Grill was not where they needed (or wanted) to be tonight. "Probably got a better gig somewhere else," Danny-boy thought. Danny had no idea who the hell The Firestones were, nor did he particularly care. The time for music in his life had passed. And as far as he was concerned, a better gig could include pulling your fingernails out with a pair of needle-nosed pliers. Tonight was a night for heavy drinking. He raised his glass to the meager crowd in the run down bar.

"To The Firestones!" He hollered to anyone who would listen.

"Screw The Firestones!" was the response he received from young Jack Doinen, whose whore of a wife was probably at the local No Tell Motel screwing whoever would pay her for her time.

Jack either couldn't register this as a possibility or didn't care one way or the other. He just kept up his commiseration with his two all-time best buds – Jack & Jim. He would even mix in a frosted mug or two of Bud, just to make sure not to leave anyone out.

Ahh, the frosted mugs of beer. Those were the best thing about The Texan as far as Danny was concerned. "Liquid Nourishment," he mumbled to number thirteen of the evening and finished it off with one big gulp.

He was doing pretty well tonight. Since arriving at 7:00 or so, he had drained thirteen, hadn't passed out yet, and it was only 8:45. Or did the clock say 9:45, or 6:45? He couldn't tell for sure. The damn numbers kept moving around, like when you get water in your snorkel mask while you're still submerged.

"Who cares," he mumbled, "Della will come get me when it's time to go."

Danny looked up from his empty beer mug just as Jack Doinen was pulling out the chair on the other side of the table.

"Oh shit," Danny mumbled under his breath.

Jack was the guy in the bar that wanted to be best friends with everyone. He typically started off in the corner booth, slowly migrating to each table and booth in The Texan until he had spoken to everyone, or passed out (usually in the only stall in the men's room). Jack had personal problems, and he liked to be able to share his problems with whoever would listen. As far as Jack was concerned, Danny was a best listener in the place. Hell, he even answered occasionally, which was more than most of these drunken mutes would do. Danny didn't figure that he was a particularly good listener; he could barely remember Jack's name. *Thank God he was named after a liquor brand.*

"Haylooooo, thar litow Danny-boy," came the mutilated greeting from doubly-drunk Jack Doinen. Danny was just about to run him off when he recognized that Doinen had brought an extra mug of beer and was holding it out to him. As drunk as Jack was, he was really waving it at Danny, beer spilling from both sides of the glass mug at the ends of the shallow arc he was unconsciously tracing. As everyone in the bar, especially drunk and pitiful Jack Doinen, knew, Daniel Bramstow was not one to turn away a free cocktail, regardless of who was offering or what strings were attached.

"Have yourself a seat there Mr. Doinen," came the response from drunken Danny Bramstow. "How's it hangin?"

"Whaaaale, you can not imagin, mah deeah littow Danny boway." Jack said with a tilt of the head that Danny found to be somehow unnatural.

Danny thought Jack might tip over and fall square in the middle of the barroom floor. But instead, he spent the next 30 minutes relating how his "bitch of a wife" had better be home "mindin' da rug rats" and cleaning "dat shit hole ova house" or he was "gonna beat sumbody's ass!" As any good listener would, Danny sat at the table looking around the bar and nodding at regular intervals, not particularly caring if Jack had noticed that he was talking to a man who was paying absolutely no attention whatsoever.

When there was a lull in Jack's story, Danny spoke up. "Who is that fucking guy running his mouth off to Sherriff Bergdolt?" He asked with an edge in his voice that cut through Jack's drunken stupor, "And why the hell does he keep lookin' over here?" That was the exact moment that Daniel Bramstow's life took an unfortunate turn and began to get very complicated - again.

III. Drivers License and Registration Please

His eyes brimmed with moisture as Emery thought again about his beautiful wife and the years that would be stolen from them if he didn't do something quickly to save himself. Thousands of other random thoughts swirled through his head like a runaway tornado destroying the scenery of his mind. Nothing made any sense to him anymore. ....*How could this happen? What am I going to do? How is Julia going to react when she receives the news? Can I make it out of this? It's not fair! Did the Bears play today? Maybe I should just jump....*

"Yeah, maybe I should just open the door and jump out," he mumbled to the picture of his sweet Julia. "I could get the rig onto the shoulder and maybe land in the grass median alongside the road."

He was gripping the wallet-sized picture so tightly that the ink was beginning to rub off of the picture and onto his thumb. He reconciled that this plan was his best chance at survival. The truck was moving so fast that the scenery had become a blur outside the windows of the big rig. Of course, it didn't help that darkness had already banished the last rays of the daylight and obscured the backdrop for the day. Emery couldn't see any of the landscape outside the window of the big International semi-tractor. He could see that there was no guardrail, which was positive. Beyond that, it was just a guessing game.

Emery thought about the rig and the possible damage it could do. First, if he didn't jump far enough, he could be run down by his own semi. He contemplated this and quickly decided that by standing on the side step outside the door, he could easily jump far enough away from the vehicle. There was no one else on the interstate, which was another positive. Maybe he could make it out of this after all. If he could safely jump into the median grass, the truck might just run off the side of the road and total itself out. Unfortunate, but better than the alternative.

He placed the picture in the breast pocket of his shirt, eased the rig onto the shoulder nearest the median and unbuckled his seatbelt. The rumble strips blared their loud, repetitive warning "rrrbbbpt, rrrbbpt, rrrbbpt," as if to wake up the sleeping driver in the cab. Emery held the big steering wheel steady with his right hand and slowly pulled the handle that unlatched the driver's door. The door cracked open easily at first, but then the wind bore down on it, making it difficult to push open. The wind blew hard into the cab, swirling the trash in the floorboard and flipping the pages of his log book, which sat in the passenger seat.

He redoubled his grip on the wheel and steeled himself against the wind, pushing the door further open. The semi truck weaved in and out of the shoulder, with the rumble strips still singing their irritating chorus. Emery slipped out of the seat and onto the side step, the wind blowing fully in his face. The wind felt like it was actually burning his face. Tears streamed from the corners of his eyes and across his burning cheeks. He could feel his heart beating - not in his chest, but up somewhere between his Adam's apple and the top of his rib cage. He could hear the pounding in his ears over the screaming wind.

"Dear God, I know it's my time to pass. I only ask that you take care of my Julia after I'm gone."

Emery had taken two seconds to make his peace with God and was now resigned to the distinct possibility of meeting his maker. Just as he was about to close his eyes for the jump, he saw a flash of red and blue behind him. He shook his head as if to break free from the fog clinging to him and refocused on the mirror.

"Thank God!" Emery shouted into the wind.

He could see the flashing lights of the police car barreling down the interstate behind him. As the police cruiser made up ground on the International, Emery carefully made his way back into the cab. He slammed the door closed and exhaled a huge sigh of relief. He glanced up into the mirror, still afraid that he might be dreaming.

Nope, the white and brown car with the red and blue lights was still there, still making up distance. Emery sat back into the seat and realized that his legs were about as solid as rubber bands. He didn't think he would have the strength to do that again even if it was necessary. He pulled the picture out of his shirt pocket, looked Julia in the eyes, and gave her a gentle kiss before returning her to the breast pocket of the yellow button down, now soaked with sweat. His hands were slick on the wheel, sweating with the realization of just how close he was to a one round bout with the grim reaper and the eminent ten count that could have followed.

The state police car was now just a few car lengths back and a crackle came over the CB.

"Hey there truck number 871. This is the state police officer behind you. Need some help?"

Emery quickly lost himself in another dreamscape. Number 871 – it had been Julia's idea to use the month and year of their marriage for the truck number. He couldn't help but smile, thinking of the day they had bought the truck and trailer and placed those big black and gold stickers on the back. That was so many years ago. It was funny how impending death can make memories seem so vivid and recent. He snapped back to reality as he again heard the voice of the state trooper screaming over the CB.

"Truck 871 – pick up the CB and reply now! This is state police trooper seven, seven, nine and I am ordering you to respond!"

Emery fumbled with the CB and finally got the button depressed. "Thank God! This is truck 871. Emery Mathis here! My throttle is stuck and I've got no brakes and no clutch. I can't stop this son of a bitch! I've got to make it home to my wife. I don't know what to do. Please help me! Please help me!"

He was babbling, but he couldn't help it. He was overcome with fear and exhaustion. He was a wreck. The sweat had completely drenched his shirt and pants. Beads of perspiration ran down his temples, neck, and chest, finally stopping at his waistband. He itched all over. His eyes were bloodshot and his head still pounded with a headache that had started behind his eyes but now traveled all the way through his ears, down his neck and seemed to have settled between his shoulder blades.

The trooper replied, "Keep 'er steady there 871. I'm going to pull up alongside of you in the left lane so I can see your face. It'll be good to finally meet you."

"Great! Come on up, but hurry."

Emery was relieved, but still on edge. Something didn't seem right about the trooper's reply. He seemed to be overly pleased with himself. Why would he be that happy? He ignored it - too much stress. It must have just been his imagination.

Emery watched the state police car pull alongside the International rig. As the trooper got closer, Emery squinted to see him better. Everything seemed normal about him. He was wearing the standard issue trooper's uniform. He even had the goofy, wide-brimmed hat on. "Why would anyone wear that thing," Emery thought, "especially in the car?" Just as the trooper pulled close to the door, the CB twittered again.

The same overly pleased voice coming over the airwaves, landing in the rig's cab, "You left one hell of a mess a few miles back, son. How'er we gonna get this thing shut down?"

A flash of green sign caught Emery's eye from the right side of the road. The road sign was now proclaiming that Benton Grove was 9 miles ahead. At his current rate of speed, that was not much time to solve this problem. He hoped the trooper had a good idea and would let him in on it soon.

Emery had forgotten all about the Toyota Camry that he had practically run over just a few minutes ago.

"Please tell me they're not dead," he mumbled into the CB.

Silence. Then the reply came. Though not at all what he had hoped - not exactly what he had expected either.

"Oh come on 871, you don't really think you could level a family car and not have anyone get hurt do you? You must be dumber than I thought."

The CB clicked off with what sounded like a stifled chuckle of laughter.

"What do you mean? I didn't do that on purpose. I don't have any brakes!! Are they really dead?" All of the lights in the dashboard were starting to blur as the tears began to well up in his eyes.

"Ring around the rosie, a pocket full of posies. Ashes, Ashes, we're all run down," came the reply from the CB.

Emery looked out the window, but the trooper's car hadn't quite made it up to the window of the rig. The statie was just out of sight behind the wheel of his police cruiser. Emery's stomach was beginning to knot up. He couldn't figure out what was going on.

"What the hell is going on here? Are you going to help me or not?" Emery was on the verge of losing it. "What the hell kind of cop are you," he screamed into the CB.

"This is officer fucking friendly, what did you say your name was… Chicken shit?"

Emery slowly moved the CB back to his lips. He was beginning to hyperventilate. The air in the cab of the International tasted stale and old, almost devoid of oxygen. This was a nightmare. In his most desperate time, right when he needed help the most, the one person, the only person that he thought could give it turns out to be absolutely insane. But then again, weren't all cops crazy to some degree? He supposed so. Emery held the CB microphone to his lips and debated whether he should even give his name to this maniac.

Finally he said, "Emery Mathis is my name, now are you going to help me or not?"

As if with great pleasure, the state trooper replied, "What? Help you like you helped me? You should have kept your fucking mouth shut, Emery. You didn't have to tell, you know. You could have just told me you knew and I would have moved on. No one would have ever had to know. But that wasn't good enough for you was it? Good ole Emery. Unfortunately for you, you had a case of diarrhea of the mouth, huh? Well, you're in one hell of a pickle now, aren't you son?" Abruptly, the CB went silent.

Now Emery was totally lost. He had no idea what this lunatic was spouting about, but it was clear that this guy was incredibly angry. Benton Grove was coming up in a hurry; they were probably less than 5 miles away now. Emery tried again to get a look at the trooper, but still couldn't see the driver. He couldn't even place the voice. He wasn't even sure he'd ever heard that voice before.

"Please… Who are you?" he whimpered into the CB, his knuckles white from gripping the damn thing so hard and his voice trembling with fear and anxiety.

Emery was pleading - maybe for his life. As he looked out the window, the brown and white Crown Victoria began to speed up. The CB crackled again and the response sent chills down Emery's back.

"THIS IS STATE POLICE OFFICER DANIEL EDWARD BRAMSTOW."

Emery knew by the tone of the voice that this should register somewhere in the depths of his mind, but it didn't. The Crown Vic was right beside him now. Emery looked into the car, at the driver. He thought he could almost recognize the man driving, but still couldn't place the voice, name or face.

IV. Take the Wheel

Joe Landis had seen a lot of wrecks since joining the State Police, but never anything like this. He had heard stories that detailed accidents like this one, but he never really believed that they were as bad as they sounded. Each time, he listened, nodded his head, and voiced the obligatory wows at the appropriate times. All the while, he told himself that they were exaggerated for effect. He even rebuffed some of the storytellers with his patented, "Oh, bullshit. That's a load of hairy crap!" In some twisted part of his psyche, he'd always wanted to be called to a wreck such as the ones described to him. Then, he could be the one telling the story - the guy that everyone looked up to. In short, the guy who had seen it all. He wanted to be able to add that bullet to his morbid résumé.

Now that he had gotten the call and proceeded to the scene, it was a much different story. Joe had a strong stomach, one that would hold up to any rollercoaster or the sight of a nickel junkie, but not this. He was still lightheaded as he walked back to his police cruiser. The memory of this balmy summer night would not leave his mind for a long time indeed. It would remain in the mental file cabinet drawer labeled "Scary Shit" only to be dredged up every once in a great while for effect.

The wreckage was strewn along the roadway for nearly three-quarters of a mile. The vehicle, probably a mid-sized sedan, had been completely decimated. It was as if the car had been crushed in some oversized garbage compactor and then thrown onto the highway like litter. Most of the body panels had been removed from the frame and each of the doors had been completely bashed in. Not a single shard of glass remained in any of the six windows. Each of the wheels on the passenger side had been twisted off of the axles like bottle caps, and the driver side wheels were bent almost underneath the main carriage.

Officer Landis had initially thought that the car had been black. As he put his hand on the side of the wreckage to lean in and look inside, he almost fell down as his hand slid across the slick metal. He looked down to see his palm colored in deep crimson, an eerie shade that was almost black in the moonlight. It was then that his stomach wretched for the first time. He wiped his hand on his pant leg and carefully leaned in again, steeling himself against the carnage that he was certain to find.

Fortunately, it wasn't what he had expected. There was very little blood in the interior of the car. However, there were three mangled bodies; one lying in the front floorboard and two in the back seat. It appeared that the mother was the front seat passenger, judging by the angle of her head - dead from a broken neck. The two daughters were a tangle of arms and legs, obviously trying to hold onto one another during the terrible accident. Joe could see the fear in one girl's eyes, while he couldn't see the face of the second daughter, who looked to be the older of the two, judging by size alone. Even though Joe had no children of his own, it stopped his heart to see these two girls robbed, in an instant, of their futures.

Looking back down the highway, Joe could see black streaks on the pavement for what seemed like an eternity. He told himself that the debris had to be rubber from the semi's tires. Had to be. However, his mind wrestled with the idea of what really was lying in that deserted stretch of highway. He took a step in the direction of the streaks and away from the metal coffin where three young women were now lying, and his stomach wretched a second time.

Joe sat on the pavement and breathed deeply. He waited a few minutes for the others to arrive, which seemed like an eternity. He had to keep his head between his knees to steady his stomach, which was now vigorously somersaulting like a three-year-old at a family picnic. Finally, the flashing lights brought him back out of his trance. He walked up to meet State Trooper Mike Menzter and give him a report.

"You don't even want to go back there," he told Mike.

Mike replied, "You OK Joe? You look terrible."

"I'm worse than terrible Mike. I thought I could take this, but I was wrong – way wrong. I've seen a lot of shit in my time on the force, but I've never seen anything like this."

He took Mike up on an offer to sit in his cruiser and describe what he had seen while the other officers got the scene under control. After two cups of coffee out of Mike's personal thermos and about 15 minutes of explaining everything that he had seen, Joe felt good enough to vacate the vehicle. Mike had listened intently and seemed as upset as Joe felt. As they walked back toward the wreckage, Mike asked a funny question.

"Joe, where's your cruiser?"

The question caught him totally off guard. His only reply had been a blank stare. He turned to point out the state issued Crown Victoria that he had parked just off the shoulder of the highway. His eyes seemed to turn toward the shoulder in slow motion. When they finally made it, they saw no police cruiser. It was gone. Vanished like a good magic trick. In its place was a rusted-out, beat-up Pontiac. Joe wasn't even sure which model. He did know; however, that the vehicle hadn't been there when he parked the Crown Vic.

"Oh shit. Shit. Shit. Shit."

Joe quickly realized what had happened. He was in such shock when he parked the car that he hadn't even turned off the engine. Sometime during his investigation of the scene or his talk with Mike, the Ford had been stolen. Stolen. *Oh Shit.* He ran across the pavement to the Pontiac parked in the place of his police cruiser; Mike not far behind. He caught himself just before he reached the vehicle. He extended both of his arms straight out to the side like a cross to stop Mike as well.

"Whoa! Don't touch it!" He was almost out of breath from his sprint to the car. "There will be fingerprints. Get one of the techs to check it out while the others wrap up the scene. It could be related."

"I highly doubt it," Mike replied. "Probably some teenager from around here that thought it would be cool to steal a cop car."

"Don't screw with me. On the side of an interstate where a fatal accident just happened is not exactly the best place to steal a police vehicle. So just do it!" He jabbed his finger into Mike's barreled chest as he spoke. Joe was exasperated with the whole situation.

"This day has gone to complete shit," he sighed as he walked back to Mike's car, shaking his head.

The reply from his partner didn't make him feel any better.

"Well, it ain't over yet."

The two officers got back into Mike's cruiser, turned on the lights and began down the interstate in the only direction the man responsible for this accident could have continued. It was slow going on the shoulder of the interstate until they had bypassed all of the wreckage that had once been a family sedan. Mike was concentrating on potential routes that the semi might have taken if it had left the interstate. He was vaguely aware that Joe was talking to himself in the passenger seat of the vehicle, staring out the window. Out of nowhere, and barely audible, he mumbled, "Oh my God, my clothes."

"What?" Mike replied.

"My uni.....um spare uniform. I picked it up from the cleaners earlier this evening. It was sitting in the passenger floorboard of the cruiser." And then in a panicked fury, "I CAN NOT fucking believe this!"

He picked up the CB and radioed back to the officer in command (OIC to all of the brothers of the police fraternity) requesting that he be notified the instant that the Pontiac was processed. He added that this should be the first thing that the techs did. He was not pleased by the reply.

"Officer Landis, this is Officer in Command Robert Valcraft. As I am sure you are aware, we are required to process the primary crime scene first. Once that has been completed, we will move on to the supposed secondary crime scene. Don't worry though; we have taped off the entire area so that it will not be compromised. I will give you a call as soon as the results are in. I expect it will be complete by noon tomorrow."

Joe Landis thought he could feel the blood vessels bursting in his brain. He grabbed the CB mic and screamed at Valcraft.

"You son of a bitch! You process that fuckin caaaarrrr...."

Joe's head whipped toward the driver's side of the vehicle like something out of a comedy act on one of those television variety shows. Mike had switched off the CB and was slowly shaking his head at him.

"Let it go Joe, we're heading in the direction of whatever caused that mess back there. People are dead and it is our number one priority to find out why. Let Val's team complete their investigation and update us later. Trust me; your stolen police cruiser will turn up soon enough. It's kinda hard to hide one of these babies, especially out on the highway," Mike smirked as he patted the dash board of his vehicle as if it were a good pet.

Joe let out a long sigh and stared blankly out the passenger side window, wondering where the hell his police cruiser was. He shook his head absently as he tried to reason why someone would steal a police car; robbery, rape, murder. Any number of devious acts could be committed utilizing a police cruiser and officer's uniform. Joe quickly cut off that train of thought before it jumped the rails and became a disaster all in itself.

"Concentrate on the task at hand," he mumbled to himself. "The rest will take care of itself."

V. Big Finale

Sweat rolled down Emery's forehead and dripped into his eyes, stinging as if they were droplets of acid instead of just salt infused perspiration. He concentrated as much as he could on remembering the officer's name or face. This was a difficult enough task without having to try keeping a forty thousand pound missile in between one solid and one dotted line while hurtling down the proverbial highway to hell. Well, maybe not to hell, but to a gruesomely painful death at the very least.

"Fuck!" Emery shouted to the empty semi cab. He couldn't remember who the hell the officer was and didn't have time to worry with it. He looked back out the window and grabbed the CB.

"What the hell do you want from me?" he shouted. "What do you want me to do?"

"Actually Emery, I want you to fucking die. You put me at risk by rattin' me out to the sheriff at that "shitty" little bar the other night, and now you will pay dearly for your mistake. I'm going to watch you die, and then I'm going to pay the sheriff a little visit. By the way, look out ahead - there's a pretty sharp left coming up. I'd say it's going to be difficult to navigate at 90 miles an hour. Might want to slow 'er down. Oh hmmn, never mind…… Goodbye Emery."

With that, the CB clicked off for the final time. Emery looked ahead. Because of the downward grade, he could clearly see the small white reflectors rounding out a quick turn to the left. He knew that his only hope was to be in the left hand shoulder when he started into the curve. The only problem was a certain police car in the left lane - between him and the shoulder where he desperately needed to be.

"FUCK YOU; YOU MOTHER FUCKING BASTARD!"

Emery half-snarled and half-screamed the expletive as he pulled the wheel to the right and then quickly back to the left. The semi rocked slightly to the left on its axles, glided to the right, and then lurched hard as it made a direct line for the brown and white cruiser. Emery was resigned to the fact that he was going to die. This was his last effort to pull this thing out, or take out this Bramstow maniac when he went down.

The reflectors in the road were a blur to Emery as the truck began to barrel to the left. He was vaguely aware of the sound of squealing tires. On the surface of his mind, he thought *maybe the brakes finally came back on line.* Below the surface, and deep in his gut, he knew this was not the case. Actually, he knew with perfect clarity where the screeching sound was emanating from.

Even as Emery violently jerked his head to the left, the world seemed to slow to an infant's crawl. He saw each detail in his field of vision with perfect clarity. He was almost at the start of the turn. The reflectors appeared to twinkle like stars and the white dotted lines stretched out in length, seemingly connecting to make a half U pointing to the left. The guardrail hung suspended two feet above the ground without the necessary anchoring poles. On the other side of the guardrail, the grassy median retreated down and into the turn and then back up again toward the outside of the protective rail and the roadway coming out of the corner.

On the outside of the highway, the shoulder quickly dropped off into dark woods. The highway was banked in the turn, but Emery was sure that it wouldn't be enough. The moonlight glinted off his driver's side mirror as his eyes quickly focused on the retreating brown and white police cruiser, blue-black smoke curling up from the back and sides of the tires. Emery thought he could actually see Bramstow smiling behind the wheel.

Danny had been quick to recognize Emery's clever plan, but not quite quick enough. The front end of the Crown Victoria dipped severely as the brakes locked up and the car made a painful cry. It slid on the highway and quickly started to fall behind the semi. He would have made it if the car hadn't begun to slide sideways. The back end came forward on the left, forcing the front end right - toward the big International. The rear tires of the semi's trailer clipped the front passenger corner and sent the car spinning end for end. It came to rest straddling the center line of the highway, front tires in the right lane and rear tires in the left, giving Danny an astonishingly perfect view of his big finale.

As the semi trailer's rear tires clipped the front of the police cruiser, the tractor's front bumper connected with the guardrail. The impact threw Emery sideways into the floorboard. The semi slid along the guardrail for a split second before ripping through the railing as if it were the finishing ribbon in the Boston Marathon. It careened down the median leaving wide, muddy tracks from the eighteen wheels. The trailer shuddered and abruptly tipped over, pulling the tractor with it. The square front end of the truck planted itself in the incline of the median traveling back toward the roadway casing the rig's rear end to rise over the front, jackknifing the trailer in mid air.

The pressure exerted on the junction of the tractor and trailer was too much and the rig ripped free of the trailer, tumbling up the embankment and onto the highway. The trailer slid up the median embankment on its side and onto the roadway, heading directly for the International's cab, which lay on the far side of the highway near the shoulder.

Amidst a shower of sparks, the front of the trailer collided squarely with the top of the rig, crushing it like an aluminum can clamped in a shop vise. The momentum of the heavy trailer catapulted the semi over the edge of the roadway. The trailer came to a halt, partially hanging over the edge of the shoulder. The road glittered in the moonlight, decorated by the shards of metal and glass that lay scattered on its surface. The International rig tumbled down the side of the embankment, ripping a pathway through the high grass and small saplings, finally crashing to a stop 30 feet below, leaning on its side; passenger wheels against the trees.

VI. That Sinking Feeling

Danny had to admit, the crash had been better than any fireworks display he had *EVER* seen.

"Holy Mary, mother of ….. That was fucking awesome!"

He sat there, almost stunned by what he had witnessed. The carnage was better than he could have imagined; certainly better than he had planned. He was even convinced that it would look like an accident to the police. Now, he just needed a place to ditch this *piece-of-shit* cop car.

His skin felt cool as a soft breeze blew in the window and brushed against his face, which was damp with perspiration. His whole body was numb and yet tingled as if it were *all* asleep. He felt exhausted and was vaguely aware that he was "sportin' wood" as they had said in high school. Against his will, he flushed in embarrassment. He had always been shy and quiet. Relationships had been difficult for him throughout his young adult life, and continued to be now. All the girls had thought he was weird in high school. He had dated two or three women in the last few years, but each relationship had ended badly with raised voices in the middle and screaming at the very end. He'd almost had to kill one who had threatened to go to the police. He just couldn't have that; not with everyone looking for him.

It always ended with the screaming, but it always began with one phrase. The phrase burrowed its way into his brain like some kind of insect and stung madly, creating unimaginable pain.

"You are *sooo* paranoid," they would say. He could usually control the first two or three times this phrase was uttered by using his patented comeback.

"When everyone's after you, paranoia is just good sense."

Inevitably, this was followed by a giggle and some irritatingly stupid phrase like, "Oh, you're just being goofy," or "You silly man."

He never let the women see the real Danny; the Danny who had been running for so many years and was resigned to the fact that he would run the rest of his life, eliminating anyone who posed a threat to him. He would not be brought in - not under any circumstances. He was careful. He took no chances. And he covered his tracks - *all* of them.

Danny looked again at the wreckage and wondered what kind of shape that dirtbag Emery was in. Surely he was dead. He looked back down the highway from the direction they had come. How long would it be before someone made their way here? He knew that he couldn't be here when they arrived. As much as he wanted to check on Emery, he knew that he shouldn't. Of course he was dead. No one could have survived that crash.

But what if he wasn't? He could ID you for the cops.

"Shit," Danny muttered. He looked again back down the highway, squinting in order to pick up on any lights that might be headed his way. Nothing.

"I better walk down there and make sure."

If you do, they will see your tracks, not to mention the disruption of the debris if you drive up close.

"Shit, shit, shit," Danny moaned under his breath, "What am I doing? I gotta get the hell outta here."

Yes. Better go. But there's always the chance that he made it. If he did, I could be totally fucked.

"Screw it."

Danny carefully drove the police car through the median and headed back the opposite direction. He remembered seeing an exit just a little ways back. He drove the speed limit with the lights off, so he could more easily see anyone coming from the other direction. The moon cast its pale yellow light on the highway and Danny drove as fast as he dared toward the exit. Just as he got halfway down the off ramp, he saw headlights coming down the highway toward the wreckage.

Oh shit. Here they come. Has to be them; I'm in deep shit now. I've gotta get out of here right now.

He stomped the gas pedal and hit the lights - time to get gone.

VII. The End

Emery lay in the grass of the embankment looking up at the full moon. He was just a few feet away from the smashed sardine can that had almost become his coffin. It was a miracle that he was still alive. He could only recall a snapshot of the crash. He remembered seeing the police car vanish behind the rig after the rear wheels clipped the front end of the black and white. He also remembered the front end of the International colliding with the guardrail. At that point, he was violently thrown into the floorboard, hitting his head hard on something solid, maybe the fire extinguisher he kept bolted to the floor in case of emergencies. The whole world began to first spin wildly and then swim crazily before finally going dark.

When he awoke, he was laying half in and half out of the cab. His feet and lower legs dangled out the driver's side window, which had no doubt been shattered during the wreck. The rest of his body lay at a crazy angle under the dash. He hurt from head to toe and wondered how much damage there actually was.

He'd gently lowered himself out of the driver's window and fallen to the ground in a heap. He found that he did not have the energy to stand up, so Emery had crawled away from the truck and finally lay on his back against the bank. He looked back at what was left of his life on the road. What began as dull pain as he climbed out of the battered vehicle was quickly becoming something else entirely. Emery could feel a growing fire in all of his limbs, but especially his legs. His midsection was already ablaze with excruciating pain. He turned his head away from the semi and vomited. His arms now hurt so badly that he could barely lift his hand to wipe the wetness from his cheek. After he did, he noticed that his cheek wasn't covered with vomit after all; it was foamy crimson. Blood.

As he looked up at the stars, Emery couldn't help but think of the words of the maniac who had gone to such lengths to orchestrate this nightmare.

"You put me at risk by rattin' me out to the sheriff…." He could easily recall both the fear and anger in the officer's voice.

"This is state police officer Daniel Edward Bramstow." Emery pictured the officer screaming so smugly at him.

Emery still couldn't put the conversation with a face. However, his mind was much clearer now than it had been back on the highway just a few seconds ago. He kept returning to the first phrase. *Rattin' me out….the other night….Sheriff Bergdolt…*

Emery coughed violently, his stomach erupting in pain. His body convulsed against the coughing fit. He could taste blood in his mouth now. There would be no stopping this train; it was coming into the final station, and quickly.

Emery laid staring at the moon; clouds slowly drifting in front of the big white sphere against black space. The clouds cleared and the hazy smoke in Emery's mind cleared with it. He saw the picture of a barroom, blurry at first, but the details slowly came back into focus. He saw himself sitting at a table talking with Sheriff Bergdolt. What were they discussing? He couldn't remember and couldn't hear in the half dream he was having. It was like watching a muted television program with bad reception.

He consciously looked around the dream bar. At first, nothing; then, there he was! He saw Bramstow. He was dressed in casual wear, just like everyone else. Jeans and a plaid button-up, white t-shirt visible only at the neck. He was sitting at a table across the room with Jack Doinen, whose mouth was pistoning up and down like a jackhammer. God only knew what Doinen was rattling on about. Emery had listened to Jack's banter many times, nodding and drinking as was the common courtesy.

Bramstow was just sitting there, oblivious to Jack's melodramatic buzzing, scanning the night's patrons. He made eye contact with Emery as his eyes swept across the faces in the bar. It only lasted a second, but Emery now remembered it well. Initially, Bramstow looked ashamed, as if Emery had caught him up to no good. Then there was a flash of fear, as if some terrible secret were sure to come out. Finally, Bramstow's face contorted and rage poured from his eyes. The final look had given Emery the feeling that he had done something terribly wrong. As quickly as it had come, the look disappeared and Bramstow turned back to Doinen, engrossed in conversation. Bramstow hadn't turned his attention toward Emery again the rest of the night.

Emery coughed again, this time weaker, but the blood was immediately present in his mouth. It was becoming harder to breathe. His chest felt heavy and his lungs made a sickeningly wet gurgling sound when he tried to inhale. He opened his mouth to wretch, but nothing came out except wet, sticky, red strings. He relaxed and lay there on the bank, breathing shallowly. He was relieved that he had remembered where he'd seen Bramstow, even though he was unsure what exactly had transpired in that brief moment of eye contact to cause a fury such as the one he had so recently endured.

Emery could now feel the warmth and strength draining more rapidly from his body. He was beginning to feel cold all over and didn't have the strength to even lift his head. His arms and legs were dead weights attached to a torso so weak that they could not be budged. His breathing was so shallow he doubted his ability to fog a mirror. The rise and fall of his chest was barely visible, and if present at the scene, one might think that it was just an illusion of the moonlight and clouds moving across the sky.

His eyelids gradually gained enough weight that he could no longer will them open. They drifted closed, slowly blotting out his view of the harvest moon. Darkness and cold enveloped him. Emery heard a siren in the distance, soft and quiet, drowned out by the silence of his dark, cold world. He ignored the sound, so small and insignificant. He was finally able to rest, and he would. In his mind, he saw an image of his beloved Julia, the one true love of his life. It was the same image that had hung for so many years in the cab of his big International rig. He saw it so clearly now, as if on a crisp, clear winter's morn. And in the cool damp grass of the highway embankment, Emery was still.

VIII. Race

"Oh shit, there it is Mike," Joe said with a mixture of nervous energy and trepidation. "Come on, let's go. Hurry."

Mike turned on the siren and sped up. As much as he wanted to get to the bottom of this, he was also nervous as to what he might find at the wreck ahead. The semi appeared to be turned over in the middle of the highway.

As they got closer to the hairpin turn, the vehicle's lights played across the median and they could see the path of the semi through the median and back up onto the roadway. Joe's mouth hung agape; he was shocked at what he saw ahead of them.

"Good God, he must have really been movin'. Look at the ditch he dug in that embankment."

Joe was reeling from the sight before him. Mike kept quiet. He knew from this small glimpse of the accident what they were going to find when they got all the way to the truck.

They pulled up as far as they could to the overturned trailer blocking both lanes of traffic. As they got out, Mike killed the sirens but left the flashing lights on. He also called for an ambulance, backup, and a semi wrecker, giving the appropriate mile marker and direction to aid the drivers in finding them. Together, they blocked off any potential traffic with the orange cones that Mike kept in the trunk of the police cruiser.

With all this formality completed, they rushed over the edge of the pavement and looked down the slope. Immediately, they saw what was left of the semi tractor, leaning awkwardly into the trees lining the edge of the foliage.

Joe grimaced and shook his head. "We've got to get down there in case he's still alive."

"If he is, he's probably trapped. The whole roof looks like it's caved in. You go on down; I'll get my crowbar from the car in case we have to pry him out." Mike quickly headed back toward the car.

After three steps down, Joe saw a man lying against the base of the embankment. He immediately shouted back to Mike.

"Mike, he's out! He's lying on the side of the bank. Get back here. Hurry!" He slid the rest of the way down the bank on the seat of his pants toward where the man lay still.

As he reached him, he immediately assumed the worst. He was careful not to move him, but leaned over placing his right cheek no more than 3 inches above Emery's lips. He listened quietly, in the silence of the night. Joe could not feel any breath on the side of his cheek, but unbelievably, he could hear the faintest wheezing coming from Emery's chest. He leaned even closer to make sure that he was not imagining it.

Once he was sure that the driver was still alive, he said, "Sir, this is Officer Joe Landis. Can you hear me?"

No answer.

"Sir, this is Officer Landis. You've been in a very bad accident. Can you hear me?"

Still, no answer.

"Sir, I am going to take your hand. If you hear me but are unable to speak, squeeze my hand. He gently took Emery's hand in his own and asked again, "Sir, can you please let me know if you are awake?"

In response to his question, he felt the softest of grips from the poor man's hand. If his hand hadn't been limp as he placed it in his own, Joe might not have noticed the change.

Where was Mike? "Mike, he's alive. Get your ass down here now! I need your help."

As if in response, Mike came hurtling down the embankment in such a whirlwind of motion that Joe thought it a miracle that he didn't end up in the trees.

Mike sat down on the opposite side of Emery and looked him over. The truck driver was in pretty bad shape. Mike could only imagine the beating his body must have taken inside the cab of the truck.

"Sir, do you mind if I check your body for injuries?"

Emery's eyelids slid open. He looked Joe directly in the eyes and hoarsely whispered. As he did, blood began to run from his nose and the corners of his mouth. Both Mike and Joe had seen this enough times to know what it signaled. They were completely still and listened with every ounce of their attention focused on the dying man. Emery's message was delivered with the last breath that he would take from this earth.

"Dying now. Save Sheriff. Go. Hurry. Bergdolt."

Mike and Joe looked at each other, dumbfounded. They had no idea what Emery was trying to tell them.

"Sir, what do you mean? Save the sheriff from what?"

Mike posed the questions to himself while Joe verbalized them aloud. Unfortunately, they would get no answer from Emery Mathis. The injuries he suffered in the wreck were more than his body could overcome. They sat with him for the few minutes it took for the ambulance to arrive. While they waited, they puzzled over his last words.

Although the time they waited for the arrival of the paramedics totaled less than four minutes, it seemed like hours to Mike Menzter and Joe Landis. They were silent until they heard the sirens in the distance, as if it would be impolite to be the one to break the silence. Finally, Mike spoke.

"What do you think he was talking about," he asked.

"I don't have any idea. Maybe we should head out to the sheriff's place. You know, just in case."

Mike shook his head and looked back up the embankment. He stood and said, "Joe, I'll go flag down the ambulance. You check him for any ID. We'll give it to the backups and get the hell out of here. We'll also have Stacy patch us through to Bergdolt's house and let him know that something might be up."

When they had informed the backup officers and paramedics of the situation at hand, Joe and Mike headed off to the sheriff's house on the outskirts of town. During the drive, Mike called back to the station and asked to be patched through to the sheriff's phone line. The telephone rang four times before it was answered.

"Hello, this is Sheriff...."

Mike quickly broke in, "Clancy, we may have a situation here."

The voice on the other end of the line did not stop to listen. ...Clancy Bergdolt, I'm unable to answer the phone right now. Please leave a message and I'll get back to you as soon as I can. If it is an emergency, please call the Sheriff's office and ask to be patched through to my radio. Thanks."

Mike left a short message and quickly called back to headquarters to get Bergdolt's cell number. "Damn," he said under his breath. He hadn't thought to get the cell number on the first call. Once he had the number and dialed, he waited for the sheriff to answer. With every ring, Mike pressed a little harder on the gas and the speedometer needle crept a little higher in the police cruiser. Once again, after four rings, he got an answer and recorded message. Mike closed the phone, flipped on the sirens and lights, and urged cruiser on with a deep gulp of unleaded. They were pushing 75 mph on the ribbon thin back roads, headed toward the sheriff's home residence.

Joe looked over at Mike and confirmed the levity of the situation with just one statement. "Something is definitely fucked up here." Mike did not answer; he only drove on.

"Do you think we should call for backup?"

Mike replied, "That's a good idea, go ahead and do it. I've got to keep my eyes on the road. I'm also starting to wonder if your little car thief had anything to do with the Camry or International, or both. Your original thought may have been more accurate than I was willing to admit. Call Valcraft and get the scoop on the abandoned car, if there is one yet.

Joe summoned the officer on his CB.

"Valcraft Here."

"This is Joe Landis. Any word on the beat up Pontiac?" Joe waited in anticipation, his heart beating fast. He had now broken into a sweat and could feel the beads of perspiration on his forehead.

"Yeah Landis, we've got a little, but its confusing. We processed the car. We pulled prints from the dash, mirror and door handles."

Joe was excited now. Prints were always good. Why did Valcraft seem so tentative? That was not his personality. He broke in before Valcraft could finish his report, "OK, did you run the prints - any hits?"

"Landis, give me a second and let me get to it for Christ's sake. I'm still reading the report for myself. Anyway, we got good prints, not just a ridge here or there. We ran 'em back at the post and came up with a Joseph Pratt. No previous record."

Joe couldn't wait any longer and broke in again, "OK, good. Did you try to locate him, put out an APB, anything?"

"He should be easy to locate, but we're probably not going to bring him in," Valcraft mocked. "Said suspect is deceased."

"Deceased? What the hell do mean deceased? Who was driving the car then?"

"Joe, we checked it out. The prints belong to a Joseph Pratt, born in Evanston, Indiana, August 8, 1972. Died July 23, 1992. Cause of death was cardiac arrest."

This time, Joe was silent. Finally, he muttered, "Cardiac arrest. Ninety two minus seventy two....You mean he had a life ending heart attack at 19 years of age?"

"That's what the cert says. I can't explain it. Sometimes, it's just your time to go. We're giving the car another once over, but I don't expect to find much. Must've been stolen and is just now turning up. I don't know how he did it. It's almost like the perp didn't leave any prints, but didn't wipe off the previous owners prints either. Listen Joe, I gotta go. I'll radio you when we know more. Talk to you later."

"Thanks."

Joe's mind was racing at the same speed as his heart now. He was so wrapped up in the mystery and anticipation of what they would find at the sheriff's place that he forgot to ask for backup. It was as if he was operating in a fog and only one thing mattered: finding out what the hell was going on here. Mike had heard the conversation and drove, slowly shaking his head back and forth but never letting his eyes leave the road.

IX. The Big House

Mike slowed to make a left hand turn. After the turn, he pulled onto the shoulder and shut the lights off. Up ahead, they could see a large clapboard farmhouse with two vehicles in the driveway. Both cars appeared to be police vehicles. Joe and Mike could both make out the big six pointed star on the door of the first cruiser. That made it the sheriff's. The second car appeared to have been in some kind of accident. The front fender and bumper were badly deformed and there was mud all down the side of the vehicle.

They each looked back at the house. There were no lights on and the place looked deserted except for the two cars in the driveway. The sheriff's two kids were grown and had moved away years back. He had been widowed for several years, so he would have been the only one home anyway. However, he would not have left without his vehicle, and the house looked deserted. A little closer inspection revealed that both porch windows were open, and the door was ajar.

"How do you want to handle this?"

It was clear by Joe's voice that he was nervous. His heart was still racing and he was sweating profusely. There were wet rings around the armpits of his shirt.

"You go around to the back door to stop any kind of escape attempt. I'll go in the front and flush 'em your way. Don't let them out the back without a fight."

Joe looked back at the farmhouse, mentally psyching himself up for action.

He nodded and replied in a quiet voice, "OK. Let's go."

They both got out of the cruiser and walked to the front of the vehicle, staring intently at the house. They paused at the head of the car before crossing the street. Each of them flipped off the safety strap that held his gun in place and un-holstered the weapons. Mike looked at Joe with a nervous smile.

"Ready?"

"Ready."

"Be alert in there. Here we go."

They crossed the street toward the big, whitewashed clapboard farmhouse with guns at the ready. The night was quiet except for the clicking of their shoes on the pavement. They reached the rock driveway and walked in the grass next to it on their way to the house. They paused at the front of the wrecked state police car. Joe pointed to the number on the front fender.

"Yep, that's mine," Joe said quietly. "Son of a bitch."

They split up, Joe heading toward the back of the farmhouse and Mike creeping up toward the front. He paused again at the steps that led up onto the big porch. He gave Joe a few seconds to make it around the house to the back door.

Joe moved quickly around the side of the house. He slowed briefly to look in a window to try to get a picture of what might be going on in the house. With no lights on in the house, he could see only shadows so he continued to move ahead to the back door. As he arrived, he slowly reached up and grasped the handle. It felt cool in his hand. Trying desperately to calm himself before entering, he counted.

"One….Two…Three…" and leaned into the door while attempting to turn the knob. The knob didn't budge and his shoulder bumped the door softly.

"Dammit," he cursed under his breath.

He hadn't even thought about the possibility that it might be locked. Joe quickly retreated and headed back around the front toward Mike. He was running, afraid that Mike may already be in the house.

After waiting a few seconds for Joe to reach the back door, Mike proceeded cautiously up the wooden stairs and across the porch to the front door. He leaned against the clapboards and exhaled quietly, gathering his wits and courage for his entry into the house.

"So far, so good," he whispered to himself.

He had made it across the wooden porch without producing so much as a squeak from the wooden planks that formed the floor. That was a good sign. Maybe luck would be on their side. It hadn't been on the side of the family that had owned the smashed Toyota Camry. Or the truck driver's either. *What is going on here?* Mike thought. *OK Joe, I hope you're in position and ready - here we go.*

Mike quickly looked through the opening between the door and doorjamb. It was difficult to make anything out in the shadows, but he did not see any figures. He pushed the door open further and stepped across the threshold. He waited briefly for his eyes to adjust to the dim light of the interior of the house.

Mike had entered directly into the living room. There was a small television against the wall to his right in front of the window. There was a sofa and recliner in the center of the room, both angled toward the TV. There were bookshelves on both side walls. The shelves were neatly arranged with family pictures and simple figurines to decorate the room. Despite these adornments, it was obvious that this house was devoid of female touch. The room was very functional, but had a cold feel despite the family photographs.

The back of the living room opened directly into the kitchen area with a hallway leading toward the left. *The hall must lead to the bedroom,* Mike thought. He could see the back door from where he was standing. Joe was not there. *Where the hell is he?* Just as he took his first step toward the kitchen, a loud **Creak!** came from the porch. Mike whirled and pointed the barrel of his standard issue revolver directly at the chest of the approaching figure.

He began to squeeze the trigger; the hammer retracting in slow motion, preparing to swing back into the closed position and propel a shot toward the intruder.

The shadowy figure quickly raised his hands and said in a hushed voice, "Fuck! Mike, it's me! It's Joe!"

Mike motioned Joe into the house and held one finger to his lips while slowly shaking his head in disgust. When Joe reached Mike, he prepared to speak again, but Mike silenced him again with the gesture. He shook his head at his partner again as a mother would when quietly scolding her child during church. They walked side by side to the back of the family room, Joe taking cues from Mike as to where and how to step to keep the noise to the minimum. The air was thick with tension. Mike leaned around the corner to check down the hall. He saw no one.

The hall looked to be nearly 15 feet long culminating in two doors, one directly ahead and the other on the left. On the right side of the hall was a staircase that led back in the direction of the living room. There was no doubt that it led to a second bedroom over the living room and kitchen.

Mike signaled to Joe that he should go down the hall and check out the bedrooms at the end. He himself would proceed up the stairs and check out the bedroom or rooms. With the two of them splitting up, they could maintain the element of surprise if someone was still here, which Mike believed was the case. Although the house was quiet and the lights were out, he could feel a presence in the house. He could feel it in the air, as if it imparted extra weight, making it heavier in his lungs.

He stepped into the hallway first, with Joe right behind. The moment they broke cover from the living room, they heard a loud **Thud!** upstairs. They quickly looked at each other and bolted up the stairwell, Mike still in the lead. The stairwell ended at a T, with a short hallway extending to both the left and right. On the right was a large open room. The left side of the hall ended in a small bedroom. They paused briefly at the top of the stairs. Mike pointed at Joe and then at the bedroom as he quickly took off toward the other room. He nearly lost his breath when he stepped into the room.

The room was in total disarray. It was clear that it had been used to house the years of memories from the sheriff's married life. The memoirs were now scattered across the floor. A set of bookshelves that had been against the back wall were laying face down at one end of the room. Lamps, candles, and ceramics were smashed with the pieces littering the floor. A desk was turned on its top to one side of the room. And in the middle of the floor, lying in a naked, crumpled heap was Sheriff Bergdolt. Hanging from the light fixture above him was fifteen inches of light gauge chicken wire freshly snipped at the end.

Mike was in total shock. His senses could not interpret all the data forcing its way in through his eyes. The sight was purely shocking. He could hear the sheriff whimpering, softly gasping for breath, lying there on the wood planked floor. But of all the senses, the smell of the room was what almost overwhelmed him. It reeked of a mixture of sweat, blood, piss, and sheer terror.

Mike quickly worked his way through the mess and over to the sheriff. When he got there, he saw more clearly what had happened in the room. The sheriff had been stripped to his bare skin, tied by his wrists to the ceiling with what appeared to be braided chicken wire, and badly beaten.

Mike thought with some certainty that Bergdolt had been interrogated. He found the wire cutters that had been used to cut the sheriff down and leaned over him, cutting the bindings from his hands and feet. He also cut off a double strip of barbed wire that had been wrapped around the sheriff's chest and apparently beaten into his flesh. He grabbed the sheriff's shirt from the floor and wrapped it around him to try to help with the shock. As he did, he heard shots from the room at the other end of the hall.

Mike got to his feet and fled toward the other end of the hall. As he entered the room, he was confused by what he saw, or didn't see. No one was in the small room. It was completely vacant. Mike's frantic eyes focused on the open window toward the back of the room. He raced to it and looked out. His partner was poised on the roof outside the window with his gun extended and at the ready.

"Joe, what's going on?"

Without even turning his head, Joe replied. "When I got to the room, there was nobody there. I walked over to the window and saw the perp climbing over the edge of the roof. He got down to the ground before I could stop him, but I got him. Shot him in the leg.

He's lying right in the back yard, about half way out. I'll keep an eye on him from here; you go down and cuff him. What the hell took you so long?"

"Later. I'll tell you when we get this guy cuffed. Maybe we can make some sense of it then." With that, Mike rushed out of the room.

Mike exited the back door and quickly moved toward the man lying motionless in the grass. He estimated the yard extended about eighty or ninety feet behind the house before coming to an abrupt halt at the base of the first row of corn. The criminal had made it better than halfway across the yard and was within thirty feet of the corn. In the dim light, the stalks resembled a seven foot wall of darkness that separated the Bergdolt residence from the rest of the world. Mike briefly remembered that Clancy did not farm the land himself, but rented the property to a local sharecropper as a supplement to his income as the sheriff. He continued his cautious walk toward the suspect.

From the rooftop, Joe watched with pride and relief. Not only had they caught the bad guy, but he had been personally responsible for bringing him down. It felt good - no it felt fantastic. He couldn't help but replay the events in his mind. Entering the room, making his way first to the window, then out onto the rooftop, shouting at the perpetrator before finally leveling the revolver and clipping him with one shot to the right leg. Thank goodness for the moonlight on this clear night or he wouldn't have even been able to see his target as he ran across the backyard toward the cornfield. And if he reached the corn, there would have been no stopping him. He would have either made it out scot-free, or gotten lost and wandered around for days in the vast field of America's number one crop.

Daniel Bramstow lay wounded in the grass. He thought to himself, d*amn these fucking cops. Can they not just leave me the fuck alone?* Amazingly enough, Bergdolt had revealed nothing during the interrogation. Daniel had done everything he could think of to persuade the poor sheriff to talk and yet he continued to plead,

"Please, I don't know what you're talking about. I have no idea who you even are. Please...Please."

Bramstow was just about to give up and finish the sheriff off when he heard the noise from the porch. He had been quiet and listened for a long time, hoping the intruders would just leave. When he snuck over to the window and looked out the front, he saw the state police cruiser so cleverly parked across the street and had bolted for the window at the back of the house. At that point, his mind had been running in overdrive.

Should he flee? Did he have time to kill Bergdolt first? Maybe he should ambush the pigs and kill them all. It would be harder, but it might be the better solution to his problem. No, killing wasn't his style. He only killed when he was forced into it; that was his rule. He hated them for that. The only thing that made it palatable for him was that he knew it was either them or him - the bastards. They had been after him for a long, long time.

Maybe today is their day. Maybe it's all over and I just don't know it. They have more resources than I can even imagine. Maybe I should just stop here and turn myself in - end this life on the run. Just as these thoughts swirled through his head, he'd heard soft footsteps in the hall at the bottom of the stairs. His flight instincts kicked in and he took off for the back bedroom window.

And now here he was, lying in the back yard just 30 foot from escape, with a bullet lodged in the back of his leg. He rolled his eyes as far to the side as he could and slowly turned his head in the direction of the house. The first bastard of a cop was still on the roof watching him. *Shit.* The second was slowly making his way from the house toward him, gun at the ready.

What am I going to do now? They've got me. Shit. How did they know I'd even be here? Bastards, they seem to know everything!

Joe silently smiled as he continued to watch Mike make his way toward the crippled man in the grass. He could see that Mike had pulled his own revolver and held it at the ready in front of him. He stepped slowly toward the figure in the grass. When he was within 10 feet of the guy, he did the unimaginable. He stepped in the line between the perp and Joe. Joe lost sight of the man in the grass. He was hidden in the shadows. If something went wrong, he wouldn't be able to help.

"Shit," he cursed under his breath. He couldn't let this happen so he shouted at Mike. "Mike, move over, you're in the….."

Naturally, Mike turned to see why Joe was shouting at him. As he did, Daniel Bramstow broke from his paralysis, spun over to his backside and leveled his own handgun at the cop and fired. On the rooftop, Joe heard the loud clap and watched his partner's head jerk back violently before his body crumpled and he fell dead to the ground.

Danny scrambled to his feet and made a mad dash toward the safety of the cornrows. The dull pain in his hamstring burned intensely, nearly bringing him back to the ground in a heap. Danny knew that he couldn't give up now; this would be his only chance for escape. He focused on the corn. The flames of pain continued in his leg and began to spread up his back, but he was less aware of them as he focused even more on the corn.

His focus was so strong that he was unaware of his mumbling, "Got to….. make it…..to…the..coooorn."

He was vaguely aware of the gunshots ringing out behind him and the exploding pain in his backside as his leg buckled under him and he half fell/half dove into the corn. His senses were so attuned to the first row of corn that he could feel the leaves softly cutting slits into his hands, cheeks, ears, and neck as he plunged into the field.

Danny knew that he could not regain his feet, so he crawled as fast as he could in the corn rows, cutting from row to row and dragging his lame leg behind him the whole while. He continued his frantic crawl/drag, listening for the other cop in the corn and fighting off the pain in his leg and lower back. Then, he heard rustling from the corn behind him. He had two choices: continue crawling and risk being heard, or lay still and risk being seen. With it being dark and the corn making it even darker in the field, he chose the second option. He lay still in the cornfield and closed his eyes, concentrating on the sound of the rustling corn behind and to the left of him.

At first, he wasn't sure which way his pursuer was moving, but after a few minutes of panic, he was able to discern that the cop was moving further to the left of him and away from his hiding place. Danny decided to lie still for awhile longer to regain his strength and hopefully avoid being spotted. As he closed his eyes, his breathing evened out and the flashbulb parade that was taking place on the back of his eyelids slowly faded and then ceased altogether. He breathed more deeply as the rustling footsteps continued to move away from him; the sound retreating, retreating, and finally stopping as he drifted into sleep.

As Danny slept, Joe Landis searched frantically in the corn for the man who had so brutally punished Sheriff Bergdolt and killed his own partner. After nearly 2 hours of wandering through the corn, he resolved to call in a search team to help. Maybe he had actually killed the son of a bitch and just needed to find him. As Joe stepped out of the corn and back into the moonlight, he was shocked by his surroundings. After a minute or two of orientating himself, he realized that he was a good 3 or 4 miles east of the Bergdolt place. He reached for the radio on his belt only to come up empty.

"And the hits just keep on comin," he said miserably.

Before leaving the cruiser, he and Mike had resolved to leave the radios in the car for fear of alerting the perp that they were coming for him. He dejectedly began the walk back toward Sheriff Bergdolt's house and the police cruiser. If the intruder wasn't dead in the corn, he would surely be gone by the time the search team arrived.

X. On the Road Again

Danny abruptly awoke from his nap in a panic. He had been dreaming so vividly that he couldn't convince himself it wasn't real. He was lying in the grass in the sheriff's yard and the second cop was slowly walking toward him. But, instead of the events unfolding as they actually had, the cop leveled the revolver square with Danny's eyes.

"Fuck you, Danny boy. I know all about your bullshit. But I can fix it," he said to Danny and the gun exploded with a wisp of smoke and death.

Danny could hear the gunshot ringing in his ears as he hysterically looked around, puzzled by all the cornstalks in his field of vision. Finally, his panic broke and he realized that he had been asleep and dreaming. *How long had he been asleep? Where were the cops that were after him? Surely reinforcements were on the way. How long until they arrived?*

Danny inspected the back of his leg as best he could through the small rip in his jeans where the bullet had entered. Luckily, the blood seemed to be confined by his jeans and had stopped flowing. Good. He didn't want to leave any more information for the cops to dissect than absolutely necessary. Danny slowly got to his feet and tested his wounded leg. Sharp needles of pain shot up from his hamstring.

"Well, it looks like I'll be gimpy for a while," he mumbled as he took his first step/hop back toward the road that he had driven in on.

He would have to be careful, but he also had to get the hell out of here. Danny's hopes were confirmed when he finally exited the corn and stepped into the street. He found himself well to the west of the Bergdolt house. He couldn't tell for sure how far west, but it didn't matter. The distance would give him a head start on his pursuers. He just had to get a car, get back to his place, grab his "Red Bags" and get out of town.

As a precaution, in case he had to leave town quickly, Danny always kept 2 bags filled with his most personal and private possessions and a map highlighting the lowest risk, most direct route out of town. He called them his "Red Bags" and "Express Route" respectively. Together they made up the "Red Ex Package."

After quietly hot-wiring one of the sheriff's distant neighbor's cars, Danny returned to the small dilapidated house he called home. He collected the Red Ex package plus a few other souvenirs and hit the Express Route out of Graisville, not stopping for several hours and only then to piss at the gas station, "trade" cars and get back on the highway. This one was an out of state late model Pontiac Gran Prix. Pontiac seemed to be his style lately.

Danny drove in silence down the long stretch of highway toward his next destination. In an earlier part of his life, he had worked part time as a travel agent and had plotted out a list of towns where he could take up residence if he found it necessary. To validate his plan, he had taken over two weeks to scout out the towns and drive his Express Routes so that he could precisely plan out the order in which he would move from one to the other if or when trouble presented itself. His diligence was certainly paying off now.

As he drove, Danny recounted the events of the last 36 hours. Everything had worked perfectly up until the police had interfered. The backstabbing truck driver was dead in what Danny was sure would be ruled an accident. He had spent weeks researching semi tractors and meticulously planning the event and it had come off without a hitch. It was unfortunate that the trucker had denied Danny his reasoning for running his mouth to the sheriff. Danny had thought briefly of the possibility that the trucker was telling the truth, but he could not allow the mere chance of more information on him being handed over to the authorities. No telling how much trouble he would be in if the truck driver knew very much at all about him.

After he had finished off the trucker, Danny had progressed to step two of his plan. He had to find out from the sheriff what the trucker told him and if he had passed anything along to the higher authorities. After a long interrogation, which had yielded only lies and denials, he had been interrupted by the two state cops. He hadn't even had time to finish off the sheriff. Thanks again to meticulous planning, there would be nothing at the house to lead the cops back to him. He was a ghost. Any evidence they found would only baffle and confuse the sorry sons of bitches.

He had barely escaped with his life, or worse yet, without being captured. Who knows what fun they would be having with him if they had been able to stop his escape? Capture was something that Danny had resolved never to let happen. Daniel Bramstow would die by his own hand before going through the hell that *they* had planned for him. And he would be damned if he didn't take a few of the bastards with him.

After settling into his hotel room at the Imperial Inn, Danny pulled out his laptop, plugged into the internet connection, and logged onto www.npac.com. On the *Newspapers across the Country* website, he scanned through the last week's stories from the Graisville Gazette. He found several articles concerning the deaths of one truck driver named Emery Mathis, State Police officer Mike Mentzer, and the local sheriff, Clancy Bergdolt. The articles stated that the truck driver died from internal injuries resulting from two successive accidents, one involving another vehicle with fatalities and the other involving only the semi tractor. A separate article stated that the sheriff died from injuries and trauma suffered in a homicide and the state trooper from a single gunshot to the head. The local police had no suspects, but the investigation was ongoing. The most recent article suggested that the police were making no progress and that the investigators were theorizing that the evidence was somehow compromised, accounting for the lack of suspects.

Danny shut down the Dell laptop, leaned back in his chair, looked out the window at the well manicured landscape and smiled. He leaned a little further back, smiled a little wider and said, "I'll probably like it better here in North Carolina anyway."

Summer of '99

I. Rain - Soft on My Window

I sat in my tattered, one bedroom apartment and listened to the rambling of *SportsCenter* while the rain pecked at the window outside. The constant tapping of the droplets seemed to carry me back on a foamy wave, back to another place and time. I wondered what part I had actually played in my grandmother's passing out of this world. Looking back on all of the events of my life, that night at the hospital with my grandmother seems the most unreal. It exists in a fog, cowering in the shadows in the very back corner of my mind. For years it had been too painful to even think about; now I couldn't dredge up all of the details if my life depended on it. But that wasn't totally true was it?

Some things came back easily. The drab green halls of the hospital and the off white tile floors. The clacking sound of footsteps in the hallway, always moving slightly faster toward the exit than when entering from the elevator. The low murmur of televisions from rooms up and down the hall, not loud enough to actively invade our privacy, but hovering at the very edge of acknowledgement, like wolves at the edge of camp.

These are the memories that come to me on nights such as this. Nights filled with light rain, fog, and Budweiser. The King and I made friends shortly after Mammaw was admitted to the "hopspital," as my youngest brother Chris would call it. Bud and I have been close ever since. The memories don't come all at once as you might expect. They start slowly, a trickling stream of water in a nearly dry creek bed. The smallest details are the ones that seep through the cracks in the mental dam that I had constructed so long ago. *The raindrops, always those God Damn raindrops clicking softly on the window; beckoning me back to another place and time.* Next, the sound of the television seems to gently retreat to that low murmur at the edge of my subconscious. Creeping away softly, slowly until it's the same faint murmur from my past. *Faster now* - the footsteps in the hall, some slow and cautiously approaching, others quick and thankful to be leaving. The walls are a drab green, almost the color of olives, yet not quite as dark. Ever so often, a picture hangs to break the monotony of color. A reproduced oil painting of Jesus in a gold frame is on one side of the hall. On the other side hangs a color print of a farmer's field, golden with rows of wheat ready for harvest. The sunset on the horizon paints the clouds a deep plum against the blue sky.

The picture inevitably triggers a shut down mechanism deep in my subconscious. As I am drawn into the picture of the field, I can almost feel the spray of the rushing flood on my neck. *I have to escape before the dam breaks and I drown in my own memories!* It's almost like waking from the "falling" dream that we all have occasionally in the deep of night. At the very point when the water fills my lungs and my mind fills with memories of that night, I snap back to the rain on the sill and ESPN on the television. As I come to consciousness, I can feel the cool sweat on the back of my neck. The splash of cold water on my face and neck never feels as good as on nights like these. So close, yet saved again from the torrent.

At a very early age, I became very close to my grandmother, "mammaw" as she was later known by not only my self, but my two siblings as well.

Mammaw lived in Ridgeton, Kentucky. Ridgeton was 134 miles northeast of our southern Indiana home. I recall the drive being one of extreme anticipation. My brothers and I would load our sleeping bags and toys into the back of the red Chevy station wagon as soon as dad would return from work on Friday night. Dad had a Friday ritual of having "a cocktail" with the other foremen of the local construction company on Friday evenings. Except, that is, Fridays that we were slated to go to Mammaw's.

Dad knew that if he took too long to get home on trip night, the anticipation of heading toward Ridgeton would most likely make all our heads explode. Occasionally, I felt that my head might explode before he got home even on a day when he wasn't late.

The trip was one of complete and utter boredom for a young child. Along the roadside, there was nothing but green fields inhabited by forever grazing cattle. On one such memorable trip, we were cruising down Highway 44, bored to tears when my 5 year old brother began laughing hysterically.

"Chris, what in the world are you laughing about," Mom asked with a puzzled look on her face?

His reply caused a clamoring so loud that it blotted out the radio in the interior of the station wagon.

"Mom, look at that one cow riding that other cow."

I guess Mom and Dad decided that no reply was better than the wrong reply in this situation.

Mom would try to help us pass the time in the station wagon by playing games. Most of the time, we played Riddley Ree.

"Riddley Riddley Ree, I see something you don't see and the color is......Red," Mom would say.

We would guess everything under the sun, red in color or not. I generally won these games of nonsense, not that we ever kept score. Eventually, I got to be the Riddler; and boy was I a good one. I would start out slow, maybe with something in the car, but the game always ended with my brother Jeff hollering, "OK, OK, I give - what is it! You're cheating, I just know it. You don't see nothin' that color!"

I walked to the kitchen to get a beer. Budweiser was still my favorite, although they were never cold enough coming out of my pale green Whirlpool Classic fridge. Maybe I could drown the memories with a beer or five. Some of the memories – flashbacks – refused to go away forever, but they would vanish for at least the night. Usually I could suppress them enough to keep from emptying the fridge of Bud, but occasionally it took the full strength of the Anheuser Busch Brewing Company to empty the storehouse of unpleasant images.

On bad nights, I could hear Mammaw's shallow breathing in my ears and feel the cool clammy skin of her hand on my forearm as

I sank deeper and deeper into the one night that had shaped me so completely.

The fun began almost as soon as we walked into the door at Mammaw's. She always had pie or cake prepared for us when we arrived. Most often it was cherry pie for us kids and pecan for the adults. My brothers and I would be eating pie before Mom and Dad got all of the stuff out the wagon. After scarfing down at least two pieces of cherry pie - Mom would allow no more than that - we would rush into the living room and turn on the television.

Mammaw only got six television channels, but the only one that mattered was channel 31 – WTVQ. On Friday nights, WTVQ aired Championship Wrestling, or "rasselin" as my dad called it. We always watched rasselin on TV and frequently practiced our moves on each other until either something got broken or someone got hurt, sometimes both. Most of the time it was Chris getting hurt that set the stage for Mom to break up the fun.

"If I have to get your dad's belt and come in there, I guarantee you'll be sorry. I brought you into this world and by God I can take you out of it!" And we knew without a doubt that this was the absolute and undeniable truth.

Tonight, the memory was more clearly in focus. I listened intently to the soft patter of rain outside. Tap… Tap…. Tap. I floated down the green hallway; moving ahead, ever so slowly. None of the lights in the hallway were turned on, but it was not completely dark either. There was a dim quality in the vision; like the darkness was there at the edges of my mind, relentlessly pressing to get in. It was just bright enough to see. I focused on the rain; holding on to it like a rope in a tug of war contest, to keep from losing control and falling in (or out) of the dreamscape. It seemed to be raining more slowly now, maybe helping in my travel down the hallway. All the rooms were dark except one. A sick yellowish light spilled out of the room and fanned across the wall opposite the door. I focused on it and floated to the doorway of Mammaw's room.

As I reached the threshold of the room, the sensation of floating vanished and I was left standing in the lit doorway. The room reeked of a blend of smells that I couldn't quite place. The best description available to me is a mixture of bleach, flowers, and fear or death. With some effort, Mammaw called to me weakly in her frail voice, "Oh Joey! So good to see you; come on in and sit with me for awhile."

I looked over to Mammaw and took in the view. She was lying in the automatic hospital bed, propped up on the pillows behind her head and shoulders. She had moved the bed into a half seated position so that she could sit up better. There were flowers and balloons lining the window sill at her right. Needles, tubes, and wires ran from all types of machinery into Mammaw's bed and disappeared under the covers, which she had pulled up to just below her chin. I could see that she had removed her oxygen mask so that she could talk easier.

"So cold in here, they are trying their best to make me suffer before I finally pass," she told me.

I walked across the room with its striped wallpaper and waxed tile floor and sat in the mustard recliner at Mammaw's bedside.

"I've been waiting for you to come back," she said. "It seems so long since you've visited. You know how I like to visit with you."

During Mammaw's long stay in the hospital, I visited her every day I could. I had the sense that she had lost track of time, and it was evident even in my dream. I smiled at her and reached up to take her hand.

"I love you Mammaw," I said with tears welling up in my eyes.

"I love you too honey, but I need to talk to you about something serious today. Can we do that?"

There was an urgency in her eyes that made me uneasy. As I prepared to answer, the darkness pushed in and threatened to drag me away from the dream. It started slowly, but began to push forward more quickly and my view of the room dimmed and started to fade from the edges of my vision. I was losing it. The black closed in until I could see only through a hole in the darkness about the size of a dime. I had lost track of the rain drops; I couldn't hear them any more. I listened intently for them on the window.

Tap…..Tap……Tap. The soft pattering of the droplets came back to me and I was propelled back through the tunnel of darkness and into the hospital room with my grandmother.

II. Book of Memories

"…..sure he would have adored you the same way I do. What happened to him was a tragedy and I'll hate the men responsible till the day I finally pass from this world."

At first, I was confused as to where this was headed. I focused on Mammaw and thought about what she had just said. She sat in the hospital bed and looked out the window. I could hear her quiet sobs and knew immediately that she was speaking of Josef, my late grandfather. I had never met Josef and knew little about him other than he was a career military man. I wasn't even sure which branch of the service he had served. I knew that he died before I was born, but knew nothing of the circumstances. Mammaw rarely spoke of Josef and hadn't remarried. I never asked her about it either. It was obvious that his death had affected her deeply.

At this point, I was still not sure where the conversation was headed, at least not consciously aware. I stayed focused on Mammaw; convinced that something important was about to surface. She dabbed her eyes with the sheet and turned back to face me.

"I do love you Joey. You've been as close to me as anyone these last few months. That's why I want you to have something, but I need you to do something for me."

"Mammaw, you know you don't have to give me anything," I insisted. "I'll do whatever you want."

She pointed at the only closet in the room. "In the closet, on the top shelf," she said simply.

I slowly stood and walked over to the closet. I opened the door and it struck me how sad it must be to spend twenty four hours a day in a hospital. My grandmother had been in this same hospital room for 4 months and all she had in the closet were two housecoats, a pair of slippers and on the top shelf, a square white cardboard box a little larger than a shoebox. The outside of the box was unmarked, but severely worn at each corner. I reached up and slid the box off the shelf. It had some weight to it, and I wondered what it contained.

I carried it back over to the chair and sat down with it resting in my lap.

"Go ahead and open it," Mammaw said with a timid smile.

I slowly slid the lid off the cardboard box. It held what appeared to be a scrapbook. Much like the box, it was unadorned in any way and severely worn at the edges. It was a dark blue, almost black in color with the brown cardboard exposed at each corner from the wear. It had an old and musty smell, like what you might find in the cellar of an old, deserted house.

"It's your grandfather's journal."

Even though Mammaw's eyes were clear and dry, I could sense that this was very emotional for her. The air in the room felt heavy all around us.

I slowly opened the cover and looked at the first page. It was a heavy grade of paper that was fuzzy around the edges and had not a single line. I didn't know if the paper had always had the fuzzy edges, or if that was also from the wear. I suspected the latter. There was only one marking on the first page of my grandfather's journal; centered on the leaf. It read, in carefully articulated print:

$$論 証$$

"Don't look at it now. Take it home with you, but don't let anyone see that you have it. Not even your parents. When you read through it you'll know why."

As these last words floated in the thick air of the hospital room, the darkness closed in on me again. This time I was unable to stop it and my field of vision went completely black. I opened my eyes and was back in the apartment. It was still raining outside, but Sportcenter was over. ESPN was showing the World Championships of Badminton. I clicked off the television. Sports were no longer a priority in my life. Staying alive and remaining free were numbers one and two on that particular list.

I walked into my mostly barren bedroom and over to the closet. I had not done much decorating in the few months since I'd moved in. I had never been much on decorating anyway. The paint on the walls was an ugly beige and looked like it hadn't been fresh in over a decade. There were no pictures and the sole window was covered by two navy blue pillow cases tacked to the window molding with heavy duty staples.

I continued to the closet, opened the door and was greeted by a loud *creak!* The small closet was filled with a disorganized scrum of clothes and miscellaneous items. I pulled out two black suitcases, still filled with clothes and personal effects from my arrival here forty three months ago, and moved them into the room. I pushed aside the clothes pile in the floor of the closet but didn't see the white cardboard box. A wave of panic washed over me. I had made a promise to Mammaw that I would protect the journal at all costs. Now I had lost it? I quickly began pulling clothes out of the closet in handfuls and flinging them over my shoulder and on to the bed. As I pulled the last pair of jeans out, the tattered box was revealed. At the sight of the journal box, my heart slowly returned to its steady rhythm.

I grabbed the box and carried it over to the bed, now covered entirely with clothes. I absently pushed aside the mess to make myself a place to sit. I opened the box and removed my grandfather's journal, replaced the lid on the box and placed it on the floor. I flipped again to the first page of the journal and softly traced my fingers over the Japanese script that loosely translated "The certain truth." I sat there for a few moments and let the memories quickly enclose me again. As the feeling of lightheadedness left me, I slowly turned the first page and began to read the script.

III. War Stories

This personal journal and scrapbook are unknown to the U.S. government and armed forces. They should remain as such unless you are willing to accept extreme and swift repercussions. I know, I have witnessed the consequence of such actions first hand.

This is my story, though I am hesitant to believe anyone will accept it as truth. This journal has been written well after the events told within, though I still remember every detail with excruciating clarity. I would strongly caution against investigation of the events contained within this manuscript. I assure you that they are accurate. I also swear to you that the strongest divisions of both the government and the forces of the military will squash any hint of this and erase anyone who openly speaks of it without prejudice or concern.

I'm not even sure where to start. The events take place beginning October of 1944 and ending with my dismissal from the military in May of 1952. Believe me, there is much more to tell, but I won't convolute the issue at hand with my own plight from being involved. That's a story for another time, as they say.

1944: The world was a different place then, and not just the obvious stuff like elected officials and the price of gas and milk. The country had a different feel. It was a feeling of pride. In the military, we were the best of the best; the best in the world. We were highly qualified, trained to the highest standards and ready for any and all missions, and I do mean *any* in the purest sense of the word.

I had finished my training and completed several successful missions as a part of the black ops group known as the Epsilon Force, EForce as we soldiers called it. In that day, black ops were a common occurrence. Hell, we were the United States of Fucking America. We answered only to ourselves. The military leadership knew that the only way to really get things done was to take ownership, make the tough decisions and execute the plan. The country was so bound up in politics, you couldn't expect the political leadership to know what to do, much less give you the authority to do it.

During our last assignment, EForce got caught in a pretty nasty situation. We were sent into Europe to assassinate a high ranking military advisor in the Third Reich. We had intel from the home base that indicated he had a meeting scheduled to review the progress of their offensive in Europe. The meeting was to take place at a privately owned restaurant just outside of Munich. Per our instructions, we arrived at the meeting site 2 days in advance, prepped, and waited. As our base of operations, we had chosen an abandoned and condemned office building across the square from the designated restaurant. Tensions were high, but we were informed, equipped and trained to execute tasks just as this one. There were 4 E's assigned to this mission. We were paired together; each of the higher ranking men with one of lower rank. Of the 4, I was the second highest in rank.

The night before the scheduled meeting we were attacked by German assassins. I don't know how many there were, probably 10 or 12; it seemed like 50 or 60. The odds were definitely against us. Luckily, the building had been chosen well by our OSS supervisors. There was no good way for the Germans to surprise us. We huddled close to one another in the front office and traded gunfire with the Germans for what seemed like hours. Bullets flew and ricocheted all around us. My training had turned me into an expert marksman and I knocked off several of the Nazi bastards myself. I remember hearing the sound of their bullets cutting through the air just inches above my head as I fired round after round out the windows and directly into multiple groupings of Nazi soldiers.

I was vaguely aware that at some point I had lost my partner to a German bullet, but I knew things were really screwed up when I heard Carl screaming. Carl was the man with the lowest rank of the four of us, but he was a good soldier. He was also good under pressure, so I was startled to hear his wails. I quickly looked to the other side of the office where he was posted. I first noticed that he was no longer shooting. He held his hands up to me as if to play patty cake. His face was a contortion of horror and fear. His hands were dripping with blood, black as the night. I fired a couple more shots to keep the Germans from moving any closer and then risked a second look.

This time, I noticed our captain lay across Carl's legs. His chest glistened black in the dim light of the office building. With only two of us left, it was time to cut bait and get the hell out. I signaled to Carl and screamed, "HE'S DEAD CARL! EVAC NOW! LET'S ROLL!" Per protocol, we had a preplanned escape route in case the mission went south, and this one certainly had.

As soon as the Nazis realized that we had stopped shooting, they rushed the building. Carl and I retreated from the office and down the back hall. We followed the stairs to the basement where we had previously opened a hole in the floor just wide enough for a man to slip through. We each jumped down the hole; Carl first, then myself. We dropped directly into the sewer system. It was cold, dark and smelled exactly like what you would expect, shit. We ran 10 or 12 foot down the sewer line and I stopped.

Carl kept moving while I finished off the job. I pulled the pin on the small egg shaped grenade and pitched it back down the sewer to where we had dropped through. I could hear the Nazis and their German gibberish just before the grenade exploded; collapsing the building's floor, killing the remaining Germans and closing off the tunnel to our escape point. We sprinted to the extraction point, climbed up the ladder and radioed for our extraction team.

Within a couple of hours, we had showered, eaten, been debriefed and were on a military plane back to the Gitmo, where our task force was stationed. Our mission had been a failure, but Carl and I had survived. I was glad for it at the time. Had I known what the future held for me, my outlook may have been quite different.

Just thirty minutes after arriving at base, I was called into an excessively large conference room that held nothing more than a podium - sans microphone. To my surprise, General Mays stood at the head of the room. I remember it vividly. The room was so cold that I could almost see my own breath. *The A/C must be working double time,* I thought. I stepped into the conference room and saluted. Someone pulled the door closed behind me. *What was this about?*

"At ease soldier," the General said.

I relaxed ever so slightly, my heart still machine-gunning within my chest. A frozen silence permeated the room. General Mays held an envelope in his right hand. He opened the unsealed envelope, unfolded a crisp, white sheet of paper and reviewed it briefly before addressing me.

"Son, you did good work over in Germany. I'm sorry about the rest of your force, especially Captain Miller. I know you two were close."

I took a deep breath and replied, "We were all close to Millie. He was a good man. His death will be a loss for the force." I had more to say, but I stopped for fear of exposing too much emotion to the General. In the armed forces, you get ahead by being a rock, having no emotion. You have to know your mission, have the skills necessary to perform, and the ability and fortitude to execute the mission no matter the circumstances.

General Mays took a deep breath and nodded his head in agreement. "You're certainly right. The captain was a good soldier. It's unfortunate that he's gone, which brings me to my next point of business." He paused, stared hard into my face and spoke again. I could tell from his eye contact and tone that something serious was on the way.

"Son, your work over the past few years has been exceptional, and believe me, it's been noticed at all levels. Your proficiency reports are outstanding. Your conduct under pressure is without question. You're as good a soldier as we have. All of these qualities put you in the same class as former Captain Miller.

My breathing was noticeably faster. I was pretty sure I knew where this was headed. It's funny how these things play out in our minds. Although I was pretty sure I was about to be promoted, part of my mind refused to believe it as truth. It was like a small child huddled in a dark corner just out of sight, tormenting me in my special moment.

"Bullshit, you're not good enough for promotion. Hell, you let them all die in that fucking office. Do you really believe he's going to promote you after that fucking disaster? He must have found out something else you've done and he's going to discharge you, and probably dishonorably you fucking pansy!"

As the demented fantasy played out in the recesses of my mind, I tried desperately to concentrate on the General's words.

"Congratulations on a job well done. I would like to recommend you for promotion to Captain of the Epsilon Task Force. Captain Josef Wilden, it has a proper ring to it don't you think?"

General Mays smiled and extended his hand as he completed the question. Without even thinking, I reached out and shook it. With that single arm motion, I had condemned my very future without even knowing it. The events of the next few years would nearly end my life, and many times I've wished they had. It would be better than knowing that they were out there, awaiting even the slightest misstep. And when I finally did, they would erase me from the face of the planet. Why? The secret, of course. Anyone who knew the secret of the Black War had to be eliminated. The secret could never make its way back to the public, *never*.

Haven't heard of the Black War? Not in any of the high school text books? *Exactly*. To the common American, there was no such war. Mission accomplished. I'm not sure where the name came from, but it fit perfectly for all of us in EForce. Black it was. Black because it went on in complete and utter darkness. Outside our commanders and us, nobody knew what the hell was *really* happening in Japan. Black because the operation could only have been dreamt up in the black, cold darkness of the devil's own heart. The things I saw, the things we did ....

Though I had read the text countless times, I still found myself in disbelief as I read the words. I continued reading and my anger and distrust escalated as it had so many times before. Surely this couldn't be real. I had done some checking, as much as I could without raising suspicion, and had not turned up anything to prove the validity of my grandfather's journal. For quite some time, I had strongly believed that the government was after me for some reason, and this *had* to be it, didn't it? The journal *had* to be right.

They were good, but not good enough. Mammaw had prepared me well by giving me the journal to help protect me. I often wish she was here now to help guide me. Sometimes, I wonder if they would still be after me if she hadn't given me the journal. *Surely they knew about it didn't they? Isn't that why they were after Mammaw?*

I had been "living quietly," as Mammaw called it, for four years. I hadn't spoken to my parents since I left. It was better that they not know where I was. Mammaw made it very clear that Mom and Dad didn't believe her when she tried to tell them Papaw's story. Because of their refusal to believe, they couldn't be trusted with the truth.

I turned back to the journal and started to read again. I was instantly drawn back into my grandfather's grim, terrible story.

IV. The Job

Just 22 hours after accepting the position as the captain of the Epsilon Force, I was back on an airplane, headed to a training base on a small island near the Philippines. Our next mission would be somewhere in Japan, but that was all I knew for the time being. I was to be reunited with the rest of EForce and introduced as their new captain at 0600. I would also get to meet the new members of the force and our training would begin in preparation for our new mission.

As we flew over the small island, I took in the view. It was crescent shaped with dramatic cliffs jutting several hundred feet out of the South Pacific on the back side of the island. The rocky land mass was smaller than I'd anticipated, but nearly three quarters of it had been cleared of its native foliage. Only the southernmost tip was still forested. The base occupied nearly all of the cleared land. Peculiarly, it appeared to be more urban than military; with neighborhoods that closely resembled those of current day Japan dominating the landscape. Another section of the compound resembled a small fishing village.

After the plane landed, I was escorted via jeep to my quarters in a nondescript concrete block building. The building was deserted; all the bunks and lockers stood empty around the main cabin room. *Must be the first one here.* I unpacked what little gear I had and used the map that I got from the drop off private to get to the mess hall. I hadn't eaten in over 14 hours and I was famished.

The mess hall was bustling with men hurriedly eating their dinners before they were required to be back at their posts. Time down was precious in the military and the men used their appointed meal times for not only eating, but writing to family members, reading return letters, reviewing training protocols, weightlifting, gambling, or sometimes catching up on a little shuteye.

I made my way through the line and found a table at the back of the room with just a couple other men at it. Just as I began to introduce myself, a tall, well-dressed man walked up and asked if he could join us at the table. He wore a black, double breasted, tailored suit and carried a matching leather attaché case. His hair was coal black and held close to his skull with a copious slathering of tonic. His eyes were a pale blue and were almost shaded by his heavy brow. This was no military man, but he exuded power and authority not unlike that of the best that I had witnessed in my time in the service.

As he pulled out a chair to sit, the others at the table promptly arose and departed. The dark haired man smiled wanly and introduced himself as Dr. Martin Price of McCline Pharmaceuticals. Now I was lost. *Why would a pharmaceutical company have someone on an unacknowledged military base on a small island off the coast of Japan?* Worse yet, why did everyone practically *run* for the exits as he sat down?

Dr. Price sat the attaché on the table and opened it without another word, removing a small file and passing it across the table. The file was stamped **CONFIDENTIAL** across the front. I was no longer hungry, and picked up the file that lay in front of me. As I began to open the file, Price roughly grabbed my arm and shook his head.

"This mission is highly confidential," he hissed. "This file contains information that not even your soldiers will be privy to. I suggest you guard it with your life and not share it with anyone. And I mean *anyone*. Truth is, it's above your pay grade, but your commanding officer insisted we bring you inside the tent. Read the file tonight - alone. I will meet you in the briefing room of the main building near your barracks at 0800 tomorrow. Be prepared. And be prompt, Captain."

With that said, he arose from his chair and left the mess hall without additional comment or pleasantry. I was at a loss for words. This mission was getting stranger by the minute. I picked at my food, looking over at the file in frequent intervals. I couldn't open and read it in the mess hall, but I was dying to know what it contained.

Finally, I resolved to give up on dinner. I left the mess hall and headed for the main building, where I could find a private briefing room to read the mission training file uninterrupted. I have recreated a copy of the briefing below.

UNITED STATES DEPARTMENT OF DEFENSE
CONFIDENTIAL

October 12, 1939
To: Captain Josef Wilden
From: Colonel Norman Correli
Re: Operation Incivility

Captain,
I am quite sure you have now met Dr. Price. Despite his cold demeanor, he is very adept at his trade, which you will no doubt witness in the not too distant future. From this point forward, you will be taking your direction from Dr. Price. He has been hand picked, as you have yourself, to carry out this operation. I must stress that this mission is of the utmost importance to the United States Military and our young country as a whole. These are frightening times we live in and desperate measures are sometimes required to ensure continued freedom.

The mission your task force has been selected for is one of the highest secrecy. Of the EForce members, you are the only constituent that will have access to this briefing and your discretion is mandatory. You will not share this brief with anyone, and you will return it to Dr. Price in your individual briefing meeting at 0800 tomorrow. Do not at any point copy the materials in this brief. At the meeting you will receive the final details of your mission. You will attend a second briefing with your EForce companions at 1500 hours. In this second briefing, the individual members of the EForce will receive the information they require for the operation.

It has become obvious that the world is headed toward a war of unimaginable proportions. We are unsure of the extent of U.S. involvement, but do not doubt that we will be engaged in some capacity. Our most current intelligence indicates that the use of biological and chemical weapons may be inevitable. To that end, the military has been investigating the development of chemical weapons of our own. As a part of Operation Incivility, your task force has been selected to advance the testing and deployment of these agents at an undetermined location within the borders of Japan. You will conduct multiple, small scale operations to deploy the agents in the Japanese public and record the effects of said deployment. You will report the most effective deployment methods as well as the resulting level of effectiveness of the agents.

Again, I must stress the importance of your discretion in this matter. We have determined that this discretion will allow for a more controlled and predictable response from your men, which will result in the utmost effectiveness for the operation. Should the operation be compromised, the U.S. government will disavow any knowledge of your citizenship or allegiance to this country.

Good luck and God Speed Captain.

At this point, I needed a break. I put the journal down and walked to the fridge for another Bud. I felt numb; disassociated from reality. I wasn't exactly cold, but my skin felt cool on the surface despite the perspiration on my brow. The hair on the back of my neck stood at attention. It is a difficult story to believe, and I knew it would get even stranger before it was over. My grandfather had tested biological weapons on unknowing Japanese civilians. It sickened me to think that he had been party to that despicable part of our country's history. It was no wonder that the government had worked so hard to keep this a secret. I drained these thoughts from my head with the last drops of the sweet nectar of Budweiser and went back into the bedroom, grabbed the journal and returned to the kitchen table to continue reading. This way I could be closer to the Bud. I popped open another bottle and took a long draught, refocusing my attention to the words.

V. Simple Orders

During my individual briefing with Dr. Price, I learned the details of the operation. Our force was eight strong and included not only myself, but several men I had served with in the past. There were only two new faces to me. Daniel Jeffery was a stocky, but solid soldier from Leesburgh, Virginia. He had been in the military for 8 years and was still young enough that I was sure he had joined at the tender age of 18, likely the morning after his high school graduation. His training was extensive and his focus was explosives. The second was a 42 year old chemical engineer specializing in mind-altering drugs. Mike Martin was tall and slender; what the army boys commonly called wiry. His head was shaved clean and gleamed in the sunlight. He was enthusiastic enough about his expertise that it made me more than a little uneasy.

The others included a sharpshooter named George Williams, our communications officer Billy Bidwell, Kevin Hawkins, Carl Conner, and Jim Atwell, all experts in close quarters combat. I had worked with George on two other operations and knew that he was also one of the best snipers in the military. Billy and I had worked together only one time. It was a larger operation, and our paths rarely crossed. As long as he could keep us linked to the base, we would get along fine. Mike, Carl, and Jim were all excellent soldiers. We had come through Basic together and knew each other well. I knew that I could rely on any one of the three if things got sideways.

Phase I of our operation was to take place on the base in the mock Japanese village. We would be investigating the deployment of chemical weapons under different circumstances and weather conditions. Phase I would be closely supervised by none other than Dr. Price. Phase II involved the deployment of the perfected chemical agents within the borders if the actual Japanese village. As the agents were deployed, we were to observe and document the reactions of the villagers. My specific task was not only to oversee the operation from the ground, but to document the effect the weapons and stress had on the soldiers. Dr. Price informed me that the soldiers would be outfitted with protective gear, but would not be completely impervious to the chemical agents.

At the second briefing at 1500 hours, I heard a similar story. Of course, Dr. Price conveniently omitted that little part about my men being exposed to the chemicals. Phase I would begin at 0600 hours at "the village." After their briefing, the men were going to the exercise facility in the main building to work out. Although they invited me along, I declined. I wanted to get back to my barracks to digest the information I had been given. I could not get my mind around the idea that we were going to test dangerous chemical agents on human beings, much less my own men! I knew that once I was on the inside of an operation like this, there was no backing out. My only option was to go to Price and convince him to better protect the men or use non-invasive materials during Phase I of the operation. I sat on my bunk and made notes and a list of questions to ask Price. With that complete, I double timed it over to the main building where I had read the Operation briefing.

I had no idea where to find Price, but I figured that if he had an office, it would be here. As I entered, I asked the MP on duty if Dr. Price had an office in the building. He directed me up the stairs to the first door on the left. I climbed the stairs and briskly walked to the office as directed. It seemed there was no one else in the building, but then again, it was well after 1800. Office folk generally had fully evacuated by this time of the evening. The upstairs hallways were carpeted in dark navy and accented with cherry wood. The heavy wooden doors were polished to a shine that made them appear wet to the touch. Dr. Price's office door was closed, but I could hear someone inside rustling papers and talking in a low voice. I rapped twice and tried the doorknob. The knob turned and the door opened smoothly into the interior of the huge office.

I had been in some powerful men's offices, but none could compare to this. It had the same plush navy carpet and polished cherry wood trim that resided throughout the hallways, but there was so much of it here that it had a cold and intimidating feel all its own. The office was pie shaped with the entry door residing on the curved wall. Dr. Price's behemoth of a desk was set at the apex of the office and faced the door. Between the desk and the door was a large conference table that was littered with papers and open books. At Price's back, a bank of windows overlooked the lobby on the first floor of the building. I estimated the office to be nearly 500 square foot in total. The other straight wall contained a bookcase that extended the length of the wall and up to the ceiling. It had a built in ladder on wheels to make the uppermost manuscripts accessible to the good doctor. I was awestruck.

"Well, come right in Captain. I wasn't expecting visitors, as you might have guessed by the closed door."

Price's voice was laced with poison and I knew immediately that my trip here was in vain. There was no way that this man was going to allow any changes in protocol for the operation. I was sure that he had planned each specific detail of the mission with a precise purpose in mind. This was, after all, an experiment to him.

I cleared my voice and began as best I could, "Dr. Price, I'm sorry to interrupt. I know you're busy, but…"

Price cut me off before I could even finish. "Captain, I know you are concerned about your men. Let me guess, you came here to ask for better protection for them. Wait. Better yet, I bet you would like me to use some kind of fake chemicals for Phase I of the operation. Is that correct Captain?"

I was stunned. How could he have predicted that I would come to him with this request? I opened my mouth to explain all the reasons that it was a prudent course of action, but the bastard cut me off again.

"Captain, let's get something straight here. This operation is essential to protecting the freedom of the American people. Maybe you haven't heard, but there is a brilliant and perfectly ruthless Nazi in Germany who is quickly taking control of Europe.

We know that both Germany and Japan are testing chemical and biological weapons just as we are. However, they are much further along than are we. And let me tell you son, they will *not* hesitate to use them against us. So don't try to convince me that I should give a shit about your seven little soldier buddies. What we are doing here is much bigger than them. Shit, it's bigger than either of us. This could be the biggest threat that our fledgling country has ever faced. We must be ready. We *will* be ready.

I know it is difficult for your little brain to comprehend, but you don't have to understand, thank God. You only have to obey my goddamn orders. So here are two that are simple enough for even you to understand. Number one, shut the fuck up. I give the orders around here and you will not question them. Ever. Number two, get back to your goddamn barracks and get ready for the beginning of Phase I tomorrow morning. Is that understood?"

For one of the few times in my life, I was completely speechless. My head was spinning and I didn't know what to say. To my surprise, I was still standing there, jaw agape when Dr. Price said, "Son, get the fuck out of my office. You are dis-fucking-missed."

I turned to leave and was stopped cold when he followed up with one last comment, "And you will share none of this with the members of your force. Not a goddamn word." I was so stunned that I left the room without even muttering a reply. I heard the door slam shut as I turned the corner and headed to the stairs. With surgical precision, the good doctor withdrew every ounce of courage in my body.

It was obvious from my conversation with Dr. Price that he did not give a damn about the soldiers who were about to give their lives for nothing more than a science experiment. My men and I were completely expendable to him. Unfortunately, I had already bought in. In the military, *especially* Black Ops, once you were in, you were in until the end. There was no escaping my commitment;

no way out. All I could do now was exercise as much caution as possible and perform my duty to the best of my abilities.

VI. Phase I

As promised, the first phase of Operation Incivility began sharply at 0600. By then, my men and I had already been out of our bunks, showered, and double-timed it over to "the village." The men were keyed up and ready to perform their duty for their country, no matter what that entailed. They had no idea that their very lives would be in such grave danger; a danger invisible to their sense of smell, taste, and sight and thereby impossible to defend against.

Dr. Price greeted us that morning and explained the protocol for the upcoming months. We would be testing delivery mechanisms in the village facade that had been created on the southern section of the island. We were broken into two teams of four and separated into to different sections of the village. At the rally point, each team would be issued protective gear and clearly labeled boxes of what Dr. Price referred to as "the package." My orders were to oversee both teams and verify that the experimentation was being carried out per regs and that all observations were thoroughly documented. Dr. Price ensured the men that the protective materials issued to them would be more than effective in safeguarding them from harm. He went on to say that we would not be using the actual chemical agents developed for this operation. However, each different delivery mechanism would require unique protective equipment in the field and we would be using it in these exercises in preparation for the final operation.

I knew from my briefing with Dr. Price that several men would receive protective materials that were in fact just placebos and would not be effective in blocking the harmful chemical agents from entering their bloodstreams. He did not release the number of placebos in each experiment, nor did he tell me what the chemical agents were or how the men would likely react to them. I just knew that each new experiment was intricately devised to study not only the delivery methods, but also the most effective agents, the varying reactions of the men, and our ability to operate under the stress that this complicated and delicate situation would create.

Initially, I traveled with alpha team to the rally point. After arriving, we found our gear waiting for us. Also awaiting our arrival was a large sealed crate labeled "Agent 1." We knew that packed inside the crate under a bedding of straw were multiple gas canisters containing the chemical agent. Each canister was a miniature version of the propane tanks that occupied all gas grilles. The first agent was gaseous in nature and the delivery method was through timed release. For the experiment, the agent had been artificially colored amber. In its natural state, the gas would be both colorless and odorless. Alpha team spent 3 months testing release methods including explosion, spray, and cloud. They tracked the development of the agent cloud under conditions of no wind first. Following that series, an artificial wind was applied using huge fans located around the village test site. During these experiments, alpha team tracked cloud longevity, exposure rate, and analyzed dispersing patterns using a complex series of computer models.

After several days with alpha team, I traveled to the beta team site and worked with them. I would return to alpha team later. When I arrived at beta site, I found that the team was well underway with their testing. Beta team was working with the same chemical agent, but in the liquid form. Their experimentation was similar, but had been modified slightly for the liquid nature of the agent. Beta team tested spray and misting patterns, injection, consumption, and dispersion into water and other liquids. Beta team also analyzed concentration patterns and degradation, dispersion in stable waters vs. flowing streams, and exposure rates.

To my surprise, not one soldier questioned their orders or the potential for exposure to the chemical agents during my involvement at the two test sites. I didn't hear any bitching or complaining at the barracks either. My blood was boiling with the knowledge of what was going on here, and I knew that no one would ever know the truth about what really happened on this small island in the South Pacific.

After each team had completed the required testing with Agent 1, they were given two weeks "leave" to rest and prepare for the next round of testing. There was nothing on the island but the base, so most of the men did a combination of finalizing reports on Agent 1, writing letters to family members and friends, working out, and hanging loose. Really, those were the only choices available to us.

We returned to duty two weeks later and repeated the cycle of testing with Agent 2. Since the men had been through the routine once already, they were completing the testing much faster than the first iteration. To my surprise, Dr. Price slowed both teams' progress by limiting the amount of testing that could be completed in a day and extending evaluation periods. After just day 4, he called me to his office for a briefing.

"Your men are completing the testing well ahead of schedule, Captain Wilden."

I responded with pleasure, "Yes sir, they are fine men, as I am sure you are aware." His response was completely bewildering.

"Captain," he said, "normally the initiative of your men would be commendable. However, the delicate nature of this research requires the highest level of precision in execution and flawless record keeping."

I waited a second before answering so that I could absorb what Price was saying. "Sir I assure you that my men will make no errors. They are well aware of the need to perform their duties at the highest level. I….."

Before I could finish, Price cut me off in what was becoming typical fashion. "Captain Wilden, I'll make this a little more clear, since you seem to be a rather slow learner. Slow….Them….Down. I have issued you and your men a schedule of events for the testing. Follow the schedule as it is written. That is an order."

"Yes Sir," I conceded.

I wasn't sure where this was heading, but I certainly was not going to argue with Price. I had already seen where that would get me.

After several days of his controlling orders, the men became restless and their dislike for Dr. Price was growing (mine had reached a fevered pitch). At first, I couldn't figure out why he would want to slow our progress. About halfway into the testing of Agent 2, Dr. Price's agenda became painfully obvious to me. I think it was during week seven of testing Agent 2 that it happened.

VII. Infected

I woke to the soft sounds of whimpering coming from the bed closest to me- Carl's bunk. Carl Conner was from Ft. Lauderdale, Florida. He was of medium build, had sandy blond hair and green eyes that were as intense as any I'd ever seen. In our short time on the mission together, I hadn't gotten to know him well, but I instantly knew that he was a good soldier. He executed orders quickly and flawlessly. I also knew that he had a wife and two children back home. The classic American family: mother, father, son, and daughter they were. I tried to ignore the muffled sobs and go back to sleep, but the whimpering was just loud enough to keep me awake. I turned and looked at my alarm clock; it read 0327 hours. I lay there quietly for 30 minutes longer as I listened to Carl's mumbling. No one else in the barracks appeared to be awake, or at least they were not stirring.

As I listened to Carl, he began to get more and more agitated. Initially, I couldn't make out what he was muttering, but as his agitation level rose, he began to speak more clearly, and in louder tones.

"No, no, don't do that. I didn't do anything. I did the job, just like you ordered."

I had no idea what he was talking about. It was probably his anger at Dr. Price provoking the nightmares. Carl's sobs continued to grow louder.

"I swear to God I didn't do it. Stay away from me you bastards! I'll defend myself if I have to. Stay back, and leave my family out of this!"

He was loud enough now to wake the others. I rolled out of my bunk and went over to him. I was going to have to wake him before he woke everyone in the barracks. I hurried over to his bedside. Carl was completely covered by his bed linens and curled up in the fetal position with his back turned to me. Not even his head was exposed. I whispered, "Carl, wake up. You're having a nightmare." There was no response. He continued his ranting.

"You mother fuckers, stay the fuck back or I'll put a bullet in each of your God-damned skulls!"

I reached out and put my hand on Carl's shoulder to gently rouse him from his dreams. At my touch, he spun around in the bed, enclosing my wrist in a grip that threatened to cut the circulation off to my hand. As he screamed at me, the lights in the barracks flicked on and I felt my heart stop in mid beat.

Carl Conner stood at the side of his bed in just his boxer shorts, left arm extended and holding my right wrist in a death grip. He had twisted my arm to the point that I was helpless to move against him. In his right hand, he had leveled the military issued Colt 45 at my forehead. He had cocked the hammer so quickly that I hadn't even seen the movement. His eyes were open, but the sharp lucidity that normally resided there had vanished. The look was a strange combination of mortal fear and loathing. The pale green of his irises gave me a feeling of sick green sliminess. The whites of his eyes burned fiery red as if he hadn't slept in weeks.

I could hear the other guys shuffling in the background as Carl screamed at me.

"You mother fucking son of a bitch! I told you to stay the fuck back! Where is my family? WHAT THE FUCK DID YOU DO WITH THEM?"

I tried to reason with Carl, uncertain how far I could push him without being shot dead in my bed clothes.

"Carl, it's me Josef. I'm sure your family is safe at home. It's just a nightmare Carl, wake up."

But it was obvious that this was no mere dream to Carl. He was prepared to kill me on the spot. His eyes widened further until it seemed that they were actually bulging from their sockets. The veins on the side of his neck pulsed as Carl stared at me, gritting his teeth loud enough that I could actually hear them.

"I know who you are. You are a lying stack of shit! You took my wife and kids from me and you *will* give them back. Now where are they?"

I had no idea what he was talking about. I had to try to reason my way out of this. What do you say to someone who is sleepwalking and completely irrational? I took a deep breath and looked Carl in the eye. I knew that in order to be successful, I had to regain Carl's trust. This is the first rule of truth in hostage negotiations. You must develop trust with the suspect.

"Carl, listen to me. It's Captain Wilden. You don't want to do this. I don't know what you're talk…"
Carl's anger boiled over and he exploded at me this time, twisting my hand further to the side. My wrist screamed in pain and I went to my knees.

"Shut the fuck up! If you're not telling me what you've done with my family, then you shut the fuck up!"

I could hear some soft shuffling in the background from the other men. Carl must have heard it also, as he focused his attention over my shoulder and shouted, "Don't you fucking move. I'll blow your heads off just as quickly as I will his. Hell, you fuckers are probably in on it anyway." He was waiving the gun madly, pointing it at every one of his teammates, unrelenting and totally whacked out.

He refocused his attention on me. Looking directly into my eyes with bulging red and green egg-shaped projections, he spoke more softly this time. It was quickly apparent that he had decided how to handle the situation. As he spoke, it was as if a calm had come over him.

"Josef, you really must understand that you mean nothing to me," he calmly said. "I will kill you and everyone else in your family if you don't tell me where they are. And believe me; it won't be pleasant for your wife and children. I'll take my time, but I will get them to talk. I will find out where you're hiding them, even if it takes the life of every single person in your entire family."

There was muted confusion from behind me. Carl again looked over my shoulder and pointed the gun into the crowd of men behind me.

"Whoa. Whoa, mother fuckers. Stay the fuck back!"

I stole a look up at Carl. His eyes protruded impossibly from his head. It was as if they were going to explode at any time. Carl blinked hard and I could see a tear fall and start its way down his cheek. He wiped it away with his gun hand, but something was wrong. Instead of disappearing, the tear smeared a dark red streak across his cheek. A slow stream of dark red tears began to trace a red line down Carl's cheek from the corner of his eye. *The stress was actually causing the blood vessels in his eyes to burst.* I had never seen anything like it in all my years of military service.

I could now feel the presence of my men and I knew that they had been inching up behind me while Carl had his attention focused on me. I was certain that this was going to be my only chance to get away. I had to make a move while Carl's attention was divided.

I moved my weight to my right side so I could free my left leg for a swift kick to Carl's knees. Hopefully, it would be enough to bring him down. I prayed that at least one of the men had pulled their Colt out and had it leveled on Carl. Just as I prepared to make my move, Carl made his.

Carl screamed again. "I said fucking stop!" As if in punctuation, The Colt 45 exploded in his hand with the smallest of blue flames licking the black hole in the end of the barrel. The bullet from the Colt traced an invisible line across the barracks and thumped into the center of Jim Atwell's chest. He crashed to the floor, landing on his back, eyes staring at the ceiling. The other men scattered behind the closest bunks, turning them over on their sides for protection from the gunfire. *The whole situation was way out of control.*

"Shit," Carl muttered. "See what you made me do? Just tell me where my family is Josef. I know you did it, God damn you."

Carl reached up to wipe the bloody tears from his right eye. I kicked out with my left foot and connected squarely with Carl's right knee. It made a terrible chorus of cracking and popping sounds as the ligaments and tendons snapped and his kneecap dislocated. It was enough. Carl toppled to the floor, his leg bent at a terribly unnatural angle behind him. He tried to stop his fall with his gun hand, smashing his fist into the cement floor. The gun clattered across the floor.

I dove for Carl to secure him before he could do anything else. My battle training had taught me to see the world at a much slower pace than the normal person. When the adrenaline rushed through my veins, as it did then, I could see everything going on around me in great detail. As I glided over the short distance between where I crouched and where Carl was lying, I saw him pull his knife from the sheath strapped to his left leg. It entered my left side just below my rib cage. The pain was intense and immediate. The serrated edge at the top of the blade ripped at the skin and organs in my abdomen. I could instantaneously feel the warmth of blood flowing freely from the open wound.

I grabbed hold of Carl and my momentum carried us into a roll. The world spun out of control and my head was swimming in pain and fear. As we came to rest, Carl had the advantage. He was on top of me and had me by the throat, choking me and screaming into my face.

"God damn you Wilden! I'm going to kill everyone in your family for this!"

Blood dripped from the corners of both of Carl's eyes and fell on my forehead and cheeks. I closed my eyes against the small shower of blood droplets and tried to roll Carl off of me, but I couldn't budge him. My throat burned and my head pounded as he continued to wrestle the life from me. I could feel the strength draining from my body as if someone had pulled the invisible plug that kept it full. Just as I was prepared to give up, I heard a second gunshot.

VIII. Unexpected Help

Bam! Bam! Bam! I almost screamed when I heard those crashing sounds and my breath caught in my chest so that all I could muster was a tiny squeak. As usual, I had gotten so far into the story that I had lost contact with the real world. I actually believed that a gun had gone off. *Bam! Bam!* It was just someone knocking at the apartment door. I hurried over to the head of the room and hollered through the steel door that kept the rest of the world out of my little safe haven.

"Who is it and what do you want?"

"UPS pickup for Clark Kent," came the reply.

I immediately undid the bolt locks (there are three - just in case), removed the chain, and unlocked the door, opening it for my visitor to enter. George McClory stepped through the door and brushed passed me, heading in the direction of the kitchen. George was in no way what you would expect of a big time operator. He was six foot nothing and weighed 170 pounds soaking wet. He had the long slender face of a horse interrupted by a hooked nose similar to what most kids would visualize on the wicked witch of the west (without the nasty mole, of course). George was almost as pale as a life-long vampire and I often wondered how he made it through the southern summers without his skin peeling off from third degree sunburn.

If you took him at his appearance, you would consider him light work, especially in a fight. However, it was obvious when he spoke that he was one hundred percent business one hundred percent of the time. He addressed everyone in a low husky voice that he controlled just above a whisper. In all my time with George, I never heard him raise his voice; I didn't want to.

George opened the refrigerator and pulled out a Budweiser. This exact series of events had been taking place on the first Tuesday of the month for nearly four years now. He arrived at varying times, but always sometime on the first Tuesday, and always during the daylight hours. It seemed that George was a busy man after dusk. He rarely spoke without first journeying to the fridge for a cold one. I told George that I would be right back with the pickup and walked down the hall that led to my bedroom. I grabbed the black knapsack from the floor under the bed and headed back to the kitchen, careful to close the door on my way out. I dropped the knapsack on the floor next to George's chair and sat down opposite him at the table.

I had dealt with George (if that was really his name, which I had seriously doubted) since I had first gotten involved in "the business" as I liked to think of it. A man on the run has very few options when it comes to employment. Through the IRS, the government could easily have found me. So, I was forced to find another opportunity to make a living. I had gotten hooked up with some small time dealers shortly after arriving in Nashville, Tennessee. They were into mostly nickel and dime stuff of no consequence. However, I met George through my main supplier after just a few months of supplying hash to some dirty business owners in the area.

We struck a deal, and I have since been distributing a myriad of designer drugs to dealers in the area. George collects the cash generated from the sale on the first Tuesday of the month. I receive a drop shipment of new product on the corresponding Thursday of same week. Nice, clean and easy. Plus, I keep two percent as my fee. In addition, George had been able to help me create a new identity for myself. He is very resourceful man - a good man to have on your side. And according to the stories, a very bad man to be on the wrong terms with.

Over the course of our time in the business together, George and I had developed a mutual respect, if not friendship for one another. George looked across the table at me and took a long drink of Bud.

"Jimmy, you don't look so fucking good. What the hell's going on?"

Shit. I should have known it would come to this, sooner or later. Even though George and I knew a lot about one another, I had been able to keep him in the dark and off the subject of this little situation of mine. He hadn't asked and I hadn't volunteered; even when he had helped me with my new ID papers. But here it was. He had come on the wrong day and caught me in one of my valleys. I took a couple of minutes to debate with myself whether to open up to George. Points and counterpoints, benefits and drawbacks, which side outweighed the other; what made the most sense?

"Nothin'." I told him. "Just havin' a rough day, that's all."

George took another long drink of his beer. It was always amusing to watch him drink his one beer. Couldn't be more than one or he would "lose focus." Each visit, he would finish off the bottle in just three drinks. Always just three drinks. The first drink was a primer, the second was the main course, and the third was just a quick finisher to be sure the bottle was officially emptied. I watched him work through the second act, his Adam's apple bobbing like a yo-yo on a three inch string.

"Jimmy, we've known each other for quite a while now. You know you're my best guy and besides that, I like you. So when I see you like this I get worried. Tell me how I can help. And I don't want to hear any bullshit about how it's "just a rough day.""

I shook my head and tallied the pros and again – about even. *Shit. Shit. Shit.* I looked over at George and he was holding the back of his left hand up at me, curling and uncurling the fingers – universal sign language for *Come 'on an spit it out*. I caved. I summarized the reasons for moving away from home, taking an alias and staying under the radar. At least, I gave him the highpoints. I had to get it out. I felt as if the story was burning a hole in me searching out fresh air. I couldn't even contact my own parents for fear that they would turn me in to the cops for what had gone down with Mammaw. Hell, they already thought I was responsible. *I wasn't was I?*

I instantly decided not to show George the journal. It was a unanimous decision; no hung jury here. I couldn't show him; it was just too risky. When the story was told, George looked me in the eyes, stared out the kitchen window and did something he had never done before. He got up and retrieved a second beer from the fridge. After downing his second Bud, George did another unexpected thing.

"I think I can help you," he said.

George told me that he had a "contact" inside the armed forces that might be able to pull together some information on my grandfather. He put heavy emphasis on *might*. I told him I understood and greatly appreciated anything he could do. With our business officially completed, George grabbed the black knapsack and left me alone again.

"I'll contact my man and let you know something next month." He said as he left the apartment.

I told him thanks, shut the door and returned to the kitchen for a Bud of my own. As I had told George, I was certainly grateful for any information that he could uncover on my grandfather. Unfortunately, I had put myself in debt to someone who would certainly collect on the favor. Sooner or later I would have to pay up – and probably more sooner than later. I also knew that this was no small favor for which I had indirectly asked. In addition, he would also be indebted to someone, which doubled the value of my IOU. I prayed that I hadn't just sold my soul to the devil and was at the same time afraid of what might happen when the devil came collecting.

IX. Recovery

As I savored the last swallow of Budweiser, I told myself that this could be for the best; that it could lead to the truth. If that was the case, at least I would know for sure. I wouldn't have to continue hiding from my unseen and unacknowledged governmental enemy. If I was really lucky, I could even go back to my old life; minus my parents of course. Surely they have given up looking for me by now. I returned to the bedroom and picked the journal back up and began reading again. I was immediately drawn back into my grandfather's desperate situation. I read on and on....

In my panicked mind, I was sure that Carl had somehow reached his Colt and was in the process of putting a bullet in my brain. I couldn't comprehend the sudden crashing weight on my chest until after Carl was dragged off of me. I lay there on the concrete floor with my men gathered around me. I could see that they were talking to me, but I couldn't hear what they were saying. It was like when I was a kid; my friends and I would rig up a telephone out of string and empty vegetable cans. The concrete floor was cold on my back and everything went hazy before the light of the bunker blinked out.

I awoke later that evening to the base nurse cleaning my wound and replacing the bandages. Apparently the knife had done enough damage that it required 12 stitches to close properly. The nurse informed me that I had lost a lot of blood and should just rest for a few days. She also had me plugged up to an IV. She let me know that I should expect to see her twice a day for cleaning and bandage changing.

Dr. Price informed everyone that the final 3 days of the current trials would be finished in my absence, and that the next set would not start for 3 weeks to allow me time to recover from my "unfortunate accident." He made no mention of Carl or the circumstances of his death. I can only imagine what they might have told his family.

Over the course of the next two weeks, I had a lot of time to think about what had happened. It didn't immediately become clear to me that Carl's raving might be directly connected to what we were doing here in the Philippines. At first, I thought that Carl may have had a nightmare terrible enough that he couldn't separate reality from dream. Then, my perception changed. I remembered Carl's eyes. The burning red veins that eventually burst and bled down his cheeks. I recalled the blood vessels in his neck rhythmically bulging and flexing, sending blood to and from his heart. Those veins were pulsing at a rate much higher than normal; they were almost spastic. His pulse had to be approaching 200 beats per minute. It occurred to me that maybe he was taking drugs. This seemed unlikely as he was extremely lucid during the testing and he had shown no other signs of drug use leading up to his breakdown, if you could call it that.

I continued reviewing my memories of the events and finally had my debriefing with Dr. Price. As I recounted the events of Carl's attack on me, I had a very strange feeling about Dr. Price's reaction. I expected him to be interested in the events, but he was absolutely enthralled by the story. He peppered me with questions and excitedly scribbled notes on his legal pad.

I also expected Price to be shocked, or at least surprised, by the aggressiveness that Carl displayed. He wasn't. In fact, he acted as if he actually anticipated it. He asked multiple questions about whether Carl had revealed anything about the reasoning behind his accusations, which of course he hadn't. He encouraged me to recount in detail the whole story from Carl's behavior the week previous to the episode and through the final gun shot ending his life.

At the time, I was still in shock over the ordeal that I had just been through. I guess I was too shocked to put all the pieces into place and realize what was really going on. It finally sank in as I finished the debriefing and was dismissed by Dr. Price. As I left his office and entered the hallway, I heard him mutter to himself in a low voice, "Well, this little development is *very* encouraging."

The words stopped me in my tracks. Like a complicated jigsaw puzzle, every piece finally clicked into place and I knew the truth. Carl Conner was Dr. Martin Price's first victim in this experiment. Price had slowly but surely poisoned Carl during the experiments that we were running for him. I was furious. I turned and strode back to Price's office. I couldn't contain myself. I wanted a piece of him and a small piece just wasn't going to be enough. I couldn't restrain myself and the questions and accusations streamed from my lips as I turned the corner and entered his office.

"What did you just say? Are you saying that you meant for him to die? And you put me and the other men in danger's path so that you could observe the outcome?"

As soon as the last word left my lips, my brain registered what my eyes were communicating. There was Price, standing in the middle of the room with his pistol drawn. The firearm was trained right at my chest. He walked slowly toward me and spoke as if we were sitting in lawn chairs in the back yard, having a beer and enjoying the setting sun on the horizon.

"Josef, as previously discussed, it is necessary that some of your men are put at risk during these exercises. We must assess their ability to perform under the conditions that will likely be present as you complete your mission. And to that end, you have performed admirably. You kept your head during this most unfortunate turn of events and were able to escape the situation with minimal complications.

Now, I am charged with a mission that is critical to the survival of this great country. And you in turn are charged with helping me complete that mission. As the Captain of your special task force, I ask that you perform your duty to ensure that the mission is completed as intended. Josef, these men will be put in extreme danger. I need to know exactly how they will react and I need you to be prepared to lead them out of danger when the situation arises. The exercises that we are undertaking are critical to the success of this operation.

As stated previously, you report to me, and you will not question this mission nor the way in which I choose to conduct it. Should you have another bout with morality, I suggest that you keep it to yourself because if you don't, you will have failed me. Failure will not be tolerated and will be rewarded with death. Please understand that should the need arise, I will deliver demise to your doorstep summarily and without hesitation. Now, I want to be sure we are absolutely crystal clear. We will not have this conversation again. Is that understood?"

I opened my mouth to speak, but only a faint breath of air escaped. I couldn't move. I couldn't speak. Everything seemed miles away except the black oiled barrel of Price's Colt. The gun had drifted up from my chest to my forehead. You can tell when a man is bluffing a kill by the way he holds his gun and the tone of his voice. During the exchange, Price was cold and collected. His voice was quiet but confident. It held a cold, metallic element not unlike the sidearm he carried. The barrel of the Colt, though it had drifted from my chest to forehead, never wavered. The finger on the trigger was firm and poised to cut the bullet loose that would end my life. No way was he bluffing. This man was no scientist, he was a cold blooded killer.

Price had casually walked across the room and was on top of me now, just an arm's length away. Again, the calm voice remarked.

"Josef, are we clear?"

I looked into eyes that seemed to be devoid of color, the irises appeared steely gray and the pupils as black as onyx. The cold, round barrel of the Colt seated itself in the center of my forehead and exerted the tiniest of pressures on the surface of the skin. He leaned into me until we were almost cheek to cheek, the gun still seated on my forehead and he made his final statements. I could feel his hot breath on my skin as he spoke.

"I will assume from your stiff and quiet demeanor that I have made myself utterly and unquestionably clear. You are now dismissed, Captain Wilden. You may go. Oh, and have a pleasant and productive afternoon."

X. Green Jacket

I read many other stories from my grandfather's journal that night. Most followed the same plot line as the story of Carl Conner. The circumstances were always slightly different, but the basic theme was the same. Dr. Price slowly decimated my grandfather's squad, killing nearly all of the men that were recruited for the mission. I don't remember when I finally succumbed to sleep, but I awoke the next morning dazed and disoriented.

The sun streamed into the room through the tattered blinds that covered my solitary bedroom window. I looked around the room and did not immediately recognize my whereabouts. My memory finally restarted and I recognized the small bedroom and the open journal lying face down on the floor. Next to the bed, an old fashioned clothes trunk stood on end. I stole a glance at the clock radio perched atop the makeshift night stand. It was nearly four o'clock in the afternoon; I had slept most of the day away. I couldn't recall how late I'd stayed up reading the journal, but I distinctly remembered the terrible stories of fear, anger, and disillusionment that were recounted in horrific detail.

I climbed out of bed and made my way to the kitchen for a pot of coffee. I started the coffeemaker and went to the bathroom for a hot shower. After waking myself up with the necessary shower, shave, and coffee (as usual, I drank the whole pot), I spent the rest of the day making calls to several of my customers to determine their needs for the upcoming week's deliveries. I phoned in the required quantities to George and was pleasantly surprised when he mentioned my grandfather.

"Good news skippy. My man came through for you. I have a full jacket on your beloved grandfather Josef. Quite a man he was, apparently. I'll talk to you tomorrow."

I hung up the phone and spent the rest of the evening in anticipation of George's arrival the next day. I tried everything I could think of to occupy my time that evening, but nothing worked. I tried the television, video games, laundry, radio; all without success. Finally, I gave up. After finishing off several Budweisers, I headed to the rack. Unfortunately, things didn't get any better there. I lay awake in bed for hours, staring at the blank ceiling in the semi darkness and wondering what would be in the paperwork that George was bringing. Somewhere between 3 and 4 A.M., my mind finally let go and I fell asleep.

George finally arrived at eleven o'clock the next morning. I was so keyed up that I had the door open before his knuckles rapped the steel a second time. I didn't even remember to go through the safety exchange to verify that it was, in fact, George.

"Just a slight bit anxious are we?" George asked as he stepped into the apartment.

He carried the black knapsack in one hand and had a black filing envelope in the other. It was the kind that expanded to its contents and each end had a string tie off to keep it securely closed. On the way into the kitchen, George pitched the knapsack onto the recliner. For once, the drugs that it contained were not the most important business of the day. Still carrying the black file folder against his chest, George walked over to the refrigerator and pulled out two Buds.

We sat down at the kitchen table and he held out one of the brown beer bottles. As I reached out to take it, I noticed that my hand was shaking. I was so nervous that I could hear my heart beating in my ears and feel it in my temples. It was as if the muscle supplying the much needed fluid had recently relocated to my head and taken up full residence. My breath was short and I could feel sweat beading up on my forehead and upper lip. I looked across the table at George. He had sat the black folder on the table and continued holding it securely under his right palm. He smiled slightly. He was obviously enjoying this.

"Well," I said. "Are you going to pass it over or just sit there with it?"

George's eyes bored into mine. His smile slowly faded. I knew the moment was short, but it felt like days – no weeks – to me. George slowly slid the file across the table toward me, never taking his hand from the top of it. I reached across the table and greedily snatched the corner of the file. Before he let go, George spoke.

"Jimmy, before I give you this, I need you to know something. I took a quick look through the file. I'm sorry, but I couldn't help myself. I must say that there is not much in there to corroborate a large scale conspiracy theory like the one you described to me."

I nodded and George let go of the folder. I had figured that this was the way it would turn out. I had been telling myself that I wanted it to turn out this way. But somewhere deep in the recesses of my soul, I felt the smallest twinge of disappointment.

"Well that's good news in itself," I told George with a forced smile. "Maybe I had it all wrong."

And maybe you didn't. In the movies, this voice always comes from deep inside. Often times, it is the character's own voice. That wasn't the case here. The voice, barely above a whisper, seemed to emanate from the very air around me, coming from nowhere and everywhere at the same time. It was as if it was carried to me on a summer's breeze, but at the same time I didn't feel the air brush against my skin. It wasn't my voice either. It was the voice of my dead but never forgotten grandmother. It was so real that I had to look over at George to make certain that he hadn't heard it also. If he did, he wasn't letting on.

George's beer bottle was empty and I couldn't even remember seeing him take a drink. He stood up and said, "I gotta go. Take care of yourself Jimmy. And I mean it."

With that, he walked over to the door and let himself out. I don't know how long I sat there gripping the file folder before I got up and went over to lock the door. When I finally did go to the door, I locked all the locks. I had some serious homework tonight; it would probably be an all-nighter. I was going to read through the entire file and see if any of the information matched up with that in my grandfather's journal. It was doubtful after hearing George's brief description of the contents. Did that mean that the conspiracy was all just a sham and I needed a reservation at the funny farm?

Or maybe it confirms everything that you already know. Maybe this thing goes so far up that you don't want to know where it ends. Maybe this black file folder is the entrance to the fabled rabbit hole to Wonderland. The only question left is whether you will play the part of Alice or turn your back on your grandparents and forget what happened to us – both of us.

I loosened the ties on the black file folder and opened the flap that held it closed. I pulled out a single file wrapped in a green jacket. It was filled with loose papers, making it about 2 inches thick. I sat there at the table for several minutes, willing my hand to open the file so that my eyes could begin their task. Finally, my hand seemed convinced and the folder slowly opened to the first photocopied page of the file.

Whoever had gathered the information had done a good job. The file went all the way back to my grandfather's entry into the armed forces. I read through his basic training proficiencies, which were all outstanding. I continued on to his early life within the ranks of the military. Much of the early stories in the journal were ones that I knew from my grandmother. It was pretty common stuff for a soldier of his rank and by no means privileged information. My pride began to swell as I read about my grandfather's promotion from rank to rank and the corresponding commendations.

About half way through the file, I had to take a break. I had a pounding headache, my eyes were burning and my stomach was making noises that were more common in horror movies than my apartment. I looked up at the clock. Nine thirty; I had already been at it for over nine hours straight and there was still no end in sight. I went to the bathroom for a piss and some aspirin and then made my way back to the kitchen to look for something other than the liquid nourishment that filled the fridge. I settled on microwave popcorn –

two bags. I washed it down with my old standby, but limited myself to just two bottles. Just for good measure, I finished my hiatus with a double splash of cold water on my face to ensure focus.

I checked my time with the clock on the microwave. Ten-o-six it proclaimed in not-so-bright blue numbers. *Good, I only wasted about a half hour.* I sat back down at the table and resumed reading. I took in every word and detail in the file. So far, George was right. There was nothing that corroborated the story that Josef told in his journal. I kept telling myself that I just hadn't gotten to it yet, but frustration was beginning to work on my mind and exhaustion was making a full out onslaught on my body, draining it of the energy it needed to drive on.

Further and further I paged through the photocopied sheets; learning more and more about my grandfather, but still not gaining the details that I so desperately wanted to uncover. I looked again at the microwave for the time. My eyes were seething with pain and it took me several seconds to focus in enough to read the numbers. It was just after three A.M. I wanted to give up for the evening, but couldn't force myself to do it. I had to keep searching. Something had to be in the file. It just had to be.

I read on. Now, I was fighting sleep with everything I had. I was having serious difficulty focusing on the words and had begun to just skim the pages for the key insights that I sought. I skimmed and flipped, skimmed and flipped. Several times I dozed off for minutes at a time, waking up and not knowing where I was and having to restart at the top of the page. At just before six in the morning, I found the commendation letter and proficiency report from General Mays along with the paperwork for my grandfather's promotion to Captain of the Epsilon Task Force. My pulse quickened. This had been in Josef's journal.

I was starting to get close to what I wanted, but the folder was becoming anorexic. It felt like I was racing against one of those hourglass timers that you found in popular board games. And the level of sand was getting pretty low. There were only a few precious grains of hope left in the file. I read through the commendation letter, the proficiency report, and the promotion paperwork paying particular attention for anything that might correspond to the mission in the Philippine islands. There was none. Also, I noticed that nowhere in the file did it mention why the Epsilon Task Force was formed or what their purpose was within the military. It didn't even mention which branch they reported to. I thought back and realized that Grandpa Josef had not mentioned it in his journal either. It didn't make any sense, but I couldn't focus on that. I had to push through this and look for more evidence of the "Black War" my grandfather had fought.

I paged through the next sheets more slowly, desperately searching for anything else that connected Josef to EForce, or EForce to the Black War in Japan and the Philippines. My heart was pounding so hard that it sounded like drums in my ears. My headache was really going now. My arms and legs felt like rubber and my head felt like a throbbing chunk of lead. There was nothing. The rest of the file contained generic proficiency reports. The writing in the reports didn't discuss any of the missions that Josef was assigned to. Each one was a carbon copy of the previous, differing only in the date of the report. Each of them stated that my grandfather was performing at satisfactory levels, blah, blah, blah. The frustration was back now and my head was still pounding like a bass drum at a *Stones* concert. As I flipped the last page over, I couldn't hold it in. I screamed as loud as I could.

"*SON OF A BITCH!*"

As I screamed at the file, I shoved it off the kitchen table with a violent sweep of my arm. My hand crashed into the corner of the wall with a "*crack!*"

"Fuuuuck!" I screamed. Now, my hand was bleeding and hurt like hell. Tears welled up in my eyes as I flexed it to make sure that it wasn't broken. Nope; I was okay from that standpoint, but boy was it going to hurt later on. I went to the bathroom and ran cool water over my injured hand and I watched as the blood swirled down the drain in the sink. It was a fitting sight as it seemed like my life was headed the same direction. My psyche was battered and hurt almost as much as my hand, which was already bruised and swollen.

After bandaging up my wound and preparing myself an icepack using what little ice I had and the only clean dish towel in the house, I grabbed a Bud and sat back down at the table. I looked at the mess I'd created. Most of the papers from the file were spread out over the floor in a fan pattern propagating from the green folder. They made a simple, monochromatic rainbow. And worse yet, there was no pot of gold at the end. There was only the almost empty green file folder jacket. Several of the papers were scattered at odd angles away from the white fan, almost as if they didn't belong with the rest of the group. One of those sheets appeared to be from a yellow legal pad. *That's odd, I don't remember a yellow sheet in the folder.*

I left the table and walked over to pick up the yellow sheet, ignoring the rest of the mess. The sheet contained hand scribbled notes. And it was an original, not a photocopy like the rest of the contents of the file. Was it from the original file where George's friend had gotten the rest of this? Before the question had fully formed in my mind, I read the top line scribbled on the paper and had the answer. And a hell of a lot more questions.

I looked over at the clock on the wall in the living room. It was almost eight in the morning. Good, I could call George. He would surely be up at this hour. I went back into the kitchen and grabbed the phone. My mind was racing as I dialed his number. There were so many questions that I needed answered. I needed to talk to whoever had retrieved the information I had just gone through so exhaustively. The phone rang and rang. I had a lump in my throat that threatened to choke me. I wasn't sure that I was going to be able to talk when George did answer. It felt like all of my questions were caught in a big hairy ball directly in the middle of my neck. The phone rang again and again. *Shit.* He wasn't answering.

Finally, I gave up and put the receiver back in its cradle. In the very beginning of our relationship, George had explained to me that he didn't believe in answering machines so I shouldn't expect anyone to answer the phone when he wasn't there. I would just have to call back later. All the better; I needed some sleep anyway. I was working on my second 24 hours without any shuteye and couldn't even think straight; some rest would do me good. I gathered up the rest of the leaflets of paper and shoved them back into the green folder. I put the yellow sheet right on top where I could easily pull it out when I finally got a hold of George.

With that done, I took the folder with me into the bedroom and placed it under the mattress. I then placed my wracked body on top of the mattress and immediately succumbed to deep sleep. I didn't wake up again until after sundown.

XI. No One's Home

George's phone rang and rang. Again and again I called, allowing the phone to ring ten to twelve times each before hanging up and redialing. Still there was no answer on the other end; just the annoying ring tone repeating itself in my ear. *Dammit! Where the hell was he?* It wasn't like George to be out so much. I checked the time. It was just past eight. It was still fairly early evening, but there was no reason for him to be gone, especially with this going on. George almost never went out on the town; he was close to being a recluse. Nothing like the flashy dealers you always see in the movies. Also, he would have expected my call.

I plopped down in my Lay Z Boy chair and reclined it as far back as it would go, letting out a huge sigh. I reached over and grabbed the remote from atop one of my mismatched and out-of-style end tables and flipped on the television. It was on HBO. There were only two channels that ever got any show time on my television: HBO and ESPN. There was some sappy love story on HBO so I flipped toward ESPN. I can't say exactly why I stopped on the local network station, but the news was on. Apparently, murder was the news of the day.

"A local man was found shot to death today in his home on the south side of Nashville. The man, identified as George McClory......

My heart stopped in my chest and my breath caught in my throat. George was dead – shot to death. I listened to the rest of the story in complete shock. What was I going to do now? How could I get to the guy who had photocopied my grandfather's file?

They switched to a reporter "on the scene." According to the reporter, George had been killed in an apparent drug deal gone wrong. He was found dead in his very own living room with one bullet hole in his chest and one additional in the middle of his forehead. Without even hearing the reporter's words I knew the story here. He had been executed, and I knew the reason behind it. George was as careful as they come. He wouldn't have done business in his own house. It was the file, had to be. As I watched further, I realized that I had never even been to George's home. Not that we were particularly close, but if anyone was going to be welcomed into his home, I would have thought it would be me. I still couldn't believe what I was hearing. By getting George involved, I had killed him.

The reporter continued with details of the murder. She mentioned that an undisclosed amount of designer hallucinogens had been found hidden in the small townhouse. There was also over a quarter million in cash. Maybe this was the truth, but I was having a very difficult time believing it could be a drug heist. If it was a drug hit, why hadn't they taken all of the drugs and the money? If it was a deal gone wrong, it seemed logical that the dealer would have taken the money, drugs, or both. In this case they hadn't, which opened the door to another possibility. Maybe it didn't have anything to do with drugs. Maybe it had to do with a bunch of photocopies in a green file jacket delivered to a certain James Davenkish in a black folder. And *maybe* was probably the wrong word.

The news story changed to some nonsense about the stock market sinking and pushing the mighty U.S. into a recession. I switched off the television and slammed my head back into the soft padding of the chair. *Shit.* What was I possibly going to do now? I had a lead on confirming my grandfather's story and I had no way of further investigating it. I sat in the Lay Z Boy for a long time, trying desperately to think of some way to figure out more about the yellow legal paper that I had found in the file. I had been lucky. I had almost missed the most important sheet in the whole file. And now that I had it, I had no way of tracking it to its origin. Well, only one thing left to do tonight.

In less than an hour, I was one hundred and thirty percent inebriated, completely *bombed.* Beer bottles littered the floor all around the recliner and the fridge was completely empty. With that monumental task completed, I passed out in the ratty beige recliner –

satisfied that I was now completely fucked. And not just from the beer either.

I woke up early the next morning in full hangover mode. I took a shower and a cocktail of drugs from the medicine cabinet. In my time, I had developed the perfect cure for a hangover. Take one scalding hot shower, four aspirin, two ibuprofen, and one 8 oz glass of water followed by a two mile jog and a second shower. Oh, and don't call in the morning.

Next, I made my deliveries. Each of my customers were glad to see me, but very disturbed about the news that I would no longer be filling their orders for them. How could I? My contacts didn't reach any higher than George and he had been put out to pasture. The fact that George was actually dead didn't fully sink in until the third or fourth delivery. The previous night seemed like a very bad dream, but I knew it wasn't. After completing my last delivery, I had a crazy notion. As crazy as it was, it was quite possibly the only way I was going to get to the bottom of this mess. I had to go home and confront my parents.

As risky as this would be, it was still no riskier than staying here. Obviously, they had found out about George's little investigation on my behalf and were sending a clear message for me and anyone who was helping me. Whomever they had sent must have been good. George would not have been taken easily. Obviously, my time in Nashville was D-O-N-E.

I stopped by a pay phone on the way back to the apartment. After inserting the required coinage, I dialed my old home telephone number. On the second ring, a familiar voice answered on the other end.

"Hello?"

I hung up. The voice on the other end of the line was my mother's. A small tear welled up in my eye and threatened to wet my cheek. I wiped it away with my shirtsleeve. As dangerous as they were to me, I still loved my parents very much. And I missed them greatly. They hadn't moved over these last four years, which was good. When I had dialed the number, I really didn't know what to expect. My parents could have moved, or even died and I wouldn't have known. I'd severed all ties to my family when I left home.

I hurried back to the apartment and packed all of the necessities for my next move. Luckily, I had kept most of it close together in case I ever needed to leave in a hurry. This had been a little fatherly advice from George; George who had done so much for me; George who was now dead because of me. All of the unnecessary bullshit that I had collected since my move to Nashville I stuffed into black plastic trash bags and threw in the apartment complex's dumpster, which just so happened to be conveniently located directly below my second story balcony.

I threw away everything that I could handle with relative ease. Dishes, clothes, towels, supplies, bed linens, and food all found their place in the dumpster. The furniture was too heavy to dispose of without help so I left it in the apartment. With the space almost completely emptied out, I went back through and did a thorough cleaning. I wiped all the surfaces, vacuumed all the floors and gave it an all around once over. With that complete, I locked the keys in the apartment and left Nashville for good.

XII. Homecoming

I pulled up in front of my parent's house at 8 A.M. the next morning, parking on the opposite side of the street. My plan was to observe for awhile before going in, a classic rule I'd learned from my grandfather's journal. I'd spent the previous night in a cheap motel about 20 miles from the house; just far enough away to give me some cover in case things went poorly.

It was Saturday and mom and dad were up and about as I expected. They had been early risers as far back as I could remember. You could hear them milling around in the kitchen between five and six in the morning even on the weekends. Actually, it was pretty infuriating for a teenager trying to get some sleep. Sometimes I wondered if they weren't being loud just to punish me for returning so late the night before.

I could easily see Mom through the screen door; sitting at the kitchen table, drinking coffee and perusing the morning paper, her lips a blur of movement. Though I couldn't see Dad in his normal seat at the head of the table, I could easily picture him sitting there reading the paper while Mom talked away, filling the room with empty words and rhetorical questions. It was impossible to tell if Dad was responding to her constant jibberish. When I was young, it was a fifty-fifty shot. Flip a coin - today he's answering, tomorrow you're "shit outta luck." The house looked so peaceful sitting behind its black wrought-iron fence. It wasn't likely to be that serene when I left this afternoon.

I took a deep breath, closed my eyes and lay my head back against the headrest. This was going to be the most difficult thing I had ever done. Even if they welcomed me in, they would not be pleased when I brought up the subject of my grandfather. That was one sore spot that penetrated well beneath the surface. It was the reason that I left home, changed my name, and began my current life. Ironically, it had now become the very reason I sat here in front of my parents' house preparing to have the exact same conversation with them a second time.

I tried to envision how the discussion might play out. Worst case scenario, they don't recognize me and I have to convince them who I am before they deny me entry into the house and close the door in my face. Best case, they immediately recognize me and are overcome with emotion at my return. And for their tears, I will reward them with a long discussion about the one topic that they would never expect and at the same time refuse to acknowledge.

I knew that my father wouldn't believe a word in the journal. When we talked about it before I left, he denied that the events in the journal could possibly be true. His explanation was that grandfather was emotionally scarred from his time in the military and that those scars took the form of stories, lies, and nightmares of things that never happened. He believed that grandfather was weak of mind and could no longer tell reality from fantasy. As for the notion that the government was trying to shut up both he and my grandmother, dad believed that there was a simple explanation. They both suffered from bouts of delusional paranoia.

We had argued for hours that night; most of it at the top of our voices. At several junctures, mom had to intercede to keep it from turning into an all-out street fight. Even now, I could still hear his voice in my ears, telling me that my grandparents were both crazy and it was not going to change, no matter how much I wanted it to. I can't recall how many pieces of furniture got broken that evening, but I distinctly remember one television, one coffee table, and a dozen family pictures and frames that lay in fragments littering the floor as I left.

During most of the argument, my mother stood in the kitchen doorway, her skin alabaster white, her hands clasped together and covering her mouth. She was not one to openly disagree with my father. What she said behind the bedroom door, I couldn't guess. Although my father rarely changed his mind, so I can't believe that it was much. That argument was no different. As my father's decibel level increased, my mother seemed to disappear into the very wallpaper that covered the walls, mimicking her environment in an attempt to avoid the predator that shared her bed each night.

When it was over, I was gone. I left for good that same night. If my parents couldn't believe my grandfather's words, then they would eventually think I was crazy also. God only knew what would happen if the truth came out about mammaw. So I left. I packed up what I could and took off for a new life; one devoid of family and friends. I couldn't have guessed that I would come full circle; right back to this very house.

I opened my eyes and looked back into the house where I grew up. The scene was blurry from the tears in my eyes. I could see that mom and dad had left the kitchen, but I couldn't tell where they were in the house. I wiped the tears from my eyes and tried to shake off the heavy feeling of dread that had come over me. I felt as if the car I sat in was filled with fog and I was choking on it. While my skin felt cool, my head was hot enough to cook my brain. At the same time, I knew that there was no question; this was something I simply had to do. Even if it went badly, which was likely, it was the only option I had left. After George's untimely demise, it was obvious that they were moving in on me. I had to make my move, and quickly.

I reached into the back seat and grabbed my grandfather's journal and the green file folder before I exited the car. As I crossed the street, I looked to the sky with its white cotton candy clouds drifting softly by. I wondered how my parents lived in such complete and utter denial of what was going on around them. *How could they turn their backs on their family?* I guessed it was easier for my father since they were his in-laws. As for my mother, Dad must have convinced her of my grandparent's senility or sheer loss of mental incapacity. He could be very persuasive when he wanted, especially with mom.

I opened the wrought-iron gate and began my approach to the house. Moving down the short sidewalk to the front porch took enormous willpower. Willpower that I was not sure I had. *How could they ignore what seemed so obvious to both of my grandparents and myself?* As I reached for the doorbell, another question hit me square in the gut, almost knocking the wind out of me. *What if my own mom and dad are involved in this thing?* I sucked air into my lungs and cursed under my breath. I wanted, no *needed* to turn around and run back to the car before they saw me at the door. I *needed* to get the hell out of here and sort this out before I did something really dumb. *How could I have not seen it before? That was the only explanation for my father's denial wasn't it?*

It was too late; I had already rung the bell. My mother quickly materialized from somewhere out of sight and was slowly reaching for the handle to open the screen door. It had been four years since I'd left, but it looked as if my mother had aged twenty five years in that same span. Her hair was almost completely gray and her skin was dotted with liver spots. Her brow was deeply creased and her eyes seemed to focus somewhere in the distance, peering right through me. They were nothing like the bright, animated eyes of the mother that resided in my memory.

As her left hand turned the knob, her right hand went to her mouth, covering the words that lingered there. I saw tears form at the corners of her eyes, and her brow furrowed as she began to weep. After one second of panic, I steeled my resolve and stepped through the open doorframe into my past.

XIII. News

My mother quickly attached herself to me, wrapping her arms around my neck and burying her wet face in my shoulder. We stood there holding one another for several minutes. When mom finally broke away, she held me at arms length with her hands on my shoulders and her eyes washed over me. She then pulled me close again and held me tight.

"Oh Joseph, I've missed you so much," she muttered in a soft and tear soaked voice.

My skin went cold and I stiffened involuntarily. I hadn't been called by my birth name in a long, long time.

"I've wanted to contact you so many times but didn't know how. Ever since your father's been gone…"

I quickly pulled away from Mom and looked her in the eyes. "What?" I asked. "You mean he left you after all we went through?"

I couldn't believe that the bastard could leave my mother with all she'd been through, including the ordeal with my grandmother and my leaving. She must have been close to her breaking point. No wonder she was so happy to see me. I stopped the questions as I saw her slowly shaking her head.

"No, it wasn't like that at all," she began. "He was great to me, especially after you left."

"Then what happened?"

"He was killed about six months after you left in an automobile accident."

"What?"

I was completely lost now. The whole room was spinning out of control. I felt like a character in *The Twilight Zone*. Of all the things I had anticipated, this was not one of them.

"Yeah. He was out front getting the mail and …"

Mom was starting to break down again. The tears were flowing freely from her eyes and her voice was cracking. She had her hand over her mouth, her head down, slowly rotating it from side to side without looking up.

"Come here mom." I said, pulling her close.

As I held her, I tried to put together what had happened and the effect it would have had on my mom. I was confident that whatever effect it had, it probably would not help my cause. It was obvious that the conversation that I came home to have was not likely to happen until much later than I had hoped. I stood in the living room holding my mother for nearly forty minutes while she cried softly into my shoulder.

We moved into the kitchen and mom finally composed herself. She poured two cups of coffee and brought them to the table, continuing her story.

"Anyway, after you left, I was heartbroken. I couldn't understand why we couldn't work it out between the three of us. But your father was a rock. You know how he gets. He said that you'd realize we were right and come back soon enough."

"Mom, I'm sorry."

"No. Let me finish. I spent weeks moving through life in a haze. Your father had to take care of your brothers because there were days when I couldn't even force myself out of bed. He did all the housework, yardwork, schoolwork, bills. He did everything, all the while reassuring me that you'd be back; that you just needed some time alone to sort it out."

Mom looked me square in the face while she recounted the events of that dark chapter in her life. It was all I could do just to look in her general direction. Knowing that I caused her so much pain was killing me. My insides were twisted in knots. I felt like I was choking on my own breath and my eyes were starting to fill with tears.

"After three or four months of that, I finally came around to the realization that you weren't coming back. I resigned myself to the fact that I'd lost my firstborn. After that, things slowly got better. Over the next couple months, I started seeing a doctor who prescribed me some kind of medication. It helped me get back on my feet. I couldn't even tell you the name of the stuff. Actually, I still can't. I even got off of the medicine without much problem."

Mom's eyes now left my face and wandered around the kitchen, lost and looking for someplace to settle. I tried to apologize again, but the words stuck to the end of my tongue. My mouth hung open stupidly.

"Then on a beautiful warm day that June... I'll remember that day for the rest of my life. I woke up before your father and started the coffee pot. I was standing in the screen door enjoying the morning when he snuck up behind me, sliding his arms around me and holding me tight. He could be quite a romantic you know."

Mom's face was now a mixture of adoration wrought with pain. Her eyes were dreamy and distant, remembering a time long ago. The corners of her mouth angled slightly up in a thin smile; but they also trembled ever so slightly, betraying the grief that she still felt for her husband.

"After a little kiss, he pushed past me and went to the mailbox to retrieve the morning paper. You know how he loved to read the classifieds every morning to see if there was anything that qualified as 'a humdinger uva bargain.' As he stood in front of the box, pulling the paper out, this beat up brown pick-up truck comes roaring out of nowhere and blind sided your father. The truck knocked him clear over the fence and into the flower bed. The driver never even slowed down."

The tears were flowing again and I reached across the table and held mom's hand. I knew it was hurting her to tell the story, but I needed to hear exactly what happened to my father that fateful day in June.

"Before even going outside, I knew it was bad. Your father lay in a heap and was completely still. I immediately called 9-1-1 and rushed out to the flowerbed to check on him. It was even worse than I thought. His arms and legs were all twisted and his forehead was nearly caved in. I checked his breathing and listened for his heart, but they were both gone. I knew he was dead. The authorities never found the pick-up or the driver. The officer said that it was probably a young kid that just got scared and fled the scene of the accident. The officer assured me that they would find him, but they didn't. Just 30 seconds earlier we were hugging at the door and then…. He was gone; just like that."

I held my mother's hand firmly and looked away, obscuring my face from her. I didn't want betray my thoughts. I had listened closely and on the surface it did seem like an innocent accident, assuming you didn't know what I knew. I was convinced that the events in my mother's story were no accident. In fact, I contemplated if the whole story was a well rehearsed performance from my beloved mother. What I couldn't figure out was how she could have known I would come to see her. That would mean that they knew my movements. And if they knew that, why not just pick me up? No, mom seemed pretty shook up. If she was acting, it was an academy award winning performance – Oscar for sure.

But why kill my father? He didn't pose a threat. He was convinced that my grandparents were both paranoid, delusional, and possibly schizophrenic. *Maybe mom convinced him of the truth.* I decided it was worth finding out for sure.

"Mom, you said that dad was super helpful to you after I left. Did you guys talk any more about the argument we had that night?"

Mom paused for just a second before answering. *Gathering her thoughts or making up a lie?* I couldn't tell for sure, but I might have struck a nerve. I let her take her time to answer. There would be plenty of chances to push harder.

"I'm sure we talked a little bit, but I don't remember what was said. I was so distraught over your walking out."

The tears began to flow again. I was really beginning to think that they were manufactured now. Mom looked at me with pleading, bloodshot eyes. She was a pitiful sight; acting or otherwise. Before I could say anything else, she tried harder to convince me.

"Your leaving pushed me into a place that I almost didn't make it back from. You don't know how much I thought about whether death would be better for me than life!"

I watched her performance with the toughest critic's eye. I still couldn't tell. But something seemed just a little off. I got up and walked back into the living room where I had left the journal and file folder. I brought them back into the kitchen with me and sat back down at the table. Mom's eyes bored into me with the exact look that I had hoped for. The confusion was clear in her face. She obviously didn't know where this was going, and that was just the way I wanted it.

XIV. Ancient History

Without a word, I dropped the journal on the table, keeping the file folder concealed in my lap.

"I don't want to talk about this anymore Joe. It's ancient history. Can we just talk about something else now? Please?"

"No." I replied coldly. "We're not done talking about this yet. You know what's in this journal don't you? You do remember don't you?"

"Yes. It's a bunch of garbage written by a man that lost his mind. In the end, he was so paranoid that he ended up killing himself."

"That man happened to be your father, mom!"

"I know. Don't get upset. I just don't think of him as being my father. It's just too crazy."

"Mom, it's not crazy, it's the truth!"

"No, it's not Joe."

How can she be so cool about this?

"Mom, you listen to me. This is the truth – every word! That's what the symbol on the first page is for."

I flipped open the page and held it up to my mother. She looked at the black figure against the white page and shook her head.

"No Joe. It's just another testament to how crazy he really was. He wrote this doomsday story and then killed himself. What kind of man does that? Tell me; what kind of man does that, Joe?"

"I'll tell you what kind - the kind that has been a part of a black ops group that experimented with biological weapons - and not just on the enemy either Mom. They were experimenting on their own team. I can imagine it probably did just about drive him insane. Hell, we don't know for sure that Grandpa wasn't affected."

"Stop Joe, I'm not listening to this any longer."

Mom made a move to leave the table. I reached over and grabbed her by the arm, stopping her before she made it to her feet.

"Joseph, you're hurting me!"

"I'm not done yet. Mom, the journal says that after the tests were complete, they actually went on a mission into Japan. All the history books got it wrong. I hadn't read that part before I left home! That's why they had to kill him and anyone else who knew the truth.

"What are you talking about?"

"Yes. Pearl Harbor wasn't an attack, it was retaliation. After the testing was complete, Price refined the biotoxin and sent Epsilon Force into Japan to use it. If it worked, our government was going to issue orders for a biological weapons strike on Germany."

"What do you mean?"

"EForce went in to Hiroshima and poisoned the water supply, which had proven the most effective way of distributing the toxin. Most of the people that came in contact with it went crazy and ultimately attacked one another. That was the end result of the experimentation. Operation Incivility; Price had found a way to turn an entire country against itself. He just needed to verify that it could work on a large scale population. It says in the journal that the agent would cause symptoms ranging from paranoia to full blown cannibalism."

"Oh my God. C'mon Joeseph, that can't be true."

She was acting confused and denying the truth. I still couldn't tell whether she was acting or not. I continued – foot fully on the gas pedal now.

"Not only is it true, but it gets worse. Operation Incivility had gone to complete shit. All of the other soldiers on EForce were either killed or got infected through scrapes, bites and blood spatter; something Price obviously hadn't accounted for. Grandpa was the only one to make it out alive. Next, that fateful attack on Pearl Harbor – a brutal retaliation for our terrible attack on Japan.

After Pearl Harbor, our government had no choice but to up the ante! What better opportunity to cover up the mess they'd created? That's where Little Boy comes in. The only way to fully clean the slate, destroying all the evidence was the most destructive force the world had ever seen - an atomic bomb. See, the history books captured everything that the government wanted, but nothing more. As citizens, we got 95% of the story, and really the only part of the story that we would want anyway. We got the outcome, but not the cause; a cause that our government would do anything to bury for good."

My mom's face was ashen. She didn't speak.

"Mom, it's the truth. And I'm close to proving it."

"Joe - stop. This is the same craziness that your grandfather suffered from."

At this point, I pulled the file folder out and held it at eye level, but did not set it down.

"This has the answers. It's a copy of grandpa's military file. It has all the evidence to corroborate his story."

Of course I was bluffing, but she didn't know that. If I was right about the whole thing, this would force her into doing something to either confirm my suspicions or prove that she wasn't a part of a much larger conspiracy.

My mother wasn't budging. She was still wearing a mask of dismay and confusion. It was like she had always warned me about making faces when I was a kid. Someone had snuck up behind her and slapped her on the back of the head, freezing her face in that exact position.

"Mom, I can prove this thing out, but I need your help. They killed the guy that I got this from. I don't have anywhere else to go."

"Tell me what else you have," she replied noncommittally.

I opened the file folder and passed the yellow sheet of paper across the table to her. She read the handwritten comments softly to herself and then passed it back to me.

"….display psychotic disorders or other symptoms emanating from the central nervous system. Paranoia, psychosis, schizophrenia and mania, are just a few of the possible effects of exposure. Effective doses could be as small as 10mg.

There is a high potential match for psychotomimetic agents including derivatives of Pecyclidine, 3-puinuclidinyl-benzilate (BZ) or LSD. Compounds of the LSD derivative are most likely, but combinations of these agents cannot be ruled out."

"What is this? It doesn't make any sense."

"I know. I don't think it was supposed to be in the file. Don't you see? Something huge is going on here. Mom, I need your help to unravel this and solve the riddle."

"Son, this piece of paper still doesn't prove anything. It looks like someone's notes from either a research project or some kind of psychiatric evaluation."

My mind raced. When I had originally read the handwritten comments, I had thought the same thing; they were most likely research notes. But I hadn't connected it to a psych visit. That was it. That was the connection. These notes must have been from one of my grandfather's psych visits either shortly before or shortly after he was discharged. It was unfortunate that I didn't have the entire report. There was no date, no signature or anything to help lead me to the doctor who had written it. Worse yet, I was pretty sure that the rest had been either confiscated or destroyed. But someone had finally slipped, even if it was just a little.

XV. A Mother's Passing

I had only one option - force my mother's cooperation. I knew that it wouldn't be pleasant, but I didn't have any other ideas. I certainly couldn't leave now, revealing so much and gaining so little. Worse yet, I still couldn't tell what Mom thought about this whole thing. I wasn't convinced that she was as innocently perplexed as she acted either.

"Mom, listen to me. There's one other thing I need to tell you and you'll see that I'm right. You'll have to."

I swallowed hard; my mouth was suddenly as dry as sandpaper. My tongue felt limp and swollen, like a wet sock stuffed between my lips. My mother looked at me intently, waiting for me to begin. I opened my mouth and with the first word, I was immediately transported back to a familiar place.

The dim green hallway, tiled in sickly off-white once again stretched before me. As I told the story, I also relived it in waking dream. I turned the corner and entered the hospital room and the smell hit me. The putrid smell of fear and death mixed almost equally with the fragrance of fresh cut flowers and the bitter odor of bleach. I was instantly nauseous. I crossed the room and sat in the cream recliner, taking mammaw's hand and expressing my love for her.

We spoke of my grandfather, Josef, and the great things he had done. We also spoke of the wrongs that were committed against him. Mammaw spoke vaguely of the Josef's poisoning before he was discharged and his inevitable demise at the hands of the very government which he had served for so long. She cried softly as she recounted the night she found him after returning from an evening with the girls. From the note he had written her (*under duress, of course*), to his being in full uniform, pressed and perfect, except for the bullet hole in his forehead (*those bastards*), ringed with caked and brownish dried blood, she left out not one detail. I recounted to my mother the whole exchange with Mammaw, including her passing on the journal to me and telling me not to share it with anyone for fear of leaving a trail for them to follow.

I paused and took in mom's reaction to what had been recounted thus far. I needed to understand her potential openness to the rest of the story because it only got worse from here. I had already made the decision that I would not continue if I wasn't sure I could get some additional information from her. I looked into her eyes and saw the sadness of loss. She appeared to have aged further in just the short time of our conversation. She was obviously shaken. I instantly decided to continue. I had nothing to lose. I hoped that the rest of this terrible story would release the lynchpin that had held my mother back from helping me.

As I finished the tale, I felt as if I was not talking at all, but sharing the experience of the events all over. My skin turned cold, while perspiration yet covered my body. The hairs on the back of my neck and arms were standing at attention. I could feel my lips shaking as the words poured out.

"After giving me the journal, mammaw weakly held my hand and told me that she had to ask me to do her a favor."

"What was that?" Mom asked.

As I spoke, I was again taken back to the antiseptic smell of the hospital room where my grandmother lay in her bed. It's a strange feeling each time I'm transported back in time like this, a feeling of being in two places at one point in time. My mind is split; I am mentally conscious of the fact that I am in the kitchen at my mother's house, but all of my other senses tell me that I am at the hospital. All the smells, sights and sounds are from years ago. It's a sense of déjà vu, only much stronger. *Déjà vu on steroids* as my father might say. In the hospital room, mammaw looked solemnly at me with grey, veiled eyes. Those eyes were breaking my heart.

"Joey, you know how much I love you, right?"

"Yeah, I love you too mammaw."

"Then, I'm going to ask you to do me a big favor; one you're not going to understand or like very much."

I nodded, eager to comply.

"Joey, you are more than a grandson to me. You're the best friend I have left on this earth, and I love you deeply. Since your grandfather died, things have gotten very dim for me. Your mother and father have abandoned me. You see, my heart attack was not so much of an accident as you might have thought."

I nodded again. Instead of lying to me as my grandmother thought, mom had actually told me the bald truth about the heart attack. Mammaw had gotten a hold of a bottle Tetrachloridine, a supplementary medication for patients with pacemakers. We didn't know how mammaw had obtained the drug, but it really was immaterial. When taken regularly, Tetrachloridine helps maintain the heart rythmn of the patient. In healthy people, the pills will trigger the heart to beat at a much faster rate. If taken at very high levels, the drug can induce a breakneck pace that ultimately ends in heart failure. Mammaw had taken half of the bottle, going into cardiac arrest almost immediately.

It had been a miracle that she didn't die on the spot. By pure dumb luck, mammaw's neighbor came over to borrow some vegetable oil for the evening's dinner and was alarmed when she didn't answer the door. Mrs. Miller could hear the television through the door, but there was no answer after several bouts of knocking. She then returned home and immediately phoned the house. When mammaw didn't answer, she called emergency 9-1-1. The paramedics had responded just in time; knocking the door in and saving mammaw's life right there in the bedroom.

"Anyway," mammaw continued in a voice just over a whisper. She took breaths from her oxygen mask after each comment she made. "After that little incident, I've only seen them once since I've been in this God-forsaken place. But, you have come to see me many times, which is the only thing that's made it bearable. I thank you for that Joey."

"You're welcome Mammaw. And I love you too. Now, what is it that you need me to do?" I asked eagerly.

"Wait a second now grandson. I've got some more left to say. You see, you need to know what you're getting into before I ask you this terrible favor. I've told you your grandfather's story. I fear that the same fate is befalling me. I've been in this hospital for months now. The doctor's aren't doing anything to make me better. They're just watching me, making sure that I stay here for safe keeping. I feel like I'm losing my mind just a little at a time. My life has passed me by. Everybody that I care about is dead, except you.

These doctors are not going to let me go Joey. They are going to poison me until I slowly fade away. Well, I'm not going to let that happen. I won't."

I nodded that I understood all of this even though I had no idea what she was saying. As soon as I completed whatever favor she was going to ask, I planned on poring through the journal for the information that would clue me in on our conversation.

"OK, with all of that said, here's the favor. I need you to unplug these bloody machines and pull this damn needle out of my arm."

I could literally feel the blood drain from my face, even in my dreamlike state. My limbs went slack and I again felt like I was going to pass out. Instead, I blinked back into the present and looked to my mother, still sitting across from me at the table as quiet as grim death. Slowly, her face filled with color; first a little pink in the cheeks and finally red from hair to chin and ear to ear. She looked as if she had spent several hours out in the hot summer sun without the protection of her Banana Boat sunscreen. She abruptly rose from the table, knocking her chair over backwards. She backed up against the stove and her hands again covered her open mouth. Her eyes bore into me brimming with anger and disbelief. I couldn't speak or move; it was as if her gaze had turned me to stone. Finally, she stormed out of the room shaking her head and clenching her fists.

I sat at the table for a few seconds to let her cool down. I knew that her reaction would be extreme, I just hadn't been sure if it would be one of anger or grief. Apparently, anger was the correct answer to the fifty thousand dollar question. I snapped out of my stupor with the slamming of a door somewhere down the hall. I took a deep breath, gathered myself and left the table for the hallway. Now the real work began. Obviously, she still didn't believe what I believed. In any case, I had to get her back to my side so that she could help me get the information that I needed.

I stepped into the hallway. There was only one closed door and it lay at the end of the hall. The doorway led to the bedroom that had belonged to my parents for as long as I could remember. I slowly made my way back to the door and reached for the knob. Locked. I took another calming breath and called to my mother through the door. There was no answer. I called again and again; each time losing a little more hope that she would respond. *Shit.* I had lost her. I leaned against the wall and let myself slide down until I felt the soft carpeting that covered the floor of the hallway. I sat there for several seconds before calling through the doorway again, apologizing and asking her to come out so that we could talk. Again, there was only silence from the interior of the room.

I leaned my head against the door and softly willed my mother to come out of her room. It was no use; she was not coming out. *What could she be doing in there?* I thought about it for a second and decided that she must be crying. I could see the image of her in my head; lying on the floral comforter with her face buried in a pillow, whimpering softly.

XVI. Unwelcome Guest

As I sat slumped on the hallway floor with my head resting against my mother's bedroom door, I could faintly hear muffled noises from the interior of the bedroom. *What is she doing?* I straightened up and put my ear flush to the door to listen more intently for the sounds. It was very quiet on the other side of the stained oak door, but I could barely make out the noise. It was my mother's voice. I was initially confused, but I quickly realized what was going on here. *She was on the telephone!* I quickly got to my feet and took several steps back, lowering my shoulder and preparing to rush the door and break it open.

Just as I started to take the first step, I had an idea. I rushed down the hallway and back into the kitchen. I had to find out who she was on the phone with. I rounded the corner of the hall and lunged across the kitchen at the phone. I gently lifted the receiver off its cradle and moved it to my ear, covering the mouthpiece and hoping that they didn't notice my intrusion into their conversation. All I caught were the last three words before the line went dead.

"Okay. Please hurry," I heard my mother say just before hanging up the telephone.

I rushed back down the hallway and kicked the door just below the knob. It swung inward and slammed against the interior wall. My mother was on the other side of the bed. Her face was wrapped in a blanket of pure terror. *She was afraid of me? What the hell was going on here?*

"Who were you on the phone with?" I screamed.

She said nothing. Her knees buckled and she dropped to the floor, curling up in the fetal position. I jumped across the bed and went down to one knee and grabbed her by the arm. She sat up, but still buried her face in arms wrapped around her bent knees. I was absolutely furious with her. My skin burned like it was on fire. My eyes stung and felt as if they may burst. I couldn't believe that she would betray her own son.

"Mom? Who was on the telephone? Goddammit mom; tell me right fucking now!"

She looked up at me; her cheeks tear streaked and rosy red from her crying. She opened her mouth to speak, but just shook her head and replaced it in her arms.

"What the hell are you thinking?" I asked her. "Don't you realize that they'll come and get me? Is that what you want?"

She looked up at me and replied. "You killed mammaw. How could you?"

"I didn't kill her," I said. "I did exactly what she asked of me. It was what she wanted. Don't you see? They were going to kill her."

"No. You killed her. *They* don't exist. For God's sake Joe, she could barely breathe on her own."

"I said I was doing what she asked. I loved her and was the only one willing to do what she wanted. Now, who did you call?"

She said nothing. I was afraid that it may come to this. I pulled the gun from my waistband. It was a Colt 45, just like the one my grandfather carried with him in Japan. I was proud to have one like it. I cringed at the idea that I might have to use it against my own mother.

As I pointed the gun in her direction, I spoke to her again. "Mom, you'd better tell me who you called. Don't make me do this."

She looked up. As her brain registered the circular barrel of the gun pointed directly at her, her eyes widened in fright. Her hands flew up beside her face as if she were preparing to be arrested. Her expression was still a mask of fear and shock. She spoke, her voice small and strained.

"I didn't call the cops. It was ahh....a friend. A man I met awhile back."

"What's his name, mom?"

She didn't answer, contemplating if she could avoid me knowing.

"What's his God-damn name!" I screamed.

"Mike; it's Mike."

I couldn't believe this. How in the hell did it end up this way? This little trip to my parents had become a nightmare of grand proportions. I shouldn't have even tried coming here. *But I didn't have a choice did I?*

"Why would you call him?" I mumbled aloud.

"Don't worry son, he's a good man. Just relax."

"Don't tell me to relax," I told her. "Will he call the cops?"

"No. I told him not to."

"Well is he coming here then?"

"Yes."

"God damn it Mom! What else did you tell him?"

"Nothing. Some things. It's okay. Don't worry."

"I'm not worried Mom. But you should be. You should be worried for your little boyfriend. Why would you do something stupid like call him and ask him to come over here? I hope for all of our sakes that he didn't call the cops."

"He didn't. Trust me."

"Trust you? After you just told some stranger that I killed my grandmother? Wait. Call him back and tell him that you were wrong. Tell him not to come over here."

Mom slowly picked up the telephone and dialed the number. She waited and listened as the answering machine picked up and went through its routine followed by the proverbial beeeeeep.

"He didn't answer. He must already be on the way over here. Please put the gun away Joe."

Shit. What was I going to do now? I lowered the gun and sat down on the bed. This was getting worse by the minute. There wouldn't be a good way to get through this one, especially if what's-his-face had called the cops already. If he had, they would be here soon with the feds in tow. My goose was cooked. My mind was racing, and I kept coming back to just two options: stay or run.

I could take my mother and head for the interstate, never looking back. But I would always be afraid, considering that her boyfriend knew enough to get us caught. Or, we could stay and wait for him to get here. *But then what do I do?*

I decided to stay and wait; it was the only way I could ensure our safety. My mother and I sat opposite one another in the living room, silently waiting for our guest to arrive. I watched her closely. I didn't think she would run, but she was obviously a liability if she did.

"What are you going to do?" she asked.

"I don't know. I have to know exactly what you told him and if he told anyone. And since you won't tell me…"

My mother fell silent again and looked out the front window and into the distance. As we sat there, I contemplated whether it would be necessary to bind and gag my mom while I spoke to her beloved Mike. As it turned out, I didn't have time for any preparation. Mike's blue Camaro slowed in the street and pulled into the driveway as I was still considering my next actions.

Mike took a couple of seconds to gather himself up and finally exited the sporty blue car, double lined down the hood with racing stripes. The vanity plate on the front read "Mike's Cam." *How fucking gay.* As Mike walked up the sidewalk, I sized him up. Five foot nine or ten, medium build, late fifties with a full head of silver-white hair. Mike looked like he was having a mid-life crisis at retirement age. He wore blue jeans, a button-down peach shirt with a sailboat print, open almost to the breastbone, and white Velcro-closing sneakers. *Double fucking gay.* I opened the front door to greet our new guest.

The door opened right as Mike Monroe reached out to grab the knob. It was obvious that he was terrified since he nearly jumped out of his skin at the site of me. *How could my mother be dating this lame ass prick?* Mike reached out to shake my hand in an uncertain gesture of kindness.

"Get the fuck in here," I said as I drug him in by the shirtsleeve.

Monroe quickly crossed the living room and sat in the chair that I had just recently vacated. Good. This way I could keep my mother under close supervision as I questioned Monroe. He opened his mouth, but I cut him off before he could speak to my mother.

"Tell me what you know; what she told you and who you've told since the telephone call."

"Ummn... I don't really know anything. And I didn't tell anyone. I just came over to check on Leeny."

I felt the anger swell within me, bubbling to the surface like hot acid. Leeny had been the pet name that my father called mom. It was short for Eileen, her given name. I backhanded Monroe, cutting his lip and honing his fear just a little more. He made no move against me, *the spineless prick*.

"Don't call her that." I told him. "You will address her as Eileen around me. You haven't earned the right to call her that name. Do you understand me?"

Mike Monroe nodded slowly, his gaze burning holes in the carpeting of the living room.

"Now I will ask you again, Mr. Monroe. What did my mother tell you? And who have you communicated with since then?"

"I don't know what your..."

Before he could finish his sentence I whipped the Colt out of my belt and had the barrel jammed between his teeth. Monroe was so scared that his teeth were actually chattering on the barrel of the handgun. I had to bite my lip to suppress the laughter that was quickly filling my throat. Mom jumped out of her chair in protest.

"Sit the fuck down!" I screamed in her direction.

My mother quietly sat back down in her chair and looked out the front window, as if nothing bad could happen to her boyfriend while she wasn't looking. I glanced briefly in her direction before continuing my conversation with Monroe. I could see her cheeks were wet with tears. *How could she really care for this guy?* It didn't make any sense to me, but I was willing to concede the point. It didn't matter; the two of us were going to be gone soon enough anyway. And Monroe? He was either going to be quiet or dead. Either way, he wasn't going to tell anyone about my presence here at my mother's place.

XVII. Reckoning

How do you force information out of a scared shitless, sniveling little maggot? I thought briefly about what my grandfather would have done in his black ops days and the answer I got wasn't a pretty one. I wasn't ready to torture and beat this man for the information, but I was working my way up to it. I leaned in close to Monroe, shoving the gun barrel into the back of his throat, and whispered in his ear.

"Are you ready to answer the question now?"

He nodded, so I slowly removed the handgun from his mouth. As if a drain plug had been pulled, he quickly sucked in air, his eyes wide and panicked.

"OK. You win. She told me everything – that you came here to kill her. She also said you're a crazy, sick fuck that…"

I was shocked. *Why would my mother say such things?* I couldn't move. I took a step back and looked over at my mother. Her face was once again twisted into that unrecognizable mask of anguish. She had her arms raised to the sides of her head and her hands buried in her hair, grabbing handfuls of graying curls and threatening to pull them out, roots and all. Her mouth was shaping the words that she desperately wanted to say, but they were completely inaudible – choked off by her own fear and pain. She mouthed the same word over and over.

"No, no, no, no…"

What the hell was going on here? I saw a flash of peach and blue from the corner of my eye. Mike was rushing me. Maybe the old bastard had more gusto than I gave him credit for. He had grabbed a brass candlestick holder and was now on his feet, preparing to lunge at me. I stumbled backward clumsily and then he was in the air, quickly descending toward my knees. If he impacted me at knee level, he could easily hyperextend or even break my knees. If that happened, things would get bad for me in a hurry. I took another quick step back and lowered the Colt, firing just once.

Mike collapsed at my feet. Well, on my feet actually. His head hit the floor solidly with a wet, sickening *whack!* that I thought only existed within the carpeted walls of the movie theater. His shoulders rested awkwardly on the tops of my shoes. I slipped my feet out from under him and stepped backward carefully. A dark red puddle had begun to form around Mike Monroe's head. A grapefruit size hole was visible in the back of his head, just above the neck. There was also a rip in his shirt just below his collar where the bullet must have re-entered his body. Because of the trajectory of the shot, Monroe's body had absorbed most of the spatter. There was very little blood in the living room, other than the puddle forming at the head of the still body lying in the floor.

I looked across the room at my mother. She was completely frozen in her chair, as still and silent as the deep night. *Shit.* How was she going to react? I certainly hadn't planned for our meeting to go this particular direction, although I knew that Mike's death may not only be possible but necessary. I just didn't anticipate it to be so sudden, ugly and final.

Mom's hands slowly drifted to her mouth, and she began to rise from the chair and walk toward Mike's body. She looked at me blankly and continued tracing her path to Mike's side. I quickly stepped over the body and stopped her progress. Mom had regained her voice, quiet though it was. She mumbled softly.

"Mike. Oh, Mike. It was never supposed to be this way."

I put my arms around her and she collapsed against my chest, almost knocking me down. I carefully walked her back to her chair and sat her down, kneeling in front of the chair and taking her hands in mine, trying to explain.

"Mom, I'm sorry. It all happened so suddenly. I didn't mean for this to happen. You have to believe me."

No answer. Mom stared blankly at me, her mind thousands of miles away.

"I understand how you feel," I told her. "But this is for the best. He could have ruined everything for us."

She looked away and closed her eyes. When she reopened them, there was something new there. Something I couldn't quite comprehend. It was like Mom's personality and character had split at that very moment in time. I then recognized what I saw in her eyes – hate. She grappled my hands tightly and spoke in a low but forceful tone. It was a tone no one had used with me for many, many years.

"What do you mean you understand? You cannot possibly understand how I feel. You just killed the only person I had in my life; and you did it in cold blood. You don't understand anything. You made a big mistake coming here Joseph. And you're going to have to pay for that mistake in blood."

She quickly reached to the end table that sat between the two chairs and grabbed the Colt that sat there. *How did my gun get over there?* I instantly realized my mistake. I had sat the gun on the end table as I lowered my mother into her chair, so that I could help her more easily. But the whole fainting episode had been a charade to take my mind off of what was happening. And she had played me like a master musician plays an instrument in the philharmonic orchestra.

My mother trained the gun on me, holding it at eye level. The hatred that she felt was obvious as it burned in her eyes, threatening to escape into the space between us. Her breathing was short and frenctic. Her lips quivered, infecting her hands which caused the barrel of the Colt to waver, tracing tiny circles in the air.

"Mom, you don't want to do this. Think about it for just a second. I'm your son; your own flesh and blood. I love you. You don't want to kill me."

The color in her eyes seemed to fade slightly. The mask of hatred that she wore eased and she lowered the gun, shaking her head all the while.

"You're right. You are my son and I do love you." She looked down at the floor as if ashamed of her actions. "But you came here and all you brought was pain and suffering. I'm sorry…"

With that, she again raised the gun and fired at me. I never even saw the gun barrel. I saw my mother jerk her arm up and I dove for the floor. The gun was loud enough to make my ears ring. The bullet passed by my neck so closely that I could feel its heat as it raced past and into the wall. I don't know whether it was my swift reflexes that saved me, or my mother's nervousness causing her aim to be off just enough to spare my life.

As I hit the floor, I immediately kicked out at my mom's legs. I connected firmly, sweeping her feet out from under her and bringing her crashing down on top of me. Somehow, she managed to hold on to the weapon as she fell. I found myself pinned on the floor by my very own mother with just a few inches separating our faces. She quickly brought the gun back within my line of sight, trying desperately to get the barrel pointed back in my direction.

We each had two hands on the Colt; she trying to force it in my direction, me trying to force it anywhere else. I could now feel the sweat beaded up on my forehead; my arms and torso already slick and salty. My hands were also getting slick with moisture. It was becoming difficult to hold on to the gun. Mom was leveraging all of her weight against me, pushing the gun closer and closer to my cheek. I could see it coming around, one degree at a time. I mustered a what strength I could and pushed it further away. Then, pain exploded in my groin. My stomach turned somersaults. Dark rings formed at the edges of my field of vision. The pain was excruciating. *She kneed me in the balls!*

Here came the open end of the gun barrel again. I tried to lean further to the right to give myself more room. My groin and stomach were warm with pain that had receded from sharp stabs to a dull throbbing. I could feel the strength slowly draining from my arms. If she got anymore leverage on me, I was a dead man. The gun was less than five inches from my left cheek. I mustered as much strength as I could, but it simply wasn't enough. My mom was too strong; her attempt on my life fueled by anger and grief. Three inches now. Panic was setting in. My mind was racing, trying to find some way out of this. Two inches away; I was beginning to see the hole in the end of the barrel.

If she was able to twist the gun much more, I was done for. If I didn't make my move now, I wouldn't be able to. I closed my eyes and focused all of my effort into pushing, not with my hands and arms, but my body. *One, two, three...Go!* I pushed and rolled with every last drop of energy I had in me. At the same time, I focused on the gun barrel. It was just an inch from my cheek. My mother and I rolled quickly in the direction of the chairs. Her body was jarred by the collision and she hit her head on the corner of the end table. The chair where her lower back hit turned over backward and crashed to the floor with a *Bang!* that seemed too loud to be real.

XVIII. Blackout

My mom was unconscious; her body limp in my arms. As I started to roll away from her, I saw the smoke floating up from the gun barrel. *Oh Shit!* I immediately ran my hands over my body. I was wet with perspiration, but didn't find any blood. I quickly scanned the room for evidence of the gunfire. I found no holes in the ceiling or walls. *What the hell...*

My mother lay on her side, supported by the end table at her shoulders. She was wearing a light blue pullover blouse that was almost the exact color of the day's summer sky. But on her right breast, there was a quickly expanding red splotch the size of a toddler's play ball. My heart sank and my breath caught in my chest. Mom's neck was limp and her head lay flush against her shoulder; her face was pale and slack. I shook her limp body by the shoulders, but got no response.

"Mom! Mom, are you okay? Talk to me!"

Still, there was no response from my mother. I pulled back her eyelids. Her pupils were completely dilated. I put my fingers to her neck to try to feel for a pulse – nothing. I shook her again; but she was still and quiet. I lowered my head over hers and tried desperately to feel her breath against my face while I watched for the rising and falling of her chest. I felt only stillness against my cheek and I couldn't determine any movement in her chest.

Heat spread throughout my chest until it felt as if it would explode. My vision began to blur as tears flowed freely from my eyes. I scrambled backward across the room until my back slammed against the wall, knocking picture frames and sconces to the floor. I slumped there, planted my head in my hands and cried. I'm not sure how long I stayed there, alternately crying and staring at my mother and her boyfriend, both dead in the floor of my childhood home. My insides felt as if they were being wrenched out. I was sure I could actually feel my heart breaking and the last ounces of precious hope evaporating from the pores in my skin.

That was it – game, set, match. This ballgame was over. *What the hell was I going to do now?* My mind was starting to race again. *What if someone heard the shots? They could be coming over here right now. Or calling the police!* I felt like giving up; turning myself in. I had just killed my own mother. What was the official word for it – matricide? There was no hope now of getting to the bottom of the conspiracy that had plagued my family for so many years. *Maybe I should just kill myself and end this whole ordeal.*

I felt so sorry, so pitiful; I was utterly helpless. Then, a curious thing happened. My sorrow and fear began to turn into something else entirely. Those dull, nagging feelings slowly morphed into a sharpened blade of fury and revenge. I realized that I could turn this thing around on the bastards that drove my family to this point. Yes, it would take time, probably years. But it could be done. It had to be done. My mother's blood was not really on my hands. It was on the hands of the government bastards that started this nightmare. The ones that sent my grandfather to certain death, forced me to kill my grandmother, murdered my father, and then forced me to kill my own mother. *Fuck them! They will get what's coming to them; it's just going to take some time.* But for now, I had to stay low - disappear. That was the only way to stay alive.

First, I had to figure out what to do about this mess- and quite a mess it was. I had two dead bodies and two large puddles of blood to somehow eliminate. *Or maybe I don't have to eliminate them after all.* If I could set this up to look like a double murder, or murder-suicide, I wouldn't have to dispose of the evidence. I just had to make sure that the evidence would tell the story that I wanted it to. *What about my brothers?* I remembered mom telling me earlier that my brothers had both moved away and she hadn't spoken to either of them in several years. Mom had also confessed to me that she had no one else in the world but Mike. And he was likely to be in the same position. So, murder-suicide it was. That would be the easiest to explain and the cops wouldn't continue to look for a suspect. *But how do I set it up so that there are no questions?*

In the end, I left the bodies exactly where they lay. It was okay that the room revealed a struggle. I went to the kitchen and sat down with a pen and paper. I wrote a short, but distressed suicide note addressed to Mike from my mother. I used my mom's rubber dish washing gloves to keep my finger prints from incriminating me. I then impressed both my mom's and Mike's fingerprints on the note, carefully putting them on opposite sides so it would appear that mom passed him the note to read. I dropped the note on the floor between the two bodies, letting it flutter to rest where it may.

With that complete, I wiped down the Colt and put it in Mom's hand. I set the chair back up right, but slightly askew so that it would appear that my mother shot herself in the chair and then slid out and onto the floor. Luckily, the bullet that killed my mother did not exit her body, so the setup was plausible. I stepped back and checked out my handiwork. After several minutes of contemplation, I decided that this was as good as it was going to get. I scanned the house for anything else that may signal my presence, moving from room to room and all the while listening intently for any unwanted callers at the door. Exiting through the back door, I left my childhood home for good; satisfied that the police would find nothing there to cause further investigation. I carefully made my way out the back of the neighborhood and around to my vehicle, still parked in front of the house, where I had left it this morning.

It was now mid afternoon and the summer sun was shining brightly, warming the heavy moisture in the air to a virtual boil. Since my early teenage years, it had confounded me how the Midwest could be so damn hot and humid at the same time. The humidity made the summers miserable with each degree of temperature increase feeling more like ten or twelve. It was strange how the heat and humidity had no effect on you while you were a child, but could make your adulthood completely miserable, sucking the very lifeblood out of you each afternoon.

I looked down both sides of the street; but saw no one was outside on this blistery afternoon. I guess that is one blessing that the heat brings – no bothersome friends or neighbors. The only place hotter than the outdoors on an afternoon like this was the inside of a locked car. As I opened the door to the stolen white Ford Escort, I felt the oven-like heat push against me hard enough to be a physical presence. *Oh well, no time to start the car and let the air run to cool it down.* I hopped in and fired up the little compact thinking to myself, "If the FBI really wanted to be invisible to the public, they wouldn't drive those oh-so-obvious big gray sedans, they'd drive little white piece of shit Escorts just like this one."

As I pulled out onto the street and away from the house, I looked back one final time on the place where I grew up and had my heart broken so many times. My head was aching terribly; I had a virtual drum squad in there playing their award winning solo at full volume- a painful ten on the dial. It felt like my head was going to split right down the center. *Must be the stress of what I just went through combined with the scalding heat in the cramped space of the car.*

I still didn't know what the hell I was going to do next, so I just drove. Down the highway, to the interstate, and out of town I went with absolutely no intended destination. After about 200 miles, I pulled over at a rest stop and tried to formulate a plan, but it was impossible. My mind was breaking. I couldn't think clearly; I kept coming back to my mother's death. I saw the chair falling to the floor and heard the loud crash that accompanied it. Then I saw my mother lying there, her blue blouse slowly turning a sick purple as it soaked up the oozing fresh blood from her wound.

The feeling was exactly as it had been when I pulled the plugs to all of my grandmother's support machines and removed the IV needle from her arm. Exactly the same; except significantly more intense. It felt more *real* if there was such a feeling. Thoughts exploded in my head at a rate too fast to understand. It was like the finale of the Fourth of July fireworks display dad took us to each year when we were children. Pop, Bang, Boom, Pop, Pop, Pop, Kapow. *What the hell was going on? Was this a stroke coming on?*

Surely not; I'm way too young to be having a stroke. Maybe I was having a psychotic break. Is this how it feels to go crazy?

The pain in my head was building; swelling and pushing at the inside of my skull with savage cruelty. Finally, I blacked out. When I awoke, my mind was clear and I felt reinvigorated. I awoke ready to drive on and begin a new chapter in my life. I quickly realized; however, that I was no longer in my car at the rest stop. I jumped out of the bed in which I lay and quickly took in my surroundings. It was a dingy hotel room. I saw a small notepad on the bedside table and quickly picked it up.

Motor Inn Hotel
"The Best Rest in the West"
7942 Grandport Dr.
Elkston, Colorado

How in the hell had I gotten here? There was no sign of anyone else being in the room, so I must have come in by myself. I peeked out the front window of my room and saw the white Escort parked in the space directly outside my door. After another ten minutes of trying to explain away my passage to the Motor Inn Hotel in Colorado, I finally gave up the ghost. Besides, I had much more important things to do. Things like figuring out where I was going to live and how I was going to keep myself hidden from the sons of bitches that were slowly exterminating my family.

I went outside to the Escort and grabbed the Road Atlas. Back inside, I opened the Atlas and began to plot the path to my future.

Summer of 2005

I. Happy Returns

Lindsey Macallum turned off the warm spray of the shower and pulled the towel down from it's hanger outside the clear glass shower door. She closed her eyes and dried her face, deeply breathing in the sweet flowery scent of the fabric softener on the soft Egyptian cotton of the bath towel. There weren't many things better than a warm shower after a three mile run at daybreak. She had been able to maintain her running while on the ship, but the shower and towels were a long way from what she was used to. This was what she missed more than anything else while she had been on the cruise, the warm spray of her own showerhead, which had just the right water pressure, and the perfect smell and feel of her luxurious bath towels. It was great to be away on vacation, but it certainly was also good to be back at home, enjoying the everyday creature comforts that she had worked so hard to provide for herself.

She wrapped her long wavy hair in the towel and stepped out of the shower. She was sure that her hair color had lightened a couple of shades from its original deep brunette in the Caribbean sun. She caught a glimpse of herself in the mirror. Wow! She really had gotten a good tan. Her smooth skin was evenly tanned to the perfect shade, almost matching her hair. The only tan lines on her deeply bronzed body were the ones for her string bikini bottoms. Lindsey had been pleasantly surprised that the cruise ship had an adult deck for topless sunbathing. She had committed to herself to get the best tan possible, which meant the less tan lines, the better. When she had suggested topless sunbathing to "the crew" as they liked to call themselves, they had each nodded eagerly with looks of mischief covering their faces.

"The crew" consisted of Lindsey and her four best friends. Dru and Megan she knew from her days at UT – Longhorns Forever. Although both were getting masters degrees in business while Lindsey finished her psychology PhD, they were bound together by the sisterhood of the Omega Chi Gamma sorority. Amy was

Lindsey's right hand and assistant at her private practice. Finally, "Peachy" had been Lindsey's closest friend since grade school. Her real name was Julianna, but she earned her nickname early in life due to her unquenchable hunger for peaches. More specifically, she craved the peaches that grew on the peach tree in Lindsey's back yard. Every time she came over to Lindsey's house during the summer, which was pretty much every day, Julianna would raid the peach tree within 15 minutes of her arrival.

The cruise had been Amy's idea. And a fantastic idea it had been indeed. Over margaritas and Mexican one evening in the fall, she had blurted out, "We all need a vacation; let's go on a cruise." The statement had been greeted with smiles and nods and the following June, they headed for the Caribbean. Now here Lindsey was, back in the grind again. The vacation had been good for her, putting her back in the right frame of mind. Amy had been right; she had definitely needed the time off. It sounded funny when she said it out loud, but her psych patients were driving her crazy!

Lindsey grabbed the bottle of moisturizing lotion from the vanity top and began applying it to her tanned arms and legs. As she rubbed the smooth cool cream across her firm, round bosom, she couldn't help but think back to the nights on the cruise and the man she had shared her bed with. Lindsey was not normally promiscuous, but what happens in the Caribbean, stays in the Caribbean, right? She had always been self conscious of her breasts, feeling that they needed to be one cup bigger to give her the perfect figure. But Mike seemed to like her C cups an awful lot. Mike - that was his name, wasn't it? No, Mark. She couldn't remember for sure, and didn't much care. For three days, he had kept her nights full of passion and intrigue, and that had been enough. At the end of the cruise, they had exchanged the obligatory phone numbers and email addresses. His was no doubt correct; hers – maybe not so much.

With her skin now clean and moisturized, Lindsey brushed her teeth and applied her deodorant. With that complete, she removed the towel from her head and wrapped it around her figure;

preparing to dry and style her hair. Fifteen minutes later, she left the bathroom, hair styled and makeup applied. She stepped into the closet, let the towel drop to the floor and picked out her clothes for the day. She was feeling quite fine today, actually. She chose a lacy G-string, matching lace bra from Victoria's Secret and her favorite white pant suit from Neiman Marcus. The jacket was cut a little low in the front, but what the hell; she was fresh off of vacation. There was no reason to get back to normal quite so quickly, was there? She finished the ensemble with a pair of white, four inch heels from a designer that she couldn't even pronounce. She had purchased them from a quaint little shop in Paris just last year and wore them every chance she got.

Lindsey looked at the bedroom clock – 8:42. *Shit!* She had a 25 minute drive ahead of her. She was going to be late for her nine o'clock with Tom Denton, a seventy two year old widower who had so many phobias that he was too scared to even list them out. Well, at least he wasn't the type to try to come onto her. She'd had several of those in the past and had transferred each of them to different practitioners in order to keep the doctor-patient relationship problems to a bare minimum. Lindsey grabbed her keys and purse from the hallway table on the way out and jetted off to the office in her black convertible Jag, top down and a smile planted firmly on her face. The sun shown down from the cloudless blue sky and the temperature was quickly rising toward the mid nineties, but without a drop of humidity on the air. *Man, this was going to be a great day!*

II. And in this corner...

The call came in at 7:28 pm. Officer Robert Trasker, or "Big Papi" as his friends liked to call him, eased the police cruiser into the parking lot in front of the *Water Buffalo Saloon* at 7:39, exactly 11 minutes after the call. The *Buffalo* had been the bar of choice for as long as Bob could remember. To the local drunks, this was the only place to go. First, the *Buffalo* had every brand and type of booze one could ask for. Second, there was rarely a night that the *Buffalo* didn't have a live band. And finally, it had a second room connected to the main saloon designated for "takeout".

Occasionally, this secondary operation caused a problem for Bob and his fellow officers, but that was a rare night indeed. Most everyone who drank at the saloon didn't drive themselves home. When the 3 am last call took place, the taxis would be lined up out front, waiting for their evening fares. To aid in keeping the drunks off the street, the *Buffalo* had a clothes line wire that stretched the full length of the bar. To get a third drink, the patrons were required to pin their keys to the clothes line.

It looked peaceful enough from the parking lot, Bob thought as he pulled into an empty space near the front. The saloon was an enormous structure that most closely resembled a brown cedar-boarded pole barn. There were twin doors straddling a huge stained glass picture window depicting an Old West scene where the barn door would normally have been. Light flickered from behind the stained glass creating a kaleidoscope of colors on the concrete sidewalk. Tonight appeared to be a relatively busy night, even if it was Monday and before eight o'clock. Bob recognized many of the vehicles scattered throughout the parking lot, as they belonged to regular patrons of the *Water Buffalo*. The sun was starting to get low in the western sky, but still burned bright red, casting shadows across the parking lot.

Papi opened the door and rose from the police cruiser just as a skinny blonde-headed man came crashing through the brown glass buffalo in the picture window, leaving a ragged hole just left of center. Shards of colored glass sprayed across the sidewalk as the man rolled clear into the parking lot, finally coming to rest against a parking block in front of a beat up, rusted out Chevy Cutlass with only three of its windows remaining intact.

Seeing this happen, Officer Trasker rushed over to the man lying face down on the pavement. He leaned over the man and quickly saw that he was okay other than a few cuts on his face and arms, but he was going to need a new drinking outfit for his next visit to the saloon. His shirt and jeans were riddled with cuts and rips, not to mention the numerous blood spots that had appeared out of nowhere. The man sat up and shook his head as if to clear the fog. If it was from the booze or the fall Trasker wasn't sure, and he didn't have the time to spend finding out.

"Stay right here."

The man nodded but said nothing in return. He was now wiping blood from his face with one of his shirt sleeves. Bob stood, turned, and strode toward the doors of the saloon. He could see a huge melee taking place inside. He unclipped his radio from his belt and quickly radioed back to the station for backup and turned again for the door. Just as he started to reach for the handle, another man crashed through the picture window, shattering the rest of the glass into a thousand falling stars twinkling in ten thousand colors. The second man landed awkwardly; audibly snapping the bones in his lower leg and careening into Bob, knocking him to the pavement as well.

This was way out of control. Should he go in or wait for back up? Bob quickly decided that he was obligated to go in. He jumped back to his feet, verified that the second guy didn't have any life threatening injuries, instructed him to stay outside with the first fighter out of the window, and lumbered over to the door, ripping it open with a swift jerk. The door slammed against the outer wall making a loud *Smack!* that would normally have turned everyone's eyes to him. Not tonight. Not one person's gaze came to rest on the big man in the blue uniform as he stepped over the threshold and into the saloon.

The bar room was even worse than he'd anticipated after looking through the broken window. It seemed that everyone in the place was in on the fight. As he looked closer, he realized that wasn't actually the case. The women in the bar were huddled against the exterior walls and in the corners; either rooting their men on or screaming for them to get out of the fight. There were as many men lying on the floor as participating in the fight. And the floor was the worst place to be; those poor bastards were getting trampled to death by the mob of fighters still on their feet. Bob could see several men on the floor grabbing and tripping others to try to increase their odds of getting up and rejoining the melee.

Somewhere near the center of the mob was Hank Marin. Hank had been in a lot of fights; some worse than others. More than once, he had narrowly escaped with his life and limbs intact. This one wasn't such a big deal, other than the sheer number of people involved. Drunks were easy to kick the shit out of; the problem was that he wasn't sure how many drunks there were and even the best of fighters had trouble winning a fight with more than 50 men; drunk or otherwise. Besides, Hank had been taking better care of himself the last year or so. He worked out regularly, ate a healthy diet and had significantly cut down on the booze. Even though he had limited his alcohol consumption, he did not have the willpower to eliminate it all together. There were too many memories and troubles in his life that needed help staying buried in his sub-dermal cortex.

An overweight, middle aged, sloppy drunk man swung his meaty right fist in Hank's general direction, hollering obscenities all the while. Hank let the punch glance off his shoulder and delivered a powerful right hook to the man's face. He felt the cartilage give way as the man's nose turned to mush and blood spattered all over his fist and arm. The fat man swore just once more and crashed to the floor face down. Hank stepped over him and punched the next guy square in the gut, lifting him off of the floor. The man made a *whooshing* sound and went down like a wet sack of shit.

The barkeep was standing at the far end of the bar, screaming for the stupid bastards to stop before they completely destroyed the damn place. Another drunk took the chance and launched a fist at Hank, this time from behind. The blow caught him in the back of the head, pushing him forward into the bar. The man took this opportunity to rush at Hank, head down - preparing for a football tackle of grand proportions. Hank looked quickly down the bar to his right and found a half empty fifth of Jack Daniels within reach. He grabbed the black-labeled bottle by the neck and brought it crashing down on the man's head, shattering the bottle and spraying everyone within spitting distance with the sweet smelling whiskey. The man lay still at Hank's feet, bloody and moaning. With the broken bottle in hand, Hank made his way through the crowd and toward the exit. No one, it seemed, was quite drunk enough to want a piece of the guy carrying a broken liquor bottle.

Hank pushed his way through the melee and toward the door, trying to get the hell out of the place before the scene disintegrated into a full-on battle for survival. Bloody fists and faces were everywhere. This was not his fight and he wasn't planning on being here when the cops finally arrived to break it up. It was clear to him that some of these guys were not going to make it out of the bar under their own power, if at all. And he couldn't afford to be connected with a bar fight that involved anyone dying.

Just as he was about to push through the final wave of drunken fighters, Hank's eye caught a glimpse of flashing lights. He was stopped cold by the white and blue beams, distorted by the small transparent shark teeth that still hung in the broken picture window framing. Hank took two quick steps back and began scanning the crowd for police officers. The hairs on his neck and arms stood at attention and his already shallow breathing further quickened. How had his luck gotten to be this rotten? *He had just stopped by the Buffalo for a quick drink to ease his nerves!*

Hank wasn't even sure how the brawl had started. He had been near the end of the bar, drinking his first beer and trading pleasantries with an attractive young lady. He hadn't even had time to ask her name before the shouting started somewhere toward the middle of the bar. Emboldened by this fine young woman's willingness to chat with him, Hank had excused himself and trotted off to prove his manliness by separating any would be fighters before their issues, whatever they may have been, progressed to the point of punches.

As he approached the source of the shouting, he quickly surmised that he was too late. There was a small group surrounding two obviously angry men. As news of a possible fight filtered through the room, more patrons began to crowd around the group at the middle of the bar. They pushed forward, each trying to get a ring side seat for the bout. Hank was now having trouble getting through to the men shouting at one another. A string of insults and obscenities rang out against the walls of the saloon. Hank was afraid that his chance to stop this from coming to blows was quickly slipping away. The murmur of the crowd was growing into a most familiar playground chant.

"Fight. Fight. Fight!"

Hank pushed harder toward the center of the ring and the epicenter of the yelling and cursing. He found himself completely surrounded by the chanting crowd. He looked back toward the end of the bar, hoping to catch the eye of his new drinking partner, but he couldn't see over the growing flood of wide eyes and open mouths, their chants now reaching a crescendo. He edged up on his toes to see how much further he had to go when he got a firm two-handed push in the lower back.

"Hey shithead, get the hell outta the way; unless you want to fight too!"

Though he tried, Hank couldn't keep himself balanced. He fell, crashing into the back of the man directly in from of him. The whole throng swayed forward and then returned upright. The man in front of Hank spun on his heel and swung a fist in his direction. Hank quickly ducked, avoiding the blow by a fraction of an inch. The punch connected firmly with the loudmouth behind him and it was on. Punches rained down on the crowd. Fists flew in all directions. Satisfied that he had fully lost the opportunity to impress the young maiden at the end of the bar, Hank tried to crawl out of the melee without getting trampled. As he reached the outer perimeter of the human bullring, Hank received a helping hand - two actually. He felt the strong hands grapple him under his armpits and help lift him to his feet. He turned to thank whoever had offered the aid and was greeted by four knuckles across the bridge of his nose.

He went down in a heap, the shock and pain of the punch shooting through his head and settling behind his eyes. He could now feel the anger welling up in him; anger that he had suppressed for a long time. It rose and expanded, filling every corner of his body, threatening to bubble from his very pores.

The anger gave him strength, sharpened his senses, and drove him to his feet. But it was not anger anymore, it was fury; a fury that demanded recompense. The man that had extended a helping hand only to then deal a nose crunching blow to his face still stood over Hank, glowering above him. He was a full eight inches and outweighed him by at least sixty pounds. But he lacked the one thing that Hank had in excess. Hank allowed the rage to flow freely from his fists, pounding them into the huge man's swollen gut.

The man doubled over, exhaling loudly enough that Hank could hear it even with the din of the barroom fight escalating. He delivered a powerful uppercut and connected with the man's jawbone. A loud *crack* accompanied the blow and Hank was unsure whether it was the man's jaw or his own fist that had broken. He felt no real pain in his hand, just a tightness that kept it rolled into a fist. That was perfect, for the need for those fists it seemed was not over.

III. Run

Officer Trasker pushed into the angry mob, pulling it apart person by person. That was really the only way to separate a mess like this; one drunk at a time. Each time he pulled a guy off of his opponent, he felt pride swell in his chest. He grappled drunk after drunk by the arms, shoulders, or chest; however he could get the best grip on the bastards. In several cases, he pulled men back from the fight by a handful of hair. In each case, the men would turn and begin to lunge at the officer only to have their ire drained by the sight of the deep navy uniform and badge. After conceding defeat to the lawman, they each headed for the door. No one wanted to be around when it came time for a ride in the paddy wagon.

One by one, Bob went about the business of dismantling the drunk and swollen fracas. He wished his backup would get here; it was going to take all night to sort this out alone. As he reached out to grab another fighter by his shirt collar, he made eye contact with a man a little deeper in the throng. Bob had never seen him before, but there was a look of recognition on the man's face that was unmistakable. It was a look of acknowledgement and fear bordering on panic. The man's eyes went wide and his mouth formed the tell-tale words that every officer of the law sees on a consistent basis: *Oh Shit!*

In a situation like this, the reaction could be from the fear of being caught in the midst of wrongdoing. But it felt stronger than that. It was the reaction of someone hiding from the law, of someone who's done something very wrong and is terrified of being exposed. The look of a criminal, maybe even a felon. The man turned and took off pushing through the crowd with disregard for the men around him, fighting or otherwise. Bob knew he couldn't leave the bar to chase this man down unless his backup had arrived to fully secure the scene. But he had to do something. *Dammit, where was his backup!*

He tried pushing through the crowd to get at the man running ahead of him, but he was having much less luck than the he would have liked. The bastard was losing him. Bob quickly surveyed his options. He could continue to break up the fight, surely losing his quarry in the process. He could pursue the fleeing suspect with disregard for the bar fight which didn't much improve his chance of catching the perp and almost guaranteed him a suspension. Or he could ….

Bob pulled his service pistol from its holster. Every officer on the force had been issued a brand new Glock just two months earlier. Bob had fired the sidearm many times at the range, but never in public. Hell, he'd only had to use his gun once during his 18 years on the force. He aimed the coal black weapon toward the roof and fired. *Wrong answer.* The crashing of the gun caused an immediate panic.

Bob had also forgotten to check his firing line. This was the cardinal sin of a police officer; the eleventh commandment the chief would tell each new officer trainee. *"Thou shalt not fire thy sidearm without first checking the firing line!"*

The shot buried itself in the huge antler chandelier that hung from the exposed wooden beams of the ceiling. Chips of wood and glass sprayed across the bar and sparks rained down on the dispersing crowd. The pit of Bob's stomach went into a freefall as he witnessed several tiny orange-red points of light gently gliding down from the chandelier toward the bar, still wet with spilled drink. As if in slow motion, the seemingly insignificant flames landed on the bar, briefly blinking out before the entire length of the bar ignited. The new flames leapt into the air, instantly four foot tall, devouring the accelerant and the wooden bar alike. Men and women ran in all directions, further trampling anyone that lay at their feet. They burst through the shattered picture window at the front and crammed through the fire exits at the sides of the saloon.

Bob looked around frantically for the runner, but to no avail. Surely all was now lost. There was no way he could find him in this mess. Bob's heart again leapt and he reflexively ducked low at the crashing sounds from his left. Pow, pow, pow in rapid succession. *The bastard's shooting at me!* He looked toward the sounds, but saw no one there. What he thought were gun shots, were in fact exploding liquor bottles; the flames licking the mirrored shelves that held them in place above the bar.

Bob scanned the exits again for the progress of the evacuation, if it could be called that. Everyone was nearly out of the burning building. It was a miracle, but it appeared that everyone was going to be fine. Bob headed for the front door, helping the last of the recently passed out drunks along his way. He cleared the building and pushed everyone in the parking lot back to a safe distance. Yep, everyone was okay. Astonishingly enough, no one seemed to be seriously injured - from the fire or the bar fight.

From the west came the sound of sirens as lights panned the crowd. Finally, his backup had arrived. Two additional squad cars pulled into the parking lot followed by an ambulance and the fire engine. As Bob walked over to apprise his police colleagues of the situation, movement caught his eye from around the side of the building. *Nobody should be over there*, he thought to himself. Bob focused on the movement, his eyes squinted to see better with the bright light and heat of the blaze in his face. *It was the suspicious guy from inside the bar!*

Bob took off in a dead sprint toward the large patch of brush where the man was headed. He hoped the man wouldn't turn around and see him coming. He had to catch up with him before he entered the overgrowth or he would likely not be able to find him for questioning. Only forty or fifty yards separated Bob from the suspect, with an additional twenty or so to the overgrowth. Even though he was out of shape, Big Papi was sure that he could get there in time. No doubt the man expected him to be tied up with the evacuation of the saloon; he had the element of surprise on his side.

Bob could feel himself getting winded about half way there, but he was sure he could catch his quarry before he entered the brush. He had a cramp coming on in his side, a "stitch" as his mother would have called it. The heat from the burning building was immense and he could hear the rapid popping of additional liquor bottles exploding and the crackle of burning wood as he passed by the open emergency doors. He was certain that this little incident would be on the front page tomorrow; all the more reason he had to catch this guy and find out what was going on with him.

These thoughts screamed through Trasker's mind as he continued to cut the distance between himself and the fleeing man. His lungs burned like hot coals buried in his chest, but he was narrowing the gap. There were less than twenty feet separating the officer and the runner. Bob's head was now pounding with every footfall. The adrenaline was pushing him on, but his body was starting to give out. The years of inactivity had taken a toll. *Good God am I out of shape!* he thought as he sucked in the smoky air and pushed his big body even harder.

The man was about to make it to the overgrowth. *He was going to lose him!* Just ten feet separated them. *Shit!* What was he going to do? If he made it to the growth, it would be very difficult to catch up to him. Bob prepared himself to lunge and dive at the man, hoping to drag him to the ground before he made his last steps and entered the thicket. Just as he started his lunge, Big Papi realized that he was too late. The runner stepped into the brush and disappeared.

Bob barreled into the growth, pushing branches out of the way and feeling sticker bushes grabbing at his shirt and pants, trying desperately to hold him back. Luckily, the thicket wasn't as dense as he had guessed and the runner was just up ahead. Bob could still see him clearly. He also saw that the brush was only twenty or twenty five feet deep and there was a splash of color just on the outside. *A car! The bastard had parked his car out behind this mess to keep it hidden!* Something strange was definitely afoot. Trasker pushed on, ignoring the bushes' sharp thorns scratching at his face and neck.

IV. Faster, Faster

Hank was halfway through the brush when he heard the loud cracking of sticks and leaves behind him. He turned sharply and what he saw, he could not believe. It was the cop from inside the saloon. How could that burly, out of shape goof have found him? He couldn't even get control of the fight at The Buffalo, and yet here he was right on Hank's tail. Luckily, he'd had the foresight to stash his car on the other side of the thicket patch behind the bar. Otherwise, the situation would be even more calamitous.

Hank knew that he couldn't be caught here - not now. If he was caught and taken back to the station on some stupid charge like disturbing the peace, there would be trouble. It was also quite likely that the officer would try to pin the whole fire on him. It was obvious that he was not the sharpest knife in the drawer, so he would be trying his best to pin this fiasco on someone else. Hank almost laughed out loud as he pictured the scene inside the saloon again. The crack of the officer's pistol, the shower of sparks, and the general panic of the patrons had been a comical enough situation, but the look on that cop's face when the bar went up in flames was, in a word, "priceless."

Hank turned back toward his vehicle and bounded out of the thicket with his keys in hand, ready for a clean getaway. Behind him, he heard another crash and saw that officer not-so-friendly had tripped on a downed limb and fallen face first into the thicket. The officer was looking at him with a snarl that was not quite as amusing as the "holy shit" look he had displayed back in the flame engulfed saloon. It was a look of pain and defeat. But also a look that said, *I'll get you boy, just you wait.* Hank allowed a slim smile, certain that he was going to make it out of this without all of the problems and questions that came along with a trip to the police station.

He hopped into the driver's seat of the ever-faithful Chevy Camaro and took a quick look out the passenger side window as he turned the key in the ignition. The officer had regained his footing and was again barreling ahead through the thicket. The chase had reminded him of something out of a cartoon. He, running gracefully toward a clean escape and Officer *I-deserve-to-be-a-rental-cop* fumbling along after him, nearly killing himself trying to catch up.

The comical little cartoon came to an abrupt halt as the Chevy's engine cranked loudly, but didn't catch. Hank turned the key again, producing the same vomit inducing result. He took a quick peek across the interior of the car and out the passenger window. Officer maybe-not-so-dork-a-lot was pushing ahead and was about to make it out of the foliage. The officer would be on top of him in just seconds.

Hank cursed under his breath and applied pressure to the key. The starter cranked and the motor finally caught. The Camaro roared to life just as the officer broke through the edge of the thicket. Hank slammed the stick into first and the engine roared, spinning the wheels and throwing gravel at the pudgy uniformed man chasing the car's rear bumper like a mangy, unwanted pet.

The Camaro burst around the side of the Water Buffalo, sliding sideways as if on ice and leaving a white cloud of dust and gravel behind. The black hot rod was roaring down the service drive that circled behind the saloon and was headed directly for the parking lot where what was left of the bar crowd were gathered, mouths agape at the sight of their favorite watering hole burning to the ground. The Buffalo was now fully engulfed in flames; black smoke billowing from every window and door. The roof had collapsed in several places and flames shot toward the sky, filling the holes left by each new cave-in. Hank had never seen anything like it before, but he didn't have time to stay and watch; he had to get the hell outta here.

In a scene out of *The Dukes of Hazzard*, the Camaro's wheels finally caught in the rocks, stopping the skid and sending the car careening directly for the crowd. Trailing behind was Officer Trasker, running at full speed, almost totally obscured from view by the plume of white dust trailing the Camaro. Hank pulled the wheel of the car hard to the left as he approached the parking lot, jerking it toward the street and away from the crowd. With wheels squealing and the reflection of the blaze in the windows of the black Camaro, he sped off into to the road and away from the crowd, the bar, and his pursuer. Hank had to smile as the sight of the burning building retreated in his rear view mirror and his heartbeat slowly returned to its normal rhythm.

Back at The Buffalo, Bob Trasker finally made it to the front of the burning building, his heart threatening to explode from his chest. He watched the late model Camaro peel out of the parking lot and head into the distance on Hwy 108. *Shit, not even close enough for a shot.* He looked down at his hands, which were shaking uncontrollably. *Was this what it was like to have a heart attack?* The way this guy took off from the scene, he had to be involved in *something* shady. And it was Trasker's job to find out what. He was going to be on thin ice with the captain either way, but if this guy got away, he'd be looking for a new job tomorrow morning.

Bob sprinted for his cruiser, still parked near the entrance of the saloon. He could feel the heat from the blaze as he pushed through the crowd. Suddenly, it dawned on him that all of these people had to be moved before he would have room enough to leave. *Dammit! He was going to lose the perp if he didn't get a move on.* He made his way through and saw Eddie and George a little further down but still at the front of the crowd, holding everyone back. It was Eddie that recognized him as he approached.

"Jesus Papi! What the hell happened here?" Eddie shouted over the din of the crowd.

"No time to explain Ed. Just move these people back so I can get my car out!"

Eddie gave him a bewildered look but obliged his request, parting the crowd like Moses, though just enough so that Bob could back his police cruiser through and easily get to the road.

After safely backing through the crowd and swinging the vehicle toward the road, Bob hit the lights and stomped the gas pedal to the floor. The big blue and gold Crown Vic leapt onto the highway with lights flashing and sirens blaring. The speedometer climbed and climbed, blowing past fifty, sixty, seventy miles an hour. Bob wasn't sure he could catch the Camaro; especially if the guy was smart enough to get off the highway at the first opportunity.

Bob slowed the car slightly, safely navigating a shallow curve, but immediately buried the pedal again and sent the flashing blue and gold bullet careening forward out of the turn. He had never driven a vehicle this fast before. Then again, he had never been involved in a high speed chase either. Hell, he hadn't been in a *low* speed chase! Until tonight.

Bob squinted ahead and thought he saw taillights in the distance. He quickly glanced down at the speedometer. Ninety five, ninety seven, one hundred miles an hour. Man, he was really moving! Despite the circumstances, he felt the corners of his cheeks rise in the slightest of grins. *Holy shit!* He was actually enjoying this. He finally felt alive and had a purpose toward which he could direct his full attention and energy. *This must be what it's like all the time in the big cities,* he mused.

V. The Morgue

Special Agent Doug Stunkle looked around his small office, scanning the pictures, crime maps and notes that covered every conceivable inch of the small space, including the back of the door. *Where to start today?* His eyes poured over the case names, each posted near the ceiling. He liked to name each case himself, something with just one or two words that could trigger his memory of the cases that he had reopened.

It was tough to keep track when your case load was every unsolved murder that had an interstate blood trail. The names reflected in Doug's steely blue eyes: *Antique Guns, Pedo Monster, Bible Slasher, Experiment, and Cop Killer* were the latest and not-so-greatest hits of the not-so-famous Special Agent Doug Stunkle. But he loved it. Doug reveled in the challenge that the job presented to him. Find what nobody else could find, do what nobody else could do, and make sure the bastards didn't really get away. The absolute best part was the look on their faces when you slapped the cuffs on 'em. In every case, they are so sure that they had gotten away clean; that it was over and nobody could touch them any longer.

Doug was in a haze this morning, not quite sure where to start when there was a brisk knock on the door.

"Come in," Doug called without getting up from his perch on the corner of the desk.

The door opened and in walked Al, grinning from ear to ear. Doug couldn't help but smile. Albert Cauhall had signed on as the file manager well before Doug accepted his position there. He spent all of his time (about 65 hours a week) tirelessly organizing and filing hard copies of case files and the plethora of miscellaneous information that the office endlessly collected.

"Good morning to you Mr. Bright and Early." Al said, leaning against the now open office door.

"Yeah, couldn't help myself," Doug quipped. "Got up at quarter to four this morning and decided to come on in. You know, that might be the best way to beat the traffic."

"You're a workaholic."

"Just because I come in *early* sometimes, doesn't make me a workaholic. I saw you were still here at eight thirty last night when I left. One might call that a tad over zealous."

"Yeah, speaking of which, I'd better get to it. Later, gator."

And with that, the tall, wiry haired file clerk ducked out of the office and headed back into the gloom of the fileroom, which consisted of the rest of the poorly lit basement. Doug and Al had become quick friends when he'd joined the Springfield, Illinois office of the FBI. Doug would never forget his initial meeting with Cauhall.

As a new hire, the first thing on Doug's orientation schedule had been a meet and greet with his new colleagues. Special Agent In Charge Colin Milner had introduced him to everyone on the main level first and then led him down two flights of steps (the old building didn't have an elevator) to meet who he called "the real character of the bunch."

Just a few short steps from the base of the stairs, the SAIC stopped and smiled. The expansive basement stretched out before them, seemingly reaching to the ends of the Earth. Immediately to their right, a small workstation comprised of a telephone, laptop computer, and a curious switchbox, with a single red button mounted where the switch should have been, jutted from the concrete floor. Between the phone, laptop and the switchbox, the little metal table almost seemed overwhelmed. Milner pointed toward the left wall and Doug got his first look at his new second home.

"That's your office over there." Milner said. "I know it's probably not what you were hoping for, but we're a little tight on office space in this old building, and you're the FNG. We'll go over there in a second. But first…"

With that, the SAIC pushed the red button.

"Don't freak out Stunkle, I'm not issuing a nuclear strike against the Middle East," he joked with a chuckle.

As Milner depressed the button, an air horn sounded somewhere deep in the basement, scaring the shit out of Doug just as the acronym registered. The FNG: Fucking New Guy. *Wow. It's really going to be great working for this tool.* Doug thought. As if on queue, a lone figure emerged from the maze of filing cabinets ahead of them. He was a tall, sinewy character with a wiry gray afro and glasses that looked like they came straight out of a *Revenge of the Nerds* movie, tape wrapped and all. The man quickly strode up to Milner, the bottom hems on his *Dickies* workpants swinging back and forth against his black-socked legs like the Liberty Bell in Philadelphia.

"You rang boss?"

Milner introduced Doug as Special Agent Douglas Stunkle, somehow forgetting that his full name was actually Doug and not Douglas, and explained his responsibilities were all cold case files that involved multiple state homicides, serials, and other crimes of interest. The clerk extended his hand and smiled warmly.

"I'm Albert Cauhall," he said. "I am in charge of all case files and intelligence that relates to this field office. If you need anything researched and pulled, I'm your guy. By the way, you can call me Al."

At this, SAIC Milner began to chuckle, smiling broadly. As if in return, Cauhall's lips parted and revealed a yellow toothed grin. Doug was lost. He intently searched both men's faces for a clue to their good humor. Finally, he couldn't help himself and asked what was so funny. Cauhall responded.

"Didn't you get my name? Al Cauhall? You know, as in liquor?"

All three men laughed out loud and exchanged smiles. Doug, assuming he was the butt of some long standing rookie humor, prodded the file clerk for his real name.

"No really," he said, still laughing. "My name really is Albert Cauhall. I like to go by Al, but you can also call me the name of your favorite cocktail. I've heard them all. And I meant it. If you need any research, I'm your man."

Doug lightly chuckled again, shook Al's hand a second time, and followed Milner over to the small square office that had been set up at the front of the basement especially for him.

From that day forward, Doug and Al had been friends. The basement was always just a little too cool and the lights were always just a little too dim, but the company was good and Doug liked to work on his own anyway. Tucked away here in *The Morgue*, as he and Al liked to call it, Doug could concentrate on his cases and hopefully make a difference.

In each case that Doug solved and closed for good, Al had played a part. Many times, he had played a large part, finding the exact piece of evidence or information that was required or linking two or three seemingly unrelated facts that would blow the case wide open. Yup, Al Cauhall was an asset that was sorely underutilized by his Illinois FBI counterparts. And that was exactly how Doug liked it; all the more time that Al could use to help him break these cases.

VI. Good Day

As the cool wind blew through Lindsey's hair, she reflected on her day at the office. As she'd predicted, it had in fact been a good, no, a great day. She was headed to meet the crew at their favorite hangout. They'd been having dinner and drinks at Mario's for…well since they came of age, so to speak. Thank God for phony ID's; they were the only thing that could help get a college student through the semester.

Lindsey pulled off the interstate and took the accustomed right on First Central Boulevard. First was normally bumper to bumper traffic, but was almost devoid of vehicles on this Tuesday evening, probably because rush hour was long over. Traffic tended to slow down around seven; and it was after eight now. The girls had a standing reservation at the little Italian restaurant and it always included "their" booth, the prototypical dimly lit table in the back corner of the place. She found a parking place on the street, hopped out of the Jag and headed into the restaurant with wine and grilled chicken fettuccine on her mind.

She blew a kiss to the maitre'd and floated toward the back of the restaurant. She could already see her best buddies sitting there laughing, drinking wine and talking about God only knew what. There was already one empty bottle on the table and a second victim was nearly half gone. She quickened her pace, not wanting to miss out on the gossip. She hopped into the booth, sliding into Dru and pushing her further into the horseshoe shaped seat.

"Hey" she squealed.

"Horses eat hay. Straw's cheaper, and grass is free," came Lindsey's retort.

"Now Linds, you know I gave up weed months ago."

With that, the girls were all cracking up with laughter. Dru was the officially recognized queen of one-liners and generally kept everyone else in stitches. Lindsey knew that she couldn't ask for better companions than the ones seated around this very table. While they were still cackling, their favorite waiter appeared at tableside and asked if they were ready to order. In turn starting with Megan, the girls ordered their favorite entrees. Brad wrote down the orders absentmindedly while his eyes kept drifting over to Lindsey. He didn't really have to pay too much attention to the orders since the girls had the same thing each week and he'd been waiting on them as long as he could remember. *Lucky stiff,* his waiter buddies would tease and joke. *Early bird plants the worm,* his dad would always say.

When he got to Lindsey, he tried his best to look her in the eye, but failed miserably despite his best efforts. His gaze sank like a lead weight in a fish tank, coming to rest on the soft V of her cleavage.

"I'm up here young Bradley," Lindsey prodded at him.

The waiter blinked hard and his eyes reluctantly met hers. Fortunately, she was smiling. He hoped he hadn't just lost his tip; but if he had, it was well worth the price of admission. He could feel the heat in his cheeks as he scribbled down her order for grilled chicken fettuccine and tossed salad with the house dressing. When he finished writing, he immediately headed toward the kitchen, embarrassed beyond belief, and put the order in. He would check on them in a few minutes to see if they needed more wine.

Back at the table, the ribbing had begun no sooner than the instant Brad had turned to leave. Dru jumped in with both feet.

"Ooohh, I think our young man-boy of a waiter might be a little sweet on you Linds!"

"And he's cute too," added Megan.

"Gimme a break," Peachy broke in. "He might have been a little sweet on her tits, but I don't think he ever made it much above that. And he looks like he's about eighteen or nineteen anyway."

"Mmmm…Looks legal to me. Yummy" Dru joked.

"Maybe next week you should go home to change before coming, Linds" Amy teased. "You know; maybe wear that pink string bikini from the cruise."

The whole booth roared with laughter. People around them were looking over and smiling; their good cheer permeating throughout the restaurant.

"Ha ha," Lindsey replied. "Very funny girls. Can't a gal wear clothes that make her feel good anymore?"

"Not when you look like that!" Amy proclaimed. "Can I get an amen from the congregation?"

"AMEN" came the overwhelming response from the crew and maybe even a few women at the tables adjacent to the booth.

Lindsey just shook her head and poured herself a glass of Cabernet. The teasing came with the territory. She had been through it countless times before and actually enjoyed it immensely. Tonight it was her, next time it would be one of the others. She'd get them back, and then some. The girls continued to chat and tease one another until the food arrived, making good use of the wine the whole while. They also flirted terribly with Brad each time he came to the table to check on them. He was eating it up; as were they. It was turning out to be a good night; good enough that they may have to order coffee at the end of the meal to help sober up so that they could drive home.

The food arrived and each of them tore into their dishes with fervor. About half way through her meal, Lindsey's cell phone rang. The ring tone was a Jamaican melody that she had downloaded especially for the cruise. She pulled the cell out of her purse and looked at the green lit screen for the caller ID.

"Shit," she grumbled. "Sorry girls, but I've got to take this."

If it had been any other number, with maybe the exception of her mom, she wouldn't have answered. But it wasn't any other number. It was Beth from the precinct. Beth rarely ever called, maybe once or twice a year. But when she did call, Lindsey knew that it couldn't wait.

Five years ago, Lindsey had agreed to consult on an as-needed basis for the local police department, sheriff, and state police post. Occasionally, one of the three departments arrested someone who gave them a difficult time. If they were too much of a problem, they would call Lindsey in to give an opinion. The calls came at all hours. They tried to call during the day (thank God), but occasionally, it couldn't wait until normal working hours.

Of all the calls that she'd received over the past five years, only one of the arrested men appeared to have any kind of mental illness to Lindsey. Most were feigning illness in an attempt to avoid incarceration. Beth was the evening assistant at the police department. She asked Lindsey to come as soon as she could. Apparently, there was a big problem....

VII. Victims

Doug lifted the big oversized legal filing box from the floor and set it on his over-crowded desk. Each end and side of the box had been labeled "Bible Slasher" with big red letters in Al's familiar, if difficult to read, script. He began pulling files out of the box and placed them on the desk in neat, orderly rows in the exact sequence in which he wanted to review them this morning. Even in today's high tech FBI, there was still a need for the old trusty, dusty files and filing boxes. Sooner or later, they would all be replaced by fancy laptop computers and on-line networks, but that day wasn't today.

Doug knew that all the high tech stuff had its place, but there was just something about sifting through all the paperwork that stirred the juices in him; making him sharper somehow, more creative, and ultimately better at his job. He liked his IBM laptop for email and report writing, but he couldn't get his mind around doing his research in a vast, manila file-less, digital library in space. He would be one of the last dinosaurs to give in and move on to fully digital documentation. It was common knowledge that if Al found anything in the online database for Doug, he was to print it on hardcopy as well as sending it via email. Until he was forced to abandon paper altogether, Doug would rely on his acute sense of facts and knowledge of research; and of course, he would rely on Al Cauhall.

Ten minutes and thirty three files later, he pulled out the most unpleasant folder in the bunch. The tab read plainly "Scene Pics." In it were contained the crime scene photographs for each of the four women that were brutally tortured and eventually killed. He sat it off to the side in a row all by itself; he would get to that file soon enough. In Doug's opinion, never would be too soon to look at the disturbing images again.

Doug scanned the backgrounds of the four women again, searching for a common thread woven through their lives. Unfortunately, it would be a thread that no one else had seen during the initial investigations. That was the trick to unsolved cases, you had to see more than everyone else, work harder than everyone else, and be better than everyone else.

In comparison with his other cases, this one had been particularly unsavory. Each of the women had been brutally punished and murdered for their "sins against God." Apparently, this killer's god was not the same god of love and grace that so many Christians worshipped each Sunday. Instead, he was a God of wrath and revenge in its most elemental form. *A bad-ass on steroids,* Doug's father would have said. Doug had never really been a strongly religious man, and the atrocities committed against these women made him wonder if there could be a God. If there was, how could he allow this kind of monster to exist? And worse, how could he just turn his head while these defenseless women were savagely murdered?

Doug read and read, skipping from file to file comparing notes on any number of things including appearance, occupation, income level, marital status. He found nothing that he could even follow up as a potential lead. It was infuriating. He felt helpless, and that was a feeling he was sorely unaccustomed to. And he didn't like it in the least.

Gail Crosby was the first woman murdered by this nameless monster. A single mom with two kids, Gail worked two jobs trying to make ends meet. The story was so common; it was the life of women across the country. The divorce rate was higher than the gross national product these days. Gail had been abducted on her way home from work late one evening in October of '88. Her night job as the late shift manager at the local electronics superstore on the northwest side of Chicago kept her out late each night. The store's records showed that she had clocked out and left work at 11:18 pm that evening. Electronic time clocks that you swiped with a magnetic card to clock in and out - what would they think of next?

At 11:43 pm, Gail had paid for gasoline at the BP station not three blocks from her townhouse. The camera footage had been confiscated in the original investigation and Doug had reviewed it multiple times. It in no way implied foul play. Yet, thirty-eight year old Gail Crosby never made it home that night. The baby sitter called 9-1-1 at 3:22 am to report her missing. According to the teenage girl's account, she'd fallen asleep on the couch waiting for Gail to return from her shift. She said that Gail normally returned between 11:30 pm and 12:00am on the two or three nights a week that she "closed." The baby sitter obviously had opportunity to commit the murder; she had no one who could confirm her whereabouts, but she had been thoroughly investigated and found to have no motive. Her relationship with Gail had been good, and was even better with the kids.

The ex-husband wasn't a suspect as he had been out of the country on business. Davis Willins was questioned upon his return and again at semi regular intervals; each time conveying the same story with the same emotion. He didn't know anyone who would want to kill Gail. They'd been through a no fault divorce three years prior and had been on speaking terms the whole while. He was an executive vice-president at a relatively small paint company there in Chicago. Willins had been traveling to business meetings in Europe for nearly a month and was genuinely shocked when the officers had delivered the news of his ex-wife's disappearance.

Six weeks later, Davis had nearly undergone a nervous breakdown when he was called in to identify the body of his deceased ex-wife. He refused to leave the Medical Examiner's office and had to be escorted out after over forty minutes of why, why, why's and countless sobs. He didn't fit the description of a murderer; and he certainly wasn't acting like one.

Friends, relatives, coworkers, and acquaintances were all checked and rechecked with not a single lead turned up. The neighborhoods from the big yellow gas station to the townhouse were canvassed and re-canvassed with no luck. It was as if she'd just vanished into thin air, car and all. Then, there was the dump.

Gail had been left naked, suspended from the ceiling rafters of a run down warehouse in an abandoned business park about ten miles from her abduction. She'd been found by a potential buyer for the park and his realtor. Needless to say, the deal didn't make it to ink. The buyer backed out shortly after losing his lunch upon seeing Gail hanging by her feet from the rafters, a grisly smile wrapped across her face.

Lying in a pool of congealed blood on the littered concrete floor directly below were her severed hands and two pink, slug like pieces of collagen filled skin that used to be Gail's lips. There were two words carved into her skin with a sharp but rusted drywall saw. You could barely make out the words due to the excessive blood that covered her upper body, but across her abdomen read LIAR in blackish red blood. On her back, the word THIEF was carved in the same vicious hand. The official cause of death had been listed as cardiac arrest due to severe blood loss and trauma.

At first, the meaning of these words was unclear, but the investigation eventually uncovered the fact that Gail had been embezzling funds from her employer. On her day job, she kept the books for a small, family owned furniture business. During the cleanup and removal of the body, a book page was found under the pool of blood below the body. But, it wasn't just any book page; it was page from the King James Bible. On golden edged, leafy sheet of paper, one solitary verse was highlighted in yellow.

Leviticus 19:11- Ye shall not steal, neither deal falsely, neither lie one to another.

The crime scene investigators recovered plenty of trace at the scene, but lengthy analysis of the collection of dirt, trash, and various other vials and envelopes full of unknown materials provided no new leads in the murder investigation. The Chicago homicide unit spent over nine months working the case with absolutely no progress. Eventually, it was closed and relegated to the unsolved cold case files of the department and transferred to the FBI.

Doug pulled the file of pictures and debated reviewing the photos of Gail's high wire act. He decided against it. Instead, he moved on to the next victim, Jill Connor. Jill's story was one of a normal suburban housewife. Married for eighteen years, four kids ages 5 to 14. Jill was a typical homemaker and was genuinely happy with her life by all reports. Her abduction took place in her own home one balmy afternoon in September of '90. Again, there was no evidence left at the scene of the abduction, she had simply disappeared. This time, however, without her automobile. Her Kansas City neighbors couldn't shed any light on the abduction and couldn't think of anyone who would want to harm Jill. The husband came up clean. There was no baby sitter this time; the kids were all of school age. It appeared that this was another random kidnapping. *But it couldn't be random! Serials were never random; they were perpetually methodical and predictably repetitive!*

Jill's body had been found exactly three weeks later, wrapped in a plastic bag and tossed on the side of the highway like yesterday's garbage. When state police opened the bag and removed the corpse, they had been completely appalled at what they saw. Jill Connor's torso had been branded with hot coins of all denominations. Her nose had been sewn shut and her mouth and throat were stuffed with official US paper currency including mostly twenties, tens, fives, and dollar bills, but with a few fifties and hundreds tossed in. The official cause of death was listed as suffocation. The ME's report also stated that the branding had taken place perimortem, which meant the sick bastard had branded her to keep her awake during the suffocation.

Pinned to her forehead with a safety pin was another leaflet taken from the KJ Bible. This time, it was from Ephesians: Chapter five, verse five.

For this ye know, that no whoremonger, nor unclean person, nor covetous man, who is an idolater, hath any inheritance in the kingdom of Christ and of God.

Jill had lived a life that very much resembled that of a million other domestic engineers. The phrase that summed it up best was "A race to keep up with the Joneses." She outfitted her kids in the best clothes from Abercrombie, was a part of the PTA, drove the newest and latest fad vehicle that she and her husband leased, and had a cookie cutter home with 2500 square feet that never got used in the most popular neighborhood in the city. Even with millions of people falling into the very same trap, it had been Jill that had aroused the wrath of this maniac and gotten herself brutally tortured and killed.

Sharon Cunningham befell much the same fate as that of Gail Crosby. She was abducted in November of '91 and turned up 5 weeks later in an abandoned warehouse outside of Nashville, Tennessee. She had been mutilated and hung in exactly the same way Gail had with just one difference. This time the bible verse had been nailed into her forehead with a carpenter's nail gun.

The last of the four victims had been Deena Dillings. Deena was a 34 year old, multiple divorcee with money to burn. She was very attractive; tanned, classic hourglass figure, manicured nails, artificially enhanced breasts, and long loosely curled blond locks. She liked wealthy men, and a lot of them. Each of her six marriages had ended due to the "extra curricular activities" in which she partook with other business men, lawyers, attorneys, and doctors. In each case, she was clearly at fault, but the court awarded her a windfall settlement that just increased her stockpile of cash, stock, and hard assets. It proved beneficial to have a good lawyer in your corner, or bed. And Deena Dillings certainly did.

Deena's kidnapping made the headlines in Birmingham, Alabama in March of '94 and her story was followed closely by the media. A high profile kidnapping and murder hadn't happened in the area for many years, and the public couldn't get enough of the story. At least what story there was to tell. Initially, it was scorching hot at the newsstand – big headlines, front and center on page one. Over the course of the next 4 weeks, with no leads on the perpetrator, what was left of the story line sank page by page through the newspaper, drowning in the midst of fresher news.

When Deena's body was found, the grisly murder regained its former perch across the front page. Details of the crime scene and mutilated body leaked to the press and the paper printed them verbatim in story after story. Still, there were no leads. This killer was good. He left no fibers, fingerprints or hair samples. No evidence of any kind. Or if he did, he chose his dumping grounds carefully enough that the evidence could not be recovered without extreme vigilance; vigilance that most police forces and CSI teams did not have.

A young teenager found Deena's remains while riding his dirt bike through a wooded area near his house.

"I ride through here every day to get to my buddy Jake's house," he'd explained to the officers.

Upon entering the woods on the well traveled dirt trail, he was greeted by the corpse of Deena Dillings, propped up against the dirt ramp that he had made with his friend Jake earlier that same summer. Deena's chest was emblazoned red with the sign of the cross. The ME confirmed that the killer cut the cross into Deena's chest with a large, very sharp, very hot knife; cauterizing the blood vessels on contact. He had also removed each of Deena's breasts and positioned them nipple up on the ground next to her. Her wrists bore severe ligature marks and were probably bound during her defilement. At the scene, her hands and feet were freed and she was positioned with her extremities spread eagle.

The blood red cross stopped just inches above Deena's pubic bone. Her vaginal area had been completely shaved and protruding from her gored vagina was an ornate metal cross. Later examination by the ME revealed bleeding internal to the vaginal wall and cervix that suggested Deena had been repeatedly sodomized with the cross before dying from internal hemorrhaging. There was no blood at the scene, indicating that Deena's body had been placed in the woods after her death as a bit of show. Nailed to a small sapling next to the dirt ramp was the familiar bible page that had accompanied the other murders. The highlighted verse was from Leviticus.

Lev. 20:10 - And the man that committeth adultery with another man's wife, even he that committeth adultery with his neighbor's wife, the adulterer and the adulteress shall surely be put to death.

VIII. Connection

Doug couldn't make the connection. It was nearly noon and he'd been through every file he had. He'd been at it for over six hours with only blood shot eyes and a pounding headache to show for his toil. *Maybe I should move on to another case.* As he contemplated a change in cases, Al cracked the door and stuck his head in.

"Hey Doug, wanna have some lunch?"

Doug knew that some fresh air would do him good. He could also bounce some facts off Al and maybe together they could make a connection between the women. It wouldn't be the first time it happened that way.

"Okay, let's go Bud." He said with a smile as he passed Al in the doorway.

They'd been through this drill before; sometimes it paid dividends, other times it didn't. Either way, Doug could count on two things for sure. First, it would be an interesting lunch. Second, he would be buying.

They went to O'Bryan's, an Irish pub near the office. It was always an easy choice; the food was good, the prices were reasonable, and it was close enough to walk, get some fresh air, and lay it all on the line.

"Which one ya workin on today?"

"Bible Slasher," replied Doug, closing his eyes and rotating his head on its axis. His neck popped like a ratchet.

"Oh yeah, the one with the Bible pages at the crime scenes. Man that one really is a ball buster. Any progress?"

Doug shook his head and laid out the whole scenario. Old one-twenty proof listened intently to the whole explanation, seemingly hanging on every word, even though he was the one who put the damn file together. He'd also read the entire thing from cover to cover countless times himself. But he patiently let Doug rattle off the facts one at a time, knowing that the verbalization alone helped;

just like he had on so many similar walks to the pub. Only after Doug finished speaking did he say anything.

"What about the church?"

"What do you mean?"

"Sorry, I mean the churches."

"AA, you're speaking in tongues. What are you talking about, in English please," Doug pried. He used a different nickname for Al every time he addressed him.

"These were religious murders; did anyone follow up on the churches that these women attended? Maybe some whacko from the church did it."

Doug exasperatedly replied, "In different cities? Hell, these were even different states! Are you suggesting that this sicko moved from state to state and killed these women?"

"Actually, I don't know what I'm suggesting. I'm just wondering if the religion connection is deeper than just with our 'sicko' as you so eloquently put it."

Doug thought back to the files that he'd pored over all morning, scanning them one at a time in his mind. *What about the churches? Could there be something there? No, that would be too simple. He would have found that by now. Wouldn't he?*

Finally, it came to him. Each of the churches had closed their doors due to the tragedy of losing a member in such a bizarre act of violence. *That was unlike a church wasn't it; to turn its back on its members in a time of need?*

They had reached O'Bryan's now, but before they got to the door, Doug stopped walking. Al took two more steps and grabbed the handle to pull open the door before he was aware that his lunch partner was frozen a few steps back.

Doug was no longer hungry. As much as he liked an O'Bryan Hoagie, his excitement overshadowed his need for fare. He looked through the partially opened entry door and could see that there was a crowd of people waiting for a place to sit. That was the other cool thing about O'Bryan's. There was only the bar, and four rows of booths. There were no tables or chairs. He reached into his pocket and pulled out a twenty.

Stuffing the bill into Al's hand he said, "You're a grade 'A', two hundred proof, one hundred percent fucking genius Al!" And he turned and sprinted all the way back to the office.

Fifteen minutes later, Al exited the stairwell and entered the basement carrying two French dip sandwiches with Swiss cheese, au jus dipping sauce and seasoned fries. He kicked open Doug's office door and pushed his way in. Doug was just closing the last of the files and stuffing it in his briefcase. He looked up with wild eyes and smiled.

"Thanks, but I can't one-twenty. I've got to get on the road toward Birmingham. The churches were opened and reopened in sequential order, Beamer. Sure, they don't coincide exactly with the murders, but there is definitely a pattern. The other thing is this: the churches are all non-denominational. In other words, they're not affiliated with a larger body so they're free to teach whatever they choose. I've got to go."

With that, Doug pushed past and headed for the stairs at a trot. He had a lot of driving to do and it wasn't getting any earlier out there. He took the stairs two at a time. Doug knew that this may be a wild goose chase, but it could also be a break in the case. And he desperately needed a break; the bigger, the better.

On the way down to Birmingham, his mind raced over the files again, probing and prodding at the case, hoping the crack he had opened would widen and finally burst the dam. The more he thought about it, the more questions he had. The bottom line was that he needed to find out more about the churches. He dialed 4-1-1 on his cell phone and asked for the number for Angel's Wings United Church of Christ in Birmingham, Alabama.

Doug jotted down the number on a notebook on the dash, the cell phone stuck in the crook of his neck, driving with only his left hand and one eye. He debated whether to call the church or not. He wanted to speak to the pastor, but he couldn't afford for him to be gone when he arrived; which would certainly be the case if he was somehow connected to the murders. Doug drove a little further and his curiosity finally got the better of him. He dialed the number and waited for an answer on the other end.

"Angel's Wings, this is Joanne. How can I direct your call?"

IX. Don't Get Caught!

Hank breathed a sigh of relief as he checked his rear view mirror for what may have been the hundredth time. There was nothing in the rear view but a ribbon of tree lined blacktop. He allowed himself the slightest of smiles and checked again, just to be sure. Yep, he was all alone. Both the car and his heart slowed to the speed limit as he focused on where he would head from here. He certainly couldn't stay in Crystalton Heights. He'd have to move further North; and maybe East too. He'd heard it was easy to get lost in the big cities out east.

First things first; he'd have to go back to the house, gather up his stuff and be ready to leave by morning. It would be a long night with not much sleep, but he'd have to make it work. Maybe he could stop a couple hundred miles out of town and sleep a few hours at one of those rent 'em by the hour trucker hotels.

Hank got about half way through his mental list of must pack items when he was startled out of his semi-trance by the flickering of red and blue lights against the tree lined shoulder of the road ahead. *Shit!* The cops had set up a road block; maybe the pig from the Buffalo hadn't been such a tool after all. He hit the brakes and looked for a side road where he could cut off before he was close enough to be made.

No dice. The cops had been smart enough to set up in an area of the small highway where there were no side roads, no intersections, and nowhere to go. He lifted his foot from the accelerator and ran down his choices. What could he do? Option one: make a quick U- turn and haul ass the other way. Bad choice; that would be just suspicious enough to warrant pursuit. Plus, Officer Accidental Bonfire would be bringing up the rear sometime in the not too distant future. Option two: plow the cops and continue on, hopefully doing enough damage to the police cruisers to keep them from following. Another bad choice; even if he made it through, his get away vehicle would probably be rendered incapable of whisking him away from this particular brand of danger.

There were too many mature trees to forge a new trail through the dense foliage to the side of the road and there was just no other place to go. Hank's mind was racing, but coming up with nothing new. He checked the rear view and could now see flashing lights behind him as well as in front. He considered his options one more time just to be sure he hadn't overlooked anything and then dropped his foot on the long, slender pedal with the full weight of his muscular leg. The Camaro roared like a wounded warrior headed into the fray of battle; making a bee line for the two police vehicles parked grille to grille across the roadway.

The distance between Hank and the police blockade was burning like the lit fuse on a stick of dynamite. He could now distinguish three officers at the blockade; two behind the vehicles and one in front, palms extended in his direction. The Camaro continued to accelerate; Hank was approaching ninety mph and closing on the cops even faster than his brain could process. He was just a few seconds from impact.

Hank instinctively pulled on his seatbelt. He wasn't normally a seatbelt wearer, but desperate times called for desperate measures.

"Just being all I can be, boys," he muttered against the howl of the engine.

He was close now, just a few car lengths away. Hank saw the two cops behind the blockade pull their weapons and level them at the approaching vehicle. The officer stationed in front of the vehicles was still aimlessly waving his hands at the battering ram that threatened to crush him against his very own cruiser, likely ending his life. The rest happened so quickly that Hank would later say that he couldn't remember exactly how it went down.

As Hank closed to within a few feet of the road block, his instincts sharpened and his subconscious mind hijacked his body, probably saving his life. He noticed a crevice of an opening at the right of the road between the cruiser and the guard rail. Hank instinctively jerked the wheel of the Camaro to the right and braced for the crash. The car slid sideways and slammed tail to tail against the rear quarter panel of the flashing white obstruction. The impact of the wreck swung the back end of the Camaro back around and the wheels recaptured the pavement. Hank never let his foot leave the gas pedal and the vehicle jettisoned forward again, leaving the stunned police officers behind.

Hank rolled down the window and stuck his head out to survey the damage he had caused the Camaro. The rear fender was smashed and it looked like he had completely lost his back bumper, but there was nothing obstructing the wheels and the car was cruising along. He stole a glance back at the blockade. Two of the three cops were standing behind the cars talking with the cop from the bar, who appeared to have just arrived. Hank couldn't see the third officer. He turned back to the road and sped on into the night.

After bringing his black and white to a screeching stop beside the road block, Bob Trasker screamed at his fellow officers for letting the perp get through the blockade.

"Do you realize what's going on here?" he screamed.

The dumbfound looks in their faces would have been comical in any other situation.

"Move these God damned cars! If that bastard gets away, it'll be the end of us all! Now!!"

Trasker could feel the pressure building in his skull, pressing outward against his ears and forehead. This was a stroke coming on, had to be. As the two officers quickly moved toward their car doors, the third officer instinctively moved toward his motorcycle, catching Trasker's eye. He pushed past the vehicles and commandeered the cycle.

"If you're not going to use this, I am," he spat at the officer.

Big Papi fired up the engine to the bike and laid a strip of rubber down behind him as he swung the rear end of the cycle around behind him and took off in pursuit of his fleeing quarry. He could still see the Camaro's tail lights in the darkness, which gave him hope that he may catch the son of a bitch yet.

At six foot seven inches tall and weighing in at over two-fifty, Big Papi was quite a site to behold perched atop his fellow officer's motorcycle. It was like watching an elephant ride a tricycle. It had been years since Bob had ridden, but he was pretty good once-racing motor cross in his late teens. He even won an event or two. The night wind rippled his crew cut as the motorcycle ate up the distance between him and the Camaro.

Hank swore beneath his breath as he again saw flashing blue and red lights in his rear view. He looked up and would have laughed had the situation not been so desperate. The cop from the bar was screaming up behind him on a police issued Gold Wing, lights flashing and siren blaring. Hank despised him more every second. The cop-bastard was less than a hundred feet behind. Hank pushed the gas pedal further toward the floor, but the Camaro didn't respond this time. It just cruised along at seventy five, as if the cruise control was engaged.

Hank looked again in the mirror. The prick was going to be on top of him in no time. *What the hell was he going to do?* He let off the accelerator and jammed it back down to the floor; still nothing. Something must have happened to the transmission during the accident. In any case, he wasn't going to outrun this pig. He'd have to find another solution. The cop was right on him now; he could see the lights moving to his left as the officer pulled up beside him.

Hank had to get rid of this guy. He didn't want to kill the officer, but if he had to make a choice he would. He couldn't let himself be taken in. No way, no how. As the motorcycle pulled even with his door, Hank pulled the wheel left to run the cop off the road. The Camaro's wheels squealed, and a loud thump followed. The front passenger tire blew, damaged from his masterful driving earlier at the roadblock, and sent the car into a roll. In an instant, Hank was on the worst roller coaster ride of his life. All around him, lights flashed red, blue and white, interrupting the darkness. Hank's seatbelt broke loose, and suddenly he was being beaten to death inside the vehicle.

Finally, the car came to a halt and Hank found himself lying on the ceiling of the Camaro. He didn't hurt exactly, but his limbs felt cold, wet, and impossibly heavy. His vision was blurred and the image of the vehicle interior still spun out of control in his brain. He tried moving his head to look out one of the windows, but his body ignored the orders his brain sent. *Sorry Bob, gone fishing. Back tomorrow… Maybe.*

Where was that fucking cop? Hank closed his eyes and listened intently. He could hear the click-clack of heeled boots on the pavement. *The son of a bitch was taking his time.* Hank opened his eyes and concentrated, slowly turning his head to look for the officer's black boots. He couldn't muster enough energy to lift his head from its resting place, and his chin scraped across the vehicle's glass riddled interior. Needles of pain shot up his neck and excruciatingly lit the base skull on fire. Just as he thought he could take no more pain, he saw the polished black police boots at the side of the vehicle, through what was left of the spider webbed passenger's side glass. The rear boot bent at the toe as the officer knelt to peer in the window. Hank could faintly hear the man calling to him.

"Son, don't try to move. Stay right where you are. Help's on the way…."

Just as the knee of the officer's blue pant leg touched the cold concrete of the roadway, Hank's eyes rolled back and he lost his grip on consciousness.

X. A Pleasure to Make Your Acquaintance

Lindsey guided the sleek, black Jaguar XJS into a handicapped spot near the door of the MissionView Medical Clinic. She'd broken nearly every traffic law in the book on the way over. Her heart was raced as she put up the mocha latte ragtop, checked her makeup in the rearview, and grabbed her briefcase.

She hated to be interrupted on her night out with the crew, but calls such as this didn't come often. As special consultant for the police department, she was sometimes called upon to consult on cases where the perp displayed signs of mental illness. The behavior was generally either substance induced or faked, but occasionally there really was something there that drove the individual to commit a crime.

In the five years that Lindsey had been consulting for the PD, she'd been called in on eight cases. Six of the consultations ended in a report concluding that drugs or alcohol were responsible for the actions of the accused. In one case, the perp had claimed insanity after an attempted strangling of his estranged wife. Lindsey promptly proved his declaration to be a facade and plea bargained his charge down to battery with relocation to the state penitentiary for a few months of safe keeping. Only one case had proven to have some degree of mental illness. And that one was a simple robbery. She had diagnosed the accused man of severe clinical depression brought on by the recent death of his wife and son in a vehicle accident. The guy had essentially robbed the neighborhood convenience store in order to feel alive again.

Lindsey had never been involved in something like this. Beth wouldn't give her the details over the phone, but she did divulge that the case included inciting a brawl, multiple counts of battery, arson, and a high speed chase that ended badly. Now, the guy was apparently going berserk at the clinic.

Tucking her hair behind one ear, Lindsey briskly walked through the front door of the medical center. Her heart's rhythm escalated with each step. It was exciting to be a part of a police investigation; especially one that would be as high profile as this one. It was possible that she would even make it into the paper tomorrow morning! Surprisingly enough, there was no one at the information desk at the front of the main lobby.

MissionView Medical Center was a small but orderly facility comprised of four wings on the main floor, and a basement that served mostly for storage, except for the morgue. The center could handle up to a hundred patients, but rarely surpassed the fifty mark. The décor was mostly earth tones and was warm and inviting, if not inspired. Most of the medicine practiced at MissionView was rehabilitation of one ailment or another. The main lobby was a large oval shaped area with the information station set at the front center of the room and seating situated around the periphery. The four patient wings radiated away from the entrance and information desk. Each wing was designated by its patient type, from physical therapy to psychiatric recovery.

Although she took a large majority of her appointments at the office, Lindsey had made many patient visits to the center. All of her patients were located down the right-rear hall, and she guessed that the newest addition to the MissionView family was probably somewhere along that same hall. She walked around the information desk and looked down each of the corridors, but saw none of the attendants or nurses. The scene was a little spooky and brought back memories of high school weekends watching horror movies with her pals.

"Hello?" She called down each of the corridors.

"Is anyone here?"

Beth had told her to hurry down here; surely they had already arrived. Lindsey gave up on getting help in the lobby and started down the psych hall, glancing in each room to verify that her contact, Officer Robert Trasker, wasn't in there with the "patient." After passing three rooms with no luck, Lindsey heard shouting from the end of the hall. She trotted down the hallway as quickly as she could; even Grace Kelly couldn't run in four inch, sling back heels.

She arrived at the room and quickly patted down her pant suit and hair before entering. As she did, she listened to the screams coming from the other side of the big wooden door. This person sounded more like an angry, trapped animal than a criminal. His piercing cries were like nails on a chalkboard at a volume of eight or nine on a ten scale.

"Someone help! Let go of me!" The man screamed. "I know who you are! Why can't you leave me alone? AARGHH...... Let me goooooooo...."

Lindsey pushed the rectangular door handle and the big door glided open on silent hinges. She could not have been more unprepared for what she saw. It seemed to Lindsey that it had been the chin of her gaping mouth that made the loud slapping sound on the cold tile floor of the patient's room instead of her leather attache.

Three female and two male nurses assisted as two male doctors tried to restrain the patient whose cries Lindsey had heard from the hallway. It was seven on one and it looked as if the medical staff may yet lose this battle. They'd gotten one of the man's legs strapped to the bed, but were having no luck with the other leg or his flailing body. Three of the nurses applied their full weight to the patient's free leg, holding it relatively still even though it was more near the middle of the bed than the side where the straps swung and the buckles clinked like wind chimes. The other two nurses held one arm tight while the doctors grabbed at the free arm. The patient continued to thrash wildly against the staff, crying out for help.

Lindsey was frozen in her spot just inside the partially closed door of the room. She hadn't even made it all the way across the threshold. The door was resting against her backside as she watched, captivated by the scene and, frankly, horrified and deeply concerned by what might happen in the next few seconds if the man was able to get free. Surely they would be able to get him under control; they did this kind of thing all the time, *didn't they?*

Just as the thought flashed behind her eyes, the madman on the bed flailed with renewed vigor, arching his back and craning his neck; his face turning toward Lindsey. As he did, Lindsey saw the hypodermic needle jutting from the opposite side of his neck. It was like a scene from some macabre black and white horror movie. She felt like she was in a dream. The body of the syringe still held most or all of its original amber fluid. Lindsey knew that the liquid was a tranquilizer to help sedate the patient and allow the nurses to finish strapping him into his bed.

In spite of the aggression that he showed and the needle sticking ridiculously from his neck, the man's eyes were not the eyes of a madman. They were something else entirely. Those eyes were filled with terror, sadness, and doubt. For the second time, Lindsey was reminded of a trapped animal devoting its entire essence to its freedom. Lindsey actually felt sorrow and pity for the man. Yet, she did not intervene with the staff's work. She stood quietly; observing the scene and mentally taking notes that she could later put to paper for her case file.

Finally, the doctors were able to get a grip on the man's free arm and push it to the surface of the bed. The younger (and more fit) of the two doctors pressed his weight against the man in the bed, holding him as still as he could. The older doctor reached up and delivered the full dose from the syringe. After just a few seconds, the patient's rigid body went limp and he almost fell in the floor, his body hanging off the bed from the waist up.

The ordeal was finally over. The nurses pulled the man's torso back into the bed and together with the younger of the two doctors began the work of strapping him in, cleaning him up, and tending to his wounds. The older of the two physicians, Dr. Xavier McStadden according to his nametag, slowly approached Lindsey, his face ashen.

"I assume you're the liaison that will be evaluating this man?" he said curtly.

"I am."

"Well, you've got a little while to wait; he's sedated and probably won't be awake again for several hours. He's also had significant head trauma from the accident, which will likely slow his recovery."

"Accident?" Lindsey asked. "I'm sorry, I didn't get a full briefing; what happened?"

"I don't have all the details." Said the doc. "I only know that there was a high speed chase that ended in a pretty bad wreck. He was unconscious when he arrived with the police, but when they left and we took over his care; he awoke and threw one hell of a fit. It was almost as if he was just biding his time until he had an opportunity to try escaping, the crazy bastard."

"What's his name?" Lindsey probed.

"Driver's license says Hank Marin, but the police haven't confirmed yet. A guy that tries that hard to get away may well be using a fake I.D. ya know? And besides that, the cops weren't able to get a good fingerprint from him."

"Where's Officer Trasker?" she asked the doctor.

"He had to go back to the station to file his report on the incident. Must have been pretty bad because he said he had to go right then; it couldn't wait. Said to tell you that he'll contact you in the morning with the details."

Lindsey nodded. The doctor began to speak, but Lindsey cut him off before he could.

"I'm just going to wait in his room until he wakes up if that's okay with you, Dr. McStadden."

The doctor nodded and walked away, leaving Lindsey to her thoughts. She slowly pushed open the door and moved across the dimly lit room to the small table opposite the bed. She sat down and glanced over at the patient, Hank Marin. He looked so quiet and peaceful lying there in the hospital bed; except of course for the leather cuffs around his wrists and ankles. Looking at him now, it was hard to believe that what she'd seen earlier had actually been real. She heard footsteps in the hall and watched the door, expecting someone to come in.

When the door didn't open and the silence returned, she turned back to her attaché. Removing the necessary folders, papers, and labels, she began the work of preparing the case history for Mr. Marin. Once the file was constructed, Lindsey began her notes on the case, recording everything she'd heard and seen since she first arrived at the MissionView. Three hours later, she'd entered all she could remember about the evening as well as sifting through two other client's files, updating notes and reviewing the day's appointments. The whole while, Marin hadn't even stirred.

Finally, Lindsey was overcome with fatigue and left for the evening. She glanced at the clock on the way out of the room; it was nearly three am. She stopped before exiting the front lobby and left her cell number with the girl at the reception desk and asked her to call if Mr. Marin's condition changed. Her body sank into the soft leather seat of the Jag and she vaguely wondered if Marin was again playing possum, but she was so exhausted that it was no longer top priority to get the first word with him.

Lindsey knew one thing for certain; Marin would be there when she returned later that morning. After calling in a message to Amy instructing her to reschedule all of the day's appointments, Lindsey dropped the top, entered the freeway and headed home, breathing in the cool fresh air of the early morning. An evening drive on the freeway with the top down always did her well, clearing her head and allowing her to shake whatever shadows may be following just a little too closely.

XI. Man of God

After nearly six hundred miles on the road, Special Agent Doug Stunkel pulled his government issued, gray metallic Ford Crown Victoria into the Angel's Wings UCC parking lot. He'd been on the road for over seven straight hours, but had made excellent time. It definitely helped being on this side of the law. Doug checked his watch; it was almost eight o'clock. He knew that it would be a crapshoot as to whether Father Craven would still be at the church.

Doug stepped out of the vehicle and looked around the church grounds, silently wondering if the structure really qualified as such. The parking lot was graveled and the church building was no more than a two story corrugated sheet metal clad hulk that bore no markings to distinguish it from a common warehouse. The exterior walls were painted southern clay red; there were no fancy stained glass windows here. In fact, the only breeches in the exterior walls were eight smallish rectangular openings along the top of the walls, just below the overhang of the coal black tin roof. The windows glistened in the pale moonlight, revealing no clues as to what may be hiding within the building.

At the back of the church building was a small playground with the prerequisite equipment. Doug smiled. In most children's play areas these days, the equipment was some conflagration of metal, wood, and plastic and consisted of tunnels, climbing walls and other pieces that he didn't even know how to describe. This play area could have been taken directly from the depths of his childhood memories. Of course it had the big swing set, monkey bars and merry go round, but it also had a sandbox (with sand castles still standing in it), and three wood block teeter totters.

The nostalgia was too much for him and he was halfway toward the playground when he heard someone calling to him from the side of the building.

"Memories…Much like the fruit of the Garden of Eden are they not?"

Doug turned toward the voice but couldn't locate its source. He scanned up and down the side of the building, his gaze finally coming to rest on the small garden toward the back of the structure. The area was surrounded by a white picket fence and Doug could see several ornamental trees within its confines. He could also make out a small arbor covered in vines and bright pink flowers. He could not however, see the man who had spoken to him. He heard a quiet rustling sound from the south end the garden and reflexively turned toward it.

"Who's there?" Doug called.

"There's no reason to be concerned, young man. For this is the house of God."

The man's voice was calm and soothingly unsettling. It almost seemed to have a liquid feel to it that Doug couldn't quite describe. His tone was quiet but somehow also carried with it an edge that made Doug more than a little nervous.

"Tell me your story my son. Tell me of the memories that lay below the surface just now."

The voice made Doug's skin crawl with dread. He scanned again and saw its source. The voice emanated from a tall, muscular man resting under a blooming rosebud tree in the garden. Its small, pink blooms were unmistakable, even from a distance. He focused his vision, but the man's face was just out of his grasp. The man stood, recognizing that he'd been seen, and headed in Doug's direction.

Doug didn't move. He felt his hand drift to his holstered gun, an automatic reflex when he felt threatened. *How could his voice travel several hundred feet from the garden to him and still be so smooth and quiet?* He quickly stole a glance around to be sure that they were still the only two here. He saw no one else in his field of vision. They appeared to be alone, not that it was any consolation to Doug. He could feel a thin layer of perspiration forming in the palms of his hands.

The man was almost to him now. He was even taller than Doug had originally thought; six foot eight if he was an inch; and athletic too. He was obviously in better shape than Doug. He had short cropped black hair and the fullest goatee that Doug had seen in quite some time. It too was as black as night. Doug could tell that the man's skin was tanned and weathered even in the dimming light. The one word that Doug could think of to describe him was.....well, *formidable.*

"Father Craven. Nice to meet you Doug. Welcome to Angel's Wings."

The man extended his hand in Doug's direction. Doug warily reached out and took it in his own. The pastor's grip was firm, but welcoming. Doug looked into the man's steely eyes and wondered if he could break the grip even if he tried. His hand had been swallowed like bass bait in a whale's mouth. *Don't be intimidated.* At six – two, Doug was used to looking down during conversations. This was something entirely different. He was completely out of his element here.

"I think you were going to tell me about those memories Doug. What were you thinking about when I called to you?"

Doug looked up into the pastor's eyes, still somehow lost. Though he tried, he couldn't speak. With some effort, he finally muttered something about memories from his childhood. He still stared into Craven's eyes, unable to break his gaze.

"I find memories interesting," Craven answered. "They sneak up on you when you least expect it. You're inevitably drawn in and before you know it, you're traveling down a path that you never intended. Memories, especially bad ones, can make us do absurd things, wouldn't you agree Doug?"

What a strange thing to say. Doug didn't respond. Instead, he looked directly into the preacher's eyes and fired the first shot over the bow.

"Father Craven, I need to ask you a few questions."

"I'm sure you do Douglas. Please come inside; I'll show you our place of worship. It's small I'm afraid, but more than adequate. The true house of God cannot be contained by any earthly structure. In any case, I find questions to be best tended in some level of privacy."

Doug followed the tall, bulky man into the church, entering at the rear of the building. The interior of the church was not much more decorative than the outside. Large round lights hung sparsely throughout the sanctuary and together with the windows provided just enough light to keep the interior from being too dim to see. The floor was poured concrete painted beige, the walls had been drywalled and painted eggshell white, and folding chairs of all colors and varieties were arranged in rows leading to the front of the sanctuary. Some eight or ten rows up where the chairs stopped, there stood a large altar covered in white cloth. Directly above the altar hung a huge wooden cross.

The enormous cross loomed over Doug's head and his breath caught in his throat. Standing nearly twenty feet tall, the ruddy and weathered cross was even more imposing than the preacher himself. It appeared to have been made from oversized railroad ties. The cross was like no other that Doug had ever seen during either his childhood or adult life, and he was quite sure that he would have remembered something like that. He was similarly convinced that the image of this trip would be permanently imprinted in his brain.

Father Craven guided Doug to one of the back rows of chairs and gestured for him to sit down. Doug sat, still lost in the enormity of the room. The sanctuary was so tall and airy that it seemed to be sucking the breath out of him and he was having trouble filling his lungs with oxygen. He took a deep breath and looked at Father Craven.

"Father Craven, I need to ask you a few questions about you and your church."

Before he could continue, Craven broke in and redirected the conversation.

"We all have questions Doug. It's the nature of humanity to question. Many times, the answers to the questions that burn brightest *and* darkest lay inside ourselves; cowering deep in the corners of our hearts. They're hidden in plain view, in our reflection in the mirror. In most cases, we are our own answer, are we not, Mr. Stunkle?"

The cryptic passage sent Doug reeling in a labyrinth of unease. *What the hell was he talking about? And why won't he address me directly?* Doug had tried twice to start his line of questioning and gotten nowhere both times. He heeded the voice of his father and "ploughed through."

"Father Craven, when did this church open its doors?"

"I think it was…ahhh…fall of 2000 or maybe 2001. I can't remember for sure. I know it's been quite awhile."

"You mean you can't even remember when you opened?" Doug responded curtly.

"Doug, let's cut the crap. You know as well as I do when the church opened; and when it opened before that, and before that. Why don't you just ask what you came here to ask? Trust me; it's really not that difficult. All you need is a set of billygoat nads. So either ask, or go home to wherever it is that you're from and grow a pair. Just don't come to my house and waste my time."

Doug was emboldened by the response. He had gotten under Craven's skin, even if it was just a little. Sure enough, under that creepy veneer was a man with a huge propensity for anger. *A very big man,* his subconscious reminded him. He pressed.

"Wow. Your house? I thought this was the house of *God*. By the way, I was raised to believe that we wore our cleanest mouth to church with our Sunday best. Why the sudden outburst? Is there something else I should know? Do we need to move to the confessional Father Craven?"

"Mr. Stunkle, I appreciate your traveling all the way down here to say hello, but I'm afraid I have other pressing matters to attend to. And I'm sure you don't have a warrant. So, if you'll excuse me…"

Doug rose from his chair and stepped past the man sitting to his right. He could feel Craven's icy stare on his skin as he moved toward the door. As he walked, he heard the big preacher calling to him one final time from his place sitting in the back row of the church.

"May God bless you and provide you safe passage home, Doug Stunkel."

Father Craven's voice had returned to that even, calm but sharp tone. It reminded Doug of how vulnerable he was. He was on *his* turf. In *his house* as the man had called it. And doug had provoked him. He grabbed the handle to the door and turned to address the preacher one final time before leaving.

"Don't worry Father Craven, I'll see you again soon enough…"

Before he could even finish, he saw that his new sparring partner was gone. He'd disappeared into the church without a sound, much in the same manner as he'd appeared in the courtyard earlier. Chills raced up Doug's back and he briskly exited the church, making his way back to the car. He sped away from the church and headed back toward the interstate, stopping only to pick up a value meal at Burger King before pulling into the local Holiday Inn for the night. The hotel was just under 6 miles from the church and had all the required amenities for him to be able to continue his investigation.

Doug tried to stay at a Holiday Inn whenever he traveled. They were the one hotel that was most likely to have High Speed Internet regardless of the location; and the rates were good, which fit in with what seemed to be the FBI's new motto: "Cheaper's better; you should be working not sleeping anyway." If he had a nickel for every time he'd heard the SAIC say those words, he'd be retired and living in Fort Knox – the vault, not the city.

Doug pitched his duffel bag into the recliner, got his laptop hooked up to the high speed cable, crammed six french fries in his mouth and frantically began recapping the day's experiences in Microsoft Word. He would distribute a report to his main man Al for filing and SAIC Milner for review when the notes were complete. As in typical fashion, Doug began with a bulleted list of key observations that he would follow up on later. He then filled in the rest of the pages with the events of the day- from his telephone conversations on the drive into town to the showdown with Father Craven at the Angel's Wings United Christian Church.

With the report finished, Special Agent Doug Stunkle glanced down the list of his key observations, the "hit list" as he liked to call it, before finally clicking on the send button, propelling the digital document through miles of high speed cable line toward the home office in Springfield. He had some very interesting leads from his interview with Craven today; very interesting indeed.

XII. Wakeup time

Bringggg, bringgg! The shrill cry of the telephone reverberated loudly in Lindsey's ears, startling her from her slumber. She leaned over to the night stand and checked the clock as she reached for the phone receiver. It was 5:15 am; she'd been asleep for just a couple of hours. Her eyes burned and her head was pounding to the beat of an all-drum marching band. Her eyes felt as if they would pop out of her head with each pulse of pain from the headache. Her hand clumsily knocked the telephone into the floor. Brinngggg, bringgg, it continued its nigh pitched onslaught, further encouraging the thudding in her brain. Lindsey was certain that the pounding would be audible throughout the room, had there been anyone else in her apartment to hear it.

She leaned over the side of the bed and finally fished the cordless receiver off the floor, reflexively flipping open the cell as she raised it to her ear.

"Hello?"

"Doctor Macallum, this is Amy from MissionView. You asked me to call if Mr. Marin awoke."

Lindsey couldn't believe it. Why couldn't he have woken up while she was at the medical center?

"Thanks Amy, I'll be there in 20 minutes."

"Doctor, there's just one other thing. The patient is awake, but we've had to administer another dose of tranquilizer. So he's still kind of out of it." The nurse continued.

Another tranquilizer? That seemed unnecessary to Lindsey. Just as she was going to ask, the nurse must have felt her uneasiness through the telephone handset and answered her unasked question.

"Well you see, he woke up and said he had to go to the bathroom. While he was in there, he tried to hang himself using the emergency pull cord."

Lindsey gasped. "I'll be right there," she said, absentmindedly flipping closed her cell phone and placing it back on the nightstand.

Lindsey pushed back her goose down comforter and slid to the edge of the bed, dropping her feet onto the soft carpeted floor. She sat there for a couple of minutes with her eyes closed, unmoving. Was this worth it? Did she have to get up and go back to see this whacko? The image of Hank Marin in the hospital bed with his back arched and a hypodermic needle sticking out of his neck flashed vividly behind her eyelids and his screams once again pierced the night. Lindsey's eyes popped open instinctively and she could feel the cool sweat on the back of her neck and arms. Her heart was racing.

"This sucks." She mumbled to herself on the way to the closet where she slid on a pair of her favorite Gap blue jeans, boy's fit of course, and one of a half dozen burnt orange Texas Longhorns sweatshirts. She didn't even bother to put on a bra. That was the best thing about sweat shirts – they were NBR; no bra required. Lindsey quickly pulled her hair back, slipped on her Nike cross trainers and headed for MissionView. Fifteen minutes later, she found herself parked in the same spot she'd left earlier. She reached into the passenger seat for her attaché and headed in to see Hank Marin. As the glass entry door slid open, Lindsey caught a glimpse of her reflection amidst the blur of letters spelling ENTER. She wasn't going to win any beauty contests today and her flirty playfulness at Mario's was a distant memory now. Oh well, she was here on official police business, even if she was in sweats.

As Lindsey walked down the hall toward Hank Marin's room, she saw Officer Trasker waiting for her outside the door.

"Well aren't you a fine sight this wonderful morning?" he said with a sideways smile.

Lindsey chose not to reply, only nodding her head in response. Maybe Trasker wasn't so much of a tool after all. At least he'd had the sense to go home, or wherever it was that men like him went, and rest until Marin woke up.

The officer guided Lindsey by the elbow across the hall and into an empty room.

"Okay, here's the story…" Began the overweight officer.

Trasker went on to detail the whole series of events from the initial call sending him to the Buffalo, to Marin's attempt at taking his own life, to his current status: awake, but groggy in the room across the hall. Lindsey couldn't believe what she was hearing. Nothing like this had ever happened in Crystaltón Heights. Trasker smiled wanly, now finished with his story. He was relishing the moment. This was the biggest happening in Crystalton Heights that he could remember, and he was right at the center of it. Lindsey tried, but couldn't return the officer's smile. As common as the gesture would have been; under other circumstances, it seemed utterly foreign to her. The story swirled in her head, sloshing against the insides of her skull. Maybe it was just the fact that she'd slept 2 hours in the last 30 or so. Maybe she was just in shock over the whole situation. Either way, she felt nauseous. She wasn't sure she could enter the room across the hall.

"Dr. Macallum, are you okay? You don't look so good."

"I'm fine, just a little shook up from lack of sleep and the fact that I'm going to be talking to someone who may be capable of anything, up to and including murder."

Lindsey looked through the door and into the room across the hall. She could only see the small table where she'd prepared her folder on Marin last night and the obligatory recliner that could be found in nearly all hospital rooms. Her vision blurred as she stared into Hank Marin's room, her focus completely lost.

"Dr. Macallum?"

She quickly shook it off and focused on Trasker.

"Okay. Anything else I should know before I get started?"

"That's not enough?" Trasker replied with a little chuckle. "I've got to get back to the station. You know, paperwork and all that. I'll be back around lunch to check in on you. If you get done before that, give me a call."

The officer left Lindsey and trudged heavily down the hallway toward the lobby and the exit. *I hope he realizes that it will take more than seven hours to make an accurate evaluation,* Lindsey thought to herself. It would take several trips over the course of six or eight weeks to get an accurate portrayal of *this* patient's mental health.

Dr. Lindsey Macallum took a deep breath, patted and smoothed her University of Texas Longhorns sweatshirt, gathered her thoughts and headed across the hallway to start what would turn out to be the most unbelievable adventure she'd ever undertaken.

XIII. Bad Beginnings

The good doctor gingerly entered Hank Marin's room as if negotiating paper-thin ice on a warm spring day. She stood at the foot of the bed and looked over her recently acquired patient. Hank Marin lay in the hospital bed, wrists and ankles strapped to the bright stainless steel bars that rose from either side of the bed. He looked as bad as twice reheated meatloaf. His face contained more cuts than a butcher shop; many covered by bandages and band aids and others with just a small piece of medical tape holding them closed. His hair was disheveled and matted in several places with blood from the accident. His eyes opened and closed slowly and drifted in and out of focus. His left eye was ringed in yellow-green. And finally, there was a dark purple ring around Marin's neck where he'd tried to hang himself in the shower. She introduced herself and asked permission to ask him a few more questions.

Marin's eyes drifted open slowly and rolled forward, or sideways – Lindsey couldn't decide for sure which.

"Seems like you've already started with the questions to me," Marin grunted in a low, gravelly voice.

"Mr. Marin, please don't make this difficult. I'm here on behalf of Officer Trasker and the Crystalton Height Police Department. They've asked me to talk with you a little."

"Bull-fucking-shit. They've asked you to come in here and interrogate me to figure out if I'm crazy. Well, trust me Dr. Macallum. I'm crazy; crazy for not killin' that Goddamn cop and getting the hell outta this God forsaken town."

Lindsey looked away; unable to stand against the intensity of the man's gaze. He was obviously filled with rage. Maybe this wouldn't take so long after all. If the interview continued down this path, it would take longer to type up the report than determine the patient's motivations.

"What's the matter there doc? A little too hot in the kitchen for ya?"

Lindsey turned toward the door. She wasn't sure she could handle this. What if this lunatic attacked her? He was strapped to the bed, but there were obviously no guarantees.

"Whoa there doc! You're not going to run off so soon now are you? We haven't even had an opportunity to get properly acquainted yet. By the way, what kind of doctor wears sweats to their first appointment with a new patient?"

Lindsey felt a flame of anger light in her chest. What gave him the right to torch her like that? She was the one in charge here, not this beat up, cut up whacko. She steeled herself, and turned back toward the bed. Her eyes swam upstream, finally meeting his. She put a mask of strength on and shot back at him.

"Mr. Marin, I am here on official police business. Just in case you don't remember, you're in a lot of trouble. So, it's in your best interest to cooperate and answer my questions, without objection. Do you understand?"

Marin stared into Lindsey's baby blues with his own cold, steely eyes. This time, she held his gaze, refusing to avert her eyes. After what seemed like a lifetime, and more, Marin finally looked away. Lindsey felt pride swell in her chest, replacing the heat of anger that was there just a few minutes before.

"Oooh, she does have some life in her after all. And such an attractive young lady as well, even in sweats."

At that remark, Lindsey didn't dare return eye contact. Her eyes darted all around the room, but never met his again. In the course of their little dance, Lindsey's eyes fell on the leather wrist bands that held Marin's strong hands firmly in place. They were light brown leather with big silver buckles and synthetic white fur on the inside to keep the patients wrists from chafing. But it wasn't the wrist bands that held her attention. It was Marin's hands. They were scraped and cut much like his face, but his fingertips were a dark brown, almost black. She inched closer to the bed for a better look. Marin tracked her gaze and balled both hands up in response.

Lindsey closed on the side of the bed, her interest now overcoming her fear. She reached down and grabbed at Marin's fingers, trying to pry them out of their locked position. Just before she gave up, he forfeited and opened his fist. Linsey looked closely at his index finger and realized that the color of Marin's finger tips wasn't a result of the accident last night. It appeared that he had been badly burned. The skin on each finger was shriveled and malformed to the point of virtually erasing his finger prints. Lindsey looked across the bed and saw that his left hand matched his right; all ten finger tips were a dirty brown color.

"Okay, let's start with this. What in the world happened to your fingers?" Lindsey demanded.

Marin closed his eyes and pushed his head back deep into his pillow behind him.

"You wouldn't believe me even if I told you, so go the hell away. Session's over."

"I say when the session is over," Lindsey shot back. "Now what's the story?"

"Fuck off you fuckin' shrink" came the reply and Hank Marin refused to say anything else.

After forty minutes of silence, Lindsey, exhausted on more than one level, decided it was best to give it a break and start over in the morning.

"Okay, you win," she said. "But I'll be back tomorrow and we'll have this discussion again. And the next day, and the following, and as many times after that as needed until you tell me what is going on with you. I'm *very* patient, Mr. Marin, and I *will* wait you out if I have to. You're not going anywhere any time soon anyway."

Lindsey returned to the medical center each morning for the next two weeks, trying her best to get Marin to open up to her. She found that he was mild and polite with her as long as she didn't pry into his past. Once she began to probe that subject matter, he quickly became agitated and his manner rapidly degraded into the equivalent of verbal bludgeoning that ultimately ended in her leaving with little more than she had the day before.

Lindsey had made a few interesting observations however. First and most obvious was the burning of Marin's fingers *and* toes. His bullshit explanation was that he spilled a boiling pan of water on his hands and then dropped it on his bare feet. She knew he was lying, and he didn't try to conceal it. As long as he didn't have to tell her the truth, he was happy. *Why would someone burn the prints off their fingers and toes?* She could only believe that it was to prevent identification by the police. *But why?*

Whatever the reason, it had worked. Trasker and the Crystalton PD had been unable to confirm the man's ID. She knew that the Hank Marin ID was a phony from Officer Trasker. Marin's driver's license was counterfeited, though it was a good counterfeit job. During the cleaning of Marin's wounds, the nurses found that he wore fake eyebrows and he'd changed his natural hair color. Obviously, this man had gone to some lengths to change his appearance and conceal his identity. Why? Why, why, why?

Why had he thrown such a fit when he first arrived at the Medical Center? Maybe he was afraid of what they might do to him. Maybe he was simply afraid of being identified by the cops. Lindsey had so many questions and not a single good answer. Hell, she couldn't get Marin to do anything but make small talk with her. She needed a new angle. She'd tried approaching him as a counselor, an authority figure, and as an advisor, all without success. What else could she do? She continued to brief Trasker of her progress, or lack thereof, each day. After the third week, he was becoming visibly agitated about the lack of progress.

As her contact at the CHPD, Trasker was closely following her interviews with Marin, devouring her notes and incessantly questioning her as to why she couldn't crack him. He himself had only been back to the medical center once to try questioning Marin. And he'd had even worse luck than Lindsey was having. Marin was a tough nut to crack, but there was one thing Lindsey had learned.

There's always a way in; you just have to find the right door. And however small and hidden that door might be, a flood usually gushed through when it swung open.

Trasker hadn't called in the State Police yet, and that was a good sign. Once the State got involved, the whole thing would get very complicated and she'd likely be removed from the case in favor of a "more qualified" or "more experienced," state employed counselor. Lindsey couldn't stand the thought of that happening. She had to find a way to figure this guy out. She needed to decipher the combination to the padlock he used to keep everyone at bay. That was the only way for her to get inside and figure him out.

When Lindsey had just about given up and packed it in for good, it came to her. During her interviews with Marin, she hadn't been convinced that he was the maniac that she'd originally thought. *Was he simply a victim of circumstance?* Also highly unlikely from what she'd seen. He was a hard case for sure. He was tolerable most of the time, but when she tried to get to a place where she was unwelcome, his demeanor changed instantly and he became a foul natured, aggressive, and spiteful bastard.

The good doctor had tested this response over and over to verify that it was consistent and natural, which it overwhelmingly was - almost violently so. The more she contemplated it, the more she became convinced that this reaction was simply a defense mechanism to help Marin cope with and bury his past. This gave her all the more reason to push him for access to whatever was driving this peculiar emotional response. Finally, she decided to take a new tact. *Maybe Hank Marin just needs a friend*, she thought to herself with a smile.

Lindsey had always made it her number one rule to not become personally or emotionally involved with her patients. She certainly wasn't going to break the golden rule now. But how was she going to convince Marin that he could trust her without putting herself out there at least a little bit as emotional bait? She was running out of time too. Trasker was nearing the end of his rope and wanted results. *Damn, he could be a real pain in the ass.* He just didn't understand; these things take time. When you get a nutcase like Marin, it could take months to fully break him down.

Lindsey knew that she would have to be careful not to give Marin too much personal information, but she'd come to the realization that this was her final recourse to try cracking the code that would lead to the answers she needed. She'd also noted on multiple visits that Marin had what must amount to terrible nightmares during his sleep sessions. She'd begun logging his mumblings, and in some cases ravings, in her notes although they had been of no help so far. Lindsey had heard about "Sleepwatching," as a recently published technique that involved documenting the sleep patterns of patients. In many cases, there are distinct and documented patterns that are associated with various mental illnesses. It hadn't helped yet, but once she got him to open up, if just a little, it might become useful.

XIV. On the mat

Doug peered out the window of his office and stared at the blinking fluorescent lights of the basement file room. It had been nearly a week since his eventful trip to the south and his meeting with Father Craven. He'd stayed two extra days in Birmingham to continue his research on Father Craven and Angel's Wings UCC. Unfortunately, it had been wasted time from an evidentiary standpoint. Everything checked out legal-eagle with the church.

Doug had tried to attend an evening service at Angel's Wings. As it turned out, there was a worship service every evening at 6:30. He'd been greeted by no less than six members of the congregation just on his walk from the parking lot to the entry door of the sanctuary. He nearly gasped aloud as he reached the threshold; Craven was there greeting everyone who entered. Doug extended his hand, only to have it remain empty in the close air of the reception area. Father Craven laid his hand on Doug's shoulder and guided him back toward the exit.

"Mr. Stunkle, we would love to have you visit a service, but unfortunately tonight is members only worship. You see, as much as I'd like to, I simply cannot allow you be a part of the service tonight. I hope you understand."

Doug was floored. He'd never heard of a church that didn't welcome guests. He smiled and looked up at Father Craven who was also smiling broadly. It was obvious that he was enjoying this little show.

"Father Craven, I've never heard of such a service, and it's not listed that way on your sign. It just says 'worship every night at 6:30pm.' Most churches that I've been to welcome visitors," Doug chastised.

Craven's lips spread even wider, exposing perfectly aligned teeth that had a sick grayish yellow color that made Doug's stomach sour. Craven was bad; Doug could just feel it. Something was *off* with him; he just needed to find out what.

"Mr. Stunkle, we do, in fact, have worship every night at 6:30pm sharp. And we do welcome visitors. We pride ourselves on being one of the friendliest congregations around. Howeeeverrr, not all services are open to the public. So if you'll excuse me, I have a devoted and eager group of worshipers that require my attention. Have a nice evening."

They were at the door now and Doug could feel Craven's hand lightly pushing him in the small of the back, nudging him to leave. He stopped in the doorway and turned to face Craven.

"When is the 'open' service where visitors are welcome, Craven?" Doug prodded, struggling to maintain an even temper.

"I have been kind enough to address you as Mr. Stunkle; you will address me as Father Craven. Have a fine evening Mr. Stunkle."

And with that, he gave Doug a light push out the door. It wasn't anything violent, but Doug was so caught off guard that he almost lost his balance and fell down. He watched Craven pull the door to, locking it behind him.

"I certainly hope no one's late to *his* service…" Doug mumbled under his breath.

He waited impatiently in his vehicle and at 7:30 sharp, the church doors opened and the church going men and women streamed out of the large steel building, quickly moving toward their vehicles. From what Doug could tell, there had been between 50 and 60 people who'd attended the service. He hopped out of the Crown Vic, put on what he considered his most welcoming smile, and sauntered up to one of the couples who'd greeted him warmly on their way in to the service.

"Hi, I'm Doug Stunkle. Do you mind if I ask you a few questions about the service?"

The response was less than he'd hoped for.

"I'm sorry Mr. Stunkle," the tall, gangly man said. "But we're very busy. We have to get going."

With that, the man lowered his head and quickly pushed past him, headed toward his escape vehicle. Doug regrouped and headed over to another of the couples he recognized from before the service.

"Art and Mary Ellen right? I'm Doug Stunkle; we met before the service…"

This time, the couple didn't even look at him. They simply continued their conversation, passing within inches of him, seemingly oblivious to his very existence. The crowd was quickly beginning to thin down. Doug scanned across the last of the church goers and didn't recognize any of them. He whirled around toward the parking lot, looking for another couple that he may have briefly spoken to before the service. There were none. He was getting just a little desperate now as he drifted back toward the parking lot. It seemed that the good Father had made Doug a part of the service after all. He would have preferred just sitting in the back observing versus being the topic of conversation.

The crowd was almost gone now. Doug rushed over to a Honda Civic with a couple of twenty-somethings getting in. He reached out and grabbed the door just before it could swing shut. No screwing around this time. Doug reached into his pocket and retrieved his FBI badge, flipping it open in classic B movie fashion while still holding the Civic's door half open.

"Hi, maybe you can help me." He started, bending over to look into the interior of the vehicle.

"I doubt it," came the matter-of-fact reply, ending the conversation before it even began. "We've got to get going so that we can pick up our kids at the baby sitters on time. It's outrageous what you have to pay for just a couple of hours away."

And with that, the Civic's door slid from Doug's grasp and slammed in his face, leaving him to stare in at the driver and his wife while the small car's engine revved and then carried the couple off toward home; wherever that was. Doug guessed that it probably wasn't the Holiday Inn, which was *his* current residence.

He walked back toward the façade of the church, scanning the exterior walls for any points of ingress or egress, other than the most obvious entry/exit door from which he'd been tossed such a short time ago. As he walked the perimeter of the cold steel building, Doug had the distinct sensation that his actions were under careful surveillance. He had felt this feeling before, but it wasn't at all like it's portrayed in the movies; it never is. There was no hair standing up on the back of his neck, no extra sensory perception, or the ability to hear sounds that were normally undetectable.

As much as people want to believe that sensational picture of how it happens, it's as far from the truth as Antarctic snow from the beautiful blue waters of the Caribbean. The feeling always started as a tiny spec in the pit of Doug's stomach. Slowly, it would swell and grow, until his entire chest cavity is full, making it hard to breathe. Doug imagined that this reflex was closely related to each individual's most irrational fears. It's the classic fight-or-flight response that is taught to bright eyed college freshmen in Psychology 101. But, instead of the hairs on the back of his neck standing at attention, they always became slick and wet in a moist layer of salty sweat that enveloped his entire body, threatening to soak through his clothes.

In FBI training, they teach the newbies to harness this feeling; to channel it. When a person has mastered their emotions, they can tap into the power of their own psyche. Being poised on the very edge of the emotional knife that threatens to incapacitate in reality improves the chances of a positive outcome in nearly any situation. It provides focus, changing the agent into a stronger, faster, and more observant aggressor. But, it's a long way from the dramatic scenes that flash across the movie screen at the Saturday matinee.

Maybe it was just his nerves, or maybe he was dreaming it. *No, someone was there,* making careful note of his every move - Father Craven no doubt. After a complete traverse of the church building, Doug gave up. Round two was over, and he was face down on the mat again. He needed to catch a break soon, or this was going to be a TKO in no time.

As Doug sauntered back to the Crown Vic, the feeling of unease continued to grow. He was certain that Craven was watching closely now. *But from where?* Doug kept his head down, slowly rotating it from side to side, showing no signs that he might be wise to Craven's little impromptu stakeout. As he approached the car, he had an idea. Instead of proceeding to the driver's door and getting in, Doug walked around to the trunk and popped the lid. The car was positioned head in, towards the church structure so Craven wouldn't be able to see what he was doing in the trunk. *Just how curious was he?* He guessed curious enough to move from his current position to get a better look at what he was up to.

Doug leaned over the trunk, peering through the gap between the lid and the rear window of the vehicle. He didn't even know where to look, so he quickly scanned back and forth with his eyes, looking for any movement at all. He didn't see any. Then, he heard a rustling from ahead. It seemed to be moving to his left. How stupid was he? Craven must have been in the garden spying on him the whole time! Doug focused his eyes on the garden area, still peering under the trunk lid and through the rear window, ensuring that Craven wouldn't have a good view of him. Using his training, he mentally calmed his nerves and focused all his energy. He was making a mental recording of the entire scene, another very handy tool that was a task requirement at feebie school.

The seconds seemed to drag into minutes and the minutes into hours, even days, while Doug waited for another movement. His vigilance meter was a thirty on a ten scale. When that pompous son of a bitch made another move, Doug was going to rush him and get some answers. Then it happened. The bastard broke from his cover and headed for the back of the church. Doug leaped from behind the vehicle and bolted toward the head of the garden, desperately trying to cut off his escape route. From his position, Doug was closer to the building than Craven was, and should be able to beat him to it. It was hard to tell through the small trees and shrubbery, but it appeared that Craven had added a black hooded smock to his coal black suit. He ran awkwardly, crouched down and with an uneven gait that made him look as if he didn't have full service of both legs. *Shit!* He was still going to make it around the corner before Doug could catch him.

Doug's heart pounded as he leapt the small fence and redoubled his effort to make it to the corner of the building before the hooded figure. Dammit, this guy was fast, and Doug didn't consider himself a slouch by any means. *He shouldn't be that fast.* Doug strained to get a better look at him, but the hood cast his face in the deep shadow of dusk. He was close now, just a few more steps, but the hooded figure had already disappeared around the corner of the building.

Doug skidded around the corner himself, ready to grab the man, but he was gone. Vanished into thin air. Doug frantically searched again for a door that he could have gone into. Nothing. He looked for any place that he could be hiding. Double nothing. There was nothing but grass for another 50 yards where the treeline began. There was no way he made it to the trees. There had to be a door on the outer wall. Doug continued to search for what seemed like an eternity as the sun dipped below the horizon and left him standing in near darkness.

Finally, Doug returned to his vehicle, exhausted both mentally and physically. He'd failed again; now the third time of the trip. Apparently, third time wasn't always a charm. As he approached the car, a hole opened in his stomach and swallowed his heart. A small white slip of paper winked at him from under the windshield wiper. He jogged the rest of the way to the car, grabbing the note and sliding into the driver's seat to read it in the light of the interior roof lamp. The text was one sentence, but spoke to much more than the words that were scrawled on the crisp, infinitely thin leaflet trimmed in gold. It simply read:

Let the people of the soil of the earth mind the business of the earth, and let the people of the flesh of The Lord tend to the business of the heavens.

Doug refolded the note and gingerly placed it in the passenger seat of the Crown Vic, started the vehicle and headed back toward the Holiday Inn to settle in for the evening.

XV. Unexpected Turns

Lindsey collapsed into the big black leather chair in her office and pushed her head deep into the oversized pillow-soft headrest, breathing in the rich smell of the conditioned leather. She flipped her heels off and stretched her legs out under the desk, finally resting them on the heated foot massager that so often pulled the plug and drained the stress from her weary body. She had been at it since just before two a.m. and still had two more appointments this afternoon.

Lindsey sighed, opened her eyes and glanced briefly at the big mahogany grandfather clock that stood majestically against the wall opposite her desk. It was just after one thirty. Good, she had 40 minutes or so to rest and reenergize before her next patient. She settled back into the big, comfy chair, her eyes slid closed, and she drifted into nothingness, trying her best to decompress and process the past few hours.

Just as she reached the point of full relaxation, the door to her office swung open and Amy came clip clopping in, her favorite clogs echoing painfully in Lindsey's ears. Lindsey's eyes shot open and her back went rigid. Her mind raced, afraid that she had fallen asleep and this was her two-fifteen, ready for his appointment. Her horrified assistant and long time friend stood with her hands on the door frame and a look of horror on her face.

"Oh shit," she gasped. "I am so sorry Lindsey. I didn't know you were resting."

"It's okay Ames. I'm just exhausted. It's been a very long night; I mean day, whatever."

Lindsey allowed her eyes to slide closed again, felt the pounding of her fatigue induced headache return, and yet, still felt Amy's gaze upon her. Lindsey knew what was going on here. Amy wanted the dirt, the details of her progress with her newest and most intriguing patient. She opened her eyes and saw Amy still standing in the doorway, leaning ever so slightly forward as if in rapt anticipation.

"Okay, if you can find me three Excedrins, I'll spill the beans."

Without so much as a single word, Amy disappeared like an apparition. Before Lindsey could even get her eyes closed, she'd returned with not only the pain relievers, but an ice cold Perrier to boot. Lindsey swallowed the Excedrin, chased the medication down with a gulp of Perrier and reluctantly gave Amy the scoop.

Her last three meetings with Hank Marin had been *very* good. However, last night had been the breakthrough that she'd been waiting for. Her strategy of appealing to him on a personal level had worked like magic. Up to last night, she had seemed to be doing the bigger portion of the sharing. She told him of her job, hobbies, and general daily patterns. Marin responded with generalities about his personal likes and dislikes, his own pastimes (working out and playing pick up basketball), but he never gave her any indication what he did for a living.

Lindsey shared personal stories about herself and *The Crew*. She even told him of the big boat trip and all the fun the girls had during the cruise. This prompted an unforeseen question that unsettled her just a little.

"So you're not tied down," Marin had asked. "I mean you don't have a significant other to speak of?"

"Well,… I didn't say that… I ahh… I.." Lindsey had gotten her feet tangled good in that one.

Marin smiled and pulled her back off the hook.

"It's okay, you don't have to answer. I'm just surprised. A professional woman as attractive as yourself, I figured you'd have to beat 'em off with a broomstick. Ya know?"

"A broomstick? What exactly are you saying Mr. Marin?"

Despite herself, Lindsey felt the color rise in her cheeks. This was a complete reversal of the Marin that she had dealt with just a few days ago, and it confirmed that she was making progress. She gave him a coy smile and forged ahead.

"So tell me more about yourself Mr. Marin, if that's what your name really is."

Hank didn't respond. Lindsey watched as his eyes lost focus and he stared off into another world - likely the world of his past. She'd sat there for several minutes, just a few feet away from a man who wouldn't give her his real name, a man that had been brought here unconscious, then sedated and strapped to the very bed in which he currently lay. And yet, she felt connected to him somehow; she shared in the pain that he felt, and it gave her insight. It helped her discern the man's intentions, his personality, and his likelihood for recovery and rehabilitation from whatever it was that had so damaged his psyche.

Lindsey's own eyes drifted and then refocused on Marin's. *Were they wet with tears?* Just then, Marin blinked hard and looked back at her. His face was a twisted knot born out of years of pain and suffering. Lindsey knew she was close. Marin needed just a little nudge and he was going to let her in. But Lindsey also knew that if she pressed too hard he might close himself off again and she'd be back to square one.

She sat quietly, searching for just the right words, all the while watching as Marin visibly struggled with his past. He looked at her briefly, and pushed his head back in the pillow and focused on the ceiling above her head. She tentatively scooted her chair forward and reached out, touching his arm ever so lightly.

"Hank, it's okay. You can tell me. I want to help, and I assure you that it goes no further than me. I'm bound by oath to keep anything you tell me confidential. Please let me help."

Hank again blinked hard, this time driving a solitary tear from the corner of each eye. He looked back at Lindsey with wet, pleading eyes that held so much pain that it hurt her just to look at him.

"You don't understand," he said. "They're going to kill me. I don't know why they haven't already. It doesn't make any sense that they're keeping me here, alive."

"Who?" Lindsey asked, as gently as she could. "Hank," she pleaded, "I'm here to help. I promise."

Hank's eyes were becoming frantic, darting from her to the ceiling, to the opposite wall and back again. She was afraid he was going to have to be medicated. He was becoming extremely agitated. His forehead was now wet with perspiration. His eyes continued to dart around the room. Lindsey was concerned that he might be headed for a psychotic break.

Lindsey's whole body pulsed in time with her heartbeat. *This was it.* If Marin could hold it together, he was going to let her into his past. In that moment, she felt a huge amount of compassion for him, and just a little pity as well. She was convinced that he completely believed someone was after him. And worse yet, he was genuinely terrified of what might happen if that person or persons caught up to him.

Lindsey watched as Hank's eyes continued to shoot around the room. They went from the wall to the window, to the ceiling, finally coming to rest on her own. For what seemed like an eternity, he said nothing. Finally he began, and when he was done, Lindsey could not believe what she'd heard.

She related only the high points to Amy now, cutting out all the personal information that Hank had given her and anything else that he'd been overly anxious about. As she told the story to Amy, the gravity of it further sank into her consciousness. It truly was an amazing tale, one that Hank could easily take and sell the rights for a book and movie deal. Of course, that's assuming there wasn't really anyone chasing him, interested in completely erasing his name from the annals of the living.

Amy could not believe what she was hearing either. Her mouth seemed permanently fixed in an "0" of disbelief. She'd never heard a story of such great magnitude, of such unbelievable depth and conspiracy. Surely this couldn't be true, but she found herself believing, none the less. She just shook her head as Lindsey recounted from her notes the events of Hank Marin's adult life. At several points, she couldn't take it any longer and interjected.

"You mean to tell me that he was implicated in the murder of his own fiancée; and to improve his chances of getting away, intentionally toasted his hands with a blowtorch to eliminate his fingerprints?" Amy asked incredulously.

"Yeah, Ames, he did. Worse yet, he had to redo it once every eight weeks or so because his fingerprints would come back as his hands healed. Can you imagine a scenario where you would be willing to disfigure yourself over and over again?"

"What was the story with his fiancée?" Amy probed further.

"I don't know," Lindsey returned. "He wouldn't go there. He still seemed pretty broken up about it, even though it was 14 years ago."

This was not exactly the truth. Hank had in fact given her the gory details of his fiancé's brutal murder. He hadn't even been able to go to the morgue to identify the multilated body for fear of being identified by the authorities and tracked down by their superiors. The lack of closure still troubled him deeply.

Lindsey continued to recount the events that Hank had confided in her. When she was done, she took a deep breath and exhaled softly. Amy stared at her, but said nothing. Silence hung in the air, polluting it, making it difficult to breathe. Finally, Amy broke the silence with the one question that weighed so heavily on both of their minds.

"So, do you think it's true?"

At first, Lindsey said nothing. She looked down at her French manicured fingers, fidgeting with the black onyx ring on her right ring finger. Finally, her gaze returned to meet Amy's.

"I don't know. It seems crazy, but at the same time, it seems too real to be a lie. Usually, patients that lie about their past do so in a very distinct pattern. They 'oversell.' They give you what amounts to a shopping list of events and descriptions that include specific details from years past that they wouldn't recall under normal circumstances. I didn't get that from Hank. Several times, I had to ask him to go back and explain something that he mentioned because I didn't have a clear understanding of what he was telling me. That *never* happens with fabricated stories. In those cases, every detail is exhaustively covered so that no questions remain in the interviewer's mind."

Amy smiled and began nodding her head.

"That makes total sense. Now that I think about it, that's how it always was with Kevin."

"Your last boyfriend?" Lindsey asked.

"Yeah, the one I saw at Mario's lip locked with that silicone filled, blonde bimbo. You'd think he might be smart enough to meet her somewhere other than my favorite restaurant. He was always giving me some long winded explanation for why he was late, why he didn't call, why he was never home, yaddah, yaddah, yaddah."

Silence again permeated space between them.

"So what are you going to do?" Amy inquired of her best friend.

"I don't know. You know the worst part? I'm kind of starting to like the guy. He seems really genuine, and he's pretty funny when he cracks a joke…"

This was not going the way Amy had expected. She stared across the desk at her friend, who continued to focus on her onyx ring.

"Come on Linds. He's a criminal. What's going on in that little brain of yours?"

"I believe him, and what if he's being falsely accused? Maybe I should be helping him instead of interrogating him for Officer Dumpy."

Amy jumped out of her seat and leaned over Lindsey's desk, palms resting on the shiny wood surface.

"Stop it Lindsey. You can't be serious. You always say 'Rule number one…"

"Well he's not officially a client." Lindsey replied weakly.

Amy couldn't believe what she was hearing. She prepared to rip into Lindsey good when there was a knock on the door. Both women looked up at the clock. It was almost two-thirty.

"Oops, that must be your two-fifteen." Amy said. "I'll delay him a few minutes before I send him in, but we're way not done talking about this."

Amy left the room without another word. Lindsey spent the next ten minutes recomposing herself and preparing for her session with Mr. Clark Mifton, a thirty-eight year old hypochondriac who was convinced he was a carrier of the Ebola virus.

XVI. Big Trouble

Hank lay in his bed at the Mission View Medical Center, staring out the window of his small room. Dusk had fallen and night was quickly approaching. He looked at the wall clock, small hand at the seven, big hand at eight: seven-forty. Small leather belts still secured his legs and wrists tightly to the bed, keeping him fully restrained. A strange and unexpected thing had happened to him over the course of the last few weeks. The shrink, Lindsey Macallum, had broken through to him. She'd reached out and grasped his heart in both hands. Hank tried to fight her off, but had finally caved. *How could he resist such a beauty that was intelligent and compassionate?* It had been a very long time since he'd allowed himself to feel anything for a woman. He'd vowed never to involve another woman in his messed up life, inevitably dooming her to some horrible fate.

But he'd quickly found that he couldn't help himself with Lindsey. He felt giddy around her, like a high schooler with his first serious crush. When she touched his hand, his flesh radiated, as if she'd set him on fire. His heart raced, and his breath came in short bursts, making his chest feel tight all the time.

The amazing thing was: Lindsey saw him. She *really* saw him. She made no predetermined judgments, no self proclaimed incriminations. She saw through the burnt fingertips and scarred face into his feelings, his experiences, to his true self. He'd kept his past buried deep within for so very long that he'd forgotten how to let it out. How to share his burden; and what that could mean. When he'd finally allowed himself to share his story with Lindsey, he felt like he could breathe again, and the air was fresher, cleaner somehow. The past no longer polluted his every breath.

Since he'd begun the task of laying the truth bare for Lindsey, she and Hank had formed what he considered a unique and special bond. At least it was special to him. Hank thought Lindsey might feel the same about him, but he couldn't be sure. Of course, it could be just an act to get him to talk. She was here as a liaison to the police after all. But that just didn't feel right. It didn't fit her persona. She seemed genuinely interested in his story, even as absurd as it was. And he looked forward to seeing her each day, to continue their conversation. *She'd also shared a lot about herself, hadn't she?* She certainly had. Hank knew quite a bit about Miss McCallum, including much about her friends, family, and most importantly, her being completely unattached in any way.

Wasn't that a crazy thought; the idea that he might start a relationship with a beautiful and intelligent woman under such ridiculous circumstances; and after all he'd been through. *There's no way, Hank.* He tried to convince himself. *Just give it up.* She was too good for him, and he was in too much trouble to think about having a relationship with any woman; much less one like Lindsey. But hope springs eternal, even in someone with no hope left; someone down and out, looking at the end of the road and knowing there's no other way to go, someone just like Hank.

Knock, knock, knock in rapid succession. Hank looked over at the door, which was slowly gliding open. Then, he saw four finely manicured finger tips gripping the edge of the door and he knew it to be her. The beating of his heart began to speed. His chest felt tight and he couldn't find the words to call her in. He opened his mouth but not a sound came out.

"Hank, are you awake?" came her voice, as sweet as honey.

Hank still couldn't say anything. His mouth was dry and his tongue felt swollen, filling his entire mouth.

"Hank, are you there?"

Hank felt himself turn flush; his cheeks felt warm and fuzzy. He was thoroughly embarrassed. How was he going to be able to explain his inability to speak? *She was coming in!* He quickly turned his head toward the window and closed his eyes, feigning sleep.

Hank heard Lindsey enter the room quietly, calling once more to him in a hushed tone. He stirred slightly, and then stilled himself again, continuing his little charade. The room was nearly dark now, lit only by the last rays of sunshine stealing over the horizon. He heard her tiptoe gingerly to the window and pull the blinds, casting the room in near complete darkness. The silence was oppressive, making the walls seem too close and strangling the breath from him. He wanted so badly to speak to her, but he was terrified at the same time. If he said something now, she would surely know he'd been faking being asleep. After what seemed like a month of silence, Hank heard Lindsey's heels treading lightly away, toward the door.

Hank stole a quick glance. She looked like an angel retreating across the room. She was so graceful that she seemed to hover several inches off the floor. She wore a light colored blouse and a smart, beige skirt that showed just enough of her legs to be sexy while still being today's professional. It seemed as if she cast her own light into the room. Lindsey pulled the door about half way open and paused there. *Shit! She was leaving!* He had to do something quick or she was going to be gone before he could stop her. Just as he opened his mouth to call to her, she spun around on her heel, catching him half sitting up in the bed with his mouth wide open.

"You were saying?" Lindsey said with a smile.

Totally busted. Hank felt his body go rigid just before all the energy drained from his muscles and he collapsed back into the bed. Embarrassment washed over him like a saltwater tide. He was completely mortified.

"I uhh… I was…" He couldn't even finish and just fell silent.

"You were asleep. I know." Lindsey finished for him.

"Uhh, yeah. I was asleep."

Hank felt like such an idiot. He didn't know what to say. Then, Lindsey smiled a warm and knowing smile as if to say *Don't worry, I know and it's okay.* He gave her an embarrassed grin and looked back at the ceiling.

"Hank?"

He looked back toward Lindsey, still standing in the doorway.

"Would you mind flipping on the lights so that I can come back over there without accidentally killing myself in the dark?"

Hank smiled again and pressed the light button on the control pad that hung next to his right hand. The bright, fluorescent lights came on, giving the room a harsh and overly clinical feel. Lindsey strode back over to the bed, turned on the small lamp that sat on the nightstand and nodded back to Hank, who doused the fluorescents with another press on the control pad.

"So Hank Marin, tell me more about your seemingly dull and uninteresting history. Where exactly did we leave off?"

With a half smile and chuckle, Hank slipped right back into the story of how he came to reside in Crystalton Heights and everything he'd done since he'd been there. For over three hours, he continued on, relating his constant fear of being discovered and the ironic circumstances that had brought him to this point. He poured his heart out to Lindsey without even contemplating what her response might be. It just felt like the right thing to do. And he felt good doing it. He felt alive again.

Sharing his story with Lindsey didn't take away the pain of his past, nor did it diminish his fear of what may happen to him in the future. He was still bound to a hospital bed, under the custody of the police. His future was not in his own hands anymore; and that made him very anxious indeed. Lindsey had related to him that Trasker and his department had been unable to turn up any leads on his real identity or past. Hank was terrified that Lindsey may share his story with his captor, but she'd given her word that their conversations were strictly confidential and she'd displayed such conviction that he had little doubt of her sincerity.

With every word he spoke, he felt closer to Lindsey. In the space of just over a week, she'd transformed from a cold and tactical interviewer to a compassionate and interested friend. *Friend*; was that the right word?

Several hours later, Hank came to the end of his tale.

"And when the medicine they injected into my neck wore off, I awoke to find myself strapped to this hospital bed." He finished, tears blurring his vision.

Lindsey was softly sobbing too. The pain and fear that Hank felt was obvious in his voice. It also seemed very real; as real as any of the scars on his body or the still fresh wounds he'd suffered in the accident. She had no idea how it must feel to be living inside his skin. She'd picked out the most predominant emotions that Hank displayed. An odd combination of grief, fear, shame, and anger seemed always to ebb and flow just below the surface of Hank's being, permeating his every word and expression. Lindsey felt strongly that he was a good man and that his astonishing story was truth. Her heart had broken for him multiple times and she'd experienced the same emotions that he'd cycled and recycled through as he related the tale.

The air in the small room was rich with emotion, almost too thick and heavy to be breathed in. Both Hank and Lindsey exhaled heavy sighs, their eyes wet with tears. Lindsey wasn't sure where this would go next. For now, silence seemed the best response. They sat there in the stillness for several minutes; he bound to the hospital bed and she seated just a few feet from him. Lindsey's emotions were a jumbled mess; she didn't know what she was feeling, or what she should be.

"Lindsey, I don't wanna die. When they figure out that I'm here, they're going to come here, find me, and kill me."

Lindsey didn't know how to respond. She opened her mouth to speak, thought better of it, and closed it with another long, drawn out sigh. Without another word, she leaned over in the chair and removed her sling back heels.

Next, she put her French manicured right index finger to her mouth, then slowly reached up and unbuckled his restraints; first the one closest to her, followed by the other. Hank's eyes were wide with bewilderment, but also anticipation. He lay very still, unaware of what may happen next. The anticipation was growing rapidly and Hank's mind was already racing at breakneck speed. *This is your chance!* His brain screamed. *Get the hell outta here!*

Though his mind was in sixth gear, his body was stuck in park. He watched silently as Lindsey leaned over the bed, going about the work of releasing his ankles from the tan leather belts. He wanted desperately to leave, but he just couldn't force himself to go. The feeling was so strong that it almost nauseated him. Lindsey smiled down at him, now leaning in and sliding into the bed with him; he moved toward the opposite edge and propped himself up on an elbow, making more room for her. His body began to tremble as she slid further in until she was against his chest. She pulled the bed sheet up to their shoulders and whispered.

"Hold me Hank; hold me close."

Hank reached his arm across her waist and pulled her close. As if in return, Lindsey turned the lamp off. Only the soft glow of the hall light illuminated the room from beneath the door. Hank couldn't believe this was happening. His emotions for this woman were so strong he felt as if he would drown in them. And he was afraid; afraid of the inevitable. Something terrible was in his future, either tomorrow, the next day, or the next week. They were coming, and he was afraid not so much for himself, but for her. He knew they were going to kill him, but now he'd allowed Lindsey to put herself square in the middle of this screwed up mess. What would they do to her? But more than anything else, he was afraid of losing Lindsey, the one person in the world that really, really *got* him.

They lay like that for a long time; maybe hours, neither could be sure. At some point undetermined by time, Lindsey heard Hank sobbing softly and turned ever so slightly to look up at him.

"Hank, what's the matter?"

"Lindsey, we shouldn't be doing this. You shouldn't be getting involved with me. No good can come of it."

Lindsey was quiet; she searched but was unable to find the right words to express her feelings and she felt sure that this was one of those moments when only the right words would do. It was a moment taken right out of one of the sappy, romance movies that she and the girls had watched so many of over the years. Granted, the circumstances here were more extreme, with Hank's past and her job, but that didn't change the moment and the necessity to choose just the right words to convey her true feelings.

"Hank, when I was young I used to love fairy tales. My parents owned an Italian restaurant and my Aunt Doodle always babysat me while they worked. Doodle wasn't her real name of course - it was Suanne; anyway, she would always tell me a story before naptime. I always looked forward to her stories. As I look back on it, I often wonder if my Aunt Doodle was senile since many of her stories had the characters all jumbled up."

"I remember many times hearing about the fair maiden who was held in a tall, tall tower by the big bad wolf and the grand knight was able to free her with the help of twelve special dwarves." Lindsey smiled broadly as she heard Hank chuckle. "My favorites were the ones with the fair maiden in desperate need of help and the tall, dark knight in shining armor would come and rescue her from whatever trouble she was in." She paused for a second or two. "Hank, let me play the role of the knight for you. Let me help you out of this terrible situation."

"Lindsey, that's very kind of you, but you don't know what you're asking. This is no game. Just by my telling you of my past, I've put you in grave danger. If they find out what you know, they'll hunt you down and kill you like some rabid animal."

"But Hank… Just think. I could help you get out of here. We could run away together. You know, disappear. Start over together. Hank, we could be happy together. This thing could have a happy ending, like in the stories that my Aunt Doodle always told."

She couldn't believe what she was saying. This was crazy. How could she have fallen for this man? Hank was quiet for several minutes, as if processing what Lindsey had told him. When he answered, his voice was somber, full of pain, regret, and hopelessness.

"Lindsey, trust me. There are no happy endings; there are only brief times of happiness that hold the promise of a joyful conclusion. But it's all a sham, a big charade that we use to keep ourselves from going crazy."

"That's not true Hank. Just give me a chance, that's all I ask."

Without another word, Lindsey turned and pressed her firm body to his and lifting her lips to his, she kissed Hank softly on the mouth. Hank hesitated, but she pressed. He couldn't help himself and responded, gently stroking her back and kissing her more urgently. He desperately needed her affection and wanted to share his affection with her. In one smooth motion, Lindsey rolled on top of him, straddling his legs with hers and rising to a sitting position. She sensually unbuttoned and removed her top, casting both it and her bra aside. Her skirt had ridden up her legs and was loosely draped around her hips and waist, resting lightly on her thighs.

Hank looked up at Lindsey with a longing that he'd never experienced for any other woman. In the dim light of the room, she was a vision the likes of which he hadn't seen. Her hair seemed to glisten in the low light, her skin was soft and smooth and her bosom swelled to just the perfect size before retreating back to her flat stomach, which showed just the suggestion of her abdominal muscles.

Hank was engorged to the point that it was painful. It had been years since he'd been in the presence of a naked woman; and never one who possessed such beauty and spirit. He longed to make love to her.

"*Well* Mr. Marin, looks like you're pitching a tent there. Planning on doing some camping?" Lindsey said with a knowing smile.

Hank gave her a sheepish smile, followed almost immediately by a soft moan as Lindsey lightly pushed the gown up his stomach, stroking him delicately. He sat up, reached around her and again tenderly rubbed his hands up and down her back. With her unoccupied hand, she guided his hands to her breasts. As they eagerly explored one another's bodies, they kissed fervently. Finally, the urge was too much and Lindsey lifted her hips up and onto him, one hand firmly planted on his shoulders, pushing him back against the bed, the other moving her G-string aside and guiding him into her.

They moved together in perfect rhythm, communicating in soft moans and savoring each moment of their unlikely lovemaking session. Lindsey could feel both of them building to a climax when an unfamiliar sound floated into her dream world. *What was that?* She heard it again and this time she knew – it was a gasp and it was not coming from either herself or Hank. In unison, she and Hank both looked to the door of the room and saw the young candy-striper standing there, frozen in time with an expression of horror fixed to her face. Before Lindsey could even open her mouth to speak, the nurse had disappeared into the hallway.

XVII. Big Break

Doug bolted upright and glanced quickly around the dark hotel room, taking a mental inventory of everything that had been in the room when he'd turned the lights out for the night. He caught the time on the bedside alarm clock, two-fifty two a.m. He sat upright in the bed for several seconds, controlling his breathing and staring at the door and the adjacent window. He hated hotels where all the rooms opened directly to the outside; they always made him feel vulnerable. But this *was* a Holiday Inn, albeit an old one, and the price was right (low) so he'd chosen to stay. Two out of three wasn't bad unless you're the pitcher that gave up the game winning home run on an 0-2 count.

Doug's blood ran cold and he froze as he saw the black shadow in the window. *Maybe it's just the folds in the curtain;* his mind rationalized, trying to quell the rising panic. Generally, he left his gun unholstered on the bedside nightstand in case of emergency. Tonight, he'd been preoccupied, mentally trying to sort through the new information that Al had given him and he'd gone to bed having left his sidearm holstered in the chair, *right next to the window*. Doug strained to focus his eyes on the shadow, hoping against hope that it was just his tired and overly active mind playing tricks on him.

The shadow didn't move, but Doug still wasn't totally convinced. He closed his eyes and took a deep breath, trying to relax. When he opened his eyes, his blood turned to ice water and his heart rocketed into his throat. The shadow was gone! Without a sound, Doug slipped across the bed and glided over to the chair, keeping as low as possible but moving with purpose. He was instantly calmed as his hand closed around the cool butt of his service piece.

The cool sensation of the gun was quickly crowded out of his mind as it registered the crashing sound of the window shattering and the sting of pain in his back and left arm. He held on to the gun tightly as the shadowy figure crashed down on him, driving him decisively to the floor. Needle-like fragments of glass were painfully ground into his face and bare chest as the intruder grabbed a handful of hair and jabbed his knee directly into Doug's lower lumbar. Then, his head was lifted from the floor, arching his back at a painful angle from neck to pelvis. The "shadow man" kept his knee firmly pressed in Doug's lower back and hissed into his ear.

"Devil, drop the gun. You have no work here."

Doug defiantly gripped the gun tighter and flailed to break loose, but to no avail. *Dammit, this guy was just as strong as he was fast. How could that be?* Pain burned hot in his chest and exploded in his forearm as the shadow-man struck him with something heavy and solid. Doug heard the bones in his arm snap like popsicle sticks and it fell limply to the floor, just inches from his face. Doug bit down hard to steel the pain, and his eyes bulged as he saw the damage the intruder had caused. Doug didn't immediately understand what he saw. His arm looked like it had two elbows. The carpet darkened beneath his now useless right arm and two ragged white tips of bone protruded the skin several inches above the wrist.

Doug felt his head and neck being brutally wrenched sideways as his face was corkscrewed toward the figure standing over him. His brain, overloaded with the firing of damaged nerve endings, simply ceased to process the messages of pain which they sent. What was left was a strange feeling of disconnectedness. His body didn't feel numb exactly, but that was as close as Doug could come to describing it. The pain in his arm had dulled, but he still felt the frayed bones of his radius and ulna catch on the twisted nylon loops of the room's carpet as the limp appendage was dragged across the floor and he was turned over and dropped on his back. The pain immediately returned, and it was more excruciating than anything he'd ever felt. His vision blurred and the shadow above him wavered in and out of focus. Doug concentrated, willing the pain away, and finally brought his vision back into focus. The slumped figure began to pull back his hood, leaning closer to him.

Doug gasped as shock and fear enveloped him, closing him off from the rest of the world. He'd expected to see the familiar face of Father Craven emerge from under the dark hood. Instead, the disfigured face of a monster seemed to hover just inches from the tip of his nose. Doug's eyes bulged painfully from their sockets and he forced himself to look away. *What the hell was going on here?* His eyes darted frantically, searching for the gun, but found no such comfort. He saw only his shattered and bleeding arm creating a pool of red on the earth-tone carpet. As he turned his head to search his left side, his face was stopped short as his captor roughly grabbed him at the jaw line and drove his fingers deep into Doug's cheeks. He leaned in closer and Doug could now smell the pungent odor of the disgusting man. The stench was so strong that it rivaled the nightmarish face that now hung over him.

Doug's head was swimming and he was having difficulty focusing. *Could that face be real?* He let his eyes drift closed, but the face didn't leave him. It glowed behind his eyelids in perfect detail; which somehow made it even worse than the real thing.

"Look at me, Satan! I'm not finished with you yet," the man demanded.

Doug tried to turn away, but the man's grip was too strong.

"Look at me now, or I'll cut your eyelids off so you'll have no choice."

The words rushed to him on the stink of the man's breath. The smell was so vile that Doug's stomach began to convulse, threatening to retch. Between the terrible vision of the man, the stench that he carried, and the sight of chalk white bones sticking out of his broken forearm, it was too much to take and Doug began sobbing softly. He opened his eyes and, through tears, focused on the shadow man's eyes, which burned red as the blood that spilled from his arm. A ridiculous thought flashed through his mind as he looked up at his captor. *Better take note of everything you can for your report.* Doug knew there would be no report. He wasn't going to make it out of this one - not this time.

Without thinking any further, he committed a description of the man to memory, just in case. His height was difficult to distinguish since he slumped forward, but Doug put him at five-eight or nine and just under two hundred pounds. He was a Caucasian male in his late twenties to early thirties. His smooth, bald head gleamed and he had absolutely no facial hair. His lack of eyebrows made his red eyes even creepier; they seemed to glow in the darkness. The worst part of the face was the skin itself. Extending from ear to ear and scalp to chin was a slightly misshapen, but unmistakable bright, red cross, as if the man had been scalded, or maybe even branded. The vertical line of the cross ran directly down the bridge of his nose and the horizontal directly across his eyes. The inside of the cross was severely blistered with some spots of skin sloughing off. The burnt look of the skin was offset by a wet, oily appearance, as if it were *oozing*. It was almost as if the man's face was decaying somehow, *which might explain the smell,* Doug thought madly.

"*Demon-childe,* you have sinned against the Father and your time of judgment has come. Prepare to accept your punishment as death and an eternity in burning pitch."

"But, who are you…" Doug gasped unevenly, resigned to his impending death.

"I am the angel Gabriel, the right hand of God, sent to cleanse the earth of the evil of The Betrayer."

This didn't make any sense. What the hell is going on here? Doug gathered his strength and swept the floor one more time with his good arm. As if by magic, the cool black steel of his seemingly lost handgun brushed against his fingers. He stretched further, ignoring the pain that shot up his spine, and felt his fingers close around the butt of the gun. He swung it up in a wide arc, smashing it into the side of the mad man's head, knocking him off balance. The man stumbled sideways, tripped over the corner of the bed and hit the floor hard. He leapt up more quickly than he'd gone down and flipped the hood back over his head, once again shrouding his face in shadow.

Doug aimed the gun as best he could with his left hand, and squeezed off three quick rounds that shattered the wall mirror and exploded the picture tube of the television. The black specter darted across the room and bounded out the window before Doug could fire again. Doug closed his eyes and breathed deeply, trying to calm himself and bring his heart rate back to normal. He heard voices in the darkness, but couldn't make out the words. Then, he was enfolded in dark silence.

He awoke in his *new* hotel room at the Holiday Inn; the pain in his arm almost reaching a boiling point. The room was dimmed by the drawn curtains and Doug again shot bolt upright, as he'd done just hours before. Dazed and disoriented, he jumped out of the bed, quickly scanning the room for the hooded intruder. He knocked the bedside lamp to the floor searching the night stand for his gun. *There was someone in the room!* The figure in the chair opposite the bed quickly reached over and flipped the light switch, bathing the small room in amber light. Doug exhaled heavily as he recognized the face.

"Thank God it's you Al. If I'd had my gun on the bedside table, you'd be dead now."

Al smiled broadly and replied, "Based on the fact that you shot up you're old room and failed to hit anything other than the mirror and TV, I'm not too worried either way."

"Fuck you, Beamer."

Doug replaced the lamp to its rightful place on the night stand and brought Al up to date on the happenings of the previous night, finishing with an inquiry of the progress in processing the crime scene. Doug leaned forward on the edge of the bed, hoping for at least one lead. Al related that forensics was able to collect some trace from the room, but it had proved pretty useless thus far. There was one witness: a young female college student staying at the hotel on her way through Birmingham to her home near Biloxi. In her statement, she identified a "scary looking guy...kinda like Batman with a hood." *Great – thanks alot there Susie cheerleader.*

Just when the story seemed to reach a dead end and Doug started to lose interest, Al became more animated; finally stopping to ask Doug the question he was longing to hear.

"Okay Doug, if you want to know all the bullshit police stuff, you can read the report. Do you want to know what I've found?"

"Honestly, I'm wondering why you're feeding me 'police bullshit' anyway and not just cutting to the heart of the matter. Give me the scoop. What-uv-ya got?" Doug replied anxiously.

Al quickly jumped into the results of his investigation of the history of Angel's Wings UCC, including all of its previous incarnations and its confounding pastor. Throughout the investigation, Al had been unable to link the Angel's Wings UCC and any of its ancestors to the murders in any way other than geography. However, each murder took place within a 12 mile radius of the church location.

None of the victims could be linked in any way to the church, even though the murders appeared to be some kind of demented retribution for amoral behavior. Father Craven had been the leader of the church in each of its previous locations. He had been interviewed in connection with several of the murders, but had not been an official suspect in any of the cases. He had a rock solid alibi for each murder. In fact, he had *the same* alibi for each of the murders in which he was questioned – the church was holding service, and there were anywhere between twenty and fifty witnesses who could confirm his whereabouts.

Upon further investigation of the police reports, interviews, and case files combined with fresh interviews that AL had conducted, some strange facts surfaced. In each new interview, the story was the same. Everyone he interviewed referred to the church as a cult, or analogous closed society. The members of the church remained constant from city to city, as best Al could tell. It also appeared that there were very few new members of the church and *no one* ever left the congregation.

Each inquiry of Father Craven or the church related to the murder investigation came to an abrupt and inexplicable halt, especially considering that none of the investigations were satisfactorily closed. Charges were brought in two of the four murders, but it was obvious to anyone who knew murder investigations that the body of evidence against the accused men was circumstantial at best. The indictment of each of these men, though satisfying to the public, ended quickly and quietly in a plea bargain to a lesser charge.

Doug was listening intently without interrupting, even though the anticipation was killing him. He wanted to drag the information out of Al. He knew from experience that Al would save his best for last and his usually deliberate pace would quicken as he reached the end of his report. Doug's anticipation grew as Al began speaking faster and faster, arriving at the final and most crucial elements of his investigation.

"…and now for the best part."

Doug leaned in even further, almost falling off his perch, his eyes boring directly into Al's. Al explained how he had re-canvassed the neighborhoods where the church was located and where the abductions took place. Most of the neighborhood's occupants from the time of the abductions and murders had moved away; probably to what they considered "safer" havens. Unfortunately, it seemed that nowhere was safe in today's world.

Of those that were left, many did not recall the incidents or couldn't give him any additional information. However, during the canvassing of the neighborhood where Gail Crosby was abducted, he found one young woman who asked him to come in and talk with her. With no one in the townhouses where Gail had lived able to help in any way, this young woman seemed overly zealous to talk to him. Al had been very confused by her age until her story was fully told. He relayed the very same story to Doug now; whose eyes came alive with excitement.

"She was only six at the time Doug; none of the police would have even thought to interview her. They wouldn't have expected her to know anything," Al explained.

"And you say that she described seeing this hooded figure on multiple occasions leading up to the abduction and never again afterward. Why didn't she tell her parents?" Doug probed.

"She says that she was too scared. She thought it was the boogeyman and if she told, he'd come to get her too."

"And she still lives there? Why?"

"Her parents retired to Florida and sold her the townhouse. She's single and no longer afraid of the boogeyman - worked out perfect for her." Al finished with a shrug and a deep breath. "Do you think it's the same guy that attacked you last night?"

"Without a doubt. And he's somehow connected to that church. I just need to know what that connection is. Fantastic job Al. You're top shelf buddy, the very best."

Doug jumped up, holstered his sidearm, and headed for the door. But before he made it across the room, Al jumped in front of him.

"Whoa, where do you think you're going?"

Doug waved him aside, shaking his head. "I've got to get back to that church, Al. The only way I'm going to crack this case is by getting inside Angel's Wings."

"Doug, your arm is broken in three places. Do you not recall that the bones were actually sticking out of your skin? You're going back to Springfield with me. And those orders are direct from Milner. We can tie this case up later."

Doug shook his head and pushed past Al. "No way, Al. I'm going to that church and finishing this right now."

Al followed him out the door, ignoring Doug's objections to him going along. Finally, the agent gave in and agreed to let Al help him find the hooded man that attacked him and bring down Father Craven. Before they got in the car to head over to the church, he leaned over the top of the vehicle and gave Al the same line that he'd heard on so many television cop shows.

"But you do *exactly* as I say, understood?"

As they pulled out of the hotel parking lot and sped off in the direction of the church, a primer gray Chevy Nova eased into traffic several cars behind them, guided by a man wearing all black, his face hidden in the shadow of a black hooded cape.

XVIII. Faceoff

Doug and Al parked the car in the parking lot of the church. They'd plotted a quick and simple strategy on the way over to Angel's Wings. They exited the car together, but headed in opposite directions. Al strode right up to the front door of the church while Doug headed around the back. As he reached the door, Al pulled the door handle. Surprisingly enough, the door opened. Father Craven wasn't guarding the front door as Doug suggested he might. Al walked through the entryway and right into the vacant sanctuary. He was awestruck by the simple but intimidating room. Looking up at the huge cross and seeing the sun shining through the stained glass windows, he began to doubt Doug's certainty that this was the source of the killings.

Al spun back around to the entryway as he heard the door lock slide closed behind him. A huge man wearing all black, except for a small white collar, approached him casually. Al could feel his heart racing, but as the man spoke, his honey infused voice was soft and reassuring, not unlike the voice a parent might use with a lost and confused child.

"Oh, pay no mind to the door. I always lock it when a new parishioner comes in. I don't like to be interrupted when tending my flock."

Al began to say something, but abruptly shut his mouth again. He suddenly couldn't remember what Doug had told him to say. He only knew that he was supposed to occupy Craven while Doug made his way in through the back door.

"I'm Father Craven, and you are…"

"Ummn," Al studdered. Should he give him his real name, or make one up? He and Doug hadn't covered the details of the conversation on the short trip over. "Ahh, Al. My name is Al Maguire."

"Al Maguire as in the sportscaster? You look pretty young to be Al Maguire."

Shit. Al knew he'd blown it, but he hadn't been able to think of any other last name. He was sure Craven was on to him already. The preacher reached out and Al instinctively stepped back. Craven continued forward, extending his arm further for a handshake.

"I'm sorry, I don't mean to tease. It's a pleasure meeting you Al McGuire."

Al reached out and his own hand disappeared into the preacher's. Then, it all went wrong. Craven gripped his hand tightly and jerked Al hard towards him, almost knocking him off his feet. At the same time, the huge man applied tremendous leverage to his arm, spinning him around like a dance partner. It was like a dance step gone terribly wrong. Craven's huge left arm made a noose around Al's neck and instantly synched, completely closing off his windpipe. Al struggled, trying his best to pry the man's arm off, but it was no use; Craven was way too strong. He tried to scream, but no air made it out of his lungs. After what seemed like an eternity, his vision began to break into fragments and the world finally went dark.

Around the back side of the church building, Doug struggled only a little in finding the hidden entrance. If he'd had just a little better light when he'd been here the other night, the hooded man who called himself Gabriel wouldn't have gotten away so easily. This time, he quickly found the outline of the rear entrance; the tricky part was finding the trigger for the door, which happened to be a foot button near the ground level, just to the left of the door edge. It too was marked only by the crease that outlined the rectangular pedal. Doug pushed it with his foot; the door popped open silently and he finally had unrestricted access to the church.

He entered a thin but long room and his blood ran cold as he began to survey his surroundings. Near the doorway through which he'd entered was a small sitting area complete with a dilapidated yellow Formica table and two beat up, metal folding chairs, not so unlike the vintage that Doug had seen in the sanctuary. The table's stained skin peeled from the edges and McDonald's bags, wrappers, and cups were piled high in the center.

Doug moved past the sitting area and found a well worn, twin-sized mattress on the floor with a dirty brown bed sheet balled up in its center. Lying at the foot of the bed was a pale lavender terry cloth robe. Doug lifted the robe with one finger and dropped it again when he saw the monogram on the left breast pocket. *DD* - Deena Dillings. *Oh shit.*

Next to the bed was an old roll top desk littered with papers and more McDonald's hamburger wrappers. Doug took a second to investigate a little further. He pulled open one of the drawers and inside found a keychain charm. It could easily have been mistaken for a teenager's, except for one thing. It was a in the shape of a G – Gail Crosby. *Double shit.*

A black metal bookshelf hung on the wall over the desk. Sitting atop it were thirteen books of identical size and color. The bindings were all printed in gold leaf - The Holy Bible. Doug pulled one off the shelf and flipped through it, slowing down in several places looking for something that seemingly wasn't there. He returned the bible to its place on the shelf and lifted the next copy. It was identical to the first. Doug paged through this one as he had the first. This time, he stopped part of the way through. In the last quarter of the bible, Doug found a page missing. He looked to the top corner of the opposite page: 1219, Ephesians: 5:6. *Third shit's a charm.*

This was it - three distinct pieces of evidence that would link Craven to the man who called himself Gabriel and the murders in this investigation. But where was Gabriel? Suddenly Doug's instincts kicked in and he remembered that he'd asked Al to keep Craven busy. What if Gabriel was with Craven and they figured out who Al was? Doug scanned the room again. At the far end was a second door. He rushed over to the door and quietly opened it, slipping through into the next room and silently pulling the door behind him.

Doug was shocked to find himself in a very small room; the walls, floor, and ceiling of the room were completely covered with richly stained and heavily lacquered wood. There was a bench chair incorporated into the back wall and there were no windows in the small room. Doug cracked the small door and peered out into the sanctuary to get his bearings. *Where was he?* He scanned the sanctuary through the crack in the door; Craven was nowhere to be found. Doug opened the door quietly, slipped through and closed it behind him. He had been in a confessional! He shook his head in disbelief and turned toward the altar. What he saw there cemented his feet to the floor. Al lay strapped securely to the huge altar, as still as the dead. Above him, Gabriel loomed; dressed not in the black hood and cape, but in a blood red ceremonial garb. His face was turned to the heavens and he held a huge ceremonial knife directly above Al's chest.

Doug pulled his glock and aimed it directly into the man's chest, holding it as best he could in his left hand while steadying it with his right. Gabriel apparently didn't notice Doug's emergence from the confessional as he began to pray aloud in a tongue that Doug didn't understand. Judging by the rough dialect, he suspected it to be Latin. Al would know for sure, but was certainly in no position to help him figure it out. Doug sidestepped his way to the main aisle, moving quickly and silently, all the while mentally preparing himself for the confrontation.

"Don't move Gabriel!" He shouted. "I've got you covered; now drop the knife!"

The bald man stopped his chant and lowered his head. His eyes bored into Doug with malice and hatred. Then, he averted his gaze, looking over Doug's shoulder, and smiled menacingly. Doug spun on his heel and found Craven sprinting toward him with a replica of the knife Gabriel held raised high. He brought it down with a flash. Doug lifted his arms to ward of the attack and the knife glanced off his casted right arm. Craven's momentum knocked Doug on his back and Craven dove toward him, the knife slicing through the air, threatening to bury itself in his neck this time. Doug rolled quickly to his right, raising the glock and firing two successive shots into Craven's chest. The man fell in a heap next to him and didn't move.

A guttural scream rang out in the sanctuary as Doug rolled up to one knee and retrained his gun on the disfigured man at the altar. But he was no longer there. Instead, Gabriel was rushing down the aisle in nearly identical fashion to what Craven had just done. His eyes were frantic and his scream drew out into the high pitched shriek of a banshee. He was fifteen feet up the aisle, but closing fast.

"Stop right there!" Doug shouted.

At the sound of Doug's voice, the malformed monster of a man lowered his head, redoubling his effort, fists and knees pumping like piston heads propelling him forward at astonishing speed. Doug had little choice. He aimed the Glock and fired twice. When the man kept up his tear, he fired twice more. The first two shots had been wide, but the third rang true, striking him just above the left knee. As he fell, Gabriel immediately rolled into a ball and somersaulted toward Doug. He rolled out of his crouch and pushed off hard with his good leg, pouncing on Doug before he could get off another shot.

Gabriel's momentum carried both of them backward into the aluminum chairs that formed the "pews" inside the church. The gun flew out of Doug's hand and clattered through the chairs behind him. Before he could regain his feet, the self-proclaimed hand of God was on his knees, swinging the knife in a wide arc at neck level. Doug leaned to his left as quickly as he could and was able to reduce what could have been a mortal slash to the neck into a deep wound to the shoulder. *That's going to hurt like hell in the morning!* Doug thought crazily. The knife glittered in a mosaic of colors, mimicking the stained glass windows of the church, as it traced a fresh arc through the thick air between them. This time, Doug took the offensive. He reached up toward the knife and caught Gabriel's wrist, dodging right and redirecting the knife away from him and into his attacker's midsection. All the air in Gabriel's lungs surged out with an indistinguishable uuummpf.

Gabriel bent over the knife and looked up at Doug, fear and defeat now filling his eyes. He tugged weakly at the knife, but was unable to remove it from its place wedged between his ribs. He pulled his hands away from the hilt and held them up toward Doug. They dripped with dark red blood. Gabriel stumbled forward, groaning in the same forgotten tongue before finally collapsing at Doug's feet.

There were no arrests that day in the Angel's Wings United Church of Christ, but the Bible Slasher case was officially closed, nearly two decades after the first murder had taken place. Both Doug and Al had made it out of the church with only relatively minor injuries and a few memories that they'd both like to forget.

A week later, Doug was proofing the final draft of his report to Milner on the investigation. He stepped out of the small office and shouted into the stacks, "One-twenty, you out there?"

Al quickly appeared at the head of one of the aisle ways.

"What did you say that disease was that left the cross on Gabriel's head?" Doug asked for probably the twentieth time since he began writing the report.

"It's a rare skin condition called Toxic Epidermal Necrolysis, TEN for short. My best guess is he got it as the result of some kind of childhood infection or it was the result of a severe reaction to a medication of some kind. The research I found says that it commonly manifests around the eyes and sinus cavity; so, the cross on his face was nothing more than a horrible side effect of the disease"

There was a pregnant pause as Doug thought about this for a moment.

"And you think the TEN is what made him crazy?"

"No, I think Craven made him crazy. We'll never know for sure, but my guess is that he found Gabriel while he was still a child, maybe shortly after the onset of the TEN. He took the boy in and slowly molded him into the monster that killed those poor women and almost did us in. Craven's solely to blame here; that poor boy never had a chance."

Doug looked at Al, up at the fluorescent lights, and then back at Al.

"I'm sorry Al, I was sloppy in that church. I should have never allowed you to end up in that situation. It won't happen again."

Al just shook his head. Even from this far away, Doug could see the wetness around his eyes. He would never be the same, and neither would Doug. Without another word, they turned their backs on one another and went back to their work, both hoping that Doug's promise would not have to be tested, but knowing all the same that sooner or later, it very likely could.

XIX. Checking Out

Lindsey and Hank looked at each other with wide eyes as the wailing of police sirens filled the room. *How could they have gotten here so fast?* They hadn't even had enough time to get fully dressed yet. Granted, she'd had to help Hank out of the bed, and he'd had to find his clothes in the closet, but the cops seemed to have arrived awfully quickly.

Lindsey finished first and ran over to the windows, peeking through the blinds. She could see the front lawn and parking lot of the medical center bathed in red and blue lights. *How were they going to get out of here?* She was trying the handles to the window just as Hank joined her there. He nudged her gently to the side and tried himself. They weren't budging. *Damn.* They both rushed back to the door and exited the room. The hall was filled with commotion and as they looked for an escape route, the policemen rushed around the corner at the head of the hall and shouted at them.

"Stop right there you two!"

Both Hank and Lindsey could easily have identified the pudgy officer on voice alone if it had been necessary. It wasn't. Bob Trasker stood at the head of what appeared to be the whole police department. The other officers had fanned out behind him and filled the entire hallway at the intersection with the front lobby. He was standing still now, but Hank knew that Trasker would soon begin his advance down the hall to apprehend them.

"Miss Macallum, I must say that I'm extremely disappointed in you; how very unprofessional to become involved with a patient during an official police consult."

Lindsey opened her mouth to reply, found no words that could explain her actions, and clamped her jaw closed in anger, fear and disgust.

"Nothing to say, huh Lindsey? Well, I guess I should have expected it. A woman with your looks shouldn't still be single at your age unless she has some significant moral issues. Fucking tramp bitch."

Trasker finished his verbal jab at Lindsey by smirking at her dismissively. He was feeling pretty good about himself at this point. Instead of one arrest, he was about to make two, making him double the hero. He'd also spoken to the FBI earlier in the day and had finally convinced them *(it took nearly an hour for Christ's sake)* to meet him back at the station, take over Marin's case and validate his true identity. *This is a jackpot*, thought Big Papi.

Hank and Lindsey looked at each other and then back at the police wedge sealing off the hallway to the exit. *Shit!* The officers were now moving toward them, eating up the hallway at a slow but deliberate pace. Hank and Lindsey looked back at one another and as if in response, they both shot off down the hall and through the doors at the end. Trasker and his crew gave chase, rushing down the hall behind them and crashing through the doors, filling the small landing ramp to the stairs.

Bob Trasker knew that Hank and Lindsey could only have disappeared by either ascending or descending the stairwells to their right. Bob split the group into two, directing half of them up the stairs to the roof and signaling to the other half to follow him down toward the basement.

Trasker's group bounded down the stairs and through the doors at the landing. Ahead of them lay a long hallway which terminated in a set of gray swinging doors with big stainless steel panels covering just the bottom half. Alternating along the hallway leading to the double doors were three single man doors on the left and a set of elevator doors to the right. Trasker rushed to the elevator doors and looked up at the lighted numbers positioned over the doors. The circular "B" was lit, indicating that the elevator carriage was just behind the heavy doors in front of them. Trasker pushed the B button next to the elevator. He pulled his sidearm as the doors parted, but the elevator was vacant, save an empty gurney. Papi directed the group using only his hands and they divided into twos and headed toward each of the man doors on the other side of the hall. Trasker moved alone to the end of the hall and the double doors.

As he entered the unmarked room, he knew immediately where he was. *The morgue.* Every medical facility had one, and they were all the same. This one felt even colder than normal, with stainless steel permeating the entire room. The back and right walls were covered in square stainless steel doors with oversized stainless handles. The wall adjacent to the door was covered with glass cabinetry that housed all the tools of the modern day medical examiner; and to the left, stood two offices, each with the door shut and the lights dark.

Trasker held his ground, standing quietly just inside the doors. He listened intently, but heard only the faint pokings and proddings of the other officers down the hall. *Where were his two little lovebird suspects?* The others hadn't radioed, so he had to assume they hadn't found them yet either. Bob walked quietly around the room, checking under benches and behind carts of equipment and instruments, but still found nothing. *They have to be here somewhere.*

Hank lay quietly in his concealed hiding place in the morgue. He could hear Officer Trasker moving around the sanitary room looking for him. There was a good chance that Trasker would not find Hank where he lay hidden. He just hoped Lindsey had found a satisfactory hiding place as well. He'd tried his best to convince her to hide with him, but she'd quickly refused, rushing off to find her own place.

Click, Click. The footsteps were getting closer now. Click, Click. The cold metal of the roller bed on which he lay gave him gooseflesh and made the hair on his neck and arms stand up. *Bang!* What was that? Then the sound repeated itself. *Bang!* He heard it a third time. *Bang!* And it was getting closer. Was Trasker trying to scare them out? Then, he heard a scraping sound, like metal on metal followed by another bang. *Screeee, Bang!* Hank closed his eyes and tried to envision what the noises might be. After each bang, he could hear several faint clicking noises. His thoughts were creating a wirlwind inside his head. In his mind's eye, he saw the overweight cop dragging his gun barrel against one metal body compartment door and banging it against the next; then quietly opening the door to the small compartment and peering inside.

Maybe this wasn't such a great hiding spot after all. It was too small to do anything but lie still and Hank had to depend on Lindsey to open the door at his feet and pull out the tray/bed on wheels so that he could get out. If Trasker opened the small square door to his compartment instead of one of the others, he was dead. There would be nothing he could do. He was trapped. The sound repeated itself just to his left. Screeee, Bang! This time, the bang sounded like a cannon in his ears. *Trasker must be right on top of him!*

Hank didn't know what to do. He listened intently, but heard only silence. He could feel Trasker's presence and knew that he was right outside the little steel door. Everything was still. The seconds stretched into hours there in the darkness. Then, the click of a handle being opened; Hank drew his legs up toward his chest. He took a deep breath and watched closely for any signs of light from the door being opened. His chest was burning and his head hurt. He felt certain that the pudgy officer was about to open the door to his compartment and drag him out into the open. *Would Lindsey be safe? Would Trasker keep searching for her?* Hank prayed that she would not expose herself trying to save him.

Hank saw a bright string of light appear at the left side of the door to his compartment. *Trasker was opening the door!* As the small door began to swing open, Hank extended both of his legs away from his chest with all the effort he could muster. His feet thrust against the inside of the door with a *thud!* And the door shot halfway open before it connected solidly with Bob Trasker's face, instantly shattering his nose and cheekbone and propelling him backward onto the cream tiled floor. The damp, cracking sound it had made was awful, but Hank couldn't suppress the dark grin that threatened to turn into outright laughter as blood spewed from Trasker's nose and a long string of vulgarity spewed from his lips.

Hank headed toward the door, calling out for Lindsey on the way. She popped out from under an examining table and quickly caught up to him at the door. Luckily, there was no one in the hallway. All of Trasker's troops were busy searching the adjacent rooms or had retreated back up the stairs. Just as they made it to the stairs, Trasker crashed through the doors, screaming profanities and spitting coagulated blood droplets onto the tile floor. He fired two shots into the ceiling tiles above his head and commanded them to stop where they were. In an instant, the other officers emerged from the side rooms and rushed into the hallway, obscuring Trasker's view of Hank and Lindsey.

Hank knew they had only one chance, and it was a slim one. Luck had certainly been on their side in the morgue. There was no way Trasker could get a clean shot at them with the other officers littering the hallway between them. Hank grabbed Lindsey by the elbow and pulled her out of her daze and up the staircase to the landing above. Her eyes were as big as saucers and as blank as a sheet of fresh copy paper. It was obvious that she was having a hard time processing everything that was going on around her. *I tried to tell her...* He shook the thought from his head. There was no time for rationalizing now.

They burst through the stairwell doors and back into the medical center hallway. There were two nurses further up the hallway that, upon seeing them sprinting their way, ducked back into their patient's rooms. Behind them, a stampede of police boots threatened loudly. The group from upstairs must have rejoined Trasker and his men. Hank and Lindsey were in lockstep as they raced down the hall and into the lobby. If they could only make it out, Hank was sure that the police cars would still have the keys in the ignition, given the circumstances of their arrival.

That gave them one chance of getting away. Obviously, they would have to dump the police cruiser and switch to something a little less conspicuous. But first things first; Hank guided Lindsey across the lobby and toward the front door. The receptionist ducked behind the double sided, eyebrow shaped desk that adorned the lobby of the medical center with a startled squeal as Trasker and his men rounded the corner and entered the lobby, weapons at the ready.

Officer Bob Trasker could be accused of being many things, but a fool was not one of them. He knew that if his quarry made it out the front doors, it was going to be difficult to catch them without leaving a trail of havoc behind. That left but one option; stop them from leaving, no matter what the outcome. It was important that they take Marin alive though. Nabbing a career criminal with alias upon alias would make Trasker a superhero, not to mention a local celebrity. It made no difference that the FBI seemed to have little interest in Marin when he'd spoken to them earlier in the day. Bob was sure that the man was bad with a capital B, and he was equally sure that the FBI would eventually figure out who he really was and uncover a sordid past with a laundry list of punishable crimes. And when they did, they'd have *him* to thank for it.

The plate glass entrance doors to the Mission View Medical Center slid open at their normal, leisurely pace. Hank and Lindsey nearly collided with them before they opened enough for the two of them to slip through. Six black and whites were lined up in the entryway of the center, their lights still flashing. Another four were parked in the front lot of the medical center. *Easy choice*; Hank guided Lindsey to the very first car in the line – Trasker's. As his fingers closed on the passenger's side door handle, a crash rang out behind him and tiny shards of glass sprayed across his back and clattered against the side of the vehicle. He looked over his shoulder and saw Trasker, just twenty or thirty feet inside the lobby, gun drawn and pointed in his direction. Suddenly, Lindsey tugged his arm in her direction, collapsing over the front fender of the police cruiser and onto the hood.

Hank turned in her direction and he could not believe what he saw. *No!* His eyes must be deceiving him. Lindsey looked up at him with a blank stare as she slowly slid down the front fender and slumped against the car's tire. Her body left a glaring red streak across the white hood of the police vehicle. Hank's mind raced. *What am I going to do now?* He thought. The woman who had so easily captured his heart during the course of their short relationship was now bleeding to death on the concrete next to him. He looked back into the lobby. Trasker and his men were standing in the very same position, as if rooted to the floor. A flicker of remorse nested itself in Trasker's features before disappearing as quickly as it had appeared.

Bob Trasker had anticipated that the plate glass of the entrance doors would redirect the path of his shot ever so slightly, making it necessary to aim for the woman's trunk to ensure he didn't miss altogether. He guessed from the nurse's detailed description of their late night "activities" that Marin wouldn't leave Lindsey behind should she be wounded. That would maximize his chances to stop their escape. He knew, of course, there was a chance that she'd be seriously wounded, but he hadn't quite prepared himself for this. The blood red stripe that marked the hood of the car almost glowed in the canopy lights of the entryway. There were screams behind him, as the rubber necked nurses stared out the windows with wide eyes and open mouths. With some effort, the pudgy officer forced himself toward the entrance, his men moving in unison behind him.

"It's over Marin, or *whoever* you are. There's nowhere to go. Don't make this any harder than it already is. Give yourself up and let us get some help for Lindsey." As the officer shouted, he and his men moved toward Hank in a slow but deliberate cadence.

Hank considered this. His heart was broken, not by the woman whom he'd grown to care so much about in such a short time, but by this pudgy, simpleton police officer who'd crossed him once already. Hank had a decision to make; a serious decision with dire consequences. He could stand and fight, trading death for death and avenging his lover's ruthless and calculated murder, or he could flee. If he stayed, Hank knew that he would be staying forever. The odds of his escaping a shootout were nearly nonexistent, especially considering he'd have to find a gun first. There was probably a spare somewhere in the cop's car, but that was just a small piece of the picture. If he fled, Lindsey's blood would be on his hands, haunting him for the rest of his life. But he'd likely see another day, even if it were haunted by love murdered.

Trasker and his men were almost to the entrance doors now and must have been able to see the frenetic look that consumed Hank's face, because they slowed their approach, fearful of what this trapped and wounded animal may do next. They were just twenty feet away now. Hank's head was pounding and he could feel the boiling blood circulating through his arteries and veins. He felt as if his head was going to explode, and almost hoped that it would. At least then it would be over. His mind made up, he yanked open the vehicle door, grabbing Lindsey under the arms and hoisting her into the police car as quickly as he could without doing her any further damage. Her face was ashen and he was certain that she was gone, but he hoped against hope he was wrong.

As Hank slammed the door and sprinted around to the driver's side, Trasker and his men advanced through the doorway. Trasker's voice grew louder and louder as Hank entered the police cruiser. Hank reached under the seat and, sure enough, found the officer's spare Glock. He looked across the vehicle as he cranked up the engine. Trasker was now screeching at a decibel level that could shatter crystal. He looked like a mad man, rushing across the entry way, waving his handgun, eyes frantic and mouth open in a cry of urgency and frustration. Hank raised the Glock and pointed it out the passenger window of the vehicle, stopping Trasker and his men where they stood.

Bob Trasker knew this was the moment that would define his career, maybe his life. Now was not the time to back down, and he wasn't about to. He was going to face this son of a bitch down, right here, right now. He sighted his Glock on the man behind the wheel of *his* police cruiser.

"Listen, you son of a bitch. You get out of my God damned car right fucking now! Don't make me kill you like I did that fucking tramp bitch of yours."

A gunshot rang out, and complete silence ensued. Trasker's body crashed to the pavement and lay still on the concrete driveway of the Mission View Medical Center. The men under his command gasped at the sight of their fallen leader and were frozen in place as the man whom they were there to arrest sped off in the police vehicle previously operated by their superior. They crowded around as a pool of dark red blood formed underneath the crumpled body. In the back of the group, one of the men hollered for help from the nurses, who stood like plaster statues in the front windows of the building. The two groups were equally unable to understand what had just happened.

A few short minutes later, the spell broke; one of the nurses came forward, and the group of police officers evaporated. As the nurse pronounced Bob Trasker dead from a gunshot wound to the head, three police cruisers rifled out of the Mission View parking lot, headed in the direction of Hank's escape route with lights flashing and sirens blaring. But their chase had already ended. Hank had too much of a head start on them and was quickly putting additional distance between himself and his pursuers.

Hank stayed off the main roads as much as he could and when he was confident that he hadn't been followed, he pulled to the shoulder and put his fingers to Lindsey's throat. The lack of even a faint pulse confirmed what he already knew in his heart. She was gone and he was responsible. Sure, he hadn't pulled the trigger, but he was no less at fault. He dropped his head back to the headrest and cried - softly at first and nearly wailing near the end. *Why? Why did this have to happen?* After several minutes, Hank was all cried out. His eyes burned and his brain felt like mush. And his heart hurt. No, hurt wasn't strong enough; it ached.

Ahead, Hank saw flashing lights approaching. *Shit!* He started the Crown Vic again and pulled back onto the roadway. He knew that a U turn would be like hanging a neon sign that said "Come and get me" on his vehicle. So, he pulled back onto the roadway and continued on his way. As the vehicle on the other side approached, Hank's heartbeat quickened and he could feel the sweat beading up on his forehead. He slid low in the driver's seat. He didn't need a chase now. He wasn't far from his home, but he couldn't risk leading the cops back there. Hank exhaled a sigh of relief as they passed on opposite sides of the roadway. The vehicle had been a tow truck with flashing blue lights, not a police cruiser after all.

Hank finished packing up his spare car, a late model Pontiac Firebird that had been in hiding since he'd bought it two years earlier, and prepared to leave this place for good. He'd parked Trasker's cruiser around the rear of the house and doused it in the same gasoline that traced its way throughout the home to which he would never return. His emotions were mixed as he struck the match and tossed it onto the front porch, watching the tiny flame quickly grow into a twenty foot blaze. He was leaving behind much, but he had no choice. His life here was over. He'd made one true connection during his time in Crystalton Heights, and that relationship had ended much too soon.

Hank took one final look through the passenger window of the Firebird and stomped the gas pedal into the floorboard. The car fishtailed before the wheels finally caught and he shot off away from the blaze. He didn't look back as he sped away; the orange flames fading until there was only darkness in the rear view, and in his heart.

Present Day

I. Last Ride

They never even called him by his name. *Why was that?* They certainly all knew it. For Christ's sake, they'd been chasing him nearly his entire adult life. They should know everything there was to know about him. It was almost as if they needed to disassociate him from his name, from his humanity. *It would be easier that way wouldn't it?* That way they could hunt him down like an animal, using whatever means necessary. Animals didn't have rights, and neither did he, at least not in their eyes. He looked out the window and reflected. It was like a dream, almost real, but somehow just a little off key.

The weather seemed only to enhance the dreamlike quality that the day had taken as its mantle. A light fog still hung in the streets and the temperature was unseasonably cool. The breeze carried with it a chill that complemented the day perfectly. The fog muted the entire cityscape and even the bright colored song of the trees lining the street was hushed on this day. It was like interacting with the world through a hazy, gray filter. For at least this day, the whole town of Langley, Virginia wore the mystique of the CIA headquarters, and he felt as if he was being smothered by it.

How could it possibly end this way? In all the years that he'd dreamed of how this chase might conclude, he'd never envisioned anything remotely like this. He looked out the window of the FBI owned sedan and found that he could not take his eyes off of the mildly ornate building that housed the many branches of the Central Intelligence Agency. He saw the FBI man standing below the huge glass arch that hung over the entrance of the massive building, still talking with a group of CIA men and wondered what their conversation may have been about. He knew that he would likely never know, and it was probably in his best interest if he didn't, but that didn't stop the curiosity from gnawing a hole in him either.

He looked down at the bright reflective steel cuffs that held his hands fast. He'd been within the walls of one of the most powerful organizations in the world today. He'd also been in the presence of several of its most powerful men, although it certainly could have been under better circumstances. And now, it was all over. He'd made it through the ordeal alive, but not without the emotional and physical scars that would forever be a reminder of the journey. There had been many times when he thought he'd not make it this far with his life intact, including several this very day. He wondered what was next for him and regretted that he had no choice in the matter. Finally, one of the CIA men passed a thin black attaché to his captor, who then made his way back to the vehicle. The dark suited man slid into the front seat without a sound, glanced back at him and started the engine. As the car pulled away from the compound, his heart pounded quietly in his chest and his mind raced. He needed to know what was going to happen next. He opened his mouth to ask the FBI man, but then closed it again; afraid he couldn't bear the answer.

II. Dead Ends

Special Agent Doug Stunkle balled up the empty McDonald's bag and pitched it from his place atop the semi comfortable Holiday Inn bed across the room and directly into the small trash can that sat next to the desk.

"Nothin' but net," he called to the empty room as he pulled the laptop computer back into his lap and turned off the television. Sportscenter had only bad news to report tonight. Not only did his beloved Cubbies lose 3-2 to those damn Cardinals, but that completed a three game sweep leaving them seven games behind the redbirds with just a couple of weeks left in the regular season. Luckily, that also meant that college basketball wasn't too far off either, and the Illini had been picked to win the Big Ten in all the preseason publications. It was almost time to make the conversion from baseball to basketball again. *Oh well, there's always next year.*

Doug sat there for several minutes with his back to the headboard and his laptop resting on his thighs. He dreaded writing his daily progress report for Special Agent-In-Charge Milner, or Milly as Doug and his sidekick Al had come to call him, especially when he had nothing to report. He'd reopened this particular case nearly six months ago, but had made little progress since then. Doug tried to keep five open cases at a time. He'd solved two other cases since he'd reopened this one. He'd tabbed the first *PedoMonster,* after the suspect, a pedophile who committed his heinous acts of defilement and murder on unsuspecting ten to twelve year old boys. Even with the case closed and the sick bastard behind bars for a double life sentence, Doug still couldn't understand what could cause a man to go so wrong. Worse yet, he'd completed his rituals of sex and anger in the presence of the children's bound and gagged parents before also killing them in a fit of post-climatic rage. He'd gained no insight from the freak in this case either, only blank stares and shrugged shoulders; as if what he'd done was perfectly natural.

The second closed case had been *Bible Slasher,* and it had nearly ended both his and Al's lives. It had taken Doug several weeks to get back into his normal groove after the close of the *Slasher* case. There was his arm for one thing. His right forearm had been broken in several places during an attack by the killer, a mentally and physically scarred young man whose mind had been severely warped by a maniac priest who preached a religion that decried death as the only atonement for sin. During the investigation, Doug had asked Al to occupy the priest while he investigated the church. While he snooped around, the priest and his deranged underling had teamed up to capture Al and prepared to sacrifice him atop the church alter. Had Doug arrived in the sanctuary a moment later, Al would likely be dead now, and his blood would be on Doug's hands.

This time, the case ended in two deaths, not a sentencing for the killer and his lifetime mentor. It had taken Doug every bit as long to heal mentally as physically from the Bible Slasher case. Every time he saw Al, he felt a deep sense of regret for unknowingly putting his life at risk and the crashing gunshots that killed Father Craven and Gabriel often woke Doug in the early hours of the morning.

All's well that ends well, some would say, but Doug didn't feel that way about the case. Agreed, Craven and Gabriel couldn't hurt anyone else now, but that didn't mean that it had ended well either.

The *Cop Killer* investigation had been like none other that he'd been involved in, either from his days in the FBI or as a homicide detective in Chicago, where he'd quickly made a name for himself as a tough minded and creative investigator with a knack for always being in the right place at precisely the right time. That ability had ultimately gained him this job within the FBI, a destination that Doug had never even considered until he'd been contacted by an FBI recruiter five short years ago.

There was plenty of evidence attached to the *Cop Killer* case, but it seemed only to create a labyrinth that no one had the ability to negotiate. It was like a bowl of spaghetti; every time you grabbed a strand by the end and pulled, you ended up with nothing more than a mess on your hands and spaghetti in the floor. Most cases unraveled slowly and intricately, finally allowing you to trace your way from the victims to the killer. Not this one. This case only produced more ends, more questions, and no suspects; it was infuriating.

The case involved the murders of three different lawmen in different locations. The first two were a state police officer and sherriff from the small town of Graisville, Mississippi. The final murder had occurred in Crystalton Heights, North Carolina. Each of the three men were officers of different ranks. *Was that something to investigate?* But that was just the beginning of the questions that surrounded this case.

The connection between the murders that had landed the case in his lap in the first place was simply a hunch by a meat head South Carolina state trooper named Brady Schat (un-lovingly nicknamed Bull by his fellow officers). Bull had a college buddy on the state police squad in Mississippi. Doug had interviewed both of the staties and had his doubts that the cases were actually related. Each of the men had a different story explaining how they became aware of the "other" murder and couldn't adequately articulate why they were so convinced the two were related. Unfortunately, both state police posts had too many hours and dollars invested to just let it go. So, Doug got the call.

This was Doug's third trip to the small Mississippi town of Graisville. In his past two trips, he'd made contact with everyone named in the file having any connection to the murders that had taken place here. The investigation had focused on the gruesome murder of the Sheriff, who'd been wrapped in chicken wire and beaten mercilessly before finally being left for dead. There were many things that didn't sit well with Doug about the events that happened on the day of the Sheriff's murder. Worse yet, he couldn't find any connection between the seemingly coincidental events of the day.

First, the dead state trooper's car had been stolen shortly before the murder of the Sheriff. Second, the vehicle had also been involved in an accident with a semi tractor and trailer subsequent to the vehicle's theft. The cruiser had been badly damaged, but the semi had left the roadway, ultimately crashing into a ravine and killing the driver.

Upon investigation of the semi, it was noted that both the brakes and the accelerator had been tampered with. There were no witnesses, so it had been impossible to know what part the police vehicle had played in the accident. However, the semi left the roadway, skidding into the left median and the damage incurred by the police cruiser was on the passenger side, putting the vehicle between the truck and the median. This led Doug to believe that the trooper's vehicle had been used to aid in the semi driver's efforts to save the rig.

Was there a connection between the sheriff's murder and the wrecked semi? What part did the trooper and his vehicle play? In Doug's time as a homicide investigator in Chi-town, he'd learned one thing for certain. You could never close your mind to the possibility that what seemed certain at first glance may in fact be one hundred and eighty degrees from what actually happened at any given crime scene. So, he had yet to rule out a connection between the murders and the accident.

The file also stated that the troopers who had found the Sheriff were convinced that he'd been interrogated. *Interrogated for what?* Doug hadn't been able to make a link between the bloody and brutal murder of Sheriff Clancy Bergdolt and any information that would require an interrogation. The widower had been a stand up citizen and man of the law for thirty-seven years. Beside that, nothing of any significance ever happened in Graisville. The sheriff hadn't been involved in a case more dangerous than minor drug busts of the local teens who thought it would be cool to smoke or deal a little *Mary-Juana*. The biggest case of Bergdolt's career had been the bust of an eighteen year old highschooler who'd been farming the illegal plants in the garage attic under ultra violent lamps and fixtures stolen from the local tanning shop. *So why the interrogation?* It just didn't make sense. None of it fit together. It was like working a Rubix Cube when every square was a different color.

On the other hand, the murder of Officer Robert Trasker of the Crystalton Heights Police Department had been pretty straight forward. It was simply an act of desperation by a man trying to escape police custody, which he ultimately had. In the escape, Trasker had severely wounded the man's accomplice, a female psychologist who had been working as Trasker's liaison during his investigation into the man's identity. Neither the woman, nor the suspect had been found. The officer's vehicle had been located behind what apparently had served as the suspect's place of residence. Unfortunately, both the house and the cruiser had been torched, nothing of significance remaining of either one.

Now, he was back in Mississippi, again turning over every stone that he could find, trying desperately to locate the right strand of evidence, the one that would lead him to the truth.

Doug's eyes seemed to lose focus as he scanned the mess of paperwork that hung on the walls above the hotel room desk. If the hotel manager found out about his redecorating efforts, there would be trouble for sure; all the more reason for the Do Not Disturb sign on the door handle. After several minutes of scanning the papers, pictures, and yellow sticky notes, Doug stood up and focused on the picture of the Pontiac found near the sight of the theft of State Police Officer Joe Landis' cruiser. He read the highlighted text in the report, for what seemed like the hundredth time and shook his head.

Owner: Joseph Pratt, deceased.

It just didn't make any sense. Finally, he moved on to the timeline he'd constructed from the case files. Doug was pretty confident that the timeline was accurate based on the information that he had. He began again checking off the timing between the events scrawled across the taped together sheets of copy paper. He was getting nowhere with the sheriff's murder or the stolen state police cruiser. *Maybe it was time to shift focus again.* He refocused on the timeline. Event timelines were one of the most basic and effective tools in any investigation.

Doug had found that the timelines helped him focus on interrelated events concurrently, and often that was the key to making a connection between the events. Early in his career as a homicide investigator, he'd learned to color code the events of a case. In this case, anything related to the sheriff was in red, the stolen police cruiser was blue and the semi accident was yellow. He focused on only the yellow tick marks for a few minutes. It was probably a waste of his time, but he learned long ago not to let anything slide during one of his investigations, that was how killers got away for good and it was his job make certain that didn't happen.

Wait a second. Doug looked back at the desktop and shuffled the stacks of papers that lay there, looking for the truck driver's logs. He found them and read through the entries, scrutinizing each one. Finally, he found what he was looking for. Emery Mathis had stopped for gas just two hours before the accident that ended his life. *Where was that station?* The log didn't mention the name or location of the service station. Doug again began rifling through the loose pages on the desk until he found the list of charges on Emery's credit cards. He scanned down the document until he found it - a Flying *J* station just forty five miles from the sight of the accident. Even at 50 mph, it wouldn't have taken him two hours to fill up and cover that distance. *What the hell happened at that service station?*

Doug knew there was no way he was going to be able to sleep now; so, he hopped off the bed, grabbed his keys and badge, and headed to the Flying *J*. The night manager was eager to help, but couldn't shed any light on the events of the evening of Emery Mathis' untimely death. When Doug asked to see the security tapes of that night, a look of despair crossed the thirty year old pony tailed woman's face.

"Sorry," she said. "We only keep the tapes going back five years."

"Shit," Doug mumbled. *Another dead end.*

Doug thanked the manager for her help and headed back out to his car, not looking forward to the ride back to the hotel or the sleepless night that surely lay ahead. He stood beside his car and glanced from the bright lights of the service station to the gray-black sky overhead. The moon over Mississippi was no more than a dim white sliver tonight. And that was about as much chance as Doug felt he had of solving this case. He turned and opened the driver door of the sedan when he noticed the twinkling sign across the street. *Live music every Wednesday and Friday!* It proclaimed. Doug had an idea. *Was it possible?* He pushed the door of his vehicle closed and walked across the street to the Texan Inn Bar & Grill.

III. Reunion

He'd changed his routine this time. Normally, he only visited her at night, ensuring that he wouldn't encounter anyone who might have questions for him. Nobody ever visited the cemetery at night; well, no one except him. But today was different; no one would be there today either. Nobody visited their loved ones' grave sites on a day like today. Besides, he *had* to talk to her; had to get some things off his chest. Some very bad things had happened recently, and more were on the way. This very well could be the last time he would ever get to visit her in this world.

So, he knelt at the foot of her grave in his olive green, hooded rain poncho, tears falling from his eyes in time with the rain that streamed from the angry clouds overhead. *Ohhh, where to start?*

He raised his face to the sky and let the rainwater wash across it. Thunder crashed in the distance and lightning shot across the sky, highlighting the fading scars on his face and neck. He knew that this act would not absolve him from the things that he'd done, or was planning. But it felt right, somehow, to share it with her. During their short time together, he'd been more truthful with her than anyone else his entire life, including himself. He lowered his head and roughly pushed the water from his face with one motion of his hands. He focused his eyes on the name etched across the headstone. LINDSEY MACALLUM, it read.

"Lindsey, its Hank. I need to talk, to tell you some things. You're probably not going to like what I have to say and all I can tell you is that I'm sorry. I'm so very sorry.

I loved you from the first time I saw you Lindsey, and our time together was special to me. I don't know if there is a heaven; I'm not sure what I believe. But I'm sure that if heaven exists, then that's where you are now. I also know that being with you, even for such a short time was as close to paradise as I'm likely to get. After what I've done, and what I intend to do, St. Peter, St. Marten or St.

Thomas, or whoever's guarding the golden gates, will surely send me packing.

Lindsey, you're the only one I've ever been able to talk to. That's why I've come back again. I want you to know the rest of my story, that part that I've never told anyone. You see, the story I told you at the hospital that night was just a small piece of a larger and much darker tale. You knew that my name wasn't really Hank, but I've had many names in my time. I've lived many lives, in many places, and they weren't always pretty. I was Hank Marin to you, but you could have just as easily known me as Jimmy Davenkish, Daniel Bramstow, or Joseph Pratt.

I left home when I was just eighteen and I've been on my own ever since. I didn't even finish high school. At my worst, I've been a drug user, drug dealer, and murderer. At my best, I've been invisible to society, blending in with everyone else traveling down the sidewalks of life. But it's all been because of *them*, see, they left me no choices. How is an eighteen year old boy supposed to take on the whole world? What was I supposed to do? Where was I supposed to turn? Not even my parents believed in my grandfather's journal and his story. But it's true; all of it."

The rain never let up as Hank told the story - the whole story. He left out not one significant event that had shaped his path to this very moment. He told Lindsey about his feelings of helplessness, the sense of always being chased and the effect it had on his psyche. He related the events that led to the deaths of his grandmother and mother, Emery Mathis, State Police officer Mike Mentzer, Sheriff Clancy Bergdolt, and Officer Robert Trasker. He pleaded that she not see him as a cold blooded killer, but the victim of a much larger and more terrible monster. Several times Hank was forced to stop, when the hurt was nearly unbearable. For minutes at a time he knelt in front of Lindsey's grave, his face turned up to the sky or down to the mud, the tears streaming from his eyes lost on his wet cheeks and the wails of pain and anger blotted out by the crashing thunder.

"You see Lindsey, it wasn't my fault. They killed them; I was just the instrument that did the damage. It was unavoidable - destiny, if you believe in such a thing. I never knew before who was responsible, but now….now I know. I've pinpointed where the blame lies - most of it anyway. I just need to figure out how high this thing goes inside the government. I'm beginning to unwind the mystery and I intend to see that whoever's at the end of this string pays for what they've done to my family.

The journal was the key. I didn't see it before because I wasn't really looking. My grandfather left the clues there for me to find, when I was ready, when I could truly see. My grandfather knew all along that it would end with me. He knew that my father, as tough as he acted, was really too weak to see the truth. His mind was too frail to understand the gravity of the situation, and he lacked the resolve to right what was wrong.

Thanks to the journal, and my grandfather, I can set it right. I have to. Besides, they're getting closer. I've spotted them….following me, spying on me. I think they're planning something, probably a hit. They are constantly there, just around the corner, hiding in the shadows. Watching, waiting, scheming; they're driving me crazy. It's got to end."

Hank said no more; he knelt at the foot of Lindsey's grave, ashamed and angry at all that had happened. Telling made it easier, or at least bearable. For the last week, the truth had been welling up inside him, threatening to spill out like fizz from a shaken soft drink bottle. It had come to the point where it made his head hurt to even think about it, but at the same time, it was the only thing that he could think about; the only thing that mattered. With Lindsey gone, it was the only thing he had left to hold onto.

Hank slumped over the grave and again the tears flowed. His mind replayed his final moments with Lindsey at the Mission View Medical Center. He could see himself running through the lobby with her, rushing through the front doors and stopping at the police vehicles, lined up in a perfect row with Trasker's at the head of the line. He heard the gunshot ringing in his ears and in slow motion he saw Lindsey fall on the hood of the car and slide down to the pavement. His heart broke again, as it had so many times since the shootout. *Why had this happened?* Lindsey didn't deserve to die. She'd done nothing to warrant what had happened to her. During their short relationship, Hank had developed deep feelings for Lindsey. And since her death, those feelings had only intensified. He missed her badly, especially now.

Hank had never considered himself to be of violent nature. It wasn't like he sought out conflict; it was as if conflict sought him out instead. As his knees slowly sank into the mud, he thought back again to the journal and how the path that had been hidden from him for so long became so evident to him.

Six short weeks ago, Hank had been at the end of his rope, quite literally. He'd traveled from town to town, staying in low rent hotels and having no real idea what was next for him. The minor wounds that he'd acquired at the end of his time in Crystalton Heights had transformed into smooth, pink scars. Although his body was finishing the healing process, his mind was moving in the opposite direction. He couldn't get Lindsey out of his head, and didn't want to. It was all he thought about; all day, all night, every day and every night. He drove from place to place in a fog, unable to even remember where he'd been the night before, much less where he was headed the next day.

Though he rented hotel rooms each night, always with cash, he rarely did so much as disturb the bed linens. *Why would he?* He wouldn't sleep anyway. He couldn't. He'd come to the conclusion that he was responsible for Lindsey's death. If he hadn't opened up to her, if he'd refused getting involved with her, she'd still be alive.

Worse yet, Lindsey wasn't the first. He'd also killed his grandmother, *Mammaw* as he and his brothers called her, and his mother. Matricide - wasn't that what they called it when you took your mother's life? What the hell did they call it when you took your grandmother's life too? Grandmatricide? Grand Matricide? It didn't matter, he did it; he killed them, all three. He was responsible for each of their deaths. And it was slowly killing him now. Lindsey haunted his every minute, every breath that filled his lungs. She was every thought that gathered in his head. He would say she haunted his dreams, but without sleep, there were no dreams, were there?

Hank felt hopeless, lost, and downtrodden in every possible way. If ever there was a valley of the shadow of death, his actions had placed him square in the middle of it and the darkness was slowly, excruciatingly choking the life from him. It seemed a chore to even continue drawing breath. *And for what?* He truly had nothing to live for now. Strangely enough, he had nothing left to die for either.

So there he stood at midnight on some infinitely forgettable evening between cities, poised on the edge of the still perfectly made No-Tell-Motel bed, a makeshift double noose made from rope he'd purchased at Wal Mart just the day before, wrapped tightly around his neck. He looked up at the length of rope that traveled from his neck up through the pushed back tiles of the drop ceiling, looped over a wooden support beam, finally terminating in a second rope necklace hanging ever so snugly just below his chin. Hank had to stand on his tip-toes to keep the pressure of the ropes off his Adam's apple. He knew that his rig would not fail him. This would be different than his previous attempt at Mission View. Once he stepped off the end of the bed, it would be lights out for good; his life ending in one swift snap of his neck. It was unlikely that he'd even hear the small, sharp noise. The words of his dead father echoed in his ears. *Son, if you're going to do something this serious, you'd damn well better be committed to it.*

For the past three hours, he'd been rotating back and forth between thumbing through his grandfather's journal and the green file folder he'd gotten from George McClory, sobbing for this lost parents and grandparents; replaying his last moments with Lindsey, and cursing himself indefinitely. In the movies, these scenes always included a fifth of whiskey or tequila, but for Hank, the alcohol was nonessential. His depression was complete, maybe even more so in the absence of drink.

Hank hadn't been able to make his peace with this world, and didn't believe he'd get the chance in the next. So, prayer to God was obviously not a prerequisite to his impending passing. Instead, he prayed to Lindsey. He prayed her forgiveness for his inability to keep her at arm's length, for allowing her to get too close to him. Oh, how he regretted that decision. He could have lived with himself if he'd only forced her away, or let her go on her own accord. But that wasn't the way it had happened, and he could never take it back.

In his frustration, Hank had flung the journal and file folder against the hotel room wall. The brittle binding of the journal snapped aloud, the pages scattering across the floor of the hotel room. At the same time, the pages in the file folder fluttered to the floor like birds on the wind, almost completely blotting out the stained, sailor blue carpet.

Hank surveyed the scene one final time before he took the last fateful step of his life. As he did, he saw something curious just below his feet. At the foot of the bed, two sheets of paper, one white page from the journal and one yellow page from the folder, lay partially overlapping one another making a partial pyramid on the floor. With one foot still raised, he stared at the yellow page, a handwritten letter from his grandfather to someone named Sherwin Deadman. If it had ended up in the file, it obviously never made it to its intended recipient. Hank had read the letter before, during one of his many sessions in trying to understand both his grandfather's plight and his own. But the letter offered no help. In fact, it seemed to contain only gibberish, each sentence relating a different subject than the previous, obviously the work of a man slowly losing his mind.

Hank glanced at the journal page and again recognized the script. It chronicled his grandfather's training in encoding messages. Dr. Price had insisted that he encode his reports with detailed updates of the state of his men's physical and mental well being. Price called it "Cloaked Sequencing." The code was brilliantly simple and yet highly effective. At the start of each report, Josef listed the dates over which the report covered. Converted to numerical format, they held the code to translate the hidden report that Price could then decipher.

Hank's eyes shot back to the letter. Atop the page, two dates, separated by a colon, stared back up at him. *It can't be,* Hank thought to himself. He returned his foot to the bed and began the work of loosening the bond from around his neck. *Maybe tonight wasn't my night to check out after all.* It seemed funny (in a strange sort of way) to Hank that it took him much longer to free himself from the noose than it had taken to construct and fit it around his neck. But, after nearly fifteen minutes, he descended from the top of the bed to sit on the floor. He gingerly lifted the journal page and the letter from the floor and laid them out in front of him. *Shit.* He needed a pen and paper. He jumped up, grabbed the Bic pen and small notepad labeled *East Normandy Inn* and rushed back to the pages as if they might melt into the floor if he left them unattended. He stared at the dates again and then wrote down the corresponding numbers at the top of the 1st sheet of notebook paper.

102448021748 was the number that emerged from the dates: October 24, 1948 : February 17, 1948. The fact that the time period between October and February could not have taken place without a change in the year was not lost on Hank. *This couldn't have been a mistake, it had to be intentional, didn't it?* He looked back at the journal entry describing the encoding process. The first number denoted whether the resulting text was to be read as is, denoted by a 0, or each sentence in reverse, denoted by a 1. *Okay, so he was going to have to rearrange the decoded message after he extracted it.* Next, was the denotation for reading top to bottom or reverse. *Top to bottom. Good, the message started at the beginning and not the end.* With those two keys set in place, he began extracting the text from the letter using the rest of the code, which revealed which words to lift from what sentences and in which paragraphs.

As simple as this was, Hank found the process to be long and arduous. When he had finally completed extracting the words from the letter, Hank rewrote them in the correct order. During the extraction process, he could tell that he had been right about the letter; it did hold some kind of message for this Sherwin Deadman, whoever that might be. He'd been able to tell that the words were forming sentences, even without being able to completely read them yet. This last step in the process took just a few minutes, but it seemed like hours to Hank. His hands began to shake and his writing became almost illegible as he scribbled the words on the pad. Sweat dripped from his forehead onto the white sheet, smearing the blue ink from the cheap hotel pen. He read as he wrote, not caring that he wouldn't fully understand the text until he came back and gave it his full attention on a second read through. His heart was beating so hard and fast that he was convinced it would explode in his chest.

As you have likely guessed, this is not actually a letter to the person named in the salutation. In fact, no such person exists, at least to my knowledge. If you've decoded this message, you are either a part of this conspiracy, or you are, at least, fairly aware of it. I've lived in this hell for as long as I can remember. I've done all I can to bring these terrible events to light, but I no longer possess the strength, nor the endurance to continue the fight. What has taken place is a disgrace not only to the men and women who've served their country, but to the country itself, and above all, it's self-centered, power hungry, and incredibly corrupt leaders.....

The message went on to name the names of the accused, including their military or governmental positions. It also detailed each person's role in the scandalous events that had taken place over the course of Wilden's life in the military. Hank had almost committed the journal to memory and as he read the letter, the story seemed to come into focus more clearly for him. The journal detailed all of the events and persons that had directly impacted Captain

Wilden, but it didn't connect those persons and events to the bigger picture - the government proper. The message connected all the dots, applying broad, sweeping brushstrokes of color to the black and white picture that he previously had of the ordeal, but it still didn't clarify the detail.

Hank didn't even recognize how little he really knew until he'd finished reading the decoded letter a second time. His grandfather had even included keys to bringing the men involved to justice. Hank was sure that the letter had been written after, or at least during, the composition of the journal. *So why hadn't his grandfather carried the plan out?* A curious question. Maybe he'd tried, or was at least trying. Maybe the men he'd written about were hunting him down and he wasn't sure he'd be able to finish the task before they caught up to him. And so he'd written the letter in hopes that someone who came after him would be able to finish the job, someone with a little less mileage, someone with more strength and endurance, and yet, just as much determination. Someone exactly like Hank.

The rain still spilled from the sky, but Hank's tears had ceased. He was cried out; it was no longer the time for tears. It was now time for action. The end was coming, one way or another. He looked back at the headstone, his face a mask of grim determination.

"Lindsey, I love you more than you'll ever know. I'm sorry; sorry for what I've done, and sorry for what I'm going to do. But I have to put this right the only way I know how. I hope you can understand. I hope you can forgive me."

Having fully emptied his heart, Hank looked to the sky. Thunder threatened from the horizon. He kissed his fingers and placed them on the soaked ground that was Lindsey's final resting place. *I love you,* he mouthed silently as he stood and turned to leave.

IV. Unraveling Identities

After two hours of interviews at the Texan Inn Bar & Grill, Special Agent Doug Stunkel walked back across the highway and got into his standard issue FBI vehicle. He slipped behind the wheel and rested his head on the headrest, closing his eyes and trying to visualize the events that must have happened the night that Emery Mathis had lost control of his semi and run off the highway killing himself; the very same night that Sheriff Bergdolt was tortured and killed. Doug had gotten a few good tips during his interviews in the bar, but nothing concrete had surfaced. He tried to use the visualization process that he'd learned at the academy and used throughout his career. Often times, it led to insights that were not apparent upon first glace at any set of facts or data. He'd used the technique successfully many times in the past, but he'd also used it unsuccessfully just as often.

The best lead that he had was a local loudmouth named Jack Doinen. He was the one character that everyone in the bar mentioned. Doinen had been in trouble with the local law enforcement on many occasions, mostly brought up on D&D charges. The Drunk and Disorderlies didn't necessarily mean that Doinen had anything to do with the murder of Mentzer or Bergdolt, but it was a place to start. Several patrons, including the barkeep (or barmaid in this case), remembered seeing the Sheriff at the bar that night *blowing off some steam*, as they'd said. The barmaid, a forty-*ish* overweight woman with hair dyed the color of caramel named Della, had also been able to connect the semi driver (Mathis) with the Sheriff. Apparently, truck drivers routinely stopped in for a drink after gassing up across the street.

Doug had been skeptical of Della's seemingly perfect memory until he questioned her about her ability to remember the events of an evening that occurred several years ago.

"Mister, I've tended this bar since I was too young to order from it." She shot back. "I know the comings and goings of every casual and serious drunk in here. I know their names, faces, family histories, and in many cases, where they're going to sleep when they leave here. So don't give me any FBI bullshit about how long it's been since the '*incident in question.*' If I say the guy was here that night, then *by gawd* he was here. I know he was the truck driver you're askin' about because he said he could only have one tonight – driving you know. Hell, I can show you where they sat if you want me to."

Della seemed as certain about that night as anyone could be, and Doug had no real reason to doubt her. *So what was the connection between Mathis, Bergdolt, and the killer?* Doug visualized the bar in his mind, semi-filled with patrons and overly loud with the music of the live band, the sheriff and Mathis seated at a table near the middle of the room and Jack Doinen sitting in the back. *Sitting by himself?* Likely not, according to Della and the other patrons of the Texan. They all seemed to see Doinen as the human equivalent of a blood sucking leech, a zit on the ass of humanity, his father would have said. *So who was Doinen sitting with?* This was the million dollar question.

The next morning, Doug drove down state road 32 looking for the mailbox with the address Della had given him. Just as he was about to give up, he found it amidst an overgrowth of grass and weeds. The rusty black mailbox leaned sadly to one side; it's white plastic numbers trying their very best to run away from home.

Doug slowly pulled up the crushed gravel drive. The small farmhouse at the top of the driveway was almost completely hidden from the road by the stripped down hulks that sat rotting in the high grass of the front yard, if it could be called that. Junk yard was probably closer to the truth. Doug estimated the half acre frontage to be home to at least fifteen, maybe twenty old, rusty, torn apart vehicles; each a different make and model. Many of the steel ghosts sat atop concrete blocks with two or more of their wheels missing.

The view from the road was absurd and yet told Doug everything he needed to know about Jack Doinen. The out of repair farmhouse with its primer and rust colored children in the front yard stood against a perfectly blue sky, broken only by the occasional snow white cotton puff cloud. It seemed obvious that this was not the house of a killer. Doinen may be a co-conspirator, a grunt filling the orders of the boss man, but he could never be the head honcho.

As he stepped up the stairs and onto the porch, he could see that the house was not in much better shape than the yard. There were several boards missing from the porch floor, the swing in the corner hung askew, attached to the porch ceiling by only one length of chain (where to find the other was is anyone's guess), and the screen door was missing both the handle and the bottom screen. Doug reached up and knocked gently on the door, suddenly afraid that it may fall in if he knocked too loudly. He heard stirring inside and stepped back, taking a second look around. *Wow, this place was really a dump; almost literally!* The door opened and a five foot, eight inch waif of a man stood in the doorway, his disheveled black or perhaps oily brown hair seemingly stopped in the middle of the hokey pokey dance. *Half of it's down and half of it's up! And that's what it's all a-bout!* Doug nearly laughed aloud at the thought.

"Whut the feeuckk you laaffin' bout?" Doinen spat at him.

Doug could smell the previous night's alcohol still on Doinen. It smelled too strong to just be on Doinen's breath. *Hell, he was probably pissin' and sweatin' 80 proof.* And it was undoubtedly whiskey too. Doug had sworn off whiskey during his days as a police detective. He'd seen it do in too many good cops. *Swim in the bottle and eventually you'll drown,* he thought to himself. Doug flipped open his leather jacketed FBI identification card and moved toward the door; not really forcing his way in, but at the same time making sure that the door didn't get shut in his face. Doinen immediately stepped away from the door, a terrified look on his face.

"I ain't got no pot duuude. I dunno who tole you that sheet, but I ain't growin' or sellin' nothin' mister."

Doug was in the living room now, and it was more of a mess than the front yard. The wood floor was covered by a huge woven rug that looked about two hundred years old. There were newspapers and magazines scattered everywhere; from Sports Illustrated to Hustler and seemingly everything in between. There were stacks of plates and glasses three and four tall standing as proud as Roman statues and busts displayed so prominently in the Louvre.

"I'm not here to talk about your marijuana Mr. Doinen; although, that could become a topic of conversation should you choose not to participate in this discussion."

For the ensuing forty minutes, Doug nearly force fed Doinen the better half of a full pot of the black sludge that Doinen considered coffee while he grilled the disheveled drunkard about the night Sheriff Bergdolt died. When he left, he had what he'd been looking for all along, a name. That night, Jack Doinen had been "partying" with a young fellow named Daniel (Danny-boy) Bramstow. Coincidentally, Danny-boy disappeared shortly after the commotion of the Sheriff's murder. Doinen didn't have an address, but in today's digital universe, it wasn't absolutely necessary, it just made things simpler. Besides, he always had Della if he needed her.

As he pulled out of Jack Doinen's driveway and headed back toward the Holiday Inn, he flipped open his cell phone and dialed 1-800-Al Cauhall. Al picked up on the first ring.

"Doug, thank God you called. Please tell me you've got something important and exciting that you need me to do right away. I've been filing reports for Milner all morning. I'm not even sure where all of these frickin' things come from! You're the only one around here that ever seems to be working on a case."

Doug directed him to search the databases for a Daniel Bramstow in or near Graisville, Mississippi or Crystalton Heights, North Carolina.

"Oh and Al, look for credit cards, real estate sales, and apartment contract defaults or cancellations. Cross reference anything you get with employment records. This could be a break, Al; you'd better get to it."

"Can do Doug – I owe you one. Thanks pal."

Doug smiled as he pressed the END button on his cell phone. Al was thanking him for work, what a sick little puppy he was. But, he was a sick little puppy that had helped him crack more cases than he could remember.

The next morning, Al called. He'd uncovered a trail, or at least the start of one. According to Al, Daniel Bramstow had left Graisville in a big hurry after the deaths of the trucker and sheriff. The credit card trail led to Nashville, Tennessee and abruptly disappeared. There was no record of Bramstow after he arrived in Nashville, and no record that he'd ever been to Crystalton Heights. That could mean only one thing: Bramstow went underground; changed names. *Was Bramstow his real name, or was that an alias too?* Probably just an alias, but it was at least a start.

Doug stood at the front desk of the Holiday Inn, waiting for Al's fax to come across. He'd compiled a list of all real estate transactions and apartment rentals within a 60 mile radius of Nashville and cross referenced it against employment records within a six month timeframe of Bramstow's last charge. There were four pages to the fax, but there were only two names at the bottom. Calbert Dobbs and James Davenkish. *Was one of these two the mystery caller?* There was only one way to know for sure; a trip to Nashville.

But before he left, he needed to check out Daniel Bramstow's place of residence during his stay in Graisville. As it turned out, Bramstow had purchased a dilapidated, one bedroom, six hundred square foot shack on the outskirts of town. He'd paid twenty thousand dollars cash. The change in title was the only paperwork trail he'd left, but it was enough for bloodhound Al. Doug went through the home with a fine tooth comb, but found nothing. On the way to Nashville, he called Al back and asked him to arrange an official processing of the run down house. Unfortunately, their office didn't have the resources to process a crime scene. Al would have to contact the local FBI office and ask them to complete the processing. With it being outside their jurisdiction, it would certainly fall to the basement of the priority list, in line right after cleaning the office bathrooms.

Once he arrived in Nashville, Doug began trying to track down the two potential suspects. At his direction, Al was back at the office pulling everything he could on Davenkish and Dobbs. First things first, he headed toward the top address on the page; a condo that Dobbs had purchased two weeks after his arrival in Nashville. Doug pulled into the entrance of *The Winds* golf community. This was not a good sign. After seeing Bramstow's place of residence in Graisville, he couldn't visualize a scenario where the man would be able to afford a condo in a golf community in Nashville.

He turned on Crooked Stick Lane and slowed down, looking for the right address. He pulled to the curb in front of a condo marked 1973 on the side of the brick mailbox. As he reached for the door handle to get out, a man in his mid to late sixties strode around the back corner of the condo, his wife wrapped tightly in his arms. Instead of getting out, Doug rolled down the window and called to them.

"Excuse me, is this 1973 Crooked Stick Lane?"

The man and his wife both smiled as they strode toward the car.

"I'm Cal Dobbs and this is my wife Nita. Can I help you?"

Doug looked back down at the fax, just to confirm that he hadn't misread the address.

"Huh. Sorry, I must have the wrong address. I'm looking for a Daniel Bramstow. You don't know him do you?"

The man gave him a puzzled look and shook his head.

Doug thanked him for his time and began to pull away from the curb. As he drove off, he watched the man and his wife walk back toward the house, arm in arm. They were obviously still in love after who knew how many years. Doug felt a pang for his mother and father, who'd both died before their time. He wished for them a scene like the one he just experienced. He also wondered if he'd ever have that experience himself. Not as long as he had The Job, he knew. The Job was all consuming, all encompassing. It left no time for anything else. Right then, Doug realized that his few real friends were the men and women he worked with on a daily basis at the FBI. The closest, of course, being Al. He was like the older brother that Doug never had, even with all his idiosyncrasies.

Doug went directly from *The Winds* to *Golden Oaks*. As he weaved his way through the apartment complex looking for number 1113- J, he smiled knowing that he had his man. James Davenkish was his name, and he was about to be apprehended. He would have to answer for the murders of Emery Mathis, Clancy Bergdolt, Mike Mentzer, and Bob Trasker. The apartment was at the very back of the complex. Doug strode up to the door and knocked firmly, his right hand already on the butt of his service pistol, just in case. A man in his late thirties or early forties answered. Doug leveled the Glock at him and forced his way into the apartment.

"FBI," he shouted. "Hands on your head. Down on your knees Davenkish."

Bewilderment covered the man's face, but he complied, dropping to his knees and placing his hands on the back of his head. Doug cuffed him and read him his rights. He pulled the man to his feet and pushed him toward the door.

"You're going to jail you son of a bitch," he said as he dragged the man out of the apartment.

The man's arm trembled beneath Doug's grip as they walked toward the car. Once he got him in the vehicle, Doug went back up to the apartment and grabbed the keys off of the TV, locked the door and pulled it to. He slid into the front seat and looked through the mesh wire that separated the front of the vehicle from the back.

"Why'd you do it Jimmy?" He asked. "What did they do to deserve to die?"

The man looked back at him with the blank, slack faced stare that was so common in busted criminals.

"What did you call me?" he asked. "Did you call me Jimmy? My name is Tim. Tim Trustcoff."

Now it was Doug's turn to look confused.

"You mean you're not James Davenkish?" he asked, hoping that he hadn't just arrested the wrong man.

"No. My name is Tim Trustcoff. I don't know who Jimmy Daven-whatever is. Did I do something wrong officer?"

After confirming his ID, Doug released Trustcoff and quickly exited stage left, thoroughly embarrassed by his mistake. He headed to the apartment office where he got the scoop on Davenkish, who apparently had left Nashville in a bit of a hurry too. Davenkish rented the apartment a year at a time, paying in cash and in one prompt annual installment. The manager hadn't been aware that he'd even left until the lease came due and Davenkish didn't come to pay it. When he went to the apartment to find him, it had been completely emptied. Doug spent the rest of the afternoon canvassing the apartments, looking for information on Davenkish. Apparently, he'd kept to himself; none of the residents even remembered speaking to him.

For the second straight day, Al called early with a fresh lead.

"Doug, I pulled a list of murders within a sixty mile proximity of Nashville for an 18 month time period after Davenkish arrived. You'll never guess what I found. Another murder. One that we didn't know about."

"Beamer, you're the best. Was it a cop?"

"Sorry to disappoint, but it wasn't. Actually, quite the opposite. A local drug distributer. He handled almost anything you could want; big into designer pills. Name was George McClory. It might be worth checking out."

"Thanks Beamer. I'll do it."

By the time Doug left the police station, he had the names of two informants that were dealers in the area. He tracked them both down in hopes that they might be able to shed some light on the subject of Jimmy Davenkish. Unfortunately, they didn't. At least, nothing that he could use to track Davenkish down. Worse yet, Al hadn't been able to track Davenkish outside of Nashville. This time, he'd left no trail. Doug spent the night in Nashville and filed a report on his activities before heading back toward the Springfield office the next day. He was out of ideas for now. He had Al running a couple more searches, but there was little optimism they would yield anything of significance. Davenkish was good. And each place he went, he seemed to get a little better at covering his tracks.

V. Island Vacation

Hank stood outside the Pizza Depot on Main Street in Beachside Island, South Carolina. Beachside Island truly was as beautiful as the internet ads had described. That was the wonderful thing about the internet; in just a couple of hours, you could become an expert on the subject of your choosing. This time, he'd done his research and found a place to stay in just over forty minutes. Quick, easy, and efficient – suited him perfectly.

Unfortunately, renting a place was the only way to get on and off the island; and it was expensive. Beachside Island was wholly owned by its residents and was highly exclusive. To ensure the privacy of the residents and their guests, island access was controlled by a manned security gate. Because of the exclusivity *and breathtaking sunsets*, it had become a popular place with the *almost* upper crust. To gain access to the island, Hank had rented a small bungalow off the beach; paying dearly - even without the beachfront at his back door.

The twenty-two hundred acre island included over three miles of fantastic beach front. An equestrian center was located inland along with countless lakes and marshes. This was truly a perfect place for nature lovers, which Hank certainly was not. To make it worse, everyone on the island was a little too hoity-toity for him.

That lot included one recently retired General Robert Wadnesku of the United States Marine Corps. General Wadnesku stood a solid six foot four and maintained his "you stand at fucking attention, boy" flatop despite his being eighteen months into retirement. Hank felt a deep-seated loathing for the General as he watched him sip coffee with his wife through the front window of the Flavorful Cup Coffeehouse across the street from the Pizza Depot. The Wad may have been in top condition early in his military career, but the years as a commander had taken their toll and his physique proved that pushing papers didn't rip you like pushups did. Hank nearly laughed aloud as Wadnesku lifted his coffee cup to take a sip and his sagging triceps swung gently from side to side below his arm.

Hank tried to imagine The Wad in full marine getup - first his black and whites, then finally settling on fatigues. The man sitting across the street wasn't nearly as impressive dressed in khaki shorts and a yellow Hawaiian button up. Oh yeah, he couldn't forget the black socks and brown leather sandals. Those were the cherry that sat proudly atop the sundae that was Robert Wadnesku.

The Wad had sold his place back east and moved here to Beachside just six short weeks ago. Hank had been here five days and watched him go through this exact routine each of those days. *So predictable.* Good, that would make his job easier. After their mid morning cup of coffee, the Wadnesku's would return to their beachfront cottage, she sowing or crocheting and he wood-working in the small shop he'd built into the garage.

It seemed that The General didn't like to be disturbed during his wood-working. Mrs. Wad had yet to come within 500 feet of the garage during the hours of ten and noon. Sharply at noon, The Wad would close up shop and return to the cottage for lunch, generally served by the wife on a huge deck that jutted out toward the ocean from the rear of the cottage. Then, out to the beach for a leisurely walk in the surf. The garage sat along the side of the house, outside of view of the deck. This is where their little conversation would take place later today. If Hank got the information he needed, a conversation was all it would be. If he didn't get it; well, that would be an entirely different ballgame. And one that neither himself nor The Wad was going to enjoy very much.

Hank casually glanced back up Main and caught a glimpse of the silver-green Chrysler 300C parked a half block back and on the opposite side of the street. He'd spotted the Chrysler on multiple occasions since his arrival on the island. Now, the car sat outside The Island Beauty Parlor. The salon didn't open till eleven, but the lone passenger appeared not to notice.

Hank hadn't been able to get a good look at the vehicle's driver, but he could easily tell that it was a man from the broad shoulders and balding pate. He'd felt the presence of someone watching him for several weeks now, but this trip was the first time he'd been able to confirm his suspicions. Now, it seemed, his tail was becoming more complacent with his task, losing the vigilance that kept him fully concealed. *He was getting sloppy.*

Hank was concerned that the man was preparing to make a move on him.

Was he alone?

Hank guessed that he was. He hadn't spotted anyone else tailing him since his arrival on the island.

But he could easily call in backup.

That was true, and a frightening deduction. Hank knew that he would be no match for a group of FBI, CIA, or military personnel – whoever the hell it was following him. After decoding the message his grandfather had left him and reading through the journal several more times, he was convinced that his pursuers were very powerful men from one of these organizations; or maybe all of them. He'd barely been able to escape the grip of the Crystalton PD; and Lindsey hadn't. At this thought, his heart broke into pieces for the millionth time. They were too close; today had to be the day for his talk with Wadnesku. Hopefully, The Wad would shed some light on who his pursuers might be.

Hank returned his watchful eye to The Flavorful Cup. General and Mrs. Wad both smiled at the waitress as she refilled their cups with steaming brew and then turned to leave the table. *Cup number two*, Hank thought to himself. That meant that he had about twenty minutes left before The Wads would be headed for home. From Main Street to the cottage was no more than a ten minute bicycle ride for the retired couple. *Thirty minutes*. Plenty of time to make it to the Wadnesku's place and claim his previously scouted hiding spot in the garage. But he would have to lose his tail first.

Hank smiled at a passerby as he left the Pizza Depot and headed up Main. He was getting closer to the truth. It was a surreal feeling, like walking on numb legs. With a quick glance, he spotted the 300C pulling across the street and joining the few cars that were out this morning. The vehicle had just started heading in his direction when Hank darted between two boutique shops and headed down the walking alley. He was well on his way to the Wadnesku's by the time the 300C made it around the block looking for him.

The heat was stifling in the metal cabinet that Hank had chosen as his hiding place. In the gray storage cabinet, he was accompanied by several pairs of The Wad's cover-alls and twenty or thirty of his mistresses. Hank smiled as he thought back to the first day he watched the retired General in his wood working shop from close range. The small garage unit had a loft that the Wadneskus used for storage. Hank had stowed away there and waited for Wadnesku to come out for his daily wood working session.

He was working on some kind of elaborate birdfeeder. Hank hated birds, the messy little bastards. Eating and shitting was all they seemed to be capable of.

After about thirty minutes of sanding and hammering, The Wad peeked out the small window over his workbench and then quickly strode over to the big gray cabinet that stood underneath the loft. Hank didn't see what Wadnesku was doing, but the screeching of the hinges was more than enough explanation of where he was. When he returned to his workbench, the General laid out the patented tri fold centerfold from a *somewhat* recent Playboy magazine; at least it was from this decade. Hank nearly broke his cover from laughter when The Wad then began a conversation with Miss June 2002.

"Oh, I see from your Bio that you like men who work with their hands. Weeell, let me tell you; I'm very good with my hands. What about a man in uniform there, Miss June?....."

Hank had made up his mind then that the big gray cabinet was the perfect place to stow away and take the General by surprise. There was no question that Wadnesku's mind would be other places when Hank leapt from his hiding place. He just hoped he didn't give the bastard a heart attack doing so.

Dammit, what's taking him so long? Hank thought to himself. He pushed the small button on the side of his watch and it cast a faint green glow, illuminating the watch face so that he could read the digital numbers. It had been forty-five minutes, he should have been here by now. Hank was starting to get restless. He'd been sitting on the stack of Playboy magazines for most of the forty-five minutes that he'd been here; he was completely numb from hip to toe. There wasn't enough room in the cabinet for him to stand up, even if he crouched over.

What if he isn't coming? What if The Wad's plans were different today, shopping with the missus maybe? What if he'd been tipped off by his tail? What if this was a set-up? They could be waiting outside the garage right now...

The interior of the cabinet seemed to be closing in on him; the air was suffocatingly heavy, laden with confusion, worry, and paranoia. Hank's chest heaved and he was convinced that he was going to have a panic attack. He had to get out of this box. Being in here was worse than being in the corpse drawer at the Mission View Medical Center. Hank tried to reason with himself, calm his fears and slow his breathing, but nothing he did helped. His mind was an out of control locomotive and his body was along for the ride.

Hank was just about to kick open the doors to the cabinet when he heard the doorknob click and the garage door slide open. Wadnesku entered, whistling a broken tune that seemed familiar. He heard The Wad kick the door closed and cross the garage floor to the bench. There was a rustling, a few clicks and the sound of the General puffing. *His daily cigar.* Everyone had a vise; General Wadnesku apparently had a few.

Suddenly, it wasn't so bad in the cabinet. Hank's legs were reinvigorated with a shot of adrenaline that resulted from the excitement (and fear) that he felt. *It wouldn't be long now.* Wadnesku's chair creaked as he leaned back and puffed his stogey.

Other than the sound of The Wad's puffing, the garage stood in utter silence. Finally, Wadnesku abandoned the chair, crushed the cigar underfoot, and began his work on the huge wooden birdfeeder that sat atop his workbench. He worked for nearly twenty five minutes before silence again returned to the small garage/workshop.

Hank's head pounded to the sound of the hammer and nails even though the hammering had ceased. *It must be time for his discussion with Miss June, or July, or December, or whatever month it happened to be that the dirty old man pulled out today.* Hank concentrated on the approaching footsteps, unwilling to let this opportunity go by without perfect execution on his part. That was the only way he was going to get what he wanted, what he needed, from the man who had been in charge of the training base in the Philippines where his grandfather's worst nightmares had begun. He'd also been in charge of the missions to Japan during the Black War. The missions of which were so dark, so terrible in both their goal and execution that they literally changed the course of the global conflict that would later be known as World War II.

Hank readied himself as Wadnesku grabbed the handles of the cabinet; somewhere between the end of his cigar and the cabinet door handles, he'd resumed whistling that stupid song. *What was the name of that damn song anyway?*

The doors to the cabinet creaked open and General Wadnesku's eyes went wide as Hank exploded from his perch atop the Playboy magazines in the bottom of the cabinet. The General actually heard the *Whoosh!* as the air was violently expressed from his lungs and he was driven onto his back in the middle to the floor. He gasped for breath but could draw none. His head felt woozy and he nearly passed out. In an instant, Hank had swiveled behind him, restrained his hands behind his back and dragged him over to the workbench. He quickly grabbed the only chair in the garage and placed it over Wadnesku's legs, pinning them to the floor. The General had been completely incapacitated before he could even scream for help.

Hank leaned in close and looked the man in the eyes. Wadnesku glared back as best he could, but his eyes gave away his panic. He was frantic, eyes darting back and forth looking for a way out of this mess. Hank reasoned that this was a result of his short retirement. Now he had something to live for. During his time in the armed forces, he was surely tougher than this. Yes, now there were daily walks on the beach, coffee and scones on Main Street, woodworking (with cigars and Playboy playmates of course) in the garage, and plenty of other delightful moments with the wife. Plenty of things to be concerned about losing should something terrible happen to him.

"General, keep your voice low and answer all my questions and I'll be gone before you know it. I'm not here to hurt you. I just want some information and you're the only one who can provide it. If you'll cooperate, this will be easy. If not, well, it might hurt a little. It might hurt a lot, actually."

The General made no sound, he only nodded slowly. His eyes never left Hank's except when shaded by his eyelids. It was warm in the garage, but a cool breeze was gently blowing through the window over the workbench. Hank could hear the gentle crashing of the surf in the distance and wondered briefly how this was going to go. Easy, or painful? He returned his gaze to The Wad.

"Do you know who I am?"

Wadnesku shook his head. The skin around his eyes twitched as the panic coursed through his body. It had always been easy for Hank to spot a liar. The look on Wad's face told him that he was telling the truth. *Good, no heroes here.*

"I know you were responsible for the training base in the Philippines during World War II. It was the base that my grandfather was assigned to. He and his team were doing research in cooperation with a company called McCline Pharmaceuticals. The operation was under the supervision of a Dr. Martin Price. Do you remember this operation?"

Wadnesku nodded this time, slowly, reservedly. He appeared to be even more shaken now than when Hank had first leapt from the small gray cabinet and knocked him on his back.

"General, I need to know who Dr. Price reported to. I know most of the periphery people that were involved, but I need to know how high this operation went. Who was the top guy? Who was calling the shots?"

Wadnesku stood his ground. His resolve had solidified somehow. He sat, trapped under the chair, hands bound behind his back with plastic zip ties. The panic that had riddled his face up to this point had been transformed into something just short of terror. He was obviously very afraid. *Afraid of what, or who? Hank, or someone else?*

Hank leaned in closer; his nose almost touching The Wad's beak. He was close enough that he could see the coal black hairs jutting from the pores on the bulb of Wadnesku's nose. He'd always thought it strange that when you made it to the other side of the proverbial hill, hair had a habit of growing only where you didn't want it and falling out of all the places that you did. It was one of those ironic paradoxes of nature, proof that God (or whoever was in charge) had a *really* twisted sense of humor.

"Wad, don't screw with me. You know what I'm talking about. Tell me. I don't want to hurt you, but believe me, I will if you force me. You're going to tell me what I want to know."

Wadnesku's resolve continued to grow. He shook his head slowly, painfully. He wasn't going to talk without some help.

Hank shook his head, almost regretfully, and reached up to the workbench, grabbing a razorblade knife. He reached down and pulled The Wad's khakis taut and ran the knife the length of the leg, ripping the pant leg in half and exposing the white flesh of Wadnesku's thigh and shin. He pitched the razor knife back onto the bench top and pulled the belt sander down; checking to make sure that it was plugged in before bringing it to Wadnesku's eye level. He sat the sander on the floor next to the general's leg. Hank pulled a roll of silver-gray duct tape from his pocket and ripped a four inch piece from the end of the roll, roughly covering The Wad's mouth before returning his attention to the belt sander.

Whirrrrr... The sander jumped to life at the flick of the red switch on the back of the handle. This wasn't one of those cheap Black & Decker weekend warrior models either. This was the industrial version of made by Makita. The sanding belt alone was three inches wide and had eight inches of exposed length. It even had two handles.

"You know, the manual recommends using both hands to avoid accidental loss of control and contact with your body. What do you think would happen if I accidentally lost control of this sander and it came in contact with... say your leg General Wad?"

Hank lowered the sander, his eyes on the General's all the while. This would get his attention, no question about that. It would also show him that Hank meant business. He watched as The Wad's eyes darted back and forth from the sander to his own thigh to Hank's face and through the cycle again. He tried to kick his legs and wiggle his way out, but he was trapped snugly under the chair. He had nowhere to go. Hank lowered the sander until it lightly grazed Wadnesku's thigh and removed it again. A perfect pink rectangle appeared where the sander had just been. In an instant, the sander had erased the hair on the General's leg and raised the skin in an irritated rectangular patch.

"Are you sure you don't want to talk about it General?"

Wadnesku only closed his eyes and put his head back. He made no sound other than the slightest of whimpers.

Hank had no choice. He had to know what the General knew if he was going to move forward with his plans. In one smooth motion, Hank dropped the belt sander against Wadnesku's leg; this time with more than double the force, and he left it there. The grit of the belt ate into the General's leg like a hungry animal. Blood sprayed out the back of the tool and across the floor. Wadnesku's face went pallid and his head quickly jerked back in a grimace of pain.

When Hank removed the sander, it had ground a divot from the man's leg, again in the shape of a perfect rectangle. The flesh around the wound was stark white, matching the man's face while the wound was bright red and oozed blood. It stunk too, like burnt plastic or rubber, or worse. Beside the streak of blood radiating across the floor, a pool of dark red flesh and blood was growing beneath the General's leg. He was bleeding more than Hank had anticipated.

"Shit General, you're bleeding pretty badly and that just won't do. We can't have you dying out here. He again reached atop the bench; this time bringing down a quart can of mineral spirits and the pack of matches that Wadnesku had used to light his cigars. He doused the wound in solvent and then stood up, pulling the chair off the General's legs. He then extracted a match from the book, lit it and dropped it on the General's leg. *Whoosh!* The flame shot up nearly four foot and died out almost as quickly as it had begun, Wadnesku kicking and thrashing the whole time.

"Are you interested in talking to me now General?" Hank asked, knowing the answer before even completing the question.

Wadnesku nodded fervently. Hank ripped the tape from the man's mouth and sat back down in the chair. Before his ass-end made it to the seat, The Wad's mouth was running in high gear, fueled by the fear of what else might happen to him if he didn't talk. Besides, it was so long ago anyway, how was anyone going to find out that he'd contracted a case of oral diarrhea?

After twenty minutes of non-stop disconjointed sentence fragments, Hank was convinced that he'd heard all there was to hear on the subject of the Black War from General Wadnesku. It wasn't necessary for him to ask even a single question. He'd gotten all there was to get from the General, although it certainly wasn't the entire story. It was; however, enough to get him to the next step. Wadnesku had shown him the next door, and it was time for Hank to barge through.

The Wad sat, still pinned to the floor, looking at Hank with frantic eyes. It was obvious that he had nothing left to tell; his story was complete. Now, he had to rely on this stranger to judge if it had been enough. He continued to look up at Hank with beseeching eyes; begging, pleading to be spared without verbalizing a single word.

Hank leaned in close for the second time. He spoke slowly in a hushed tone and looked the man directly in the eyes.

"General Wadnesku, you've been most helpful. I'm sorry for the unpleasantness that I've caused you, but I had to know everything you did and you must admit your initially reluctance to share. Now, I'm going to cut your restraints and let you go in to see your wife and get that burn of yours cleaned up and bandaged real good. But before I do, you're going to give me exactly ten minutes to get outta here before you go in. You will not breathe a word of our conversation to anyone between now and the day you pass on from this world. Do you understand?"

Wadnesku quickly nodded.

"Okay. Thanks again for the information. There's absolutely no reason for anyone to know what went on here today. You continue your life, I'll continue mine, and it's unlikely we'll ever see each other again."

With that, Hank reached up to the bench top one final time, grabbing a pair of tin snips. He cut The Wad's restraints and slowly backed away from him to the door. He didn't think that he was going to get any trouble from the man, but you can never be too careful. As Hank had anticipated, Wadnesku continued to sit in the floor, still as a statue. Without another word, Hank exited the garage and was gone.

General Robert Wadnesku sat in the floor of the garage for a full fifteen minutes without moving, except for a slight tremor in his leg every now and then. The last thirty minutes or so had left him horrified. He wasn't sure if he'd ever feel safe again. *That was a pitiful reaction for a man who'd spent so long in the military wasn't it?* He looked down at his leg and felt fresh pain wash over him. That had to be at least a second degree burn. Blood was pooled in the seat of his pants along with the sharp smell of urine. Great, he'd wet himself. *Now that was really pathetic.* He'd seen men piss themselves plenty during his time in the military and early on he'd vowed never to disgrace himself that way. Well, at least he was still alive; that's what counted.

With a considerable amount of effort, the General hauled himself to his feet and limped over towards the door. He made a slight detour to shut the gray cabinet's doors tight. He'd have to clean it out and get rid of the son of a bitch next week. Otherwise, he'd constantly be replaying this day in his head. He got to the door, shut off the lights, and turned to leave. As he did, he ran square into the cold steel barrel of a coal black handgun. *Pow! Pow!* And it was over, his life ended with one bullet in the brain and another in the chest. He never saw it coming and never felt a thing.

VI. Jigsaw Puzzle

The sun was blinding, making it an abnormally warm day for early fall. Doug Stunkle pushed his FBI standard issue sedan as hard as he dared without being completely reckless. He had a lead and he couldn't afford for it to cool any more than absolutely necessary. He was starting to form a picture in his mind of the man he was pursuing and he couldn't believe what he was seeing. One man with multiple identities, committing murders in completely different states; *what was going on here? How were these people connected? There had to be some reasoning behind it, didn't there?*

As he sped down the interstate, he replayed the message from Al on the speakerphone of his cell.

"Doug, you're not going to believe this. The results of the CS investigation on Bramstow's apartment finally came back. Trace analysis contained fibers and hairs with DNA from Joseph Pratt, deceased. I checked; that's the same name that came up in the theft of that State Trooper's car; Landis was the name. Somethin' weird's goin' on with this Pratt character. I looked up his records, but everything checks out. Died on July 23 of '92. Heart Atta…"

Doug pressed the * button on his cell, cutting the message off and skipping to the next. After a short pause, Al's voice came through the speakerphone again. Al was right, Doug couldn't believe it. All along he had the name of the killer and had completely ignored it.

"Doug, it's Al again. I checked on that murder-suicide you asked me about; the Monroe-Pratt case. There were a *few* things in the case notes that didn't exactly add up. Reviewing the crime scene photographs, the body positions seem strange for a murder-suicide, but there was no evidence that they'd been moved. Also, the suicide note produced a handwriting match to Nancy Pratt, the shooter. The problem is…that it wasn't a 100% match, it was only 91%, which is borderline. The difference was attributed to her deteriorated emotional state. If you go down a slightly different route, you could make the assumption that the suicide note was written under duress.

I guess what I'm getting at is that this may not have been a murder-suicide; it may have been a *double homicide*. As a matter of note, the murder weapon was a Colt forty-five. I couldn't track it to anything or anyone - too old. I hope the info helps. Call me if you need anything else.

Oh yeah, there was one other thing. The third case you gave me, the hit and run that killed the father... looks to be an accident, but I can't tell for sure from the evidence. There were no eye witnesses and the vehicle was never recovered. Anyway, that's all I've got for now. Hope it helps. I already said that didn't I? Well, I do. Anyway... Uhmm... Good luck. Bye."

Doug exited the interstate to the local expressway and headed for the East side of Evanston. His mind was a whirlwind of possibilities. How could he have been so blind as to ignore the name the first time it came up? *Stupid. That's a rookie beat cop's mistake, you idiot,* he thought to himself. Oh, well. All he could do now was finish the investigation and not let something like this happen again. Learning from mistakes had kept several of his fellow agents and cop-pals alive over the years. He dialed up Al on the cellular, leaving it in speakerphone mode. As usual, Al picked up on the second ring. Milner had issued Cauhall a cell of his own since he spent so much time away from his desk and down in the case rows. It had probably been the smartest thing his boss had done since Doug had arrived at the field office in Springfield.

"Hello?"

"Al, it's Doug; I need some help. Can you get me an exhumation order? I need it faxed to the Rose Park Cemetary in Evanston, Indiana. No, I don't know the phone number; you'll have to look it up."

There were several seconds of silence from the other end of the phone. Then Al came back on, again tentative.

"Doug, you have to have a family member sign the order."

"I'll get it signed Cuervo. You just get it drawn up and sent to the cemetery."

"But, who's going to sign it? The guy's parents are both dead, we don't even know if he's got siblings, where they are, or anything." Al questioned.

"Al, get the damned order and get it sent. Let me worry about the signature. Okay?"

"Okay. Sorry Doug. I didn't mean to question… Never mind. I'll get it."

Doug felt bad about snapping at Al, but sometimes he just asked too many questions. He didn't always need to know every detail of the investigation. Sometimes, he just needed to do his part and not ask so many damn questions. Doug knew that Al was worried that he'd do something illegal and get both their asses in a ringer. Well, Al was wrong. He wasn't going to forge the signature anyway.

Doug exited the expressway and took Meridian Street for several blocks before reaching his destination. Rose Park Cemetery had been opened nearly a hundred years ago and was almost full now. Most of the plots that were left were reserved to ensure that the plot owner could be buried amongst family. Planning your own death; what a terrible thing to have to spend time on, thought Doug. He'd already decided that when he left this earth, he wanted his body to be cremated and his ashes spread on the four winds. The thought of being filled with preservatives, locked in an airtight box and buried in the ground was a terrible conclusion to life. Not to mention that it sure seemed like overkill to him. Ashes to ashes, dust to dust… Or whatever they say.

He maneuvered the big vehicle, tracing the curvy one lane road that wound through the cemetery until he finally found the area that he was looking for. Many people didn't know it, but nearly all cemeteries are mapped out in sections and the attendant could point you to exactly the area you're looking for given just a few seconds of patience. Doug pulled the sedan into the grassy shoulder of the lane and hopped out of the car. A feeling of morbidity clung to him like a parasite. His heart was starting to beat fast and as he walked among the tombstones, his breath came in short bursts. What was he going to find here? This would be the first time he'd performed this particular ritual. He'd heard the stories in the locker room, but never really believed that he would someday be on the telling end.

As he concentrated on pushing the thought of what was about to happen from his mind, he nearly tripped over the headstone that he'd been looking for. He staggered back slightly and took a brief look. It wasn't nearly as ornate as most of the others in the row. In fact, it was completely undecorated in any way. The engraving was plain and to the point; containing only a name and two dates separated by a dash.

Joseph Anton Pratt
October 13, 1972 – July 23, 1992

Doug stepped away from the grave, watching the John Deere tractor creep up to just the right distance so that the shovel could begin its work. Doug wasn't sure what to expect of this little excavation. He felt hollow inside and didn't know what he wanted the outcome to be. The very thought of disturbing a gravesite that had been sealed for over twenty years was overwhelming. His stomach lurched and his McDonald's quarter pounder with cheese almost came back out of the dugout for an encore. His head felt like it was on a merry-go-round. He stumbled away from the grave and tractor and looked for a shady place to sit and catch his breath. It felt like it must be a hundred and fifty degrees.

The section of the cemetery where the Pratt's were buried was within fifty yards of the cemetery's property line. Tracing the line from one end to the other was an eight foot tall concrete wall with black, wrought iron spikes on top. Just inside the wall stood a shady oak tree that looked like it was probably a sapling long before they started putting people in the ground here. Doug looked at the headstones as he strode over toward the shade. He passed the elder Pratt's headstone and the stone for Christopher Pratt, also buried with the family. Born October 28, 1979. Died April 7, 1998. He'd been just eighteen years old. Doug shook his head and continued down the row.

The air seemed even heavier as he continued to trudge down the row. The John Deere continued its work behind him, creating a pile of brown dirt that obscured his view of the grave. He passed a few empty gravesites, and at the end of the row encountered a small stone that stole the air from his lungs. Doug had to rub his eyes and look a second time to be sure he really saw what he thought he did. *Was it possible? Or could it just be a mirage from the heat?* He wiped the sweat from his brow and knelt down to get a closer look.

Lindsey Jolene Macallum
My one true love
1974 – 2006

The grave was adorned with two beautiful bouquets of pink and yellow roses; one to each side of the stone. Each looked to be composed of a dozen long stems, and not a single petal showed any signs of wilt. Doug's head was spinning and he felt like he was trapped beneath the surface of a frozen pond. He didn't know what to do next; he looked back at the John Deere. The dirt pile was huge and the caretaker was fastening some kind of cable to the arm of the Deere. Doug rushed back to the grave site, arriving just as the old tractor lifted a dirty brown, wooden box from the ground and swiveled to set it to rest in the walkway between the graves.

Doug grabbed the crow bar from the caretaker's hand before he could even get his feet firmly planted on the ground. He began prying open the lid of the pine box with the caretaker protesting at his back. The wood sounded awful as it groaned, cracked and finally splintered beneath the assault of the crowbar-wielding FBI agent.

The caretaker ratcheted his protests up another level and reached around Doug, grabbing at his sleeve and trying his best to force Doug to stop what he was doing. Just as he got a grip on the FBI man's forearm, the box lid popped up with a loud *Crack!*

Doug let the old man take the bar from his hands and slowly stepped to the head of the box. He was pretty sure what he was going to find, but telling yourself never made it a reality until it was actually real. He took a long draw of the close, hot air and lifted the lid. The caretaker had finished his protests, but stood by with his arms crossed, shaking his head in disgust.

As he removed the cover of the box, Doug leaned over to more quickly see into the interior. He smiled thinly as the lid scraped back, finally falling to the ground. Doug glanced down toward the oak and Lindsey Macallum's grave. He returned his gaze to the playground sand that filled the wooden box at his feet, grabbing a handful and letting it sift through his closed fist. He began to walk away, ignoring the further barking of the grouchy old man who minded the dead.

Joseph Pratt wasn't dead after all. In fact, it looked like he was very much alive based on the roses that adorned Lindsey Macallum's conveniently located final resting place. The murders of Sheriff Clancy Bergdolt and Officer Robert Trasker had been linked after all. And if it hadn't been for a couple of headstrong cops, the case would have never even made it to his desk. Now Doug knew who he was chasing, he just didn't understand why. And he couldn't be more than a few days behind Joseph either. He picked up the cell phone, pushed the redial button, and waited for Al to pick up. As usual, it took just two rings.

The pressure was killing him. Doug was close, he could feel it. He was getting close to figuring this thing out. He had so many questions and so few answers. As he waited for his computer to log into *AwayNet*, the Springfield office's FBI interface, he finished off the last of his quarter pounder and fries. He flipped on ESPN and watched for the day's scores. The Cubs had a day game today against the Astros; Zambrano against Clemens, back from yet another brief retirement. He watched several scores scroll across the bottom of the screen, but no Cubs score. He must have missed it and now he'd have to wait for the ticker tape to start over again. Finally, the computer beeped and he was in. He went right to his inbox and found the email from Al at the top of the list.

From: Al Cauhall
Sent: Tuesday, October 4
To: Doug Stunkel
Subject: Macallum Notes

Doug –
Here are Lindsey Macallum's notes.Luckily, the CHPD still wants to catch this guy bad enough that they didn't make us get a court order; they just handed them over.I had to get them to scan them in and email them to me.Call me and let me know if you want me to look through them.Millie's got me working on some sorting project that's taking most of my time.Good Luck.

-180 .

Doug smiled as he clicked on the PDF file attached to the email and watched it open to Dr. Macallum's notes on Hank Marin, aka Joseph Pratt. Al's best work was done over the phone, in the archives, and on the FBI network. He wasn't particularly well schooled in email etiquette, punctuation, or sometimes even spelling. But he always got Doug what he needed. Doug also knew that Al was lying about not reading the doctor's notes. He'd have them read before he left for the evening. Doug devoured the notes, breaking away only to use the restroom and refill his coffee cup. Thank God for in room coffee makers; another reason the Holiday Inn was

Doug's first choice. The PDF was thirty two pages long and Doug had read through it twice when he finally shut down his laptop and leaned his head back against the headboard of the bed.

He looked over at the yellow legal pad where he'd jotted down three lines.

Dr. Martin Price

McCline Pharmaceuticals

Operation Incivility

Doug glanced at the clock on the nightstand- one forty-six A.M. It was too late to call Al. He'd have to do it in the morning. He'd been able to cross reference the FBI database for Price's home address and the location of McCline Pharmaceuticals. He'd also gotten significant background on the company from their web page. However, he'd need Al's help with the third piece of this puzzle. He'd been able to find absolutely nothing on Operation Incivility. *Nada. Zilch.* Was Joseph delusional? Price and McCline had checked out; that certainly lent some truth to the story that Dr. Macallum had transcribed in her notes, even if her viewpoint was tainted by her feelings for the patient.

Doug flipped off the lamp, slid down into the bed and closed his eyes. He needed sleep, but sleep eluded him that night. He couldn't stop thinking about what he'd uncovered in Macallum's notes. His mind was trying desperately to put the pieces together. They seemed to fit, but he needed a few more to fully complete the picture. He turned the light back on and grabbed the legal pad to jot down a few more notes for the morning.

1.	*Price = VP at McCline Pharmaceuticals*
2.	*McCline supplies anti-depressants and other chemical balancing drugs to the private sector.*
3.	*McCline contracts ~80% government, 20% private*
4.	*Operation Incivility???*
5.	*McCline ? Operation Incivility??*
?   Talk to Price!

Doug read over the page three or four times. Finally satisfied with his notes, he again turned off the light and laid his head down on the pillow. This time, sleep came quickly and carried him away on the slow rolling tide of exhaustion.

VII. Prescription for Terror

Hank arrived outside the estate of Dr. Martin Price with a burning in his chest. Price bore a huge part in his family's terrible history, and Hank had come to collect the debt. He blinked away the tears as he briefly remembered his grandparents, parents, and Lindsey. He tried to focus on the task at hand; this was not going to be easy. The sprawling estate stood in solitude, neighbored only by three huge Cypress trees. Separating the grounds from the rest of the world was an eight foot iron fence terminating in a huge automatic gate that guarded the front entrance. Life must be good when you were a big wig at a drug firm for the government.

Hank wasn't sure to what degree Dr. Price was still involved in McCline's daily business, if at all. *He may be retired, by the looks of this place,* Hank thought as he gazed through the heavy gate. He guided his vehicle past the house and pulled to the curb a block and half further down the road. He sat in the car for several minutes, committing the landscape of the neighborhood to memory and contemplating the day's assignment.

There were only 4 houses on the entire block, each positioned at one of the corners like brick and stone impediments. The home he'd parked in front of was for sale and there was a small placard on top of the hanging sign that read *Great Bargain!!* Hank snickered to himself. The house was probably six or seven thousand square feet; how could it be a great bargain? Across the street from Price's house was a huge Mediterranean villa with landscaping that cost more than the house Hank had grown up in. It was surrounded by a six foot stucco wall that would easily work as an obstruction to anyone's view of the scheduled activities. Finally, at the behemoth adjacent to the Price home, two men worked in the yard, mowing grass and trimming the landscape.

Everything looked pretty innocuous. Hank exited the vehicle and headed down the walk toward Price's not so humble abode.

He was careful to make note of everything and everyone (which turned out to be no one) around him. When he was directly across from the estate entrance, he stopped and lit a cigarette, leaning against the stucco wall at his back. The smoke burned his throat and lungs; it had been years since he'd given up the habit, but he needed something to help still his trembling hands. He was so nervous that he was afraid to open his mouth for fear that his teeth may chatter aloud. He looked across the street and took in all he could of the big Mediterranean's neighbor.

The Price home appeared to be empty at the moment. Hank looked up the driveway that extended from the road, through the gate, and terminating in a circle in front of the main entrance to the home. Midway between the gate and the front door was a second, smaller circle with a replica of the Trevi Fountain, one of the most famous landmarks in Rome. It was amazing, even at less than one tenth scale. It is said that if you toss a coin into the Trevi fountain, it assures your return to Rome. *I wonder if the same is true if I toss a quarter in the Price Fountain,* Hank mumbled with a crooked grin atop his pursed lips.

His eyes fell on the figure of Neptune perched atop his shell chariot, charging across the water pulled by two sea horses guided by the most masculine of tritons. He pictured himself as that proud, strong figure, finally able to end the madness that had permeated his family for three generations. Tomorrow night, he would undertake his task in earnest, eliminating the first of the integral parts of the vast and undeserved governmental plot against his family.

But would the following night be soon enough? His pursuers were still at his heels, weren't they? Hank had eluded them at Beachside Island and had yet to see them here, but he knew that it could only be a matter of time before they arrived. *What was their intent?* He didn't know and certainly had little ambition to find out. From the first day he'd noticed them, he suspected their arrival would eventually signal the end of his life. Satisfied that tomorrow would have to be soon enough, Hank finished his cigarette and headed further down the street before crossing and doubling back to find a way over the wall and into Price's domain.

Hank spent nearly ninety minutes scoping the place out. Luckily, Price appeared to be a low security guy, no rent-a-cop, no dogs, and no cameras. Hank had to assume that there would be a security system on the house itself, but that would be easy to negotiate as long as he didn't arrive too late, when the system was most likely to be on. He proceeded to look through every window he could, committing the interior landscape of the house to memory. When he finished this task, he headed out. Emboldened by his little espionage escapade, Hank decided he'd walk right out the front gate. As he passed the replica Trevi, he reached into his pocket and pulled out a shiny new quarter. As it bounced around the figure of Neptune and finally plunked into the water filled bowl at the base, he muttered, "See ya soon doc."

At the front gate, Hank scanned the area, found the keypad along the wall on the right hand side of the gate and pressed the "open" button. The gate silently began to glide open, separating in two at the center. When the gate reached the apex of its wide arc, Hank pressed the "close" button on the pad. After a second of hesitation, the two iron barred panels began to return to their previous position. Hank easily slipped between them, crossed the street and returned to his car. As he swung back into traffic and pulled away, he noticed a dark gray sedan pulled to the side at the adjacent street corner. His heart leapt and his breath caught in his throat. He almost drove onto the sidewalk as he turned to look through the back window of the car for a better view of the sedan. It was empty, but he still hit the gas and made tracks, headed to find a place to stay for the evening.

Hank sat at the small desk in the tiny hotel room and looked at the drawing he'd just completed of the Price grounds. He'd been able to identify each of the rooms on the first floor by looking through the windows and he'd filled in the unknown areas in the house with dotted lines and question marks, but he could pretty well guess what was where. He suspected that the interior of the home consisted of a formal dining area, an office or study, a bathroom, maybe two, the den, and the kitchen. He had no idea what was upstairs, but hopefully he wouldn't need to go up there. He sat back in the chair, closed his eyes and mentally went through each step of the plan for the following evening.

On the edge of the bed sat a half eaten pepperoni pizza from Domino's. Hank moved it to the desk and climbed into bed. His room at the Esquire Inn had apparently been furnished sometime in the mid seventies. But the bed was clean, and the rate was low. *Matter of fact, the sign out front advertised Rent for two nights, get one free!* Hank only intended to be here two nights, so he'd bargained with the tattooed, frizzy red haired freak show working the desk to get a twenty five percent discount off the standard rate. He prepaid his bill, sixty-one dollars cash, in case he had to leave in a hurry, which was likely based on the next day's itinerary.

Hank had already been to the big box hardware store - Lowe's or Home Depot he could never keep them straight, and gotten the required supplies. He had a plan, and knew exactly what to expect. He fell into a deep sleep almost as soon as his cheek touched the pillow.

Deep into the night, Hank awoke with a start and thought he heard a loud *Thunk!* from inside his room. He shot bolt upright and looked around the semi-dark room. He saw nothing out of the ordinary. He leaned over and switched the light on, just for good measure. Nothing. Hank got out of bed and went to the small bathroom to get a drink of water. The water from the sink tasted terrible, even worse than it smelled, which was saying something. He closed his eyes and gulped down the last of the glass.

It must have been a nightmare, Hank thought back. Yes, he had been dreaming *hadn't he?* He faintly remembered a dream of being held down and forced to do something. *What was it?* He stood in the bathroom for several minutes, searching his mind for the memory of the dream. He remembered that the scene had taken place in this very hotel room. He'd awakened with a start and tried to sit up in bed as he'd just done, but a heavy arm forced him onto his back. There were two men standing over the top of him wearing crazy Halloween masks. *What were the masks? Concentrate.* One was Freddy Krueger, the knife-fingered fiend from the Elm Street movies, and the other had been... *Bill Clinton?* Yup, the other had been the former president of the United States. He could clearly recall the two faces hovering above him now. Bill and Freddy, what a combination; tearing up the town, lady-killers for sure!

But, what were they doing in the dream hotel room with him? Hank squinted, even with his eyes already closed; trying desperately to focus on the dream, but it was gone- whisked away by the light on the wall of the dingy little hotel room. Hank opened his eyes and almost gasped at what he saw. The man in the mirror had deep, black half-moons under each of his eyes and blood red lightning bolts throughout the whites. He had a half grown beard, and his hair was an oily mess. He licked his teeth and felt his tongue move across a gritty surface not too unlike wet sandpaper.

He hadn't slept well in quite some time. As he thought back, he couldn't recall exactly when the nightmares had begun, but he knew it was sometime close to his last visit to Lindsey's grave. *How long ago had that been? A week? A month?* He couldn't remember for sure, but a couple of weeks seemed about right. Hell, it may have only been four or five days. When you were as screwed up as he felt, the days seemed to drag on for weeks.

Even with as little as he could remember about this dream, it somehow felt familiar. He closed his eyes hard and strained again to remember. *There were two dreams weren't there? Yes.* This was one of them, the dream of being forced to do…*something. What was the other?* He searched and searched his foggy memory. Hank's head pounded in time with his heart. In the other dream, *he* was the one in the midst of Operation Incivility, taking his grandfather's place. He was the one being physically and mentally tested, abused. He was the one losing his mind a little piece at a time, watching his friends and fellow soldiers being poisoned and murdered.

Hank splashed cold water across his face, wiped it off with the stained hand towel that hung on the wall and shook the images from his head. He then headed back toward the bed to try getting a little more shuteye. Instead, he lay there, staring at the ceiling and going over his plan for later that evening. It was a broken record, playing over and over in his mind until the sun started to peek through the curtains across the room. It took all the strength he had to get vertical, and Hank had to lean against the wall for a second before heading for the bathroom. Today, he would take a shower. And brush his teeth, even if it was just with soap and an index finger instead of toothbrush and toothpaste. Today was a big day and he didn't want to be too crazy looking for his appointment with the doctor. Yes, today was a big day; a day of answers, and of reckoning.

Utilizing the knowledge that he'd gained the day before, Hank easily made his way onto the Price grounds, and up to house. He stood outside the window of the study at the front of the house and waited as long as he could stand it before reaching up and sliding the window open as quietly as he could. He consulted the mental drawing of the house, the three unlocked windows circled, arrows pointing away from the circles to a note stating *Entry Points.*

Hank listened intently for any suggestion of movement and heard only the faint, garbled sound of the television, most likely coming from the den. He quickly slipped through the window and pulled it closed with a leather gloved hand. He was in the house! All was going perfectly, according to the detailed plan he'd laid out for himself. He quietly made his way across the study and into the main hall. The deep red wood floor was covered with fine Indian rugs that cost more than Hank could even guess. He was glad for the doctor's extravagant tastes; the rugs were perfect for softening his footsteps.

As he made his way through the main trunk of the house and headed toward the sound of the television, his vigilant eyes and ears searched the silence, finding nothing that piqued his sense of danger. As he cautiously moved around the corner and transitioned from the main hall into the dimly lit back hallway, he saw the flicker of white light at the end of the hall. He'd been right; the television was on in the small room. Hank padded down the hallway to the threshold of the den. He stood for several minutes outside the door, waiting and listening. His heart was racing, and it felt like it had taken up residence just below his Adam's apple. The nape of his neck was wet with sweat even though the interior of the home was a cool sixty-eight degrees.

Hank put his arm behind his back, reached under the black sweatshirt that he wore and removed the Colt 45 from his waistband. He'd loaded it before he left the hotel, so he simply switched off the safety, which sounded loud enough to *be* a gunshot in the utter silence of the home. He wanted badly to check the clip, but he silently convinced himself that it was still loaded from earlier in the day.

He held the gun up to his right cheek, closed his eyes and counted to three before stepping into the doorway of the room, thrusting the gun out before him, prepared to shoot anything or anyone that moved. Hank's jaw went slack and he nearly gasped aloud as his eyes registered the fact that there was no one in the small room, only the big bosomed blond news anchor on the evening edition, chattering away about all the lives lost in the Middle East over the past decade.

"It seems you chose the wrong house to rob tonight, bub."

The voice was coming from directly behind him and Hank knew that he was busted. He felt the heat rise and wash over him in a wave.

"Go on, drop the gun and have a seat there buddy."

Hank complied. Only when he turned to sit down was he able to look up and see his captor. He was a tall man with a heavy and deeply furrowed brow. His hair was dark as night and held in place by a slathering of hair care products. Were it not for his eyes and the deep lines in his face, the man would have looked twenty years younger.

"Obviously, you don't know who you're fucking with, young man. You can't break into *MY* house, sneak around and try to pull a gun on *ME*. You see, that just won't do. So now, the question is: What do we do now? Or more appropriately, what do *I* do?"

He said nothing else for several minutes.

Hank opened his mouth more than once to try giving Price one lame excuse or another for his actions, but decided better of it each time and just sat in the leather armchair with his lips firmly pressed together and his eyes on Price. As if on queue, the man spoke again.

"Fuck it. I'm just going to kill you. You're trespassing on private property *and* carrying a gun. You have no rights here. Besides, I'm obviously doing it in self defense."

He raised the barrel of the small gun and pointed it at Hank's head. This was it, his only chance to get out of this alive. Instead of just sitting there, waiting to die, Hank dove and tackled Price. There wasn't even a shot fired. In less than twenty seconds, Hank had pinned Price to the floor and sat on his chest, knees firmly pressed against the man's shoulders. He'd knocked the gun out of Price's hand and had retrieved it himself during the abbreviated tussle. Now, he pointed it directly between Price's eyes.

During the short struggle, a government issued Gray Ford sedan pulled to the curb outside the walls of the Price Estate. Special Agent Doug Stunkle killed the lights and sat quietly, looking through the passenger window at the big house that sat within those fancy iron gates at the front of the grounds. He could see several lights on in the house, but saw no movement through the windows. Joseph Pratt was here tonight, Doug could feel it deep in the marrow of his bones. He had not a shred of evidence to prove it, but he knew it just the same.

Doug got out of the car and made his way up to the house. There was no one there to work the gate, but he noticed a speaker to the left of the gate. He pressed the "Call" button, heard the beep and waited for a response. *Nothing.* Doug's heart rate doubled. He pressed the button again, acknowledging the same beep with a nod and waited for a response. *Still nothing. It had to be Joseph. He was in the house with Price. Had to be! What was he doing?*

Doug headed down the walk and found a spot where he could scale the fence. After dropping down on the inside, Doug made his way up to the house and started checking the windows. He made it around the house quickly until he came to the bay windows of the den. The curtains were pulled, but light flickered from behind them and he could see two distinct shadows in the room; one standing, and the other kneeling.

Doug raced back around to the front of the house and tried the front door. To his surprise, it was unlocked. He rapidly but quietly made his way through the house and toward the back room that was the den. As he got close, he heard three voices. The first was the high pitched voice of a woman recounting the day's stock markets movements. The second was the loud, agitated voice of Joseph Pratt. The final was the quiet, but determined voice of Dr. Martin Price, refusing to answer the questions that Joseph fired at him in rapid succession.

Doug didn't sense that Price was in danger yet, so he waited outside the room to get a better understanding for the cause of the showdown. It was difficult to follow the conversation over the news anchor's voice on the television, but it was obvious that Price had seriously wronged Joseph Pratt, who was here to exact his revenge after he got whatever information he was after.

Doug stood with his back against the wall just outside the study for several minutes as the Q&A session in the room heated to the point of boiling.

"Fuck you, you piece of shit!" came a shout from Joseph. "I've had enough of your bullshit. I'm going to send you straight to hell where you belong!"

Before Hank could pull the trigger and put a bullet into Price, the FBI agent stepped around the doorframe and into the room, his gun extended, pointing directly into Hank's back. Doug saw the doctor kneeling at the man's feet. His glasses hung awkwardly from one of his ears, and a fresh, red line of blood traced a path from his eyebrow, down his cheek and neck, terminating in a dark spot on his shirt collar. He looked terrified.

"Hold it right there Joseph Anton Pratt. Don't move." His voice was loud and firm. The figure before him went as rigid as a steel beam.

"FBI! Drop your weapon and get on your knees with your hands behind your back. Doctor Price, are you okay?"

Only after the heavy handgun clattered on the wood floor did the doctor nod sheepishly and slide away from the man hovering above him. He regained his feet and stepped aside as the man slowly knelt and put his fisted hands to his back. As he stood back and took in the scene, a confused look creeping across his face.

At that very moment, there was a thunderous crash in the front hall as the main door was blasted off its hinges and a squad of six men covered head to shoe in black streamed through the busted doorway and made a beeline for the study.

"What the hell?" Doug said aloud, turning toward the hallway, only to be greeted by the ski masked men. Before he could speak, he was knocked to the floor by the leader of the group and everything went black as the butt end of a machine gun crashed against his temple.

Price leapt for cover behind the wingback chair that Hank had been sitting in just a few minutes earlier. It had been knocked over during their scuffle and lay sideways between the wall and door. He didn't see what happened next, but he heard the crashing of glass and the roar of six machine guns dispensing death in rapid succession.

Pow, pow, pow, pow. Pow, pow, pow, pow.... Then, silence.

Price arose from behind the chair and looked around. The men were gone, apparently having vanished though the broken window. Only he and the FBI man were left in the room together. He looked at the wall at the end of the room and the square hole that previously held the room's only window. The wall was littered with what seemed to be a million bullet holes. There were wood splinters and broken glass on the floor in front of the missing window and a trail of shell casings running the length of the room. The old man walked across the room to the window and looked out. It was fully dark now and he saw no sign of the men. He listened for them, but heard nothing indicating their whereabouts or activity.

Dr. Price crossed the room and sat down in the wingback chair that still stood upright, letting out a long winded sigh of relief. He knew that this evening could have ended badly for him. He'd been very lucky. He waited for the FBI man to wake from his little nap. He knew there would be questions to be answered on both sides when the man awoke....

VIII. Raising the Stakes

The situation room was overflowing with agents, supervisors, and department heads. The room was hot with the body heat of the nearly fifty CIA men and women crammed shoulder to shoulder in the conference room. The air in the room was thick and stale; a sense of dread hanging like a rain cloud just below the ceiling. There was a low grade buzz of conversation that filled the room and drifted out into the hallway. An agent lined tunnel formed slowly as the National Security Advisor made his way through the door and headed to the front of the room followed closely by the Director of the Central Intelligence Agency and the Director of the Washington office of the Counter Terrorist Unit.

When it came to big wigs, this was about as big as it got, so everyone that could justify being involved in the briefing had gotten themselves invited. Few people in the office had worked directly with the local CTU director; the DCIA always commanded an audience, and the National Security Advisor reported directly to the President. This was a power meeting of the highest order. As the National Security Advisor reached the front of the room, a blanket of silence fell over the group.

"People, I'm here on direct assignment from the President this morning. He sends his greetings and complements each of you on the outstanding job you do every day keeping our country safe. I won't rehash the facts of our situation since we don't know much yet and I'm sure everyone has gotten the story at the water cooler. Instead, I just wanted to let everyone know that while your DCIA will be heading up the investigation directly, I will be overseeing everything from a small workspace just down the hall."

Several of the agents exchanged glances and smiles at this comment. Many of them had noticed the "small workspace" down the hall, which was actually a situation room about half the size of this one, yet double the size of the DCIA's office.

"In addition, Homeland Security will be on apprised of progress or concerns as they arise. I know I speak for my organization as well as CTU and Homeland when I say that you have our complete and unwavering support as well as the full complement of our resources at your disposal. With that said, I'm going to turn it over to Will who will give you the critical pieces of what we know and issue assignments. Thanks for your attention and remember: we don't know the extent of what we're dealing with yet. We need to bring this to a close as quickly as possible. In short, we need each of you at your very best until this business has concluded."

William Amblin Jr. now stepped to the center of the table at the head of the room. He'd been a member of the CIA for over twenty years, his previous experience coming as a member of the Federal Bureau of Investigation, which was a very unique combination and made him an extremely valuable asset. In addition, the CIA was in Will's blood, so to speak. He was the only DCIA in history who'd taken the reigns directly from his father.

Many of the agents in the room had served under Will's father, Big Bill as he'd been so oft called and admired. And Will had continued the legacy of strong leadership; he'd gained the respect of every person in the agency through hard work, determination, and his strong sense of moral judgment. The agency had regained the bulk of public's trust under his watch, and it was certainly not by accident. They'd prevented multiple terrorist attacks and captured or killed most of the Al Qaida leaders under his direction. His contacts within the FBI had proven invaluable during his tenure as DCIA as well.

"As you well know, it is highly irregular for an investigation of this scope and importance to be headed up by someone who is directly affected. However, I've been granted the conditional role based on my intimate knowledge of the victim and experience in this type of case while I served in the FBI's missing persons unit."

Will was visibly shaken, but seemed to be keeping it together fairly well. He paused and looked down at his hands, planted firmly on the desk as he leaned over it slightly.

"As many of you know, my wife was abducted last night while she was out with friends at the Performing Arts Theater. We have very little in the way of leads. According to eye witnesses, someone killed the power to the theater at approximately 8:45 pm and pulled the fire alarm minutes later, just before 9:00. The theater's backup generators had been disconnected and the theater was plunged into complete darkness.

Eleven of the evening's patrons, including one of Di…ahh my wife's closest friends were trampled to death in the confusion that ensued and countless others were injured. When the lighting was restored, everyone that escaped had gone home. The list of the victims did not include my wife and local authorities were able to locate all the other ticket holders except her this morning.

As you might imagine, we were unable to recover any significant, useful, physical evidence at the theater. However, a ransom note, of sorts, arrived via mail carrier this morning. My wife's abductor has asked only for a private meeting with me, of which I am inclined to oblige if we can determine the sincerity of his intentions and institute the proper security protocols to ensure the safe return of my spouse. That's all we have for now. I appreciate everyone's eagerness to help, but we simply cannot utilize everyone at this time. If I call your name, report to Situation Room Three at the close of this meeting. Questions anyone?"

There was a flurry of questions of which the DCIA was either unable or unwilling to answer and then he called the "Lucky 7," as they were later deemed and the meeting finally dissolved into a disembodied crackle of voices and motion. When the room finally cleared, there were several agents at the front with Amblin trying desperately, if unsuccessfully, to get assigned to the case. With one final wave of his hands, the exasperated Director of the Central Intelligence Agency walked away from the men, his head down and his face stony.

Several hundred miles away, Doug Stunkel sat at his desk staring at his computer screen. He blinked hard and then refocused on the sea of paperwork strewn across his desktop. He'd been so close to apprehending Pratt without incident; he just couldn't believe what had happened. Just as he was about to cuff him, a team of commandoes ruined the whole thing, shot up Price's house and allowed Pratt to escape. He'd been knocked unconscious and by the time he awoke, Pratt and the commando team were long gone.

Doug had grilled Price about the commandoes, but the old man seemed to be as much in the dark as he was. He'd also questioned the doctor at length about Operation Incivility. He got little information from him other than a repeated refrain of "I'm sorry, but that's classified." Doug considered himself a pretty good judge of character and after less than an hour with him, he considered the man an ass of the highest magnitude. He seemed to take pleasure in his ability to shut Doug down without giving him even the smallest nugget of information that he could use in his investigation.

The very fact that Joseph made an attempt on the man's life confirmed that the operation had some bearing on Joseph's actions. *But why?* If he only knew the answer to that question, he might be able to ascertain Joseph's next move and catch up to or outflank him. Doug heard the familiar shuffle of loafers and looked up to see Al leaning against the gray metal door frame.

"Hear anything else from the CIA?"

Doug shook his head. Since the break in at Price's, there had been two other significant developments in the case. The first was another murder, a retired general who'd been stationed in the South Pacific during World War II. Al hadn't been able to extract his specific duties from the military, but he was able to tie him to Operation Incivility. General Robert Wadnesku had been shot twice at point blank range while woodworking in the garage his Southern Carolina retirement home. The murder weapon was a Colt 45; the same make and model that had been identified in the Monroe-Pratt case.

The second was the kidnapping of the wife of the Director of the CIA. When Doug had seen the news story on CNN, he immediately knew that it was connected to his case. Joseph was upping the ante. He was trying to get an audience at a level that would be able to react to his agenda, whatever it may be. As a missing persons case, the FBI should have been given jurisdiction in the case but they hadn't. The CIA was heading the investigation and the DCIA was in charge. Doug had been able to get an initial meeting to go over his findings with the CIA, but they were too "overburdened" to be able to act on any of the information in the files. Instead, they listened, seized his work and sent him on his way with an empty promise to "keep him in the loop." *Wow; it must be a pretty big loop because they hadn't made it back around to him yet.*

"Hey Doug, I was reviewing your reports to Millie for possible connections that we may have missed and I was wondering, why don't you ever refer to him as his real name, Joseph Pratt? You always have him in there as one of his aliases."

"I don't want to give Millie too much just yet." Doug explained. "And I've got to keep an ace in my pocket for dealing with the CIA later. You know - a little insurance policy."

Doug smiled half heartedly, but there was no optimism behind it and the smile quickly faded. Al followed with a simple "Oh," and headed back out into the stacks to search for other connections between the cases. Before he made his second step, he turned back around and stuck his head back into the office.

"How'd you ever get that exhumation order signed anyway?" He asked. "That was a pretty good piece of work."

Doug looked up and again smiled weakly. "I can't give away all my secrets Al. Let's just say I'm highly influential."

Al knew that Doug had signed the order; he just didn't know how he got it past the Medical Examiner. And he didn't like all the mystery that suddenly surrounded this case; rarely was Doug this secret. Al shook it off and headed back to the stacks, hoping to find something that would blow the case open.

At six o'clock sharp the following evening, Will Amblin strode into Clifton's, a high dollar steak and seafood restaurant where the food was first class, the service was consistently excellent, the wine was of the finest vintage, and you could still order cigars at the table - Cubans if you were a regular. He passed through the piano bar at the front of the restaurant and strode up to the Maitre'd.

"I believe the other member of my party has already arrived. Ahhh, Smith please."

The Maitre'd led him across the restaurant to a table where a middle aged man with a bad rug and mustache sat waiting patiently. The man wore slacks and a sport coat with a pressed, blue Oxford button down underneath. Amblin slid into the chair across from him, but said nothing. It was obvious that the man was trying to disguise his appearance. After a long silence, the man spoke, a regrettable expression painted on his face.

"I'm very sorry sir, but your wife..."

He didn't get a chance to finish his statement before Amblin was across the table and on top of him, pounding his jaw line with his fists, accusations and profanity streaming from his lips. The man was pinned on his back, his arms flailing aimlessly beneath the beating that he was receiving. Suddenly, a swarm of

CIA agents were at Amblin's side, pulling him off of the bloodied man trapped below him.

"The son of a bitch kidnapped and killed my wife…" Amblin explained to his men.

One of the agents stepped forward and pulled the man off the floor, handcuffed him, and carried him out of the restaurant with the help of a second agent. Amblin gathered himself up, straightened his suit coat and shirt, and began to wipe the blood from his fists with a napkin he picked up from the floor. Several agents still gathered around him but said nothing, fully understanding the gravity of the situation. No one dared question the DCIA's decision to pummel the man who'd abducted and murdered his beloved wife.

As they turned to leave, Amblin's cell phone beeped. He absentmindedly grabbed it and looked at the screen.

1 NEW TEXT MESSAGE
READ?

He pushed the "YES" button and read the message. His heart sank and he felt the warm, sharp blade of recognition rip his gut.

IF YOU WANT TO SEE HER AGAIN, SEND THEM AWAY. I WILL CALL YOU WHEN THEY ARE GONE.

From the very back of the room, Hank watched as Amblin spoke quietly to the men around him. None of them looked around, or gave any indication that Amblin had clued them in on the message. The men all nodded and turned to leave. Amblin righted his chair at the table and sat back down. Hank let him stew for several minutes before calling. Finally, he dialed the number and Amblin answered immediately. Hank directed him to his table and hung up just as Amblin bent to sit across the table from him.

The fury in Amblin's face had dissipated and was now replaced by regret and concern. He realized that he'd been bested and that he was now on this man's turf, and without back up.

"So is it really you, or is this another ruse?" He spit sarcastically.

Hank looked directly into Amblin's eyes. He expected to see hate and disdain, but was surprised to see only desperation.

"It's me. I paid the man you attacked $500 to dress up, sit at that table, provoke you, and then let you beat the shit out of him. It really is amazing what people will do for a few dollars."

"But he said my wife was dead." Amblin said with a confused look on his face.

"No, you didn't let him finish. He was saying that your wife would not be able to make it to dinner. He had no idea of the circumstances; he knew only that you were going to be royally pissed off when you found out that she wasn't going to be able to meet you."

Hank smiled, please with himself for properly orchestrating the deception to ensure a private meeting with Amblin. Before he could say any more, the waiter came over to take their order.

"I'll have the number nineteen crab cake appetizer with the number twenty seven filet, number six baked potato, and a bottle of your best red. What would you like Bill, since it's on your tab?"

The waiter turned to Amblin, who just waived him off. He turned back to Hank and said, "I'm sorry sir, but the numbers on the menu aren't for the entrees, they're the prices. The menu at Clifton's is ala carte."

"In that case, I'll also have the number fourteen Turtle Cheesecake." Hank said without a hesitation.

The waiter nodded without looking up or replying. He looked to the ceiling as he strode away from the table, appealing to the heavens for saving from these stupendously uncouth customers.

"Okay, here's the story Mr. Amblin. Your wife is safe and sound. As a matter of fact, she's been staying the last few days and nights at a certain upscale hotel chain downtown. I'll release her under only one condition. I want retribution for crimes committed against my family over the last 40 years. In addition, I want you to call off the goons that have been following me for the last several weeks."

A look of utter shock spread across Amblin's face. He'd expected this to come down to money, as almost all kidnappings do. This guy actually believed *he* was the victim. Will couldn't believe it. It took him several seconds to reply.

"I don't know what you're talking about." Amblin said flatly.

For the next twenty minutes, Hank quickly went through the story with Amblin, who seemed to be confounded by it, with one exception. Amblin's demeanor changed when he mentioned Price. It was obvious that the DCIA was unaware of Operation Incivility or any plot to either capture or kill Hank; however, Amblin openly admitted that the CIA had worked with Dr. Martin Price and his firm on multiple occasions. Further, he told Hank that he and his staff had a meeting scheduled with Price in the coming week. Hank asked to be present and Amblin immediately refused. He obviously wanted to confirm Hank's story before he would do anything. Hank had expected that a man of his stature and position would. When he was done, he looked the DCIA directly in the face.

"So, do we have an understanding then?" Hank asked.

"I assure you that I will use the power vested in me to investigate what you have told me today and verify it's authenticity in exchange for my wife's safe return. I can promise nothing more at this point."

They were both silent for several minutes as Hank's wine and the appetizer arrived.

"Oh, the story's authentic; I can assure you of that. And you'll keep this matter completely confidential until you've made your determination? I have your word?"

Amblin nodded. "My word," he said solidly.

"Call home." Hank said as he got up to leave, grabbing the bottle of wine by the neck.

"What?"

"Call home." Hank repeated and briskly headed for the front of the restaurant. He passed two agents as they exited their dark blue Crown Vic and headed into the restaurant in search of their leader.

As the men approached the DCIA, they recognized the tears in his eyes as he held the phone away from his ear ever so slightly and responded to the "I love you's" traveling across the open cellular line.

IX. Flights to Catch

Doug Stunkel and Al Cauhall rode the elevator up from the lobby of McCline Pharmaceuticals to the thirty second floor. As they did, they reviewed their plan one final time. As simple as it was, Doug hoped it would prove to be equally effective. They knew that Dr. Price was "out on business." Thanks to an ingenious call from Al to McCline, they'd been able to ascertain that Price was in fact still very involved in the business. He still had an office, a personal assistant, and kept a fairly busy schedule. Donna, Price's PA, had refused to give even a hint of Price's business dealings or whereabouts.

Al had checked all the airline passenger manifests for all flights leaving the two local airports over the past week and came up empty. That meant Price was flying on a private carrier, quite possibly a McCline Pharmaceuticals business jet. With private planes and private landing facilities, it was much more difficult to track the movements of someone like Price, especially if he wanted to be transparent.

Al stepped aside and leaned against the plate glass windows of the hall while Doug entered the office of Dr. Marten Price's personal assistant and proceeded to "raise a stink" as he so aptly called it. He smiled as he listened to Doug roar away at the poor assistant, who in no way deserved the treatment she was getting. Just a few seconds later, the two emerged from the PA's office, she spewing apologies and Doug insisting on seeing someone of equal or higher rank than Price.

As they walked down the hall, Al slipped into the office, tapped a few keys on the PA's keyboard and quickly accessed Price's schedule and itinerary. He clicked the "Print" button, grabbed the laser printed page and headed back out into the hall. After a few tense moments at the glass, Al saw Doug emerge from an office down the hall and he headed for the elevator. Doug arrived just as the elevator doors were about to close and stuck his arm through, holding the car for himself. Al said nothing as he handed the printout over to Doug.

Doug scanned the document and found the current date. It simply said:

Travel to Langley for meeting with Amblin.

The next day had one line in the box also.

Review Project Mind Trap – CIA HQTRS.

"I'll be damned. Good work Captain." Doug said, patting Al on the back roughly.

"Captain – that's a new one." Al returned. "But, I don't drink Captain Morgan."

"That's all right Al, you don't drink half the shit I call you. Come 'on, we gotta go."

Doug looked out the window of the plane and watched the clouds drift by outside. Al had been crushed that Doug had refused to bring him along to CIA Headquarters, but he hadn't argued. Doug felt bad for not being able to fulfill Al's curiosity, but he couldn't afford for him to get in the way. This had to be handled the correct way. It had to be handled quickly and quietly; too much was at stake. In the argument, Doug had touched on the *Bible Slasher* case and how dangerous it had been for Al who finally had agreed to return to the Springfield office "for his own safety."

X. Coming Together

The Marble Hall extended far above the security officer's head, terminating in a glass barreled ceiling at its height. The very sight of The Hall was inspiring beyond words. His mission was almost complete, and he couldn't think of a more appropriate place for it to conclude than CIA Headquarters. He watched the gray clouds gather in the sky through the clear roof.

"Sir, I need to see your ID." The guard repeated, breaking Hank out of his reverie.

"Oh, sorry. This is my first time to HQ," he responded while handing over the ID badge he'd just received from his contact the previous day.

The man quickly scrutinized the ID, looked up to see Hank removing his sidearm and looked back at the ID to confirm he'd been approved to carry a firearm within the building. He handed the ID back, logged the gun in a book on the counter and returned it to Hank with a smile.

"Colt forty-five," He said. "A classic."

"I'm a classic kind of guy." Hank replied as he re-holstered the weapon and entered the main hall. He walked over to the receptionist's station in the center. It was horseshoe shaped and fashioned from marble, with a black granite top. Behind it, three chairs, three computer screens, and three attractive, if nondescript, women talked into headsets and punched buttons on their keyboards with the momentum of dueling freight trains. They were impressively succinct in their conversations and the calls were answered and transferred before Hank even realized that they'd switched from one call to another. He leaned on the counter and waited patiently for one of the young ladies to look up. The brunette to his right finally did.

"Can I help you Mr. ..."

"Marin... Hank Marin. I'm due for a meeting with Dr. Martin Price, Director Amblin, and a host of others and unbelievably, I left my agenda at the hotel. Could you please tell me which room we're in?"

The young lady cocked her head ever so slightly and a confused look crossed her face. Hank's heart leapt into his throat. *He'd been found out already; and by a receptionist!*

"It looks to me like you forgot more than your agenda Mr. Marin. Would you like a pad and pen for notes?"

Hank could feel the color rise in his cheeks. Before he could respond, she'd produced a yellow legal pad and pen from somewhere behind the desk and set them atop the heavy, black counter at Hank's hands.

"It's okay; I can tell a new guy when I see one. But you owe me, and I'll remember."

Hank gave the young receptionist a smile and grabbed the pad and pen. He felt an icy bolt of lightning strike him as he remembered the yellow sheet of paper that he'd found in his grandfather's file; the file that George McClory had risked, and maybe given his life for. *Had it been CIA?* No way of knowing for sure.

"Conference Room 3B," said the receptionist. "Up the elevator behind me and back down the hall toward the front of the building. You can't miss it."

"Oh. Thanks." Hank replied, already heading in the direction of the elevator bank.

"I take payment for IOU's in Starbucks, just so you know. Black with a drop of honey and nutmeg," the receptionist called after Hank.

He didn't respond; he had payback on his mind, but it certainly didn't involve his new receptionist friend. As the elevator rose to the third floor, Hank pitched the pad and pen into the corner of the elevator and steeled himself for the inevitable confrontation that was about to occur. He leaned his head back and rolled it from side to side, the bones of his upper vertebrae popping loudly in the confined space. Out of nervousness, he felt beneath his sport coat for the Colt, still holstered safely at his side. The elevator dinged, the doors slid open and Hank emerged on rubber legs. His heart beat heavily in his chest. He walked down the hallway until he found the plaque labeled 3B.

He looked down the hall in both directions, and saw no one. Closing his eyes, he listened intently for voices wafting from the room, but he heard none. Surely, the meeting was already underway.

Hank took several minutes to gather his courage and then with one final breath, he burst through the doors, prepared to charge the front of the room and strangle Price with his bare hands. Within the conference room, eight men of varying age and stature sat around the oversized conference room table and a huge projector screen displayed the faces of three more men, obviously at a different location. Their eyes all shifted to him from Price, who stood at the front of the room, just to the side of the projector screen. Hank had never seen a picture so clear and bright from an overhead projector and the bizarre scene stopped him in his tracks.

All at once, the suits rose from their seats and applauded. Bewildered looks covered many of their faces and they repeatedly looked back and forth from Hank to Price and back again.

"That is impressive," someone at the table exclaimed.

"I've never seen anything like it," someone else echoed.

Still others continued the refrain. "Incredible. Unbelievable. Outstanding."

Hank had no idea what was going on. He was shell shocked. His legs went from a feeling of Jell-O to the weight of cement. He couldn't move; he was as still as a statue at the end of the table.

"Welcome, Subject Fourteen." Price said to him. Then to the room, "As I was saying Gentlemen, this project has been underway for well over thirty years, adapting, changing, morphing to include a much more ambitious scope. But we've accomplished our mission. Today is a day of achievement and celebration."

Hank stared at Price, his mouth agape. *What the hell was going on?* He wanted desperately to ask, but his jaw was slack and he couldn't seem to find the words to form a proper sentence.

"Fourteen, you look confused. Have a seat, and I'll fill you in."

Hank didn't move a muscle.

"Well, suit yourself; stand if you like. You see, Operation Incivility didn't stop with your feeble minded grandfather and his squad. In fact, that was just the dawning of the project. We've advanced this venture by dramatic leaps over just your lifetime. I must say, it truly is amazing to see the progress we've made since Incivility. Today was the final piece of the operation, if you will; the final step for Project Mindtrap. Both of your grandparents, your father, you, and one of your siblings have been unwitting participants in our little experiment. You see, this kind of research simply can't be done in a lab. It *must* be conducted in the field; that's the only way to obtain accurate data. That was the key that eventually led to today. Lab rats are good for some testing, but not the likes of this. Mind Control? We know we can control the minds of simple rodents without even exerting ourselves. But subverting free will; now that's an accomplishment of the highest order.

We've had failure after failure, but this time… This time we knocked it out of the park, so to speak. We broke the code. No more losses; this time we found the magic."

The last statement from Price broke Hank from his trance.

"What do you mean no more losses? You used my family members as test subjects and then cut them loose when they no longer served your purposes? You killed them?"

Price's eyes fell on Hank with a look of utter disdain.

"The termination of the other subjects, though unfortunate, was necessary to bring us to this day, to bring you to this point."

Hank was still confused, "What point?" He asked.

A smile crept over Prices face. This was his big finale. The chance he'd been waiting for all his life.

"You were programmed Subject Fourteen. Over the course of the last thirty years, my team and I have used a variety of techniques to program you to do exactly as instructed. Obviously, we can't control your every action, but we can do enough. We can direct your actions in order that you will complete specific objectives over the course of weeks, months, even years, when necessary. Your programming will override your own personal objectives. It will even override your sense of justice and morality. You will unfailingly accomplish whatever goal we set for you."

Hank thought of the dreams. The men in the masks; *they weren't dreams at all, they were real.* He suddenly remembered what they forced him to do; to breathe from a mask tethered to a tank of some kind. They were using some kind of gas to control his mind, allowing them to make hypnotic suggestions and control his actions.

"The gas," Hank muttered.

"Yes, the gas, among other things. You see, we used your whole life's circumstances to program you. We cultivated the paranoia that was passed down to you from your grandparents. We even added a few of our own touches, and whaala! A perfect mind slave!"

Hank's head was swimming. The pieces were now snapping into place. *That's why he never really knew why he was so paranoid of people and the different circumstances of his life. Why he couldn't seem to control himself sometimes.*

"The journal?" Hank spoke in a low voice, almost to himself, seemingly afraid to ask aloud.

"A fabrication. Operation Incivility was real enough, and it was very similar in scope to the description in the journal; however, the journal itself was but another tool to put you on the path." Price boasted proudly.

"George…"

"Planted."

"The men following me, they weren't after me; they were just tracking my movements?"

"...And administering the necessary pharmaceuticals."

"Lindsey..."

"That was an unfortunate and unforeseen turn of events. But we understand our mistake and have taken the necessary precautions to prevent such a sequence from recurring."

Hank looked from Price to the faces gathered around the table. They ranged from skepticism to astonishment to downright horror.

"You son of a bitch!" Hank screamed as he pulled the Colt from its holster and extended it toward Price. The look of shock and terror immediately conveyed that Price had expected Hank to barge into the meeting, but hardly anticipated he'd be armed; a miscalculation that would be his last.

Hank let out a guttural howl as he repeatedly fired the weapon until the clip was empty, but Hank's finger continued to flex and the gun never wavered. Click, click, click...

FBI agent Doug Stunkel heard gun shots and screaming as he exited the elevator. He sprinted down the hall, flung the doors open and burst into the conference room. The eyes of everyone in the room immediately shifted to him. The only faces that he recognized were that of Director of the CIA, William Amblin Jr. and Dr. Martin Price. He'd never met the DCIA, but Will was somewhat of a legend within *both* the CIA and the FBI. He had his detractors, but they were far outweighed by supporters.

Dr. Price lay on his back below the hanging projector screen. The carpet beneath him was already stained in a pool of reddish brown and a million red dots traced bright red pen strokes down the huge screen above him. The men all waited for the FBI man to make a move, terrified of the man holding the Colt forty-five, still pulling the trigger in perfect rhythm, his eyes dark and empty. Click, click, click...

Doug walked away from the door and over to Hank. He gently pried the weapon from his clenched fingers and pulled one of the conference room chairs up behind him.

"Joseph, I want you to sit down and don't move. Sit right here," he said as he guided him into the chair.

Hank looked at Doug with eyes that were unfocused and far away. He continued to look at Doug curiously as he sat in the chair, as if searching his face for something. Doug looked intently into his eyes and repeated.

"Joseph, I need you to stay seated right where you are. Do you understand?"

Hank nodded; his eyes glassy, but focused on Doug.

Doug turned back to the front of the room and made his way toward the screen and Price. Amblin had already moved over to him and was checking his vitals. Doug didn't need confirmation from the DCIA; the man's gunshot riddled chest and torso declared his fate. Doug walked back over to Joseph and put a hand on his shoulder.

"Is everyone okay?" He asked to the men in the room.

Everyone nodded, including the three on the screen, hundreds, maybe even thousands, of miles away. Doug turned back to Joseph.

"Joseph, I'm going to have to ask you to come with me, and wear these."

The FBI agent produced a pair of stainless steel handcuffs and clasped them around Joseph's wrists, who made no move to stop him. Doug led the cuffed man out of the conference room, down the hall and out to his car. Only when he had Joseph secured in the back seat of the Impala that he'd borrowed from the local field office did he head back up toward the building. He heard sirens in the distance, probably the local PD and an ambulance. *No need for them now*, he thought to himself.

XI. Last Ride

They never even called him by his name. *Why was that?* They certainly all knew it. For Christ's sake, they'd been chasing him nearly his entire adult life. They should know everything there was to know about him. It was almost as if they needed to disassociate him from his name, from his humanity. *It would be easier that way wouldn't it?* That way they could hunt him down like an animal, using whatever means necessary. Animals didn't have rights, and neither did he, at least not in their eyes. He looked out the window and reflected. It was like a dream, almost real, but somehow just a little off key.

The weather seemed only to enhance the dreamlike quality that the day had taken as its mantle. A light fog still hung in the streets and the temperature was unseasonably cool. The breeze carried with it a chill that complemented the day perfectly. The fog muted the entire cityscape and even the bright colored song of the trees lining the street was hushed on this day. It was like interacting with the world through a hazy, gray filter. For at least this day, the whole town of Langley, Virginia wore the mystique of the CIA headquarters, and he felt as if he was being smothered by it.

How could it possibly end this way? In all the years that he'd dreamed of how this chase might conclude, he'd never envisioned anything remotely like this. He looked out the window of the FBI owned sedan and found that he could not take his eyes off of the mildly ornate building that housed the many branches of the Central Intelligence Agency. He saw the FBI man standing below the huge glass arch that hung over the entrance of the massive building, still talking with a group of CIA men and wondered what their conversation may have been about. He knew that he would likely never know, and it was probably in his best interest if he didn't, but that didn't stop the curiosity from gnawing a hole in him either.

He looked down at the bright reflective steel cuffs that held his hands fast. He'd been within the walls of one of the most powerful organizations in the world today. He'd also been in the presence of several of its most powerful men, although it certainly could have been under better circumstances. And now, it was all over. He'd made it through the ordeal alive, but not without the emotional and physical scars that would forever be a reminder of the journey. There had been many times when he thought he'd not make it this far with his life intact, including several this very day. He wondered what was next for him and regretted that he had no choice in the matter. Finally, one of the CIA men passed a thin black attaché to his captor, who then made his way back to the vehicle. The dark suited man slid into the front seat without a sound, glanced back at him and started the engine. As the car pulled away from the compound, his heart pounded quietly in his chest and his mind raced. He needed to know what was going to happen next. He opened his mouth to ask the FBI man, but then closed it again; afraid he couldn't bear the answer.

He had so many questions. *What were they talking about, standing up there? Had Amblin weighed in on the final decision? Was he going straight to jail, or worse?*

The car's engine hummed as they pulled away from CIA headquarters. Hank turned and looked out the back window of the Impala at the front entrance. There were three black and whites and one ambulance parked in front of the building, lights still flashing; sirens now silent. He closed his eyes hard against the memories of all the flashing lights he'd seen in his life. There was so much pain; it weighed on him like a heavy overcoat. He let his head sink, leaned over his knees and sobbed silently; sobbed for his family, for Lindsey, and for himself. He rubbed the tears away roughly with the back of his shackled hands.

"Wow, you really did a number on Price in there, didn't you?" the FBI man called from the front seat.

Hank didn't know how to respond. Was this feeby trying to get a confession out of him? Did he really need one? The room had been full of witnesses including the director of the CIA. Hank chose silence as the best response.

"You don't even recognize me do you?"

Again, silence. They'd made it to the Interstate and the car drifted over to the shoulder. Once parked safely off the road, the FBI man turned around and looked directly at his confused vehicle companion.

"You don't. Joe, it's me, Jeff."

Hank felt the blossom of warmth in his chest. He couldn't believe it. The FBI man had seemed familiar, but he hadn't been able to place him earlier. Hell, it had been so long since he had last seen either of his brothers; they were still both kids when he'd left home.

"Ohmaaagod… Jeff, I can't believe it's really you. How did you… " Hank trailed off. He couldn't believe his youngest brother was actually sitting in the front seat of the car.

"I'm FBI Joe; out of the Springfield office. I go by Doug now, well Douglas. Douglas Jefferey Stunkel. When I submitted my paperwork, a friend of mine in the bureau suggested that I change my name to avoid any negative light from our family history. They still figured it out eventually, but I had proven myself in the interviews and pre-hire training, so it wasn't an issue."

Hank couldn't believe what he was seeing or hearing. He was overjoyed to see his brother for the first time in over twenty years. His emotions swirled in him like a hurricane. Fear, sorrow, joy, bewilderment, he couldn't keep track of his feelings and quickly stopped trying. Instead, he let the tears flow, unconcerned from where they were borne.

Doug got out of the car, let Hank out of the back seat, and released his cuffs. He was immediately enfolded in a bear hug embrace by his big brother. As they broke apart, Hank looked at the FBI man through wet, bloodshot eyes. A great deal of concern still showed in his face.

"So what happens now little brother? You taking me to jail? I deserve it, and worse. Jeff, I've done some horrendous things in my time; things no man should ever do. And I wouldn't dare ask you to risk your job by letting me go. I'm just glad to see you, spend even a little time with you - you know, with blood. I've been alone and on the run for so long... I can't remember what it's like to be part of a family. Whatever your decision, I can live with it; I only ask that you don't orphan me. Don't leave me behind."

Doug leaned in through the window of the vehicle and grabbed the black attaché that the CIA men had given him back at headquarters. He passed it to Hank, who reluctantly accepted it.

"Inside this case, you will find everything you need to start your new life. You are no longer Joseph Pratt, or Hank Marin, or any of the other personas that you've gone by in the past. Your new name is Stephen Phoenix of Boulder, Colorado.

There is banking information and a little starting cash. It's really not all that much for what you've been through, but it'll have to do. There's also a pardon for the murder of Dr. Martin Price. The Mathis, Bergdolt, Trasker, and Wadnesku cases will be closed as unsolved."

When Doug mentioned Wadnesku, Hank stiffened noticeably, but said nothing. Doug continued, moving forward at a slow, deliberate pace.

"The one stipulation is this: you must keep your nose clean from here out. You don't have to hide, but don't give them a new reason to catch up to you either. If you do, you'll be in violation of your pardon and our deal. Both the CIA and FBI will come down on you heavy, and I *won't* be able to help. Truth be known, they'll probably be checking in on you from time to time just to be sure they've made the right choice. Do you understand the deal?"

Hank nodded.

"Any questions?"

"Just one," he said. "What's the story with Wadnesku? I didn't kill him."

Now it was Doug's turn to look confused. He thought back and finally his face went from a snarled look of bewilderment to a subtle smirk.

"That would be Price's way of gift wrapping you for a trip to prison, I suppose, the final bow on top of the package. Knowing what I now do about him, I shudder to think what he had planned for the next step in his little science experiment. He deserved exactly what he got; even Amblin agreed."

"So, the CIA wasn't in on it from the beginning?"

"They commissioned the original project to develop our chemical weapons database, but everything else was Price. He was making his pitch for them to buy into the mind control project when you showed up. Actually, you're arrival was the pitch. Sorry."

Doug looked at his confused and distraught brother and realized that he still didn't grasp the whole story.

"Get in and I'll tell you the rest on the way to the airport. You've got a plane to catch."

Hank started to grab the door handle to slip back into the rear of the car.

"No, the front, you dumb ass."

They exchanged smiles, easily drudged up from their childhood time together, and each slid into the front of the vehicle, eager to gain back the lost time of the last twenty plus years. Not even the clouds and misty rain could subdue the relief that resided in their faces. At that moment, Hank knew that he could never tell his brother of his role in the deaths of their mother or grandmother, nor did he need to. Those scars would heal in time, though they would never completely disappear, like broken bones and joints that were mended, but ache with the arrival of fall rain and winter cold. Joseph and Doug had both found a brother that day; they were family again. The future was a blank page, waiting to be filled.

Acknowledgments

The author would like to extend his heartfelt thanks to all who helped make the dream of this project a reality; most of all, my wife Jennifer who nods and smiles at my most maddening plot ideas instead of calling the police station. Thanks go to the many that read, critiqued, and, in some cases, applauded this novel, especially Larry and his red pen of death. In addition, Mitzi Ferderber, who tirelessly proofed each page and patiently corrected each mistake. Thanks also to my parents, who taught me at a young age that nothing is impossible and then reminded me often. Mom, you're right; all things are possible through the Father Almighty who deserves all thanks and praise.

Printed in the United States
117771LV00001B/4-21/P